SANCTUARY BURIED

WITSEC TOWN

BOOK 2

USA TODAY BESTSELLING AUTHOR

LISA PHILLIPS

"You NEED TO GO."

Sixteen-year-old Francesca Canetti shook her head. "Mama—"

"We're relying on you, baby." Mama clutched little Isabella to her movie star bosom, both of them shaking. "I need you to be strong for me so I can take care of Bella."

Fourteen-year-old Bella had tears running down her cheeks. Mama pushed the closet door open. "Be strong for me."

Uncle Benny had shown up ten minutes ago. The look on his face made Francesca pull Isabella from the upstairs landing into Mama and Papa's closet. Mama had been in there already.

"Go, Francesca."

Frannie's nightgown floated to her knees as she stood. Her legs wobbled. Her spindly teenage knees knocked together, but she'd made it to the open double-doors of her parents' bedroom.

The shouting grew louder. Uncle Benny's voice was brittle, and Frannie could picture his big cheeks jiggling as he yelled.

"Benito—"

"No, *capo*. Do not do this."

"We have no choice." Her father's voice was subdued but still full of an authority which demanded respect and obedience, despite the fact his reputation alone commanded it. "The decision has been made, *figlio*."

Frannie stopped at the top of the stairs. Her feet sank into satiny carpet, and she gripped the mahogany rail. She should go back and tell Mama and Isabella everything was fine.

"Then I'm out," Uncle Benny said.

"No one leaves the family but the coward who turns his back on us."

Ever since one of Papa's lieutenants testified against her grandfather, Frannie's father had made it his personal mission to destroy any signs of dissent among his men. Frannie was only sixteen, but she saw enough and heard enough to understand at least part of her father's operation. And the problems he was having.

It was why they hadn't been to Florida this year—although the way her mom carried on about losing their family vacation, someone could well have been in a horrific accident which scarred them for life. When Mama was unhappy, everyone in the whole neighborhood knew about it.

Frannie turned to go tell Mama everything was fine—well, that *this* was fine at least. Life was still life, and Frannie still had to tell Papa she thought she might want to go to culinary school. He was pushing for her to start taking college classes so she could get a law degree and pass the bar as fast as possible. Because La Cosa Nostra in Baltimore needed a lawyer who would always put the family first.

Too bad Frannie would rather make cupcakes. But if she

told Papa that, she'd end up the trophy housewife of one of his business associates.

She was never going to escape.

La Cosa Nostra might be his family, but it was going to absorb her whether she wanted it or not. Mama had chosen this life, back when she fell in love with Papa, but what about Isabella? Frannie's sister was barely fourteen and already Papa's men were starting to eye her in a way that said the girl was too quickly becoming a young woman.

The gunshot cracked like a firework. Frannie jerked as though she was the one who'd been shot. But was it Papa...or Uncle Benny?

Frannie sprinted down the stairs. She slid across the marble tile of the entryway on her socks, through the archway to the living room where her father stood, the smoking gun still in his hand. Uncle Benny lay in a quickly spreading pool of blood.

Frannie gasped and covered her mouth with her trembling hand.

Papa looked at her. The mobster had struck again.

It was past midnight, but he still wore his black slacks and pale blue silk shirt. He stowed the gun in the back of his belt and motioned with his hand. "Help me move the coffee table, *angela mia.*"

Frannie didn't move.

Uncle Benny shifted and gasped. Her eyes darted to where he lay—eyes open and fixed on her. "Francesca—" He coughed.

Papa said, "Help me move the coffee table."

She looked at him.

Her father's eyes were full of impatience. "We must take care of the body, *cara.* You will help me."

He wanted her to...what?

Frannie looked aside, and promptly threw up on the back of the couch.

"I do not have time for this."

Papa was mad. Was he going to shoot her, too?

Would he do so if Frannie wasn't useful to him anymore?

She took a step back, wiping her mouth with the back of her hand.

"Francesca!"

She took another step back and ran. Pumping her arms and legs like she was running the one hundred meters, Frannie raced through the hall into the kitchen. But there was nowhere to go.

"Francesca, stop!"

The click of his shoes pursued her, and Frannie circled through the dining room. His gun fired. A bullet slammed into her shoulder and she stumbled, ice cold fire burning down her arm. If she kept running she was going to end up back in the living room with Uncle Benny. Where else could she go? The only other way out was the front.

Frannie ducked out the side door from the dining room and cut left, down the hall to the front door.

It exploded inward.

Men in black fatigues, wearing helmets and carrying huge rifles, poured through the front door in a haze of smoke.

Francesca Canetti skidded to a halt and slapped her hands over her ears to quell the shouting. The sound of her own screams tore through the haze in her mind.

Her father.

She spun around.

Armed men raced by, bumped her one way and then the other. With their guns pointed at her father, they yelled over and over until he set his hands on his head and lowered to his knees.

Frannie didn't think Nicolai Canetti had ever kneeled before any man in his life, and absolutely not since he'd been accepted into La Cosa Nostra. A gloved hand grabbed her shoulder, pulling her back. Pain whipped through her body, and Frannie collapsed to her knees. She looked up and saw "FBI" on the back of their vests.

One crouched beside her—a woman. "Everything is fine, Francesca."

They knew her name? Frannie looked into the eyes of this stranger and allowed the woman to pull her back to her feet.

One of the men surrounding her father produced a piece of paper from his breast pocket. "Nicolai Canetti, we have a warrant to search all residences, offices, warehouses and any other parcel of property owned by you or anyone in your immediate family."

"For what?" Papa's voice was ice cold.

"Any information pertaining to your shipping company and its links to your off-shore accounts in Belize and the transfer of said money to persons employed by the Hanera cartel, particularly in reference to gun running between Baltimore and the Port of Veracruz on the Mexican coast."

"Special Agent Turner!"

The man with the search warrant looked toward where the voice came from. Another agent strode out. He spoke low in Special Agent Turner's ear, but Frannie heard him say *Benito Canetti*.

Special Agent Turner turned back to her father. "You killed your own brother?"

Her father's expression didn't change. "He was attacking Francesca. He would have hurt her."

Papa was going to use her to save himself. She didn't know why she was surprised. Of course he was going to use her to save himself. That was all he was ever going to do. It was like a switch flicked inside her.

The woman agent beside her said, "Why don't you come with me, hon." It wasn't a question.

Frannie tore her gaze from her father and let the female fed lead her into the kitchen. She perched on a stool for two seconds before bounding to the sink and dry heaving into it. She heard the agent get water from the fridge. The woman handed the glass to Frannie along with a paper towel.

Acting like she cared. Mostly Frannie figured it was the lesser of two evils. She didn't want to be in the room with her father and his relentless, twisting lies. These FBI agents weren't much better. No government person or cop had ever done Francesca Canetti any favors.

"Want to tell me what happened?"

The pain in her shoulder registered. It stung like crazy. Her nightshirt was ripped and blood was dripping down to her elbow. Frannie pressed the paper towel to her shoulder and shut her eyes, before doing the very thing her father had always told her not to.

She told someone else family business.

When she got to the part where the agents had rushed in the front door, Frannie opened her eyes. The kitchen was brighter than before. The weight that seemed to always lie on her shoulders had receded, allowing her to straighten fully. To stand tall.

The swinging door wooshed open and the male agent looked beyond Frannie to his colleague.

Out of the corner of her eye, Frannie saw her nod and then she stepped away. "I'll get someone to come and look at your shoulder."

This agent in charge—the one whose name was Turner—

waited until the woman had left, and then said, "Your father is a bad man, Francesca Canetti."

His face was serious, but there was warmth in his eyes. Maybe he counseled the daughters of mafia captains on a regular basis. It was more likely he only said what he had to, to get the job done. She'd seen his type before. All this man wanted was to see her father in jail, he didn't care at all about what would become of Mama and Bella.

What were they going to do when they found Mama and Bella in the closet? What if they hurt them on accident? Frannie ran for the stairs.

The agent caught her, his thick arm banding around her waist.

"Let me go!"

"You're not leaving. Stop struggling or you'll hurt yourself more."

"I have to get them! They're upstairs in the closet."

He set her down, but didn't let her go. "Your mother and sister?"

"They'd better not get hurt."

He didn't seem impressed by her bravado, but she didn't care. He said, "If you're worried about them being hurt, the only thing you can do is help me put your father away."

"You mean testify?"

With his gaze boring into her, he nodded. "I do."

"FRANCESCA!" Papa yelled from the hall.

She jerked as her whole body flooded with dread. Could he hear them talking? The pain in her shoulder was making her want to throw up again.

"Look at me," the agent said. "Don't worry about him. Focus on me."

"I—"

"FRANCESCA, YOU BETRAY ME AND YOU ARE DEAD!"

She couldn't move. She shouldn't have told them what happened. It wouldn't do any good. She was never going to escape Papa and his reach.

The agent said, "Frances—"

"You won't be able to protect me. He'll kill all of us."

"You have to trust me. This is what we do. We keep people like you safe."

Frannie bit down on her back teeth. "Because it serves your purpose."

"No, because it keeps guns out of the hands of kids trying to prove themselves by shooting other kids. It gets drugs off the streets. And it's going to keep your father's lieutenants from destroying any more lives."

"Maybe I'm not that honorable." She tried to be a good Catholic, but she was never going to be good. Frannie would always be stained by who she was.

The kitchen door whooshed again, and Mama and Bella were ushered in by two agents. Special Agent Turner looked star-struck, even if he'd known who Mama was. That happened a lot when Mama entered a room. Frannie knew why. She'd seen the movies Mama starred in during the sixties and seventies. Mama had been all about bringing back the golden days of Hollywood, and she still dressed like a starlet.

Mama froze. "Oh, no."

"Mama—"

"You take him down and we'll go with you, Francesca Canetti. You'll ruin all of us."

Frannie honestly didn't know what she was going to do. Mama was probably just worried about her big house and the credit card Papa gave her. All she did was troll high-end boutiques and take trips up to New York to buy even more stuff.

Special Agent Turner said, "All you've gotta do is trust me. I'll keep you all safe." He really looked like he believed it. "Your testimony could mean the difference between being free of this life and living forever under his thumb."

"Maybe I want this life." Frannie lifted her chin. "You don't know me."

"We've been watching you all for weeks, Francesca. A girl who gives her lunch to the sixth grader that lives in a trailer with her druggie mom and who volunteers in a rescue shelter and bakes cupcakes for the residents of a senior center does not belong here."

Her mom opened her mouth to say something, but Papa's shout cut her off.

"FRANCESCA!"

She lifted her chin. "Okay. I'll testify."

———

DAYS LATER, Frannie sat at a huge table in a conference room at the federal courthouse...somewhere. She had no clue where they'd flown her. It felt like she'd been talking all day while the gray-haired woman typed everything on her little type-writer. The US attorney made pages and pages of notes, nodding and smiling when Frannie gave him something juicy.

The stitches on her shoulder had been removed, and she was getting better at using her arm, but it was still in a sling.

Francesca glanced at the marshal across the table and returned the woman's small smile. Homely looking, the female marshal didn't fit the part of a tough-edged fed, but maybe that was the point. It would draw more attention to

Frannie if it was obvious she was surrounded by cops. Cops who had become good friends in the last few weeks.

Deputy Marshal Sarah Harness looked aside at the US attorney. "We should wrap up for the day. Frannie's tired."

The US attorney didn't look impressed, but he still acquiesced. "Any word on the mom?"

Sarah shook her head. "Miranda still refuses to believe her only option for safety is an Alaskan tundra, or plastic surgery. She wants to be placed somewhere warm. Miami was top of her list."

Frannie's stomach clenched, and not just because she hated the idea of moving to Miami. Although that would be bad enough. She knew Mama didn't like the idea of her testifying. She just hadn't thought Mama would dig her heels in to this extent. As the marshals had explained, it was like trying to put Shirley Temple in witness protection. Plastic surgery really was the only option.

And yet her mom was refusing.

Sarah said, "I put in a call to my boss to see what we can do, but I'm still waiting to hear back."

The door opened. The two deputy marshals on guard in the hall parted, and a man strode into the room. Sarah shot to her feet. "Good morning, sir."

"Marshal Harness." He glanced around the room. "If you could all please give me a minute with the witness."

It wasn't a request. Even the US attorney jumped up, scooping his things into his arms before shuffling out. Sarah shot Frannie a smirk and pointed at the back of the man who had demanded everyone leave. She mouthed, "That's my boss. He's cool."

Frannie smiled and nodded.

The man cleared his throat. Sarah shut the door behind her, and the brown-haired man in a charcoal suit sat and smoothed down his red tie. "My name is Grant Mason. I'm the director of the Marshals."

Frannie felt her eyes widen.

"I heard about your mother's refusal to alter her appearance." He paused. "You understand it puts not only her, but also you and your sister in jeopardy?"

Frannie nodded.

"It hinders our ability to protect you when your mother's face is so recognizable and she refuses to stay inside."

Frannie didn't say anything. What could she say?

"There are a couple of options. One involves separating you from your mother and sister. We can protect them so far as we are able, but since you're the primary target of your father and his men—"

"No."

"I understand. My family is also very close."

"I know the risks," Frannie said. "I know we'll be in danger, but Mama—"

"I also understand that. Still, there is another way to keep you safe if you're interested. The risk your father or any of his lieutenants will find you is going to be reduced significantly."

She straightened, feeling safety wash over her for probably the first time in her life. "Whatever it is, we'll do it." What other choice did they have?

"It won't be easy, Francesca. But you will be safe." He smiled. "I know it feels like you're being forced into a corner, but this really is the best option."

The director opened the briefcase he'd carried in and pulled out an inch thick stack of papers. "This is an addendum to the Memorandum of Understanding you already signed when you were enrolled into the witness protection program. It details everything you need to know about Sanctuary."

"Sanctuary? What's that?"

"A state secret known only to myself and the president, Ms. Peters."

Her new last name had been used sparingly, but when he said it, Frannie felt like maybe she could actually be this person they'd created. Francesca had died when Uncle Benito was shot. This new girl, Francine Peters, could be strong. Independent.

She hoped.

Frannie sat up straighter. "So what is this place?"

"Sanctuary is our first and only witness protection town."

CHAPTER 1

Eight years later

FRANCINE PETERS JERKED AWAKE. The crash came again, the sound of something heavy falling over and splintering on a hard floor. Like the cracked tile of her downstairs entryway.

Her breaths came heavy, her mind flitting through the murder of the Mayor's wife only weeks ago, the series of break-ins and thefts at the Medical Center recently and the missing drugs. But there was likely a far less sinister explanation for this noise.

She glanced at the clock. 3:04 a.m. That was half an hour of sleep she was going to lose before she had to get up for work anyway.

The front door slammed. Footsteps were followed by giggles and loud "shushing." Frannie rolled her eyes and pushed back her comforter. In the dark she made her way to the door of her bedroom and down the stairs. Did they really think they were fooling her?

Memories from years ago washed through her mind, and her steps faltered. An entirely different scene had met her at the bottom of the stairs of her childhood home that night. A night that led to her testifying against her own father and bringing down a Mexican cartel.

Frannie blew out a slow breath and continued, gripping the stair rail to keep from rubbing the scarred skin on the top of her left shoulder. It wasn't worth dwelling on. He would never find her here in the middle of nowhere, surrounded by mountains, in a town only accessible by military transport.

Frannie's mom, Mimi, wobbled across the entryway to their tiny three bedroom house on her stiletto heels. She was barely forty-five, but swore she was still in her thirties. She didn't realize no one believed her, not when her daughters were adults. Mimi's low-cut shirt had a wet stain on the front that tracked down to the lap of her short denim skirt. Her hair had looked better earlier in the evening, before Frannie went to bed.

Frannie's sister, Izabelle, was dressed in a matching outfit, with some of their natural blonde amid the streaks of her hair. Gone were the days of Francesca and Isabella Canetti. For years now, they'd been Francine and Izabelle Peters. Frannie would never have predicted her sweet little sister would turn into a mini clone of their mom.

She stopped at the bottom step and folded her arms.

Her mom looked up, not a shadow of remorse on her face. Instead her mouth morphed into disgust. "What is that hideous thing you're wearing?"

"My nightgown." It was an over-sized T-shirt, XL being the only size Sam Tura had in stock when she'd registered for his gym, Sleight of Hand. She hadn't been back there since the older woman she'd hired at her bakery had fallen ill and received a cancer diagnosis.

Izzy, who was twenty-two, snorted. "I wouldn't be caught

dead wearing that." She shot a smirk at their mom, and both of them erupted into giggles.

It didn't take a genius to figure out what their lazy limbs and slurred speech meant. Despite there being no alcohol allowed in the WITSEC town of Sanctuary, they seemed to have gotten their hands on some—or a substance which produced similar effects.

Not that anyone had ever accused Frannie of being a genius, even though her mom always referred to her as the "smart daughter." Mama had to tell people something when Izzy was the pretty one. Especially given the fact Frannie's face looked more like her father's, despite her inheriting her mom's strawberry blonde hair. Still, Frannie was smart enough to figure this out.

Instead of waiting for them to quit laughing, Frannie went to the kitchen and hit the button on the coffee maker. It wasn't set to come on for fifteen more minutes, but she didn't want to wait. She stared at the liquid dripping into the carafe and tried to ignore the sounds of her mom and sister following her into the kitchen for round two.

Frannie grabbed the Ibuprofen from the top shelf of the end cabinet, got two waters from the fridge and set both on the breakfast bar's stained linoleum surface.

Her mom shook out the tablets. When she drank, water dribbled down her chin. Mimi lowered the bottle and swiped her mouth with the back of her hand. "Thanks, darling."

Her mom's gratitude was eclipsed by Izzy saying, "Yeah, thanks Cinderella."

Frannie poured her coffee, ignoring the clench in her stomach telling her to fire a quip back at her sister—whether it was words, or something more substantial. Too bad Izzy wasn't ugly, or Frannie's step-sister. But she was wicked.

Mimi swatted Izzy in the arm.

She shot her a look in return. "What? You're the one who came up with it."

Mimi shot her a look that said, "Shut up," her eyes wide.

Why was mom worried about offending her now? That day had long passed.

"I'm going to bed." Izzy set her bottle on the counter and water sloshed over the top. "That was a great night, Mom."

Mimi grinned. "It was. I think Diego really likes you."

Hearing the name was like a blow to the face. Why did it have to be *him* of all people? So long as he didn't come around, Frannie would be fine. She'd never cared for him or the way he looked at her—which was markedly different from the way he looked at Izzy.

His brother Matthias, on the other hand, probably didn't even know Mimi had two daughters. The brothers worked as hands at Bolton Farrera's ranch. Nadia Marie, the salon owner who'd given up trying to get the ranch boss to notice her, had told Frannie there was a lot of ignoring going around at the moment. There was probably something in the water over at the ranch that made them oblivious to interested women. What other explanation could there be?

Frannie pushed away all thoughts of tall men in chambray shirts, jeans and chaps. If she kept thinking about them any longer, she'd go into premature menopause. Her mom might claim their hair was "strawberry blonde" but that didn't make Frannie's propensity for blushing any better.

"Nighty-nighty." Izzy giggled, her unsteady footsteps retreating from the room.

Frannie held her breath and turned. Sure enough, her mom was still by the breakfast bar. "You need something, Mimi?"

It was by mutual consent that Frannie now called her mom by her given name, and it was not something she cared to dwell on. Not given everything else swirling around in her head.

When her mom didn't say anything, Frannie said, "You should probably get some sleep if you're going to be in the bakery this afternoon."

"I've been meaning to talk to you about that, darling. I—"

"Whatever it is, it's not going to happen." Frannie wanted to throw a fit. *Why do I always feel like the parent?* "With Stella in the medical center, I'm short-handed. I need you to come to work and do the job I pay you for."

Frannie was more than short-handed. Stella had, for years, been doing the work of two people, and she never said a word about it even though Frannie paid her for the work of one because she had no idea.

Then Stella was diagnosed with terminal cancer, and she kept coming to work, even up until she had to spend the day in a chair while she manned the register. Like that was the obvious thing to do when she didn't have the energy to walk up and down the space behind the display counter. Frannie never said a word, because she loved having Stella there. If the woman wanted to carry on as normally as possible, Frannie was going to give her that.

Her mom's face morphed into something meant to look either kind, or in need of sympathy. Frannie wasn't sure which.

"Darling, you work so hard. I love that you've found what makes you happy, I do. Sweet Times is a great success. Everyone says so. Especially when I tell them it was my daughter who set up the bakery. I know you need help right now, but I simply can't come in today. I really would help if I could, but there's something I've got to do. I'd get out of it if I could. You understand, don't you, darling? I'd love nothing more than to be there to help you."

Like pushing Frannie, at sixteen years old, out of the walk-in closet just in time to witness her father murder Uncle Benito. Was that supposed to be *helping*? It was on the edge of Frannie's tongue to pour the accusations out at her mother, but she held the words back. It wouldn't change anything.

"It's not even really my thing, it's Izzy. She has an appointment—" Mimi leaned close. "—with the doctor, you know?"

No, Frannie didn't know. Why did her mom think she would? The two of them kept only their own confidences, leaving Frannie to navigate life by herself. She lived in the same house with her mom and sister, but like they were the family and she was just a renter, despite the fact she paid the mortgage each month and did all the cleaning. The nickname Cinderella might sting, but it wasn't entirely inaccurate.

"Mom—" She was ready to launch into her speech about responsibility and earning the money Frannie paid her mostly out of obligation. Then her mom's eyes would glaze over...

Instead, her mom cut her off. "You're such a good girl." Mimi squeezed her in a hug with those spray-tanned, skinny arms. "So honest and strong." She patted Frannie's cheek a little too vigorously. "My brave one, taking care of us."

Unfortunately, Frannie had learned each of those weren't necessarily good things. All it meant was she was the one picking up their slack, doing whatever they didn't want to do.

Mimi tottered to the door and glanced back. "I'll make it up to you next week, when my schedule isn't so busy."

Meanwhile, Frannie's bakery hemorrhaged money paying salaried employees who barely came to work and when they did, were two hairs above useless. She needed to hire two people to replace Stella but could barely afford it, since her mom and sister were on the payroll. And she needed all her spare money to replace the broken second oven.

In the real world, Frannie would fire them both and get herself a studio apartment, followed by hiring staff who were actually competent. But this wasn't the real world, it was Sanctuary.

The town was populated entirely by people in witness protection. All because forty years ago the Marshals Service decided to experiment and see if federal witnesses could live in their own community, tucked away in the mountains. This uninhabited portion of Idaho was perfect for protecting them. Surrounded entirely by mountains, the town sat in a basin only accessible by air in what had been designated a no-fly zone. Sanctuary was where the government hid their highest-profile witnesses, household names with recognizable faces.

Which meant she was stuck with her mom and sister forever, whether she liked it or not.

Frannie dressed in her work clothes and pulled her hair into a ponytail. She rode her bike from their street, which was on the south side of town and one of five major roads in town. The streets all ran parallel to each other so that the town was an oval with the ranch at one end and the farm at the other.

Frannie pedaled along the deserted, darkened roads to Main Street, where Sweet Times was located on the west end, closest to the ranch. As she did every morning, Frannie locked her bike at the back of the building and glanced once in the direction of the ranch before going inside. Like always, the light at the ranch house was on, as was the light in the barn and the residence where the ranch hands lived—where *he* lived.

There was a sense of solidarity, knowing he was awake, even though he'd never actually said anything to her but, "Two loaves of white bread, sliced, and a dozen chocolate cupcakes."

Frannie unlocked the back door and walked through the

kitchen, flipping on lights. There was a faint smell of lemon scented cleaner, and the stainless steel surfaces gleamed. At least someone was still doing their job.

She got started, measuring ingredients for three kinds of bread, sweet rolls, cinnamon rolls and the chocolate pastries one of her customers had requested yesterday. While the dough rose, she started a pot of coffee and scrambled herself two eggs. She ate standing up, trying not to let the fire her mom had lit in her stomach flicker to life. It always lived there, never really gone. Just embers, ready to flare up at any moment. She'd lived with it for so long that when the anger and frustration stirred up, it caught her off guard with its ferocity.

She didn't want to hate them, but the reality was...they were never ever going to change.

Frannie grabbed her heaviest rolling pin and started to roll out the cinnamon rolls. Who needed therapy or a work-out? Her kitchen was the place where she could revel in the solitude. Here she didn't have to be strong, or brave, or smart. It was just Frannie and her ingredients and the infinite number of things she could create.

She rotated the board and continued to roll out the dough, over and over again.

Why had her mom sent her downstairs all those years ago? Frannie didn't have to ask herself what kind of mom did that to their child, because she knew. She lived it. For once Mimi could have stepped ahead of her children to accept what might come at them. But, no. Mimi only ever thought of herself. Izzy seemed oblivious, since she just went along with everything. And Frannie was beyond frustration, somewhere near exhausted with it all wondering why her life had to be like this.

"Did the dough offend you?"

The corner of Frannie's mouth curled up. His voice sounded even better in her head than in person. Full and smooth, like hickory smoke. She had it bad if she was imagining him talking to her when she was alone in the bakery and the sun hadn't even risen over the mountains yet.

He cleared his throat.

Frannie looked over at the door to the front of the bakery with just her eyes, seeing him there at the corner of her vision. Then she glanced at the clock. She should have already had the ovens on by now.

Frannie looked back at him. "Two loaves of sliced white and twelve chocolate cupcakes?"

She swiped her floury hands on the front of her apron. A strand of hair had come loose from her ponytail, making her itch to push it back.

"Actually..." He paused. "Um...it's Francine, right?"

"Frannie." She frowned. If the front door was still locked, how did he get in? "You're in my kitchen—"

She was struck again by exactly how dark his eyes were. He couldn't be more than a couple years older than her, late twenties probably. His brother, Diego, was twenty-four like her; she knew as much from Izzy and Mimi's conversations.

Thick dark-brown hair fell onto his forehead in disarray, as though he simply smashed his hat on with no thought to what it would do. "You're Matthias, right?"

The corners of his eyes crinkled, and the color actually lightened. There was a moment of silence, and then he said, "Tias."

It sounded like *Tee-yas*. "I've never heard anyone call you Tias." She liked the way it rolled off her tongue.

He shrugged, apparently not noticing the comment made her sound like a stalker who followed him all day, listening to his conversations. "No one does. I just decided I wanted a shorter version of my name."

"And you gave it to me?" Great, now she felt even weirder. As if this whole thing wasn't awkward enough. "Are you sure there isn't something you need? Actually, why don't you tell me how you managed to get in the locked door?"

His dark eyebrows drew together, and he motioned to the front of the store. "You haven't been out front yet?"

Frannie shook her head, already moving toward him. Thankfully he got out of the way enough for her to push through the swinging door to the storefront. She stopped abruptly so Matthias—Tias—slammed into the back of her with an "oof."

Dishware she had painstakingly unpacked was strewn across tables. There was even a mug on the floor. Crumbs littered the scene, and coffee stains marked the surfaces along with other liquids. Frannie weaved between tables where cupcake casings had been crumpled and tossed on the floor. Fabric she'd stretched on the seats herself was damp with spills.

The fire in Frannie's stomach ignited, flaring hot all the way out to her toes and the tips of her fingers. Even her hair felt like it was on fire. Boiling tears burned in her eyes. She lifted a plate and pitched it at the wall then bent double and set her hands on the table in front of her. The inferno rushed in her ears. She didn't hear the sob when her body bucked, but she knew she was crying.

"I can help you clean up."

She spun around. He was so close the heat from his body warmed her further, but the fire was excruciating. She moved back, clipped a chair with her foot and stumbled. Tias reached out.

"No." Her voice was high and shrill, and she winced. "Just go."

"I can help you clean up, or go get Sheriff Mason. He'll want you to make a report about the break in."

A report? She had to clean this up and get ready to open the store, not face the sheriff's uncomfortable questions. Matthias had already moved toward the front door. The door they'd left *unlocked*, leaving her livelihood in jeopardy. "I'm not making a report."

"The sheriff can find out who did this."

But she already knew who'd done this. "I don't need your help."

His eyes softened, and she hated the sight of it. "Frannie."

She didn't need his pity. This was embarrassing enough as it was. "Please just go."

"At least let me help clean up."

"Matthias, just *go*."

"Fran—"

"GET OUT!"

She grasped the hair on either side of her head, hard.

They didn't care about her or her life at all. They went where they pleased, when they pleased and did whatever they wanted. Broke into her store in the middle of the night and trashed the place like this was their house too, and she really was Cinderella cleaning up after them all the time.

The front door shut, and she was blessedly alone. Terribly alone.

If only.

Frannie cleaned up the dishes and swept. It was almost calming having to do it, since the work helped bank the fire. What was she going to say to them? Nothing ever helped. It was almost not worth the energy it took to yell at them when they never listened anyway.

Half an hour later Olympia knocked on the glass front door.

The woman's wide frame was enveloped by a floral dress accentuating her dark Greek features, which she'd passed on to Matthias. Frannie gave her a small smile and opened the door to admit his mother.

"Hi."

Olympia didn't reply, she simply eased into Frannie's space and surrounded her with comfort and love. Until that point, Frannie wouldn't have admitted it was what she needed, but it sure felt good.

Frannie stepped back from the hug, certain her warm face was now pink. She reached up and tucked the loose strand of hair behind her ear. "Was there something you—" That was when she remembered.

She surveyed the tables for any sign of the cupcakes her mom and sister—and goodness knew who else—had consumed last night. Blue paper casings and smudges of blue and red frosting... Her heart dipped into her stomach.

She raced to the kitchen and hauled open the fridge door.

All gone.

The two dozen cupcakes Frannie had baked for Olympia's twin grandsons' fifth birthdays were gone.

Rage burned hot in her eyes, blurring her vision with unshed tears. Her grip on the fridge door handle was so tight it made her hand spasm in a cramp. She slammed it shut and turned to Olympia, now standing in the kitchen doorway. Frannie didn't know how she was going to break the news. That was probably why Matthias had come, to pick up the cupcakes before the party later this morning. And all she'd done was yell at him.

Frannie would close the bakery for the morning before she disappointed Olympia.

The older woman's gaze softened. "Precious."

Frannie had no idea why Olympia always called her that. The Greek matron did most of the cooking for community dinners, so when Frannie provided the desserts they worked side by side. Olympia only ever called her precious.

Frannie sucked in a breath. "I'll have them ready in time. The boys won't be without cake on their birthday. I'll make sure of it."

"I know you will." Olympia nodded and then, bizarrely, rubbed her hands together. "And you'll stay for the party, too?"

"Oh, I couldn't." Mostly just because Matt—Tias would be there.

No. Thinking of him and using his nickname...she would only let it slip. Then everyone would think there was something between them.

CHAPTER 2

"Dude, what is wrong with you?"

Matthias looked back at the barn's side door to make sure it was still attached. He had slammed it pretty hard.

Bolton Farrera, his boss who was more like a partner, stood with his head cocked to the side and a frown under the brim of his hat. Matthias didn't blame him. Everything about this was confusing. "You've been acting weird since you got back from town. I thought you were just going to get the twins' cupcakes for the party."

Matthias smiled at the big, rough looking ex-DEA agent saying "cupcakes." "I had my mom go get them."

"You chickened out? You didn't even go talk to her?"

Matthias felt the smile drop from his face. "I talked to her."

He explained to Bolton about the mess and Frannie's reaction, even though it was more than humiliating she yelled at him and didn't even let him help. The woman obviously had bigger problems to deal with than his hurt feelings. Even if he knew what it meant when a woman yelled at him to get out.

Bolton didn't waste a second before he said, "She knew who did it."

Matthias frowned. "Seriously?"

Bolton nodded. "She's embarrassed. Whoever it is, she's covering for them."

Matthias pressed his lips together. He knew Frannie lived with her mom and sister. Most folks knew, although she was rarely seen with them outside of the fact they lived together, and Mimi and Izabelle both pitched in at the bakery. Occasionally.

There was a walking train wreck waiting to happen, and likely when it did, it'd have something to do with Diego.

"Just because she yelled at you it doesn't mean anything bad."

Matthias shot his boss a look. "It doesn't mean anything good, either. And why are you giving me relationship advice?"

Bolton's lip curled. It was safe to say Nadia Marie had pinged on Bolton's radar in the last few weeks. After the new sheriff arrived in town and the Mayor's wife was murdered, the chief suspect had been Nadia Marie's best friend, Andra —a former assassin who may or may not have been working for the government back when she'd killed people for a living. Matthias wasn't real clear on the details.

The deputy sheriff had been killed trying to deliver Andra to her enemy. The schoolteacher was arrested in the conspiracy to frame her. And the doctor's wife had committed suicide over the shame of implicating Andra in the first place.

Cleared of the charges by the president, Andra had recently returned to town after a long stay at the hospital. She was now happy in a relationship with the sheriff and they were getting married soon. Life had settled down, and their battle had blown over. But Andra's best friend, Nadia Marie, had remained in the spotlight—for Bolton, at least. Despite the fact she wanted nothing to do with him, the man wouldn't let the idea of her go. But neither did he seem to have any intention of actually starting something with her.

And why not? It wasn't like there was anything holding Bolton back from having a romantic relationship. Not like Matthias. There was next to no point in him even talking to Frannie. It was a nice idea, and a good dream on most days. But Frannie was like the unattainable prize.

He'd slipped, telling her to call him Tias. For a second it had been sweet hearing the nickname come from her lips, but it wasn't like he'd be around her anymore. She would hardly call him that on the odd occasion he came in the bakery because he couldn't resist the temptation to see her any longer.

He needed to let her go.

"So your girl's having some troubles."

Matthias let a snort slip out, the sound too much like his horse, Danser, when she was getting impatient. He needed to quit doing that. "Frannie isn't my girl." But she did have trouble. "If she needs anything she knows to go to the sheriff. He's the one who can help her."

"You really think she'll do that?" Bolton scratched under the brim of his black cowboy hat and then pressed it back into place. "Seems like if she doesn't want anyone involved, she's not likely to go to the sheriff. Maybe you should go over there later. Make sure she's okay."

Even before Bolton was finished, Matthias was already shaking his head. He glanced aside at the ranch house Bolton lived in. "She doesn't want my help."

Matthias stayed with his brother and the other two ranch hands across the way, in what would have formerly been called a bunkhouse. Like it was something quaint and nostalgic, instead of a basic building that smelled like the inside of his boots in June.

"Doesn't mean she doesn't need someone."

Matthias would like to see Bolton try that tactic with Nadia Marie. It was likely to go down real well with the strong-willed woman. Frannie was the type he'd have to be careful not to bully into his way of thinking. "I can't. Between the party and then tomorrow's rehearsal, I won't have time."

Bolton laughed. "Who knew you had such a busy social life?"

"I tried to get out of doing the play, but Shelby and Aaron called my bluff." Matthias sighed.

"How do you think I wound up volunteering to build the set? I'm supposed to meet with Aaron during the twins' birthday party."

Matthias folded his arms and kicked at the dusty earth under the toe of his boot. The town was surrounded by a ring of mountains capped with snow from the rain last night, but it wouldn't snow in town for weeks yet.

Simeon and Reuben's fifth birthday was in two hours, just before lunch.

Matthias turned to look where the road from town stretched out, east of the ranch. Diego should be bringing the boys to the ranch any time now so the family could set up while the twins were out from underfoot.

He glanced back at Bolton. "Have you seen Diego?"

His boss shrugged. "He was assigned to check W2 this morning, before he went to get the twins."

Bolton had divided the ranch into quadrants, W1, 2, 3 and 4, since it was essentially a rectangle before the forest started on three sides. Dan Walden, whose farm was east beyond the town, had done the same with his land, designating it E1, 2, 3 and 4. Only instead of a herd of cows, Dan had crops and greenhouses in each of his quadrants.

Sanctuary had been designed to be as self-sufficient as possible. Some things had to be shipped in on the transport which came and went every Monday morning, but for the most part their food was grown—or raised—locally. There were three trucks, five golf carts, a couple of ATVs and two dozen or so bicycles in town. Most everyone walked where they needed to go, unless it was all the way across town. Often when he was in town picking up supplies, someone would ask him for a ride.

A few of the older residents had been in town forty years, since it was first founded. Matthias had been his nephew's ages when his father testified against the drug lords he'd double crossed; mostly because without WITSEC they would've all been killed. Matthias, his brother and his three sisters had all grown up in Sanctuary. He could barely remember what the world was like beyond the mountains.

"The ranch truck is still here." Bolton walked away in the direction of the bunkhouse.

The other truck belonged to the former DEA agent. Matthias and the rest of the guys used the second truck, which was much older.

Bolton had done something in his previous life that warranted enough pull to be the only person in town who could bring their personal vehicle with them. Matthias remembered a few years ago when it was flown in by military helicopter. That had been fun to watch.

The bunkhouse had been constructed of logs using trees they'd cut down from the forest circling the town. The furniture was made by a guy with carpentry skills and then upholstered by his mom and her sewing machine. The whole place would probably look and smell a lot better if any of them knew the first thing about cleaning, or if the rest of the guys had any inclination to pick up after themselves.

Matthias was tired of being the one who mopped behind the other guys. Most of the time he cooked his meals at the ranch house, since Bolton couldn't do anything except grill a steak. In exchange he used the bathroom where Bolton had a housekeeper who came over from town once a week.

It was a good trade-off.

When they got closer, music was playing inside the bunkhouse. Bolton opened the door and it increased to deafening levels. Diego was stretched out on the ratty couch, asleep.

Matthias resisted the urge to kick his brother, but shook him awake instead. Diego smelled like...well, he didn't want to dwell much on that. Neither, it seemed, did Bolton. Though Matthias saw the curl of his lip as he inhaled through his mouth.

Diego puffed out a rank breath and opened his eyes. "What? Whaddaya want?"

Matthias decided having a brother who wasn't useless would be a good start. Instead he said, "You were supposed to be back with the twins already."

Diego looked at his watch and ran a hand down his face. "I'll go right now."

"Forget it."

Bolton said, "He's right. There's no way you're driving in this state. Guess you'll be late for the party since you'll be cleaning out the horse stalls."

"Seriously?" Diego groaned. "I can't drive when I'm tired, either. That's why I was taking a nap."

"No," Bolton said. "You were taking a nap because you rolled in at three-fifteen this morning and you're hung over. I should fire you."

"Fire me?" Diego's eyes widened. His dark hair and smooth face capped a body toughened by ranch life. Still, he was more slender than Matthias.

With his broad shoulders, Matthias would probably snap Frannie's ribs if he ever hugged her. But it wasn't like he could stop being so big. Diego could stop being a moron any time he wanted.

Diego lumbered off the couch to stand up. "I need this job, man."

Matthias shook his head. "Then maybe you should act a little more grateful for the fact you actually have it."

Diego's gaze swung around. "Who asked you, Mr. perfect-all-the-time know-it-all? No one cares what you think."

"Oh yeah?"

"Yeah, momma's-boy. Why don't you get out of my face for once? What I do doesn't have squat to do with you. You're not dad." Diego lifted both hands and slammed his palms into Matthias's shoulders, forcing him to take a step back.

Matthias curled his fingers into a fist and slammed it in his brother's face.

———

MATTHIAS TURNED RIGHT before he reached Main Street toward the residences on the south side. The town was shaped like a wrapped piece of candy. The stores, businesses and the Meeting House were along the center and the residential streets wrapped around to the north and south.

Frannie's bakery was on the west end of Main Street, so he saw it even when he didn't want to because it was on the way to...everywhere.

The twins' mom, Matthias's oldest sister, Maria, lived in the center of Third Street in one of the rare four-bedroom houses. All the residences were basic, following the same seventies-style décor with only a few exceptions. Nothing much had been updated since the town was founded on the government's spending budget. Forty years later most people's homes were woefully outdated and held together with scraps of wood and duct tape.

Maria's husband Tom was former FDNY and the town's fire chief, although he also held down a job landscaping. The flowers out front of their house were there courtesy of Matthias's other sisters, Antonia and Sofia. It was worth trying anything to cheer up Maria.

The front door opened and two now five-year-old hooligans tore down the front walk, elbowing each other to get ahead as they ran. Matthias felt the knot in his chest loosen as he caught his twin nephews, swinging them both up over his shoulders.

"Uncle Matt!"

"It's our birthday!"

Matthias mock-gasped. "It is? Did I know that?"

They started to laugh, but they were nervous—like they didn't know for sure if he was joking. "I probably should have gotten you boys a present."

Identical faces fell.

"Although, I did find two huge wrapped boxes in my closet this morning. Maybe those have something to do with your birthday?"

They both squealed.

"Birthday presents!"

"Cake!"

Matthias chuckled and set them down. This being-an-uncle gig was pretty sweet. "Hey, how about you guys call me Uncle Tias?"

Reuben started dancing, little more than a shimmy. "Tee-yas...Tee-yas..." Simeon shoved him. They both fell, and the wrestling portion of the morning commenced.

Matthias grabbed two elbows and hauled them up. "You boys want to come to the ranch for a while before the party?"

"Presents!" "Cake!" Simeon and Reuben both jumped up and down.

"I'm just gonna tell your mom we're leaving."

Both the boys reacted. It wasn't overt, but they were still young enough they didn't know how to temper their feelings so people wouldn't see. He didn't want them to be affected by how Maria was, but how could they not be? At the very least, they knew their mom wasn't like other mothers.

Simeon mushed his lips together and said, "She's in the bathroom. She's been in there for an *hour* already."

Which begged the question of what they'd been up to during that hour. Matthias wasn't sure he wanted to ask. He set his hands on a shoulder of each twin. "You boys go grab your shoes, and I'll let your mom know we're leaving."

They raced inside and through the house. Matthias jogged up the stairs, slowing as he neared the top. He had to get this done quickly if he wanted to minimize the upset it would cause the boys.

He didn't knock on the bedroom door. The curtains were still drawn, so he flung them open. Tom's side of the bed was pulled straight, like he'd made it as soon as he got out. Maria's side had a collection of pill bottles on the nightstand and the blanket was rumpled. The mattress had an indentation where she'd probably lain there for most of the morning.

Matthias trailed to the bathroom. The door was cracked, so he pushed it open. Maria was slumped on the toilet lid as though she'd simply lost all her energy and needed somewhere to sit.

He leaned against the door frame. "Ree?"

Her hair hung straight and unwashed. The sleeves of her sweater were long enough they covered her fingers. She looked up, her eyes lined with yesterday's mascara.

"You have two hours until the party." Matthias shoved aside the shower curtain and started the water. "You need to get ready and get over to the park by eleven forty-five. Can you do that?"

She nodded without looking up and lumbered to her feet like she was eighty instead of barely thirty.

Matthias sighed. "It's Reuben and Simeon's birthdays. They need you today, and you're going to have to get it together."

Her eyes lifted to him then, and the sight sliced through Matthias the same way it had every time she looked at him since that night so many years ago.

From across their father's dead body.

"I'll try."

Matthias took a step back. She needed to do a whole lot more than try if she didn't want to ruin today for his nephews. He needed to find Tom and have a word with Maria's husband. It was still early November, which meant this would only get worse over the next few weeks until the anniversary. Chances were Tom was completely aware of that, and it was why he'd chosen to work the morning of his son's birthdays, leaving Matthias to pick up the slack.

"Matt—" She clasped his still raw hand. He hissed and pulled his hand away. "What happened?"

Matthias dismissed her concern. First Diego, now Maria. He wasn't going to let her use him as a crutch any more. Not if she wanted to be strong enough to take care of her life, her marriage and her family on her own. Matthias was sick of being the good one. If it wasn't for Antonia and Sofia, he'd wonder what was wrong with him given every member of his family had a life that seemed to be hurtling along like a train wreck waiting to happen.

"I'm taking the boys to the ranch. We'll meet you at the party."

Her eyes flickered with confusion.

"You did get them a present, didn't you?" She opened her mouth, but stopped as though she didn't know what to say. His heart sank. "Did Tom get them anything?"

Her mouth jumped up in a smile. "I'm sure he did." But he saw in her eyes she had no clue if it was true or not.

"Get ready. I'll see you there."

She took a breath and squared her shoulders. "Yes. See you there, Matty."

Matthias's stomach churned. That was what his father had called him, but it had never been affectionate. He should tell her he didn't like it, but Maria had enough swirling in her head without him adding to her angst with his own issue. He could tell her to call him Tias—no. Something stopped him from doing that.

"Take your shower."

Matthias headed back downstairs and let himself out the front door. He knew the reason why he'd only given the nickname to Frannie and his nephews. He just didn't want to think on it.

There was already enough in him that made him wonder if he really, truly was a good person. He didn't need to add this slight to his sister. Maria was always and forever just going to be...Maria. There was nothing he could do about it if she wasn't willing to help herself. The only thing he could do was try and soften the blow for Simeon and Reuben.

But that would be hard if he couldn't even find them.

Matthias ducked his head back inside the house. No noise. That didn't mean they weren't in there, though. It was when their space was silent that Simeon and Reuben were up to something. The boys were smart, but it was more like a healthy knack for strategic cunning. Neither was particularly quiet, except they had moments of intense concentration when it was as if the whole world went silent around them. And it never turned out well.

The truck was still there, which was good. He didn't want to know what was going to happen when they decided to learn to drive. Matthias checked the back yard and their bedrooms. The shower was still running, but who knew if Maria had even gotten in yet. Figuring they'd run off down the street, Matthias pulled away from the curb and drove slowly through town. That was the down side of a town like this. The boys were free to roam whenever and wherever they felt like going.

Main Street was busy with pedestrians, and people milled around outside the diner, the gym—which was more punching bags than treadmills—and Frannie's bakery. Sweet Times was a favorite hangout for the boys, since they could get a cupcake and charge it to their family's account. It was how everyone paid Frannie for her goods. No one knew why she'd chosen not to accept cash or any other method of payment. Customers simply received a bill at the end of the month, which they were obliged to pay within fourteen days. But who wanted to be in debt for a cupcake?

The bakery didn't even have a tip jar.

Matthias parked around the corner and walked to the front door. The bell had been broken at some point, so there was no noise when he opened the door—at least, no noise to signal his entry.

The tables and chairs had been cleared of the earlier debris, and now Frannie's customers hung out with their desserts and coffee. He was surprised she hadn't simply closed down for the day, but she likely couldn't afford to lose business just for the sake of cleaning.

Matthias waved to the bank manager. Tacked on a board on the wall were flyers for community events. The bright orange poster in the center was for the arts group's upcoming production of Much Ado About Nothing. It made Matthias's stomach do a tuck and roll just thinking about the play. What part were Aaron and Shelby going to give him? He better not have more than one line...if that. Maybe he could be a tree.

The door to the kitchen swished open, and Frannie strode out. Her eyes locked on his, and her steps faltered. That had to mean what he thought it meant, right? Why would she react like that if she didn't feel it, too?

"Hey." He smiled. "Have you seen my—"

"They're in the kitchen."

"They are?"

She nodded, a small smile curling her lips up at the corners. "They wanted to frost their birthday cupcakes, so I set them up. They're doing fine. How's Maria?"

CHAPTER 3

Frannie felt like she'd swallowed a cactus. The bakery had customers at three tables and two more with dirty dishes she needed to clear away, and yet, she just stood there while Matthias's emotions washed over his face.

She'd never understood before how expressions could be so clear and here she was watching it. Everyone knew there was something up with Maria, only no one knew what it was.

"You want to come back here?" She motioned to the space behind the counter.

Matthias hesitated for a second and then rounded the counter. He rested his hips against the clean surface beside the computer she used as a cash register. Not that the thing was actually working. Today she was using a notebook.

Frannie busied herself, shifting cupcakes to half-empty trays and taking out the unneeded ones. "Wanna talk about it?"

He looked at his boots and shook his head before he looked back up. "The boys are really okay?"

Frannie waved him to the kitchen door where he looked in at the twins, surrounded by every color of sprinkles they'd somehow gotten everywhere—even in their hair. Her mega bowl of blue frosting was between them. He sighed, long and deep, a *soul* sigh if Frannie had ever heard one.

"I'm sure the party will be fun. Maria wouldn't...do anything. Like to mess it up, would she?"

"I hope not." His voice was a whisper.

He looked so...broken. Frannie didn't know what she was supposed to do to help. "And it's left to you to do damage control?" She, of all people, knew what that felt like.

Matthias looked up. A spark of something flashed in his eyes, and the feeling of solidarity she got every morning when she saw the light on at the ranch stretched between them like a rubber band. Frannie wouldn't ever forget that look for the rest of her life.

"That isn't it." He looked away and the rubber band snapped.

Frannie wiped her hands on her apron. "Your sister does whatever she wants. She's going to be how she's going to be, and you're left to pick up the slack and cover for her, making sure the boys don't suffer because she's selfish."

He pushed away from the counter. "That's really what you think?"

Frannie shrugged. She knew the signs. She lived them.

"You don't know what you're talking about." His face had blanked. The lack of emotion was scarier and more distressing than the flash of pain she'd seen earlier. It was like he was forcing himself not to feel anything at all.

"Maybe not, but—"

He walked to the kitchen, cutting her off. "Let's go guys."

Two sets of feet pattered across the linoleum and collided with him at the swinging door. "Uncle Tias!"

The name sliced through her. If the boys were calling him

that as well, then it wasn't a big deal. Why had she thought it was a big deal?

She watched Matthias swing them both up in his big arms, holding them effortlessly like they didn't weigh almost a hundred pounds combined. It wasn't like she'd never seen them together before. Frannie didn't know why it struck her so profoundly in that moment, but it did. She tried to suck in a breath but it got stuck. Parents came in all the time with little kids. Why did it throw her now, just because it was Matthias and his nephews? She was probably just emotional because she was so worn out.

Part of her didn't believe that lie. Something was missing from her life, something huge.

"Uncle Tias, is it time for the party yet?" Simeon—or Reuben, she couldn't tell which twin was which most days—bounced up and down in his arms.

"Almost." He chuckled, but it sounded flat. "How did you guys end up all the way over here? You were supposed to be at the house while I talked to your mom. You know you shouldn't be wandering off on your own."

The other twin piped up. "But Ya-Ya told Dad you were picking up the cake. We had to come and make sure it was going to be good. And we got to *help* and it...was...*awesome!*"

Frannie wasn't sure she was physically capable of being that excited, at least not without passing out.

Matthias, who was evidently completely at ease with their high energy, only chuckled. "Of course you did. So, is it ready now?"

Frannie nodded. "It is." She went into the kitchen and set the cupcakes she'd hidden in the fridge when the boys arrived in two boxes, along with the half-dozen they'd frosted. The boys both hugged her around the hips.

Matthias said, "You need a ride over? Mama said you were coming to the party."

"Oh." She scrambled for words. He wanted the awkwardness to continue? "I really can't. There's no one to watch the—"

"Good morning." The words were bright and cheerful, and belonged to Susan Sheraton.

The First Lady.

Frannie sucked in a breath and coughed, trying not to drop the cupcakes. "Good morning, ma'am. What can I get you?"

The first lady smiled. "Actually, I'm here to help you." She set her forearms on the counter, her manicured fingernails linked together, and smiled a natural and very genuine smile Frannie imagined had set many people at ease over the years.

Frannie didn't move. "Uh…you are?"

Matthias chuckled and rounded the counter with the boys, while Frannie set the cupcake boxes on the counter. He smiled like everything was totally normal. "Good morning, Susan."

Susan? He called the first lady, Susan? It was her name… but still. Who did that?

"Good morning, Matthias. Boys, are you having a fun birthday?"

They bounced in his arms. "Yeah!" "Birthday!"

The first lady laughed, a dignified and classy chuckle that made Frannie feel frumpy in comparison.

Mrs. Sheraton and her daughter, Beth, had arrived a few weeks ago in secret, after the newspapers reported multiple targeted attacks against the first lady. Initially it had been thought to be assassination attempts on the president until it became clear Susan was the target, and her daughter Beth had been caught in the crossfire.

The investigation had uncovered a secret service agent connected to an eco-terrorist group, which compromised the whole organization and left the first lady and her daughter with nowhere safe to go—except Sanctuary.

Frannie hoped for their sakes the whole thing was wrapped up quickly so that Susan and Beth got to return home. Plus, she was ready for the internet to be turned back on. Being on security lockdown was annoying when she needed to look up recipes. But not enough of an inconvenience to complain to the sheriff, like some people had done.

She could live with reading her news in print a week late.

Susan turned her winning smile to Frannie. "Olympia told me you have a certain party to go to, and you might need someone to watch the bakery while you're gone."

Frannie gaped.

"I don't expect you to pay me, it's just a favor. But Beth has taken over the position as school teacher, and since my daughter is working, I've decided I might need something to occupy my time. Maybe this could be a trial, and if you like the arrangement, we could turn it into something more regular."

The first lady wanted a job? A floor-sweeping, tray-hauling, crumbs, dirty dishes and frosting in her hair...*job*? There was no way Frannie was going to let her do all that. Assisting customers, maybe—she'd probably sell a lot of cupcakes—but not the other stuff. A woman like her didn't do menial labor.

Her smile faltered. "Of course, if you don't—"

"No, no." Frannie stopped herself before more words tumbled out. "Uh...yes. I could actually use the help."

Except she would actually have to go to the twins' birthday party, instead of hiding in the bakery and working.

Now she was going to have to figure out how to stay out of Matthias's way, all the while making it not obvious she was trying to do exactly that.

What on earth was Olympia up to?

The first lady smiled. "You have nothing to worry about. I'll take care of your shop. I have some retail experience from my college days. If you'll just go through the procedure with me, I should be able to keep things running."

Frannie felt her cheeks warm. Olympia was obviously trying to help, and it wasn't like she didn't need it, but that meant they all knew she was struggling. And why did it bother her so much, anyway? She didn't want to run herself ragged covering for her mom and sister; she'd rather get her life straight than continue in this mess. But admitting she needed help was a whole other story. Stella was in the medical center. It wasn't like she could just replace the woman. How did you do that?

Today, all she needed to do was accept the offer. "Yes, ma'am."

"You can call me Susan."

Frannie had to apologize for the only clean apron hanging in the closet, but the first lady didn't seem too concerned over the ragged material. She wouldn't be saying that later when she was "glowing," exhausted and with powdered sugar on her expensive blouse. She showed Susan the ledger, explaining her pricing system.

"That must give you a whole lot of accounting to settle."

Frannie shrugged, but the first lady was right. She had ordered so much of her life to make the drama of her mom and sister's behavior as minimal as possible. It meant extra paperwork, but for the sake of not having cash in the store it was worth it. And while that had been okay for a long time, now she was starting to get tired of it. After the break-in last night where they'd gone way too far, taking advantage of her for the hundredth time, the time had come for a change.

"Is everything okay, dear?"

Frannie shook her head to dissipate the convoy of thoughts and shot the first lady a smile she hoped looked nice and not scary. "If you think you'll be fine, I'll be back in two hours."

"No problem." The first lady moved toward her. Frannie braced as Susan Sheraton wrapped her toned arms around her and gave a little squeeze. Then tiny five-year-old hands grabbed hers and pulled her toward the door.

"Birthday party!"

Frannie blinked and looked at each of them. Matthias's eyes were warm. Whatever had passed between them was now gone in place of amusement. "Let's go."

She moved with him to the door, where Matthias stopped. "You want to take off your apron?"

Frannie looked down. "Oh. Right." She hung it up in back and then came back out. He was still smiling.

"I'm ready now."

They walked outside looking like a couple with two kids. Everyone in town knew differently, but it was how they would appear.

Today was turning out to be one of the strangest days of Frannie's life.

———

MATTHIAS SOAKED IT UP, since it was likely the only time in his life he would get out of his truck in the company of a woman who wasn't his sister and two kids. He took the cupcakes from her, and they walked across the grass to where the party was all set up.

The boys ran ahead to their dad, who was talking with Matthias's mom. Olympia looked up at the boys' yell, and her eyes caught sight of him walking over with Frannie.

He saw the moment it hit her, the split-second when his mom's face changed from curious to ecstatic. He pushed out a breath and tried to keep smiling. Cue the wrong idea.

Tables had been set up, covered now with food, presents and a drink station. The crowd was impressive given this was a birthday party for a pair of five-year-olds. Beside the gathering was the town's park, where someone had hooked a sprinkler to a hose, and a dozen kids were running through the spray. He'd have to keep the twins with the party or they'd wind up soaked.

His mom bypassed the cake boxes he was holding and pulled him down to kiss his cheek, a knowing look in her eye. "Matthias."

Matthias didn't want to know what she was going to say to Frannie, and he wasn't going to wait around to be embarrassed by it. He strode away to deposit the cakes on the folding-table draped with a blue tablecloth, but heard, "Precious."

His stomach clenched, and his fingers throbbed from slamming his fist into Diego's face. Thankfully he hadn't broken the skin on his hand, it was just red and sore. Matthias's mom did not need to know he'd lost his cool with Diego.

He looked back to where his mom was embracing Frannie. The look on Frannie's face wasn't entirely happy, as though she hadn't expected to be hugged. And why not? Frannie's mom and sister were pretty touchy-feely women.

Matthias set the cupcakes down. His mom would love it if he started a relationship with Frannie. She'd have the two of them married off for their happily ever after within three days, and she would tell everyone it was her doing. Matthias figured he'd be too busy being happy to complain. Too bad it wasn't going to happen. He didn't need another person to tiptoe around.

"Matthias!" Pat Mason, the sheriff's son, ran at him, full force.

Matthias braced and let his little friend slam into him for a hug. "Dude, did you grow a foot since last Sunday?"

Pat grinned. "Dad says I'm having a growth spurt."

"I believe it." Matthias ruffled the nine-year-old's hair. "How's school going?"

The kid shrugged. "Pretty good. Mrs. Myerson is cool, even if her dad is a Democrat."

Matthias laughed. Pat's father—Sheriff John Mason—walked over. John had arrived only weeks before, his arrival sparking a turn of events that left two town residents dead, one in jail and one almost convicted of a murder she didn't commit.

Matthias was glad it had all worked out, but didn't figure he'd be able to come through it as unscathed as they all seemed to be. In fact, now John and Andra were engaged it was almost like everything had always been fine. Maybe that was how it worked. And why love felt like the Promised Land he'd always been denied.

"Hey, Matthias."

He shook the sheriff's hand. "John. How's it going?"

Matthias glanced at Frannie, still talking with his mom. She was nodding her head and smiling, like she had nothing better to do than hear what Olympia had to say.

"Thought so."

Matthias looked at John. "What was that?"

The sheriff smirked. "Nothing."

"Don't you have a deer to find, or someone to give a citation to for bike riding too fast?"

"Not today." John was still smiling. "Today I have nothing better to do than hang with my boy and my fiancé, and eat cake at a kid's birthday party."

"Lucky me."

John laughed; his eyes caught on Matthias's hand and he frowned. "Is the other guy okay?"

Matthias waved off his concern. Apparently it was a little noticeable. "It's nothing. I just lost my cool with Diego is all."

"That explains the sunglasses."

Matthias looked where John motioned. Diego was talking with two women, laying on the charm as usual, but with sunglasses to cover what was likely a black eye given how much Matthias's hand hurt.

"You wanna tell me?"

About the punch, or all of it, Matthias didn't know which. He shook his head. "It's fine."

"Just let me know, you need anything. Yeah?"

Matthias kept his face straight. "You're available to help hide the body?"

John didn't react. "He's getting that bad?"

"Never mind." Matthias sighed. "You wouldn't get it."

John's eyebrow rose. "Because I don't have three meddling brothers who are a pain in my rear?"

Matthias had met John's brothers, but wasn't sure how much they could interfere when John lived in a town like this one.

Sure, one was the director of the Marshals, so he was technically John's boss, given John was the sheriff of a town of federal witnesses. But there was also the quarterback for the Dolphins—Nate—and the other brother... Well, that guy had perfected skulking for sure. Matthias had only met Ben once, but could admit at least to himself he was slightly scared of the guy, even though he'd shown up to help John rescue Andra.

John lifted his arm, and his fiancé walked to his side. Andra smiled up at Matthias. "Hey."

He cleared his throat. "Hey."

Matthias had always been intimidated by Andra. Not just because she had light skin and dark coloring that made her look like Snow White, but because until recently she'd lived a reclusive life up in the mountains.

The rumors had been more than slightly terrifying, and finding out she'd been a government assassin hadn't really helped the intimidation factor. Now Andra was living with her best friend, Nadia Marie, and planning a wedding. Matthias figured if John cared about her enough to ask her to be the mother of his son then she was worth knowing.

The tall, slender salon owner joined them, too. "Hey, Matt."

"Nadia."

She grinned. Usually Nadia Marie would object to someone shortening her name. But since she did it with his, he'd mentioned her lack of standing to complain about it. Now it had just become a regular joke when he went by her salon to get his hair cut.

Frannie stood beside her, wringing her hands together. "I should set out the cupcakes."

Matthias jumped into action, ignoring the smirks. Frannie came to stand beside him. He didn't move away but held his ground and opened a cake box before he slid it over to her.

It was torture, and he should give the whole idea of her up. Nothing was going to happen between them even though she'd given him a gift in allowing him to talk about Maria even a little. His emotions didn't usually get a whole lot of air time, so it was weird and actually nice she'd asked him about Maria.

It wasn't judgmental, even if she'd assumed Maria might cause a scene at the party.

The simple fact Frannie had understood he felt like he had to hold everything together allowed him to take his first full breath in forever.

Matthias handed her the next cake box, and she looked up at him. Smiled. "Thanks, Tias."

Movement behind them brought his attention around. Matthias looked back to where Andra, Nadia and John were smirking. Andra had her hand over her mouth. There were tears in her eyes from laughing silently. Matthias kicked out his leg in John's direction.

They all laughed.

"Huh?" Frannie turned to the group.

Nadia said, "I'll fill you in later."

Matthias's face whipped around to pin her with a look, but she didn't take her statement back. Nadia just smiled at him.

"I have to go help Mama with something." He strode away, feeling like an idiot for retreating, but what else was he supposed to do? Frannie couldn't get the wrong idea. That would just make things worse than they already were.

Diego stepped into his path, so Matthias didn't have time to move before he collided with his brother's shoulder. They both turned to face each other. Diego's sunglasses concealed both the black eye and the usual distain when he looked at Matthias. Did he want another black eye, or was this retaliation time?

"This isn't the place for this."

Diego stepped closer. "You think I'm going to let a black eye slide?"

"I think—"

"Matthias! Diego!" Their mother's voice wasn't a hundred

percent ecstatic, but it wasn't unusual given the look in her eyes. She squeezed Matthias's arm, just above his elbow. "Will you round up the boys for games, my love?"

"Sure."

Matthias caught the boys and brought them to the middle of the gathering, where his mom and Tom had set up ring toss and a sort of mini obstacle course the kids could run over, under and through. Adults mingled, snacking on the food his mom had made while Matthias was dragged through the games by Reuben and Simeon. Not that he minded, except when he stopped and saw Diego laughing with Frannie.

"Uncle Tias, come on!"

Frannie looked over then. Diego kept talking, trying to hold her attention, but it was on him now. Matthias couldn't help the small smile that curved his lips and probably made him look like a weirdo.

Simeon pulled on his arm and Reuben joined in, grunting and trying to drag him along. Frannie turned back to Diego, and Matthias's heart sank. It was for the best.

"Uncle Tias!"

He laughed and followed the boys to more games. His focus needed to be on giving the twins the best life possible.

Maria, dressed in a red floral sundress with her hair curled, strode through the crowd. "Reuben, Simeon! Mama's here."

It was so surprising Matthias actually stumbled. The boys let go of him and ran to hug their mom. Whatever was going on, he was glad she had decided to be present for this, even if he was determined to be, too. Just in case. Her yo-yo emotions had short-changed so many occasions for the boys, even when Tom attempted to cover for her. Matthias's job was to soften the blow of whatever was coming next.

CHAPTER 4

Frannie heard Maria's arrival, but Diego's hold on her arm kept her from turning around. The grip wasn't painful, but it was firm enough to let her know she wasn't getting away any time soon.

"You really should come with us sometime. We'd have a great time. Your mom and Izzy always do."

Frannie tried to pull her arm away again. He didn't look like he was all about the fun, even if his reputation was exactly that. He looked almost...predatory. Still, there was nothing special about her, he probably did this with every woman he came across. Although the thought didn't make her feel any better.

"No, thank you, Diego. That's not going to happen." Frannie pulled away then, to make sure he understood. "I have to get back to the bakery and check on things."

She turned but didn't get anywhere, halted by what was going on in the middle of the party. Maria's face had whitened to look a lot like sheer terror. The twins glanced between their mom and their dad, who stood behind where she knelt in front of them.

Maria looked up at Tom. He sighed. "Boys—"

"Found it!" Matthias's voice didn't sound like he'd had a success. His smile was almost brittle as he handed the boys a wrapped package. He stepped back, a gift tag in his hand, which he slid in his back pocket.

Maria beamed.

The boys tore the box open and pulled out boots—a black pair and a brown pair. Simeon and Reuben both took a boot in each color and kicked off their sneakers to pull on one black and one brown boot.

Everyone laughed. They reached in again and took out matching cowboy hats. "Awesome!"

They ran around, hugging first their mom then their dad. Matthias looked at Frannie then, but his smile died. Frannie felt Diego's heat behind her back, before his hand slid around her waist. She jumped out of reach, but it was too late. Matthias had already looked away.

Frannie moved. Too late she realized it made her look like a frightened mouse. She turned to face him. "That was not okay."

He looked her up and down. "I could have a lot of fun with that sweet body of yours, Frannie Peters."

Before she could retort back, her friends showed up. On either side of her, the cavalry flanked Frannie. Nadia Marie's perfume was unmistakable, and Andra stood slightly in front in a protective stance. But Frannie didn't relax, she couldn't. Not yet.

Andra Caleri folded her arms. "You say anything like that to her again, Diego, and I'm going to hear about it."

He blustered for a second, and then said, "Yeah? So what?"

"You know what."

"You're not going to kill me. You'd get kicked out of Sanctuary. Everyone knows that."

Andra smiled, but there was nothing amusing about it. "You think anyone would find your body? I don't make a mess, and I happen to have the ear of the sheriff. Everyone will assume you simply tried to leave...and got lost in the woods." She waved her arm in a graceful move, encompassing the mountains all the way around town like a moat. An impenetrable moat.

Diego swallowed and backed up a step. Frannie wanted to whoop, but that wouldn't be classy. It wasn't a good idea to catch the eye of an assassin, even one who didn't kill anymore. Well, except when the deputy sheriff had tried to kill Andra, and she ended his life in self-defense. But that was pardoned by the president, so it didn't count. Diego looked like he wanted to save face, but evidently thought better of it and stalked off.

Nadia Marie nudged Frannie's shoulder with her own. "What was that about?"

"Just Diego being Diego, that's all."

Nadia's eyes narrowed. "That's all?"

"It's fine." She turned to Andra. "Thank you."

"No problem."

"I appreciate you saying it, even if you wouldn't actually kill him." To be honest, the former assassin made Frannie a little nervous, too. Okay, a lot nervous—enough to try and laugh off her concern.

"For Diego, I'd like to think I would make an exception."

Now Frannie was the one trying to swallow. She coughed and inhaled. "I really should go. The first lady is looking after the bakery, and I need to make sure she's okay."

She wasn't ungrateful they'd come to her rescue. It just didn't stop her from being disappointed Matthias hadn't been the one to come over. If it'd been so obvious to Nadia and Andra she needed help, why hadn't he seen it?

Frannie glanced over at him and saw the muscle in his jaw move. The twins looked happy, so why was he upset?

"Maria misplaced their present, or forgot it, or didn't even buy them one." Nadia's voice was low. "He gave them the present from him and then claimed he was the one who forgot to bring his. Like we all don't know he's covering for Maria, who can remember a hair appointment she made six weeks ago without me even writing it down."

The disgust on her face was plain.

Frannie said, "You have no idea what is going on with her."

"And you do?"

No, but if Matthias was willing to defend his sister then maybe there was something worth defending.

Nadia Marie shook her head. "It's like she doesn't even care."

"That you know of." Frannie shrugged. "It's possible there's a whole lot that none of us are privy to."

Andra stepped closer to them. "What are you talking about?"

"I'm just saying, what you see isn't always a measure of everything that makes up a person. We all have things about us no one ever knows, or sees."

"So you're hiding something?" Nadia Marie frowned.

"Aren't you?"

Nadia's brows twitched like she was trying to hold the frown and it slipped for a second. There was definitely something about this woman no one knew, and it wasn't the fact she had a thing for Bolton Farrera, because that was obvious even if she hadn't come out and said it.

Andra shifted. "So you just hold everything in and never

get close to anyone? Trusting someone with the truth is harder, but eventually a whole lot more rewarding."

Frannie folded her arms. "Until they realize you're not what they thought, and then you're all alone again. No thanks."

"With the right person, you can let go of the fear."

"It's not worth it."

She wanted to glance at Matthias again. Was he the exception instead of the rule? She couldn't let herself hope for what would never be. It was fine to spend time with him when she had to, but there was zero point in seeking him out. Not when Diego was intent on making her life miserable.

If she made it clear she was interested in Matthias, things would get so much worse. Diego would get mad, Matthias would pull away and she would lose the small connection she had with Tias now. She couldn't risk it. She wasn't willing to let that go, not for the sake of what maybe could be. Not when it would end in awkwardness and a broken heart.

He deserved better than her.

"From your lips to God's ears." Andra grinned, and beside her, Nadia chuckled.

"What's that supposed to mean?"

"One thing I've discovered about God? The thing you're holding onto so tightly that you think is right? You're about to be proven *wrong*."

"No way." God wasn't like that. "I don't have that kind of faith, not like you guys. God is God and all, but it's not like it needs to be more than that."

Andra glanced at Nadia Marie, and they both smiled. "Sure." Andra laughed. "Whatever you say."

"It's not like I actually come to church. I have to work on Sundays. Someone has to bake the pastries you all eat after service. Did you think of that?"

"And then you bring them with you to the Meeting House." Nadia Marie grinned. "Maybe sometime you should sit and listen in."

Because she didn't do that when she was in the kitchen? It wasn't like she could close her ears. Church was fine and all, even if it didn't resemble anything she was used to. But she'd had religion as a child, and it wasn't going to help Frannie figure out this mess that was her life now. She was stuck, permanently holding the dissonant fragments of her existence together by sheer force of will. If she let go, even for a second, her whole life would crumble. And then where would she be?

"Happy birthdays!"

Frannie's head whipped around. "Oh, please. No."

Andra's hand touched her shoulder in a move of camaraderie, but it didn't help. Nothing was going to help the fact her mom was tottering across the grass. The stiletto heels of her red sandals sank into the ground, but from her pasted-on smile no one would ever know. She crouched in her denim skirt—which made several people wince and look away—and held out her arms.

The twins hesitated but accepted her gesture. Izzy walked over after her, carrying a present wrapped with blue paper. The boys moved from the hug to the gift and tore into it. Izzy smoothed down her hair, running her fingers through it while she smiled and looked up under her lowered eyelids at Diego.

Frannie didn't look at him; she didn't want to know what was there. Whatever it was made Izzy flash her perfect white smile at Matthias's brother.

Mimi clapped. "There's cake, even? How darling!"

Why was she here? Mimi didn't care about these kids; neither of them did. Diego held out his elbow, and Mimi wrapped her arm in it while he escorted her to the cake table. They both bit into a cupcake Frannie had baked.

Maria held out her arms to the twins. "Let's sing *Happy Birthday!*"

Tom stepped up beside her and touched her arm. "We should light the candles, so the boys can blow them out."

Her smile faltered. "Yes. Of course."

Tom shook the box of matches. Diego and Mimi strode away, tossing their cupcake wrappers in the direction of the trash. They missed, the blue-smeared casings falling on the grass.

Mimi looked up at Diego. "Kind of airy, don't you think? I like my cake rich and moist. Dark. The same way I like my men."

Frannie spun around. Nadia Marie and Andra were still right behind her, which meant she almost collided with them. "I'm going back to the bakery."

Frannie didn't much care if she had to walk back. Nothing in Sanctuary was far from anything else. The longest distance anyone could travel would be to walk in circles around town, but who wanted to do that all their life? Frannie didn't like the idea of never getting anywhere.

The beat of her sneakers on the sidewalk pushed down the frustration with every step.

One day she should take up running. It had to be easier to escape your problems when you were rushing by, leaving the world behind.

Frannie let herself in the back door of the bakery and paused by the stairs leading up to the second floor. There wasn't much up there. She mostly used it as storage, but only because the previous store owner had piled all the old furniture and scraps of material like carpet, and even some drapes and old dirty sheets, up there. It wasn't good for anything she needed. There wasn't even a working bathroom.

She had hooked up her computer in the single bedroom

and hauled in an old metal filing cabinet, but that was it. The plus side was that her mom or sister would never intentionally soil themselves by going up, so she actually had a private space. Even one that smelled like mothballs—or what she figured mothballs would smell like if she actually knew what they were.

The first lady strode into the kitchen with an empty tray. "There you are."

"Everything go okay?"

"Fine, dear. You?"

Frannie shrugged. How someone could make a look of consternation feel warm was anyone's guess, but Susan Sheraton did. Frannie figured the first lady wasn't used to taking crap from anybody. Or being lied to.

Susan set her dainty hand on her hip. "I have a daughter. I know what being brushed off looks like." She sighed. "Believe me, I know. But you don't have to tell me if you don't want to. I'm not about to pry in your business."

"Thank you."

Her blue eyes narrowed and glinted. "Ah, so there is something."

Frannie laughed, which felt good. There wasn't much in her life that warranted humor, unless it was the tragic kind. "Any idea how to escape your life when you're basically stuck with it twenty-four/seven?"

"Well, it's funny you should ask that..."

"Yeah." Frannie mock-sighed. "You probably don't know anything about being stuck under a microscope. Or having to do something because people assume you should, instead of being able to just goof-off for a day."

The first lady smiled. "Have you tried kick boxing?"

"Seriously?"

"Sam has a class on Thursday afternoons at four. It's a

great workout if you're feeling the need to pummel something that won't get mad, or hit you back."

"All right." Frannie smiled. "That sounds pretty good." She was going to have to work it around rehearsals for the play, but it might just be worth it.

"You know, I can stick around here if you have something you need to do."

"Really? You're not bored yet?"

Susan shook her head. "It's different, but I've enjoyed meeting everyone who came in. Beth is due in a few minutes. I gave her a call and said to come over. You have her favorites in the display cabinet. The chocolate croissants."

"That's right. She asked for those especially, said she had a craving."

Something flickered over Susan's face, but she shook it off fast and smiled. "I'm sure she did."

"If you're good, then I'll go upstairs and get some paper-work done." Frannie waved toward the stairs behind her. "Holler if you need anything."

"I certainly will."

Half an hour later the first lady brought Frannie a bottle of water and a sandwich. That was when she realized she hadn't eaten anything since her four a.m. breakfast. Frannie pulled her gaze from the snow-crested peaks of the mountains out her grimy window and looked at the desk.

She was still surrounded by papers. They hadn't magically disappeared while she'd been daydreaming.

Susan chuckled. "I shouldn't laugh, but you really look like you're in pain."

"I am." She puffed out a breath and then grabbed two papers that tried to blow away. Those needed to be delivered. "I really hate accounting, but it has to be done."

"And you prefer baking, or conversing with customers better?"

"Baking."

"That's what I thought."

"What do you mean?"

The first lady shook her head, but her face looked a whole lot like Olympia's had that morning. That, *I'm a mom and I'm up to something,* face. "I'll let you know when I figure it out."

Frannie should tell her everything. Then Susan could give her an answer for all of it, but she wouldn't be sorting out her own life. She would be leaving that to someone else. Again. Therein was the whole reason she was in this mess in the first place. She should have just told Director Mason to stick her mom and sister in Miami. At least they would have died happy.

By the time the sun set behind the mountains, Frannie had printed the whole stack of invoices. Tomorrow they would need to be delivered, after which, money would trickle in, and she'd be able to buy some more toothpaste. Then she'd be able to purchase more bulk baking supplies from the Air Force for next month.

Although she was out of blue food coloring now. If she wanted to make those whale cookies before her shipment came in on the delivery transport, she'd have to run to the tiny general store on the other side of Main Street and grab one of the little bottles.

The first lady had left a couple of hours before and apparently cleaned the tables and mopped the floors before she'd left. God bless the woman. Frannie double-checked the locks and tried to calculate how long it would be before she could get a security alarm. A hundred years from now, most likely. Unless she could get an oven for free, or find someone to fix the one that was out.

Dreading the idea of going home, Frannie rode her bike to the medical center instead. The light in the front windows was dim, but the security guard would let her in.

Xander appeared at the door, making her jump back even though she'd been expecting him. The whites of his eyes were the only thing visible against his dark skin. Then he smiled, and she saw the gap between his front teeth. He laughed, but the sound was muffled through the door, and he hoofed his girth back to the reception desk where he pressed the door release.

Frannie pushed the door open and stepped inside.

He stuck his thumbs in his belt. "Scared ya."

"Yes, you did. Hi, Xander."

"Hi yourself, Ms. Frannie." His belt contained a baton, flashlight and radio but no gun. Xander had been hired as a night guard after the break-ins started and the locks were broken. No one had been caught yet and things seemed to have quieted down. There'd been one more theft of pharmaceuticals the sheriff figured out had happened during the day, but Xander kept up his nightly patrols, and Frannie was glad for it. His presence meant Stella wasn't alone when her husband went home for the day.

"Here to see Ms. Stella?"

Frannie nodded. "How is she?"

His smile slipped. "Not so good."

Frannie squeezed his tree-trunk bicep, suddenly feeling like she needed to comfort him. It had to be hard to be around sick people night after night. Sure, a lot of them recovered and went home, but some didn't. She wasn't sure she could cope with that sense of finality. *Death Valley*. It was what some of the town residents called Sanctuary. Not that it was actually a valley, more like a basin. But it was where they all came to die.

Frannie made her way down the hall. The only alternative to dying here was to leave...and be killed on her father's order by his men still hunting her.

What power she had lay with the choice itself, instead of the outcome. There were people in the world who wanted her dead and would use any means necessary to see it happen. It was why she was here—why her family was here, as much as they grated against her.

Now the only power she had was in the day to day decisions she made. Like the decision to cut her mom and sister loose, fire them from the bakery and move out. She'd taken care of them for so long it was almost instinctual now. What would she do on her own? How would they pay the mortgage, and how was she going to break the news that she was cutting them off? Did anyone other than the first lady even want a job at the bakery?

Not to mention there was hardly time to worry about all that when she was running a business, working her hours in the kitchen and at the front counter. Starting tomorrow she was going to be acting in Aaron and Shelby's play. It had sounded like fun at the time, and the selection process was something like jury duty in this town, but Frannie had loved drama at school. Not that she'd ever admit that to her former movie-star mom. Heaven forbid.

When things calmed down, that would be the time to start making huge life changes.

Frannie knocked softly on the door to Stella's room. Since Stella was a permanent resident of the medical center, the room had an en-suite bathroom with a tub and a detachable shower head. The TV was a little bigger than in the other rooms. But the smell was worse, even with the fresh flowers Stella's husband brought in every week. The bouquet was all reds and gold glinting off the lamp-light, something you might find decorating your table at Christmas. It was an interesting choice.

A short, bulky figure stood over the bed. Not the doctor, someone else was visiting Stella. A night nurse? Frannie hadn't heard of anyone being hired on after the doctor's wife committed suicide. The remaining day nurse might be working late.

"I can wait outside if you want."

He turned. It wasn't bright enough to make out who it was, but he had a wool cap pulled over his face.

"What are you—"

His hand came into view, a needle clutched in his gloved fingers.

Frannie's heart stopped beating in her chest. For a moment she couldn't breathe. By sheer force of will she sucked in air...

And screamed.

The stocky man dropped the needle and ran at her. She was still screaming when he tackled her, shoving her into the wall.

The back of Frannie's head slammed into the corner of a shelf, and she hit the ground.

CHAPTER 5

FRANNIE COULDN'T TELL if someone was coming or if the pounding was inside her head. Everything was blurry until the light flicked on and Xander rushed over.

"Ms. Frannie, I heard you yell. What happened?"

"Someone...a man..." Her thoughts wouldn't coalesce, they were as helpful as yeast that wouldn't activate. But one thing rose to the top. "Stella."

"Let's sit you up, and I'll see to her." Xander grabbed his radio. "Sheriff Mason, this is Xander at the medical center. We need you over here, A-SAP."

Frannie's head spun. She leaned her shoulders against the wall and touched the back of her hair. No blood on her fingers. That was good, right?

Xander went to Stella's bedside, but didn't touch anything. "She's still sleeping. There's a needle here. What happened?"

Frannie massaged her temples but couldn't make sense of any of it. Who was that man? Had he been trying to kill Stella? She was dying. Why kill a woman with only a short time to live?

Xander picked up the phone beside the bed and punched in a series of numbers. "Doctor Fenton?"

Frannie tuned out what he was saying. Her head hurt like nothing she'd ever felt before. It was going to be a nightmare trying to work tomorrow, but that worry was for then. Right now she had to check on her friend. It took several attempts, but she managed to get her feet underneath her. Using the bed for leverage, Frannie pulled herself up. The world stopped and then rotated in the opposite direction. Her legs started to give out, but she forced her knees to lock.

"Ms. Frannie!"

Stella's eyes were closed. Her chest rose and fell with the slow breaths of someone resting. Still, relief didn't come. Stella had lost so much weight, and her color... Frannie's heart hurt just looking at her. She stumbled back, not wanting her friend to waken and see the effect being here had on Frannie. Stella didn't need Frannie to compound her suffering.

Xander took her elbow. "Let's find you a place to sit."

Frannie nodded, feeling the wet tickle of a tear on her cheek. She swiped it away as the security guard steered her out to the waiting area. A Jeep pulled up outside, and Xander hit the release button on the door to let the sheriff in.

John Mason wore jeans and a crumpled T-shirt. He'd slid his badge on his belt, and his gun was in a shoulder holster like he was some big-city police detective instead of the sheriff of a small town. Given he'd formerly been an undercover US marshal, it wasn't a wonder the man could pin her with a stare that made her nearly pee her pants and wish he'd just ask a question so she could spill her guts—even if she hadn't actually done anything wrong.

Frannie had also seen him crouching down before his son, sharing a soft smile with the nine-year-old. But that man wasn't here now. This man was all cop. He might have the same short blond hair, and his chin held a smattering of stubble, but those good looks didn't soften the authority he wore like it was a shirt. The same way his brother, Grant, the director of the Marshals, did.

"Frannie, you okay?"

Xander appeared beside where she sat and handed her an ice pack. She smiled her thanks, not sure she could speak yet, and pressed it to the back of her head. It was really cold. She took a breath and blew it out before looking at the sheriff. "No, I'm not okay."

He crouched, his mouth crimping into a sympathetic smile. "You want to tell me what happened?"

Frannie reiterated the whole thing. The man, the needle. All of it.

Sheriff Mason stood. "Xander, stay here with her for a minute."

The security guard rocked back on his heels, thumbs in his belt. "Sure, boss."

John snorted, but walked straight for Stella's room. A couple of seconds later, the doctor let himself in the front door, pocketing a key. "Frannie?"

She felt her brow furrow. She didn't know why it surprised her that he knew her name, but it wasn't like they'd ever really talked. His wife—before she died—never came to the bakery, and they didn't exactly run in the same social circles. Doctor Fenton looked like one of her mom's old boyfriends from when Frannie was in middle school, during the year her parents had been separated. He'd been a plastic surgeon. Their relationship would probably have bankrupted him if it'd gone on any longer.

Frannie wouldn't be surprised if he got his hair and nails done at Nadia Marie's salon. And if he did, the appointments had continued even after his wife committed suicide, because not one thing was out of place.

"Ms. Frannie hit her head. Ms. Stella's resting, but we're not sure if something might have been done to her."

Doctor Fenton flinched. "Done to her?" Clearly the idea of someone messing with one of his patients was abhorrent. Frannie considered that a good quality in a doctor. He reached for her head.

"No, I'm okay. It's just a bump. Check on Stella first, please."

He nodded. "Very well. I'll be back shortly."

The sheriff passed him in the hall, now coming back. They stopped and had a brief conversation, neither one looking particularly happy. Especially not when they both turned and looked at her. Shouldn't they be searching for the man who'd been here?

She shifted and looked up at Xander. It hurt her head, but she had to ask the question. "Did you see someone run out of the room? A man?"

"No, Ms. Frannie, I didn't." From the look in his eyes, that concerned him. Like he thought she was losing it.

"How could he have gotten out if the front is locked? Is there a back door that's open?"

His face twitched. "Worth checking, I think." Xander wandered off, suddenly energized. Was he hoping she was right? Which begged the question—why did they think she was wrong?

Unless they didn't believe her.

The sheriff sat on a waiting room chair across from her and rested a small box big enough to hold a butter knife on his lap. "Ms. Peters, can you tell me about the needle?"

"It was in his hand. He dropped it when he ran at me."

"Can you describe the man?"

Frannie already had, when she'd told him the first time. "Short and stocky."

"Taller than you?"

"Maybe an inch or two shorter. Heavy. Not that he looked it, but more like an impression of heaviness. Like he had trouble hauling it around, so he walked like it took a lot of effort. But he moved fast. Before I knew it, he was running into me." Frannie lowered the ice, the back of her head now numb.

Sheriff Mason said, "The man you saw, what do you think he was doing?"

Frannie closed her mouth, pressing her lips together while the things she'd seen washed through her mind. The man standing over the bed, a needle in his hand. "He was going to harm her, wasn't he?"

The sheriff gave her a conciliatory smile. "Until we can confirm what was in the syringe we can't be sure, but the doctor gave me a pretty good idea. So yes, we think he was trying to harm her."

"Like kill her?"

"Frannie, why do you think someone would want to do that to Stella?"

She frowned. "I don't know. She isn't doing well at all. Stella has been fighting, but it's clearly hard, and it's taken a lot—" Her voice hitched. "—out of her. But she promised me she's not going to quit. She promised me."

"A particular kind of person may consider it a kindness to end that kind of suffering."

"You mean like..." The idea of it broke over Frannie like an ice cold wave.

Doctor Fenton strode down the hall toward them.

Frannie shot out her chair and fought away the dizziness that momentum brought on. She planted both feet and waited for the doctor to come to her. "What is it, how is she?" Was everyone going to stop looking at her like that? She wasn't the one who was sick.

Doctor Fenton scratched his perfect hair. "Mrs. Noel is sleeping. I'm not sure she woke up, even with the disturbance, and I'm disinclined to rouse her now. At this point she needs to rest."

The pounding in Frannie's head kicked up again. "What?"

Doctor Fenton sighed. "She doesn't have long."

Her legs moved. Before she realized what she was doing, Frannie had backed up two steps. The back of her knees hit the arm of a chair and she crumpled. The sheriff caught her, lowering her to the seat.

"You stopped it, Frannie." His blue eyes were soft. Kind. "Nothing happened because you were here right when Stella needed you. Whatever that man had planned, he couldn't do it because of you."

Frannie pushed out a breath and nodded.

"You said you didn't know who it was?"

She shook her head. "He was wearing a mask." Her voice was high and tight.

"I know." His gaze softened. "If you think of anything else tomorrow, you need to come by and tell me. I'll be around, whatever you need. I don't want you to hesitate."

"Uh...okay."

"I want you to be careful. I want you to be aware of what's happening around you. Keep your eyes open."

"Why?"

"Because there's a chance this guy thinks you can identify him. We have to see how it plays out, but I'm not willing to take any chances with your safety."

"You think he's going to come after me?"

"If your life was in danger, he likely would have killed you in that room instead of just pushing you aside."

Frannie tried to swallow, but it got stuck.

John kept talking. "I think you just freaked him out, and he ran. I want you to be cautious. It's not worth being caught unaware."

"Uh..."

"Is there any way you can keep from being alone for the foreseeable future?"

It was dawning on her in increments, like pieces of a puzzle dropping into place. She had stopped an awful thing from happening to Stella, and now her life could be in danger. Again? Not from witnessing a murder, but from preventing one.

"I—" Her tongue got stuck in her mouth. She tried to breathe, but nothing was coming out. Frannie got up, but she must have done it too fast because she swayed.

Multiple sets of hands caught her, but she couldn't shake them off.

Everything went black again.

———

MATTHIAS DIVIDED the pan of eggs and sausage into twelve breakfast burritos. Sure, there were only four of them at the ranch, but they could have something else to eat mid-morning when they broke for more coffee and he went to church.

The kitchen door swung open, and Bolton stomped in from outside. "Eat up. We need to meet with the sheriff."

Matthias moved the burrito away from his mouth. "Why?"

"Didn't say." Bolton shook hot sauce on his eggs. Then

more. Then some more. Then he wrapped up the tortilla and took a bite.

Diego and Sean came in. Diego's eye had retreated to a purplish-green. He didn't say anything, but Matthias saw a look pass between Sean and his brother. Why Sean insisted on hanging with his brother was anyone's guess. One day the guy was going to wake up and realize he'd thrown away what could have been some really good years for the sake of getting into trouble with Diego.

And didn't that make Matthias sound like a bitter old man?

It wasn't like his early twenties had been all about laughter and love, and fun. He'd mostly worked, and gone to the bakery when he couldn't resist the urge to see Frannie. Maybe Diego's way was better. He was certainly living a more interesting life than Matthias's unrequited existence.

A relationship wasn't going to work. When he forced himself to face reality he could accept that. The rest of the time he was too busy wondering what it would be like to kiss her to worry about how it would turn out. Maybe it would work, if he could swallow the risks.

Bolton grabbed two filled, hot cups and motioned to the door with his chin. Matthias followed him out to the truck, and they drove into town.

Before Bolton's arrival, the rancher in charge had been barely worth anything, an old accountant who knew next to nothing about cows and left Matthias with the running of the ranch. Matthias had emailed a bunch of ranches around the country under the guise he was writing a paper for a class about animal husbandry and found out what to do.

The on-the-job learning had been rough, but between the information he got and Dan Walden's direction, he'd managed to survive enough that when Bolton came, things were running pretty smoothly. His current boss had bought the ranch and made Matthias a full partner. Everything was split fifty-fifty, and they made all the decisions together. It was more than Matthias ever expected, even if he still considered Bolton the one in charge.

Matthias hadn't been expecting any of Bolton's side activities either. Not the fact his new boss would insist they all be trained to use every one of his weapons, along with self-defense, hand-to-hand combat and basic escape and evade tactics. Or that Bolton would have Matthias help him with surveillance.

It was like Bolton was expecting Sanctuary to suffer a full-scale attack.

Bolton held the steering wheel in a loose grip. "Judging by the scene back there, you didn't talk with Diego yet."

Matthias had been expecting the question. Still, he couldn't help but react. "He never came home last night, so I didn't get the chance. He probably waited until just before we left to come to breakfast so I wouldn't have the chance."

Not that Matthias even wanted to have a "talk" with his brother. Bolton insisted they have a good working relationship, but if Diego really thought Matthias was trying to be their father, there wasn't much he could repair. Diego didn't know him, and nothing Matthias could do was going to fix that.

"Anything on the screens?"

Matthias shook his head. Their surveillance system covered most of the forest area, but concentrated on the boundaries—the highest elevation of the mountains. Last night had been Matthias's scheduled night to watch over town, but it'd been uneventful. Like always. Still, Bolton had enough weapons in place he could crush a coup if one was ever to take place in Sanctuary.

It goaded him there wasn't more he could see, since he had no idea where Diego went when he disappeared. Into the woods surrounding town would have been his guess, but who knew? They didn't watch every square foot of it. For a small town, there were entirely too many places to hide here.

As they drove past, Matthias didn't get a good look at the bakery except to see the light was on. Bolton pulled around the back of Main Street, to the north, where Frannie's bike was against the wall out back. They parked a few doors down, beside the sheriff's Jeep. The back door was unlocked. When they entered the office, the sheriff was on the phone.

"I'll let you know more later." He hung up and waved them in. "Sit."

Bolton leaned against the cabinet that housed the microwave and coffee maker and folded his arms. Matthias grinned and chose the chair behind what had been Deputy Palmer's desk, back before he double-crossed them all and tried to kill Andra. He'd heard the sheriff's fiancé had stabbed Palmer in the neck with a pen. It wasn't any wonder that no one applied for the deputy position since.

What Matthias didn't know was why he was here. Bolton was ex-DEA, so the sheriff consulted with him on any case that needed more than one pair of hands, or eyes. Bolton claimed he didn't want the deputy job, but he was willing to help out if he could walk away to the ranch and the case didn't follow him. Which Matthias figured meant that had happened before, maybe in his former life. Bolton probably didn't want a repeat here, where he was supposed to be safe.

The sheriff sat forward in his chair. "I know you both have plenty to do, so I'll cut to the chase. I'm not convinced Harriet Fenton committed suicide."

Matthias said, "The doctor's wife?"

The sheriff nodded. "It was well done, but every aspect

does not add up. In the light of this fact, I've been through the previous sheriff's files and compiled a list of five cases since Sanctuary's inception which I think were murders either incorrectly investigated, or simply closed and labelled an accident or suicide because that was what they appeared on the outside."

Matthias glanced between Bolton and John. "What does this have to do with me?"

"Two reasons. The first is that last night Francine Peters witnessed the attempted murder of Stella Noel, a terminal patient at the medical center. She walked in on what she says was a man attempting to inject a substance into Stella. The assailant ran at her and slammed her against the wall. She was knocked out, but there was no lasting damage except a bump on the head."

Matthias was up and halfway to the door. He thought they might have called his name, but he didn't know for sure. He needed to get to Frannie. Now. Bolton's arm collided with his stomach, but he kept going. Nothing was going to stop him getting out the door. She'd been hurt, and the sheriff waited until now to tell him?

Matthias grabbed for the door handle but Bolton hauled his body backward. He wrestled against his boss's grip. "Let me go!"

"I'll put you down if I have to." Bolton wasn't even breathing heavy. "Don't make me do it, Matt."

"Let me go!"

John grabbed his arm and the two of them pushed him against the wall. The sheriff got in his face. "Give us a minute before you run off."

Both of their hands held his shoulders pinned against the wall. Matthias tried to move but couldn't break free. Why couldn't he go see her?

"Matthias, calm down."

He jerked one more time and then exhaled. "Whatever it is, say it so I can go."

"Don't go to her like this." Bolton's jaw flexed and he said, "Get a hold of yourself. You go to her like this and she'll shut down. You know that. If you want to help her, you need to get some control."

He didn't want to admit it, but Bolton was right. Frannie wasn't going to respond well if he barged in. She was so private. She wouldn't want her business spread around, even if the sheriff had only told him and Bolton. The way she responded to her mom and sister wading into the middle of the twins' party by skedaddling, she for sure wasn't going to want him to barge in when she'd been attacked.

He tried to breathe, but couldn't catch it. "Back up."

Bolton's eyes flicked over his face. "You're good?"

Matthias nodded and they stepped back. "I'm good." He braced his hands on his thighs and sucked in a breath.

"She's probably home. I'll give you a ride on my way."

He shook his head and looked up at Bolton. "She's at work."

"Seriously?" John looked baffled. "It was almost midnight before she went to bed. There's no way the bakery is open this morning."

"Her bike was there. She won't let the church service go without desserts."

"Well I'll be."

Matthias nearly smiled. That was Frannie all right. There was no way she'd let a bump to the head stop her from opening her store.

Matthias needed to know she was okay. "Let's go."

"One more thing." The sheriff ran a hand down his face, looking tired now the rush had passed.

"Spit it out."

John lifted his eyebrow.

Matthias didn't apologize. He just wandered over to the four waiting area chairs and slumped into the closest one. "What is it?"

John glanced at Bolton, who nodded. So whatever this was, his boss already knew. Matthias decided he'd get mad about that later, when he knew Frannie was all right.

"The first case I found was your father's."

Matthias froze. "Mine?"

John didn't say anything. "He had a heart attack." It was the standard answer—one Matthias had said enough times the lie slipped from his mouth with the smallest measure of bitterness.

"Your dad's autopsy came back inconclusive. The heart attack could possibly have been caused by elevated levels of a medication he was taking. It was a known side-effect."

"Like someone gave him extra pills?" Matthias hesitated while his brain processed what John was saying. The fact his dad had been on medication wasn't surprising. What was surprising was the fact the doctor had called it a heart attack. "And...you think he was murdered by whoever tried to kill Stella?"

John nodded.

Bolton said, "Matt—"

Matthias looked back at the sheriff. "How many cases did you say?"

"Stella would have been number six."

Matthias squeezed the bridge of his nose. There was no way it was even possible this killer had fed his dad extra pills and given him a heart attack. The sheriff could very well be right about the others. John was a good cop.

He was just wrong about Matthias's dad.

CHAPTER 6

He had to have heard by now, so why hadn't he come? Frannie unlocked the bakery's front door early Monday morning, determined not to think any more about Matthias.

She held the door wide while Susan glided in, a wide smile across her face. "Good morning."

Frannie's head still pounded, and she'd avoided acknowledging how dark the inside corners of her eyes were. When it was three-thirty in the morning, some things just weren't worth facing.

Now it was just before eight and she needed to rustle up some "perky" fast, or today was going to seriously drag. Yesterday had been bad enough. Even though the volume of goods for the church was smaller than what she would make for the store, the down-side of delivering baked goods for service and looking rough was everyone asked if you were okay. They'd all wanted her to stop and chat. To stick around so she could "hear the message."

Frannie realized the first lady was staring at her with her head cocked to one side.

"What?" Released from her lips, Frannie heard how short her tone was. She sighed. "Sorry. What is it?"

Susan shrugged off Frannie's behavior. "Nothing, I just wondered for a second what your name used to be, that's all. You don't have to tell me, it was simple curiosity."

Frannie shut the front door and they got to work, side-by-side. "It was Francesca, now it's Francine. But I was always Frannie."

Susan looked back for a second, one hand on the fridge door. "That doesn't put you in danger, not having changed your identity?"

Frannie accepted the tray of chilled lemon bars and set them on the counter-top. "Not when you technically no longer exist. It would be hard for my father or any of his men to find us when there's nothing to find. The only paperwork that exists is here in Sanctuary. A lot of people don't bother changing their names at all. Although they're still miffed we have to pay taxes under the table."

Susan smiled. Maybe she was planning on talking to her husband about that. Frannie figured there had to be some advantages to pillow talk with the president of the United States.

"And there's no paperwork anywhere else?"

Frannie shook her head. "When the director assigns one of us to Sanctuary our WITSEC file is brought with us and given to the sheriff. It doesn't leave here, and neither do we. The only way there could be a breach of security is from within Sanctuary itself."

"Wow." Susan rested her manicured fingers on the edge of the counter, studying Frannie. "And a breach like that really happened with Andra, the previous school teacher and the deputy sheriff?"

Out of the three of them one was back in town, one was in

jail and the last was dead. Deputy Palmer had sold out Andra's safety in exchange for a life beyond the boundaries of Sanctuary's mountains. The school teacher had been duped by Palmer into believing she would go with him. And while he was dead now, she got her wish—she'd left Sanctuary—she'd just done it cuffed, facing a lifetime behind bars and a gag order from the president.

"Have you thought about dying your hair red?"

Frannie blinked. "Red?"

"You have the coloring for it, and I figured after the couple of days you've had maybe you'd like some time off this afternoon to relax and be pampered."

"Pampered?" Susan probably thought she was an imbecile, repeating everything she said back as a question.

Susan smiled. "You say that like it's a foreign concept."

"It isn't." Frannie was familiar enough with pampering just watching her mother, who took every opportunity to "treat" herself to a spa day. "I've just never actually done it myself."

Who had the time for that stuff? Most days she worked, which meant little-to-no make-up and a ponytail. It wasn't going to make any waves with potential suitors, but she had no time for that either. Especially not when she'd said yes to being part of the next theater production. Mimi and Izzy were going to die laughing when they found out about it. Frannie would—probably, hopefully—dazzle everyone during the two weeks of rehearsals and then wind up throwing up on stage in front of everyone opening night.

Susan smiled. "I can see you're thinking about it."

"Maybe." Frannie smiled back. "Right now we have a ton of work to do, though. Since its Monday, everyone will be in to get the special."

If Frannie didn't love trying new sweets recipes, she'd

probably loathe it. Dan's fresh crop of strawberries from his geo-thermal heated greenhouse had been way too good to pass up. Once the Danish pastries were fully cooled, they carried the trays out front. Sure enough, a crowd had gathered at the door.

Frannie let them in, noticing as she moved that the first lady was dumping out the old coffee grounds and filling the pot. She should have done that already, before Susan did—even though the first lady didn't seem to mind menial jobs at all.

A trio of gray-haired, knuckly old men shuffled through the door. *Sonny, Louis and Michael.* "Gentlemen."

Sonny shot her a look and went to intercept the first lady, like it was her fault Susan was making the coffee. She'd be hearing about that later.

Louis pecked his papery lips on her cheek and squeezed her upper arms with more strength than he should have had, before he broke off and followed Sonny. Probably to flash his pearly dentures at the classy woman Frannie was going to have to figure out how to pay. Was Susan going to accept a check? This whole situation was beyond awkward.

Michael stopped in front of her. His dull gray eyes pinned her in place. He hugged her with his right arm and the stump that remained past his elbow on the left side. "How is your head this morning?"

Frannie pushed back a strand of hair that had come loose from her ponytail. "I'm fine."

"That is not an answer to my question, *angela.*"

The name her father had called her sliced through her like a blunt blade, but Michael knew. He continued to use it even after she'd told him her father used to call her "angel." He'd explained it by telling her something about locusts eating years. Which was bizarre, and also not worth the effort of arguing with.

Michael turned her, and she hooked her arm above his elbow to clasp his loose bicep. "You should sit with us, take a break."

"Michael—"

He chuckled. "At least you did not begin to complain by calling me *capitano*."

Frannie smiled. He only wished he was the boss. Sonny was firmly the one in charge. Louis was the underboss, and Michael was the *consigliere* of their group. Which left Frannie as a lieutenant whether she wanted to be or not. It had taken a couple of years of push-and-pull, and their incessant attempts to give her what she'd lost, but eventually she'd succumbed to the fact she would always and forever be "family."

Michael led her to Sonny and Louis, who stood beside one of her four-person tables. The first lady walked over with a tray of coffees and four plated strawberry Danishes. This was getting worse and worse.

"Here you are." Susan set it down with a flourish. "Frannie, you too."

Sonny shot her a look.

Frannie sat down.

She waited until the men had settled, and then said, "This couldn't wait until next weekend's meeting?"

Sonny set his mug of black coffee down. "This isn't chamber of commerce business. We're simply concerned, that's all."

"The first lady is only volunteering here." Until Frannie could figure out how to give her some kind of recompense. "It's merely charity, nothing more."

Sonny's eyebrow rose. "You think that's all you are?"

The bakery door opened and Beth entered, dressed in the

cleanest jeans Frannie had ever seen, and a gray wool sweater that hung from her shoulders and down over her wrists to hook on her thumbs. She sent Frannie a smile and motioned to the back. Frannie nodded, and the first lady's daughter went into the kitchen.

Beth had been a professional ballet dancer. She always moved like she was still on stage, making Frannie feel frumpy in comparison. Yet somehow Beth managed to maintain an air of gentleness and quiet that made no sense, considering she was one of the most well-known women in the country. She should have been brash and entitled, and the lack made Frannie feel even worse.

The front door didn't shut. Nigel Billet ushered his girth into the bakery and glanced around. *Don't see me.* His attention settled on her with a glare, like he'd caught his intended prey. The former Dallas newspaper editor had beady eyes like pin-pricks in his tubby face. And his personality matched.

A voice with a thick Bronx accent said, "Francesca."

She jerked her gaze to Louis. "Don't call me that." He didn't react to her statement, he just looked at Sonny. Frannie sighed. "I have to get back to work. We're very busy, as you can tell." And her head hurt.

Sonny's hand settled on her arm. "Your life could be in danger."

"It isn't." At least, not any more than it had been before she saw someone try to kill Stella.

"We understand you have no wish to become a witness for the second time, but you must understand—"

"No," Frannie said. "I didn't see anything. I don't know who tried to kill Stella, and I have no intention of dwelling on it any more than I have to. This isn't some long, drawn out drama. It happened, and now everything is going to go back to normal."

Louis's head jerked. "You're not going to try and figure out who it was?"

"No." Again. "The sheriff has made me aware of the fact I could potentially be in danger. But I didn't see the person's face. If he tries to silence me, or kill Stella for real, he could fail and then someone might catch him. I might see his face after all. If it was me, I wouldn't risk exposure like that."

Sonny said, "You're going to gamble your life on a maybe?"

"I'm not a cop, so I can't bring him to justice. And I'm also not an amateur sleuth with bad impulse control and a death wish. I'm a baker."

"So you're going to ignore what happened."

"No." She stood then, leaning down to the three men to say one more thing before she got back to work. "I'm going to live my life."

Frannie strode to the kitchen. She pushed the swinging doors open, immediately assailed by the sound of retching. Then water running. Beth emerged from the bathroom, her face pale and the hairline on her forehead damp.

"Are you okay?"

Beth shot her a look. "Are you?"

Frannie blinked, and then smiled at her. *Touché.*

"I won't tell if you don't." Beth strode out.

Susan chuckled. Frannie spun around and saw her in the corner of the kitchen. The sink behind her was full of dirty plates and mugs, and she'd donned Frannie's pink rubber gloves.

The woman was out of control.

"What was that about?"

Susan said, "She's pregnant, but she doesn't want anyone to know yet. Not that she's going to be able to keep it a secret much longer." The first lady hesitated for a second, her face suddenly wistful. "I haven't seen her smile in weeks, but I finally managed to get her to write a letter to her husband. Even if it never reaches him, I still think it helped her to get all her thoughts down. I'm going to take a trip and see my husband soon, so I can tell him about the baby at least. I'll have to leave you in the lurch, I'm afraid, but we can't schedule it. I'll only know it's time when John tells me the helicopter is here."

"You should be with your husband if you can." What else was Frannie supposed to say? This was the president and the first lady. If they wanted to have a conjugal visit, it had nothing to do with her.

Susan smiled. "I'm hoping the president can get word to Lieutenant Myerson about the baby."

Frannie couldn't imagine having a spouse she was estranged from, or had no way to contact. Both Susan and Beth hadn't seen their husbands in weeks.

Neither could she imagine how the SEAL was going to feel when he found out his wife—who'd essentially disappeared off the face of the earth—turned up in a WITSEC town, pregnant. It sounded like Susan and Beth were assuming the baby was his, at least.

Frannie didn't know exactly what the situation was, since Beth didn't talk about her husband. Which, in and of itself, said a lot. Here Frannie would rather be anywhere else than the one place she couldn't get away from her family, and Beth couldn't even share her pregnancy directly with her husband.

Frannie followed Susan back out front. Nigel Billet had left without his Sanctuary News exclusive, but that was okay with her—even if it meant the man was going to make up whatever story he wanted. If she didn't know he'd been a huge Dallas newspaper editor in his former life, she'd probably have sworn he wrote fiction. Maybe he was living the dream now, spinning everything whichever way he pleased without repercussions.

Still, the one person she actually wanted to see never came in.

After Tias stuck his head in the day before—after church—to quickly say "hi" and ask her how she was feeling, he'd promised to come back when he had more time. Maybe that was just something he'd said to fill the conversation.

The door opened, and two families entered. Frannie brushed aside the melancholy feelings and shot Susan a smile. "Welcome to Mondays."

Susan laughed. "Just try and keep up with me."

The lunchtime rush had just died down when the door opened, and Nadia Marie walked in with Andra. Nadia Marie strode between tables, while Andra followed more cautiously, surveying the room. They looked like a famous starlet and her bodyguard.

"Sandwich?" Frannie glanced between them. "Sam brought over some barbecue chicken and it's incredible." She'd inhaled two between customers, just after twelve o'clock.

Nadia Marie grinned.

Uh-oh.

She clapped her hands together. "Makeover!"

Susan must have called the salon. "No—"

"Red is going to look *so* good on you. Trust me."

Why did it always freak her out when people said that?

Andra chuckled, like she completely understood Frannie's pain. Except her natural hair was the darkest shade of brown, so it wasn't like she knew. Not really. It would probably be that color when she was eighty.

Andra said, "If she says it'll look good, then it will. Nadia

Marie really is a master. But that's not the only reason why we're here."

Andra trailed back to the front window, and Nadia Marie waved Frannie over. Andra's attention was fixed on the road from the ranch. "They're almost here."

Nadia Marie grinned, but her gaze snagged on Frannie. "You really should come by this afternoon. Let me treat you to a hair-coloring."

Frannie turned to the window. She'd been blonde as long as she could remember, although there was a significant amount of red in it from some unknown grandparent on her mother's side. If she went fully red she would be taking steps to separate herself from her mom and sister.

In a way, it sort of felt like they'd tried to leave her behind years ago. Maybe it was time for Frannie to do it too. *I'm going to live my life.* Her own words rang in her ears. Eventually she was going to have to quit vacillating, and now was as good a time as any.

"I'll do it." She turned to Nadia Marie, who had her nose pressed to the window. "I'll come over and—"

"Here they come!" Nadia Marie squealed. She jumped up and down and clapped, while Andra stood next to her smiling.

Frannie glanced out the window. A pack of men in shorts and sweat-dampened T-shirts pounded down the blacktop from the ranch toward Main Street. The two men at the front, Sheriff John Mason and ranch boss Bolton Farrera, both wore weighted down backpacks while the rest of the guys followed without.

Nadia Marie sighed, the wistful sound of a woman with unrequited longing. "I love workout day."

The pack hit Main Street. When they reached the bakery window, Frannie saw Matthias just behind the sheriff and

Bolton. His face cracked a smile when he saw them all watching at the window.

Frannie took two steps backward. Her foot caught on something and she tripped. She flung her arms up and wind-milled before her back hit the ground with an *oof*.

"Ouch." Winded, Frannie rolled over and tried to stand. Multiple people jumped up and lifted her to her feet. Her cheeks flamed, and she silently petitioned God, if He really did exist then maybe Matthias might not have seen that horrendously embarrassing display.

"He seriously likes you." Nadia Marie planted her hands on her hips.

"Even if he did, there's no way he does now."

"Pshaw." Nadia waved away Frannie's concern. "I bet he didn't even see." She paused. "But if you let me do your hair it would make a bold statement. Frannie, the *all new woman.*"

"You realize you freak me out, right?"

Andra laughed. "Me too, but you just roll with it. She really does know what she's doing."

"I know that." Frannie grasped the hem of her apron. "It's just..." She looked around at the crowd of customers. They were a pretty good reason not to ditch on the bakery for the afternoon, but why was she hesitating to say it out loud?

"You can be back in an hour and a half, tops."

Frannie bit her lip. "You really think I'll look like a new woman?"

When had she ever felt new, even when she became someone else and enrolled in witness protection? She'd quickly realized she was still the same person she'd always been. Daddy's girl, despite betraying him. Her mother's confusing daughter. Her sister's lame older sibling.

When would she feel like the Frannie she'd always wanted to be?

"Have I ever given anyone a bad haircut, or a color that didn't suit them?"

Frannie sucked in a breath and straightened her shoulders. If she was going to make some changes... To actually *live*... "Okay. I'll do it."

Nadia Marie jumped up and down, clapping. Again. She made a noise that sounded like, "Eeeeeee!" And Frannie got caught up in the celebration.

Beth came in the door. She surveyed the scene and laughed. "I take it she said yes." The first lady's daughter had pink cheeks and a bright-eyed smile. Apparently the morning nausea had passed.

Frannie glanced between Beth, her two friends, and Susan who was behind the counter. Her eyes narrowed. "You guys planned this."

Beth strode to the counter. "Mom did. You go get your hair done and take a break. I'm going to lend a hand while you're gone."

Because what was better than the first lady doing menial labor at her bakery than the first lady *and* her daughter doing Frannie's work?

Andra stepped closer and whispered in Frannie's ear. "They want to do this for you."

Frannie swallowed. She glanced around then nodded to Andra. "Okay. Let's go before I change my mind."

Two hours later, Frannie returned from Nadia Marie's salon with a new hair style that was several gorgeous shades of red and rich copper. She didn't feel any better about making prestigious, upper class women work for her, but the time spent in Nadia's leather massage chair had almost been worth it.

Frannie locked the front door at precisely four in the afternoon and flipped the sign to *Closed*. It took a few minutes for Beth and Susan to exclaim appropriately over her hair and hug Frannie as though it had taken all kinds of bravery to make the change—which wasn't entirely inaccurate, then Frannie made her way to the stairs.

A white envelope sat on the linoleum just inside the back door.

CHAPTER 7

Matthias lifted his fist and knocked on the back door of the bakery. The sun was making its way behind the mountain peaks, though sunset was hours away still. He knocked again.

Frannie screamed.

Matthias fisted his hand and pounded on the door. "Frannie, open up! It's Tias."

The door swung open and Frannie stood there, pink-cheeked and out of breath, clutching a broom. She held the broom up, ready to swing it at him. Matthias lifted both hands, palms out. "Whoa there. It's just me."

"Tias." She blinked, and her grip on the broom slipped. Despite the fright, she looked more shiny than usual. In fact, she looked different...amazing.

"Is everything okay?" He glanced around, inside and out, but couldn't see anything amiss.

"Yeah." She pressed a hand just below her neck and sucked in deep breaths. "My head's killing me. I saw this letter on the floor, and then you knocked. It freaked me out, and I just screamed and grabbed the broom." Her cheeks pinked with embarrassment he thought endearing. "Sorry."

Matthias looked at the envelope on the linoleum.

Frannie picked it up. "It's probably just a bill, or someone's payment."

"You sure you're okay?"

She nodded. "One time, someone paid me in office supplies. I guess they had extra printer paper, and it certainly saved me the expense of ordering more for myself." Frannie swiped the letter off the floor and stepped back. "You want to come in? I have a question for you."

"Sure." He stepped inside and shut the door behind him. The lock on her back door was little better than a residential bathroom lock, and just as easy to break into. "You need better security than this."

"I do?"

"There might not be much crime in Sanctuary, but it's worth it to protect yourself better than this."

"Okay." She paused. "I have to fix my second oven, or buy a new one, first. But I guess new locks wouldn't be a bad idea."

But was she suddenly cautious about security because her sister and her mom had broken in and trashed the place? Or because she thought she was in danger? Matthias wanted her to open up and feel like she could trust him with what was going on. With Frannie there was way more going on below the surface. Would she ever let him in? Maybe a better question was, what would Matthias have to give up in order to get her to trust him? There was only so much he could openly share without betraying family confidences.

It was why he'd always assumed there couldn't be anything between them—although his resolve appeared to suck at the moment.

And...she probably thought he was a complete moron, standing there saying nothing and staring at her.

Matthias cleared his throat. "What was the question you had?"

"Right." She burst into movement, opening a door behind her and leading him up the stairs. "I had some ideas to make a few changes up here, but I don't know anything about renovating. Or plumbing. That's probably the biggest issue. The bathroom up here doesn't work at all. It never has."

They stepped into a living space full of boxes and piled up chairs that looked broken or old—the previous owner's color scheme. That guy's bread had been nowhere as good as Frannie's, and he hadn't even bothered with cake. Like no one in Sanctuary deserved a treat.

Matthias crossed to the room she'd indicated and cracked the door. The tile in the tiny bathroom was green and dusty from disuse. There was a single shower, a sink and a completely dry toilet. He twisted the handle on the tap at the sink and nothing came out.

Matthias crouched and opened the cabinet to check the pipes. Everything looked like it was connected, which was something at least.

"I can come back with my tools and check it out. It shouldn't be too difficult to figure out why there's no water coming through." He looked back at her.

Frannie's jeans and fitted T-shirt were simple but they really worked for her. She normally didn't wear makeup, but today she'd done something that made her eyes look bigger. And her hair—

"Your hair is red."

Frannie giggled and touched the side of her hair. "I was wondering if you were going to notice."

"I noticed how good you look, but I only just realized what was different." He wanted to kick himself. "So, yeah. I'm a guy. We knew that." He felt his cheeks warm and bet it didn't look nearly as good as when Frannie blushed.

She chuckled more, and he crossed the room to stand in front of her. "I really like your hair, Frannie."

It was red with some blonde and rust colored stripes. She'd curled it so it was sort of wavy and hung around her face.

"Nadia Marie did it this afternoon, so take your fill because it's never going to look this good again. It never does, no matter how hard I try to recreate what she did."

Matthias wanted to stand this close to her for longer, but if he did then he'd end up doing something impulsive—like kissing her. He'd have to apologize, and she'd think he felt guilty when the likelihood was he wouldn't regret it in the slightest.

"So what were you thinking you wanted to do with this place?"

Frannie looked aside, biting her lip. "I'm still figuring that out. I think I want another option for somewhere to stay, like if I have to work late and be back early then I won't have to go home if I don't want to."

Matthias found a folded table and perched on the edge trying to act as unassuming as possible, which was difficult considering how big he was. "Is everything okay at home?"

Frannie shrugged. "I just need some space sometimes."

"I can understand that."

"I'm sure you can. I only have one sister and my mom. You have three sisters and your brother. Your mom is really cool, though."

"When she's not complaining to all of us about the fact she only has the twins for grandkids. Apparently there should be a whole lot more by now, even though Sofia's barely twenty and Maria's the only one who's married."

Frannie chuckled. "I can see Diego wanting to spread his wild oats around town, but that'd be a little awkward if he starts building a family, or multiple families, that way."

Matthias groaned just thinking about it. "I'd like to argue he's more mature than that, but it's probably not true."

Thinking about Antonia and Sofia made Matthias want to swing by their nursery tomorrow. His sisters were a lot like Frannie, except that they created gardens instead of cake. If there was a problem they'd keep it to themselves in order to avoid the drama of asking for help. He had to pry everything out of them, but at least if he went and paid them a visit he'd be able to look in their eyes and know for sure whether everything was fine. He hadn't had the chance to speak to them at the twins' party, and they could lie way too easily over the phone.

He looked around again. "So you're looking to turn this into a real living space?"

Frannie tipped her head to the side, motioning at another door he hadn't looked in yet. "In there is the bakery office, so that's clean and usable at least. The kitchen can be cleaned up, but I can cook most things downstairs. I'd like to get some furniture, and maybe a TV out here and for the bathroom to work. The second bedroom would be a good place to have for storage, since I can get a pull out couch in the living area to sleep on." She shrugged. "I don't need much more than a studio apartment would give me."

Sanctuary wasn't a town for those accustomed to a certain level of affluence in their lifestyle. He knew from around town, and who her mom was, that Frannie had grown up rich. Her father had been some kind of big-wig, and it was obvious her bakery was doing well. But he didn't think she was in this for the sake of raking in bundles of cash. Not if she had to save for a lock, or to fix her oven.

"I can take a look at the oven for you, too. If you want."

"That would be great. But aren't you busy—" She hesitated, like she was searching for the word. "—branding cows, and stuff like that?"

Matthias pinched his lips together to keep from laughing. Yep, she was a city girl. "We only raise cows for food. We don't have to brand them because you only do that when you want to claim them as yours, like if you're going to sell them. There aren't any other ranches in Sanctuary, so if there's a cow inside these mountains then it's ours. We do count them a lot, though, to make sure none got lost in the woods. And we have the other animals to take care of."

"Oh, okay."

"I'd like to help you out, Frannie. However much you want to use this apartment, it'll just be nice for you to have personal space. Like you said." He nodded. "I'll come by tomorrow with my tools and get started with a look at your oven. Then we'll clear some of this stuff into your second bedroom."

Frannie sputtered. "Oh, okay."

"You don't want me to do it?"

"It just...uh, tomorrow? That might be—"

"Moving too fast?" Matthias felt his lips twitch. Could he help it if he wanted to jump into this? Frannie had handed him the perfect opportunity to spend more time with her. He wasn't going to dig his heels in.

He stepped closer to her then, succumbing to the temptation of seeing whether her hair was as soft as it looked.

It was.

"I'll go as fast or as slow as you want me to, Frannie." He paused, watching as her eyes flared. Here with her it was like they were the only two people in the world—a fact which could cause him to easily go against his convictions. "But not tonight."

He stepped back.

"Excuse me?"

Matthias stuck his hands in his pockets, like all that hadn't just happened. Like his heart wasn't racing. Like he didn't want to kiss her until she got that breathless look again. "I have somewhere to be tonight. I'm going to be in Andy and Shelby's play this season."

"You are?"

"Sure." He shrugged, like it should've been obvious a rancher would also be an aspiring thespian. "My name came up, and I didn't think I could get out of it this time."

"I'm going to be in it, too."

"Serious?" Matthias reacted like this was a complete surprise. In reality, the minute he'd seen Frannie's name on the list he'd jumped at the chance. "Much Ado About Nothing, right?"

"I couldn't believe they decided to do it. It's my favorite Shakespeare play."

"It's a good one?" He would have read it, but he was in the middle of a Carl Gabriel novel, and he didn't cheat.

She grinned. "The best."

Matthias rocked back and forth on his boots. "Want to walk over to the Meeting House together?"

"Sure." Frannie motioned with the letter. "Let me just toss this on my desk for later, and I'll be right out."

———

THE CHAIRS in the Meeting House were still set up from church the day before. Andy and Shelby Evangeline sat at the front. Shelby had on her usual floral cotton dress she'd sewed herself, and Andy wore an ugly brown pair of slacks with a mustard colored shirt. The strands of his hair that remained were combed over the top of his head from ear to ear.

Frannie chose a folding chair halfway back and Matthias sat beside her. There were about fifteen people scattered around. She wanted to focus, but all she could think about was how close Matthias was. They'd gone from passing acquaintances to nicknames and whispered sweet words in two days. It wasn't her headache muddling her thoughts anymore. Tias's closeness, the rich scent of his aftershave and the fact he grinned every time their eyes met was succeeding at it just fine.

Shelby stood, her blonde perm jiggling with the movement. "Welcome, welcome everyone!"

Andy removed the spectacles from his breast pocket and unfolded them to perch on his nose. "Thank you all for—"

Nadia Marie squeezed in front of Matthias and slumped into the seat beside Frannie. She grinned, out of breath, and whispered, "Hi."

Frannie grinned back. "Hi."

Nadia Marie leaned forward. "Hi, Matt."

He leaned forward too. "Hi, Nads."

Nadia Marie giggled.

Aaron cleared his throat. "As I was saying—" He narrowed his eyes at Nadia Marie. "We're glad you're all here, supporting community arts in Sanctuary. Shelby and I have enjoyed every one of the one-hundred thirty-three plays we have put on since we arrived in town over thirty years ago. You all know how this works, although some of you haven't performed with us before. If you're new, welcome."

He paused, his smile lighting on Frannie. "We'll start every meeting and rehearsal with a prayer. You will all receive your assigned part and a copy of the script tonight. We have six weeks before opening night. Bolton Farrera has kindly offered to assist us in building the set."

Both Nadia Marie and Matthias reacted. Nadia, clearly surprised Bolton would be part of the play, while Matthias snorted at Andy's explanation of the ranch boss "offering" to help. Frannie decided he'd probably found out Nadia Marie was involved.

Andy continued talking, gesturing with his long, pale fingers as he spoke. Frannie only wanted to know what part she was supposed to play. She'd told Tias the truth, mostly because she was too freaked by his behavior to do anything but react honestly. Much Ado About Nothing was her favorite Shakespeare play.

Now she only wanted to know how much stage time she was going to get with Tias and exactly how Andy and Shelby had modernized it. Not to mention they always insisted on messing with their plays so that one of the characters "shared Jesus" with another character—and the audience. Usually it wasn't too groan-worthy.

Father Wilson, the town's multi-denominational minister, stood. His grizzly face never moved, so Frannie wasn't convinced he actually knew how to smile. He resembled the priest from when she'd gone to church as a child, with a side of "enforcer." She'd be too scared to make confession with him, worried he'd probably murder her for being such a sinner. It had been years and years since her last confession. How many Hail Mary's would he make her say for that?

If Frannie wanted to find out, she'd have to miss work to make the mass he performed every morning. Ten-thirty on Sundays was the more casual, evangelical church service.

Father Wilson's words filtered through, sentiments that covered doing everything as "unto the Lord" and asking Him to bless the play. Frannie shifted in her seat. She just wanted to act. Why couldn't they get on with that? Why did their beliefs have to be part of everything they did?

Tias's warm fingers entwined with hers. His skin was rough. He squeezed her hand, but then didn't pull his back. Apparently he was fine with prayer being a part of the play. He attended Sunday services, and also mass with his family. All of Olympia's children did. What Frannie didn't know was why Matthias continued to do it even when he didn't have to. Frannie had stopped as soon as her father died. He'd been the one who dragged them all to church all the time, like paying homage to God would make him a better person.

Sins couldn't be washed away like that. There had to be a cost. It didn't make sense any other way.

Father Wilson said "amen," and Frannie looked up. His gaze locked on her. Tias moved to pull his hand away, but she held on tighter.

Father Wilson nodded to Andy, walked around the chairs and left. That was when Frannie let go of Tias's hand.

Nadia Marie leaned closer. "You okay?"

Frannie nodded, while Andy read from his clipboard a list of names and what part they would be playing. When he announced Nadia Marie Carleigh would play the part of Hero, the female half of the sweet, misunderstood couple, Nadia made a fist and punched the air. "Oh, yeah." She leaned in again and whispered to Frannie and Tias. "I gave her a free perm, and she hooked me up."

Frannie laughed, even though inside she was a little disappointed she and Tias weren't going to get to play the tragically in love couple who were messed with by all the other characters. Still, there were good parts left.

"Terrence Evangeline." Aaron and Shelby both smiled at their son, who was pushing late thirties and yet still lived at home with them. "You'll be playing Claudius."

Nadia Marie groaned, although she tried to cover it up for the sake of Terrence, who was beaming at her like he'd just won the lottery. Frannie was just glad they didn't make Tias Nadia's love interest. That would have sucked if she'd had to watch them fall in love. Why hadn't she thought of that before? Maybe she wouldn't be able to do this—not if she had to watch him kiss someone else.

Frannie bit her lip. That wasn't why she was here. She wanted to do this because it made her happy, and she needed to do that more. It didn't matter what her mom and sister thought.

"Matthias Hernandez," Andy searched the group until he found him beside Frannie and nodded. "You'll be playing Benedict."

Frannie grinned.

His gaze was on her. "Is that good?"

"That's really good." While Frannie was going to enjoy watching him be snarky, pretentious, and unwilling to admit he secretly loved...

"Francine Peters, you'll be playing Beatrice."

Frannie nearly squealed. But that would be unprofessional. Instead she grinned at Nadia Marie so hard her cheeks hurt. Nadia knew what that meant, because the only person Tias would be falling in love with during this play, was her.

Tias nudged her. "Benedict and Beatrice?"

Frannie nodded. "This is going to be a lot of fun." She was going to get to be just as snarky, pretentious and unwilling to admit she secretly loved Matthias back.

One out of three was good enough. The rest was all about the power of theater.

Andy clapped. "Frannie, Matthias. Why don't you, along with Terrence and Nadia Marie, come up to the front." He listed off a few more names. "We'll run through some lines just to get a feel for how you'll work together."

They all stood. Frannie's stomach churned as she took her script from Shelby, and they assembled in front of everyone. She was really doing this. She glanced at Tias, and he gave her a nervous smile. Frannie flipped to the right page and silently read through the scene they would be working on. She chuckled, realizing it was the first scene where the men were returning from war and Beatrice was asking after Benedict and trying not to sound concerned as to whether he'd lived or died.

The Meeting House doors flung open and her mom strode in. Hair poofed out to maximum volume, Mimi strode through the room like her tiny outfit was a gown and this was red carpet, opening night. She saw Frannie and her steps faltered. "You're in the play?"

Frannie nodded. Her stomach churned, which wasn't good since she hadn't eaten dinner.

"How...nice." Mimi sat, smoothing down what there was of her skirt. She motioned with her hand like a queen. "Please, continue."

Frannie glanced at Andy, who nodded. She cleared her throat and lowered the papers to her side, her attention on the general store clerk who would be playing the messenger. "If my lord comes, you must prepare a great feast. For he has a healthy appetite, a truly excellent stomach."

Matthias, off to one side, grinned.

The exchange continued, with Frannie and the messenger, the Lord of the manor and Nadia Marie all chirping in remarks.

"Excellent!" Andy clapped. "We're going to do well, I feel." He glanced at the group at large. "I need only Terrence,

Nadia Marie, Matthias and Frannie now. I'll see the rest of you tomorrow night."

People dispersed, but Mimi kept her seat. What was she still doing there? But then she got up, ignoring Andy and Shelby and walked straight to Frannie. She snatched Frannie's script from her hands and looked at the page.

"Mom—"

Mimi shot her a scathing look and then flipped pages, finally settling on a scene closer to the end.

Shelby said in a soft voice, "Mrs. Peters, could you—"

Mimi shoved the script back at Frannie. "Let's do this scene." She glanced at Frannie. "I'll show you how to give it some real zing."

"Mimi—"

Her mom ignored her, striding over to Matthias. He took a step back, but Mimi moved closer. She settled two hands on his chest and leaned in.

Frannie didn't hear the words. All she heard was a rushing in her ears. Matthias's ears went red, the same way they had upstairs at the bakery when he was embarrassed.

"Mom. We're doing fine."

She didn't explicitly tell her to get out, but it was implied. And everyone else knew that. So why did her mom ignore her?

"Mom!"

Mimi spun around, her face contorted with rage. "I'm only trying to help! You need more..." Her wave incorporated the whole of Frannie. "More."

Behind her, Nadia Marie smirked and shook her head. "Not with that hair."

Mimi's gaze darted back to survey Frannie's hair and widened.

Frannie said, "We've only just started. We'll let you know later if we need coaching, or whatever. Okay?"

Mimi vacillated, like maybe she wasn't going to give in. Did she ever? "Fine." She stormed back to the seats. Apparently, even with the miracle of her backing down, she was still staying.

Andy motioned to Frannie. "Please begin on page one hundred eighty-seven."

Frannie nodded. In the corner of her eye she could see her mom, seething. But she had to do this. If her mom was here during the performance she'd have to get through it. She might as well learn how to deal with her presence now.

Frannie stepped into the middle of the space. Matthias did the same so that they were face-to-face but not crowding each other like her mom had been. She could smell her mom's perfume on him.

Matthias leaned in and whispered, "You don't need more anything. You are already more *everything* than her."

CHAPTER 8

Early the next morning Matthias strode through rows of potted flowers for sale outside the nursery. He acknowledged the guy his sisters and brother-in-law had hired with what the girls called, "the guy nod."

Brian was early twenties and had a roaring crush on Matthias's sister, Sofia, the youngest of them. Sofia was twenty; Antonia—who was taller and slender where Sofia was plump—was twenty-three. There might've only been a few years between them, but it still made Matthias feel old—especially considering he'd been the father figure in their lives ever since their dad died.

Brian didn't nod back. He raised his hand to stall Matthias. "Uh…"

Matthias pulled open the door and discovered what Brian had been trying to tell him. All he could hear was female screeching. Not something he was unfamiliar with, considering he had three sisters. They just didn't do it often. And not for years.

He strode between the aisles, stocked with plant food and pet paraphernalia. "What in God's name is—"

Too late Matthias realized what he'd said. Bolton was a good friend, but Matthias had also learned some not so good stuff from him. Including a few choice phrases that liked to slip out when he wasn't thinking about what he was saying.

He really needed to quit doing that.

Matthias turned the corner at the end of the aisle to the space in front of the counter. Maria was on top of Antonia. The two of them were rolling around on the dusty floor tiles, pulling each other's hair.

Sofia was behind the counter, the phone in her hand. She replaced it in the base. "I was just about to call you." Her full cheeks had lightened two shades and she looked like she was about to start crying.

Matthias smiled, trying to reassure her, and turned to his other sisters. "Enough."

He hauled Maria up and held her back while he used his free hand to help Antonia up. She ignored his hand and stood, brushing off the seat of jeans that were way too tight for his liking. But it was an ancient argument between them.

"What's going on?"

Both of them started yelling.

"Quiet!" Matthias's bellow filled the enclosed space. Sofia hiccoughed. They all turned to her. With tears streaking down her face, their youngest sister fled from behind the counter, down the aisle.

Matthias pulled both of the girls to stand in front of him and folded his arms. "Do you see what you did?"

Antonia shot him a look. "You're the one who yelled and made her cry."

"Seriously?" He looked at Maria. "What's going on?"

His two sisters were direct opposites. Where Maria apparently couldn't care less about her appearance, Antonia took complete pride in hers.

"Someone explain this right now."

"Oh good grief, you sound like Dad." Antonia rolled her eyes. "Maria's crazy, so what else is new?"

Still reeling from the second implication in as many days that he was at all like his father, it took him a minute to realize what she'd said about Maria. Matthias glanced at the accused. Maria either hadn't noticed or didn't care what Antonia thought. He wasn't ever going to understand women.

Maria turned her tear-filled eyes on him. "She's sleeping with Tom."

"What?"

"Our *sister* is having an affair with my husband!" Maria's scream pierced his ears. "I just know she is."

Matthias looked at the other sister. "Antonia?"

"I refuse to dignify this accusation with a response."

That wasn't good. If Maria was lying, Antonia should be defending herself much more vehemently than this. He'd seen that enough times, although it was possible every single one of those occasions had been based on hormones. Was this normal, hormone-free Antonia, or was she simply refusing to deny it?

"See!" Maria yelled. "She knows she's guilty, that's why she won't admit it! She's sleeping with Tom. She's been having a sordid affair with him this whole time!"

"Maria." He softened his voice. "You need proof. Because whether this is true or not, just saying it is going to tear this family apart."

"Don't placate me. I know what I know."

Which was a problem, considering Maria's concept of reality was dubious at best.

"Where are the boys?"

Maria waved away his concern. "Tom didn't have anything scheduled for this morning, so he took them hiking."

That was something at least. Matthias turned to Antonia. "Is it true, or is she mistaken?"

There was a flicker of something he couldn't discern in her eyes, and then Antonia said, "I'm not responding to any of it. She can't just come in here and act like this. I'm all dirty now. I have soil in my hair for crying out loud."

Yes, because that was the most important thing happening right now. "Antonia—"

"No. I won't answer it." She stepped away. "I'm not going to. Not when she's acting like she always does. She just walked in here and attacked me like a banshee. She has to know she can't do that."

Antonia strutted away.

"Maria, why don't we walk and talk." He held his hand out to his older sister. "What do you say?"

Maria glanced at Antonia's back, shooting tiny missiles with her eyes. "She knows I'm right. It's why she won't deny it." Her earnest eyes moved to him. "I know it's true."

Antonia made a sound of frustration. "Talk some sense into her. She can't just walk in to my place of business and do this."

Maria touched her face, sucking in a breath that could turn into crying at any moment. "I'm not the one who will tear this family apart."

As far as Matthias could tell, they were already torn apart. On the one hand, Antonia and Sofia and Diego were all trying to live their lives—albeit they were turning out to be disasters in some cases. Maria was stuck, unable to move on from what had happened. Their mom acted like their dad had never even existed, and Matthias was stuck somewhere in the middle— honestly sick of all of it.

But was that just another avoidance tactic? The shrink

had thought it was. He'd barely told her anything, and she'd nailed it. That was why he never went back.

"Come on, I'll walk you home."

Maria shrugged off his arm. "No, I'm going for a walk. Then I'm having lunch with Mama."

"You are?" When she nodded, he said, "That's good, Maria."

She rolled her eyes and shoved at his shoulder. She might want to pass it off as no big deal, but nothing good came from Maria closeting herself at home. "I know what you did with the birthday presents. I'm sorry I forgot to get them something and you had to pretend your present was from me. Thank you."

Matthias touched her cheeks then. "Every time, Maria."

"I should have remembered."

"It doesn't matter. It doesn't make you a bad mom. You love Reuben and Simeon."

She nodded, a slight movement. "I think I do. But what if I hurt them really bad one day?"

"You have to trust yourself. Don't listen to the lies, see them for what they are."

She walked away, and Matthias glanced up at the mountains.

He always turned his attention that way when he needed to be reminded there were things in his world bigger than him. He had to recognize again that there were greater things, which called him to be more than he was. Faith was something Matthias had always had a comprehension of, being dragged to mass almost every day of his life. But something Dan Walden, the town's farmer, had said recently struck a chord in him.

They'd been having a Bible study every week for a while now, and Matthias had mostly only gone because the sheriff attended. Matthias understood religion, but this was different. Even John's excitement over his new "relationship" with God didn't completely make sense to him.

What Dan and John both spoke of was a deep connection to God that didn't require the four walls of a church, or even the elements of communion. There wasn't much that was sacred within Sanctuary, although Father Wilson performed the duties of a priest as best he could. Dan maintained they didn't even need any of that. Like Matthias could just talk to God as if they were friends, and tell God all of his problems.

It felt awkward, but Matthias did it then. He looked up, because where else was he supposed to stare?

He told God everything God probably already knew, but it felt better to lay it out. All he could think was that his life had been this way for years. Maybe it wasn't ever going to change. God didn't have to fix Maria, Tom, Antonia or anyone else in his life if He didn't want to. Maybe the only person Matthias had control over was himself, which meant he had to discover what God wanted from him.

If he didn't have to worry about his family because God was going to take care of them, then Matthias was freed up to go after something he actually wanted for himself. Something he hadn't thought was possible, given the colossal mess of his family.

Frannie would be at work right now, up to her elbows in flour. Which was good since he was due at the bakery in ten minutes anyway for another meeting with Dan and Sheriff Mason.

Matthias set off in that direction, still determined not to care that they'd smirked at him when he suggested the bakery. He didn't care what his friends thought.

Matthias knew what he wanted.

———

FRANNIE SLIPPED the letter opener into the envelope, her attention on what could almost be called her apartment. The living room had come a long way since she'd voiced her desire to Matthias to make it an actual, livable space. Since her mom had actually shown up today, Frannie was able to clear out all the junk, throw away a lot and pile the rest in the bedroom. The dust had been thick, but it felt good to sweep it away and reveal what was underneath. Personal space.

She pulled the folded paper from the envelope and coughed. It smelled almost chemical, a weird odor she couldn't associate with anything in particular though it was strong. This wasn't a payment. The paper had handwriting on it, a sprawling spidery writing she didn't recognize.

Dearest Francine,

Please accept my apology for any injury I caused you on Saturday night. That was not my intention.

Saturday night?

The night the man with Stella had pushed her into the shelf.

Frannie's stomach churned. What on earth?

Her hand dove for the phone, and she dialed the sheriff's office.

"Hello, dear." It was the sheriff's secretary—the dispatcher.

"Dotty. I need the sheriff to come to my office above the bakery immediately."

"He's already at the bakery. I'll radio him. He'll be right upstairs." Dotty kept talking, but Frannie's attention was back on the letter. She hung up the phone.

While I may have caused you harm, I do not regret my reason for being present in Stella Noel's room that night.

Yes, this is my confession.

Boots pounded up the stairs. Frannie sucked in sharp breaths, still smelling the foul odor of the paper.

As trite as it may seem, I am tired of the silence. The lies. Since my wrong to you has been great, it is my desire that you accept my explanation.

It is true, I have killed many. But not for any pleasure I take in the action. I simply perform God's work of mercy in the lives of the men and women of Sanctuary.

The door flung open, hit the wall and swung back. The sheriff burst in, gun drawn, with Matthias directly behind him. Dan Walden, the farmer, brought up the rear of their group.

Frannie jumped up. Her chair was shoved back and rolled on its wheels to hit the wall. She pointed to the letter, but no sound came out of her mouth.

Sheriff Mason holstered his gun. "The letter?"

She nodded—a jerky movement at best. Her eyes sought out Matthias, and he walked to her.

"Tias." She tried to breathe but could only sputter. Leaning forward, Frannie sucked in a breath and coughed it out. Matthias's strong hand rubbed up and down her back. He crouched beside her, sweeping her hair from her face.

The sheriff came around the desk. He used the lid end of a pen and the eraser of her pencil to fully open the paper where she'd dropped it on the desk. He held the letter open, reading it for himself.

Beside her, Matthias made a noise. He stepped closer to the paper, which meant the warmth of his body came into contact with hers. The sheer heat of him was like nothing she'd ever felt before. She was always cold, and he was like a furnace conjuring images of a warm fire on a snowy night. Or s'mores at the bonfire they'd had the one time her father actually let her go to summer camp.

John straightened. "I was right." His attention was on Matthias. "He's killed before. The attempt on Stella wasn't his first time."

Frannie gasped, coughing again. "Not his... What?"

Matthias lifted his hand to squeeze her shoulder. "Stella wasn't the first. He's killed others."

"He said it was God's work."

Dan's eyes hardened. "He might think that, but..." It was clear Dan's opinion of this person—whoever it was—and their theological convictions, wasn't ever going to be favorable.

Frannie glanced between each of them, Matthias's hand still on her shoulder. "Why did he send this? Why is he apologizing to me when he's killed people?"

"Maybe it's exactly what he said." John's eyes were soft for her. "Maybe he wants someone to talk to."

"Well, I'm not available." Frannie didn't need this. Air refused to enter her lungs. She couldn't even breathe.

"Frannie," Matthias's voice was gentle. "Give yourself a minute. This is a shock. I get that. But you don't have to accept this. We're not asking you to be this monster's confidante."

John said, "He's right. I don't want you reading this, or any more if you get them. As soon as you know what they are, just turn them over to me."

"Okay." She could do that. This crazy murderer could write whatever he wanted. It didn't mean she had to read it.

"I'll get you some water." Dan wandered out into the kitchen area.

"The faucet doesn't work," Matthias called after him. "You'll have to get it from downstairs."

Frannie caught his hand in hers and squeezed it gently, grateful she hadn't had to say all that. Matthias didn't let her hand go, he glanced at her and held her eyes without saying anything.

John said, "Do you want to read the rest before I put it in evidence and take it back to the sheriff's office?"

Matthias shifted. "Frannie—"

Maybe she should. Maybe she needed to hear, just once, what this person had to say. "I want to. I want an explanation."

"Just make sure you don't touch the paper or the envelope any more than you have to. I'll be back in a minute with an evidence bag." He looked at Tias. "Matthias?"

He nodded. "I got it."

Frannie scanned the page until she found the place she left off.

To those who no longer wish to reside in Sanctuary, I offer a way out. To the tired, the sick and despairing, I provide eternal rest.

"Wow, he's really full of himself. He thinks he's providing a service, killing people?" She couldn't even begin to comprehend what kind of a person thought that way.

I end life only after making an offer. If that offer is accepted, then I carry out that which is my duty.

"No."

Matthias gently squeezed her hand. "What is it?"

"Stella wouldn't have accepted any offer."

"She is very sick." Matthias paused. "Maybe she—"

"No. She wouldn't have done that. She wouldn't just give up and leave me." Frannie's voice hitched. She covered her mouth with her hand and tried to cry quietly. Why had she said that? There was nearly always somebody else around, even at home. It wasn't like she was lonely. Matthias was going to think she didn't have any friends. But there was something about the relationship she had with Stella that she didn't have with anyone else—and she was going to lose it.

"I won't let him take her away from me. I won't. I don't care if she did accept his offer. I'll talk to her, get her to change her mind."

Matthias sighed.

"I will. I know you don't think I can, but Stella and I..."

"I know you're close. Everyone knows. It's obvious from the way Stella is with you that she sees you as the daughter she never had."

Frannie said, "She has a son. He didn't want to come with Stella and her husband to Sanctuary. But you're right. We are family." It was unspoken, but he knew the reality of her life with Mimi and Izzy, and why she would jump at the chance to be close to a woman she considered a second mother.

John rapped on the door frame. Matthias backed up an inch, but still held her hand.

"I'm going to enter the letter as evidence. Are you finished with it?"

"Yes." Frannie braced against the shudder. "Can I go? I think I need a walk."

John nodded. Without letting go of Matthias's hand, Frannie walked to the stairs and down. She twisted the handle and gulped clean, fresh air. She just walked, without setting a destination.

Halfway down the road that ran behind Main Street, Matthias pulled her to a stop. Frannie spun back to him, mortified at the tears falling down her cheeks.

He drew her close and swiped the wetness away with his thumbs. "We'll go see Stella. We'll talk to her together. Maybe we can convince her to fight more. To hang on."

"She's in so much pain—" Frannie's voice broke. "Why am I so selfish?"

"You love her. You want her with you, not in pain. Just because you love her."

"I don't want her to die."

"I know." He drew her closer so that she rested her forehead on his chest. Frannie folded her arms around him and soaked up the warmth of his comfort.

It was like falling.

The strength of what she received from Matthias right then was unlike anything anyone had ever given her before. Even in Stella's friendship. Frannie realized she could live right here. In the place where she needed, and he simply gave. How did he do that when precious few people in her life had done anything but take from her?

Frannie pulled away. She winced at the frown that marred his features.

"What?"

She shook her head. "I'm okay now. Thanks."

"That's it? You just needed a hug?"

"Maybe you give really good hugs."

The worry dispersed from his face. "Will you let me know if you need anything else? I'm not good at figuring out what women want. I have enough sisters to know there's no hope of understanding you."

Frannie curved her lips into a small smile. "You want me to make this easy for you?"

His lips compressed. "Of course you're not going to do that."

"No way." She laughed.

Matthias chuckled, never releasing her from his gaze. "A guy can hope."

Frannie blew out a breath, remembering her earlier thought about wilderness summer camp. "You know what I really need right now?"

"What?"

"A s'more."

"I was going to fix your plumbing tonight, but I could be persuaded to join you." He paused a beat, suddenly looking nervous. "You want to come back to the ranch with me, and we'll make a fire?"

CHAPTER 9

MATTHIAS LOADED the supplies for s'mores into his backpack along with a picnic blanket. It might be chilly on the mountain. They couldn't stay out late, not when both of them had to be up early, but it would get dark quickly so they had to be prepared.

A date. They were going on an actual date. Mostly only because a killer had made contact with her. Not a great reason, but he wasn't going to pass it up.

Matthias pulled two cans of soda from the fridge, fumbled and dropped one. It hit the toe of his boot and spun across the floor. When he retrieved it, the top had popped out. Great. That was going to fizz like crazy when it was opened, and these were the last two. They'd have to share.

Matthias sighed and put the still-good can in the backpack. He zipped it up and turned to the door.

Bolton was leaning against the doorframe, one boot crossed over the other at his ankles and a smirk on his face.

"What?"

Bolton tried to look innocent, which made Matthias wonder why he even bothered. It never worked, probably because Bolton didn't have an innocent cell in his body. "Not a thing, brother. How's Frannie?"

"Frannie is fine, thank you."

"I'm sure she is." Some of Bolton's humor bled from his face. "If you're worried, I can take up some of your jobs, and you can stick closer to town for the time being."

Matthias nodded. "I was going to ask you about that. I can get most everything done early and be in town mid-morning at the latest. You'll just have to manage Diego and Sean the rest of the day."

Bolton nodded. "I know how to crack the whip."

"I know you do." Matthias chuckled. He'd had to get in line, several times, after Bolton showed up, when the man decided they were going to do things his way. But his respect for Bolton had only grown because of it.

"Hot date?"

Matthias narrowed his eyes. "None of your business."

Bolton mock-sighed, shaking his head. "S'mores and soda? You can't figure out something better than that?"

"It's what she wanted." Matthias shrugged. "It's not like there are any upscale restaurants in town I can take her to. There's only Sam's diner, where everyone's going to see us, and I won't get a minute's peace to talk with her."

"Thought about this a lot, have you?"

"Of course I have." This was Frannie, after all. It wasn't worth messing up, not when he thought he knew how good it could be. "I'm going to use the grill so the fire isn't big, and we're just going to hang out. Maybe I'll introduce her to Danser."

Bolton shook his head, like Matthias was the biggest disappointment he'd ever seen. "Take her to Rush."

"We can't hike to the hot springs in the dark."

Bolton smirked. "Clearly you know nothing about

women. First, yes it's a treacherous path. She's going to need you to hold her hand over the tricky spots. And the hike is worth it to get to the hot spring. Then you can make a fire in the clearing, thereby confirming your man card is firmly in place."

Was there doubt about that? Bolton had some random ideas about women if he needed to make a real fire instead of just using the barbecue. Matthias wondered how many women had succumbed to Bolton's tactics. "You sort of scare me."

Bolton smirked. "Back in the day, I had some major game."

"I'm not even sure what that means."

Bolton laughed. "It means I know what I'm talking about. Stay here, I'm going to get something. You'll need it."

Matthias heard him sprint upstairs and grabbed the flashlight that sat by the front door in case the power went out. Bolton came back downstairs carrying two champagne flutes.

"For the soda?"

Bolton said, "Works every time. Pickings are slim in Sanctuary, but Frannie's definitely a winner."

Matthias supposed that was a complement, although Frannie might not have seen it that way. "Thanks." He checked his watch. "She should be here any minute. I'm going to wait on the porch."

She was riding her bike to the ranch, even when he'd offered to pick her up. Maybe she'd figured it would make this seem less like a date. She either needed that reassurance and with it less pressure, which was fine with him, or she just didn't want him picking her up from her house, where her mom and sister would be.

Bolton said, "Have fun. Stay safe."

Matthias laughed. "Later."

Bolton turned down the hall to what was the dining room, where he kept his computer. All the camera feeds he'd set up on the perimeter of town showed up there, and the rancher spent his evenings making certain the town remained safe. The integrity of their security over the internet was monitored by the NSA, but part of Bolton's job was to maintain their physical security.

It had taken weeks, but eventually Bolton had been given clearance to read the new sheriff in to his assigned task. John had been grateful Bolton and Matthias would know if there was ever a breach of the mountain range. The peaks were high enough it would take days of treacherous hiking to scale them, but it wasn't impossible for someone to enter Sanctuary that way—if they knew what they were looking for.

Something about Bolton, and his situation, made him the perfect candidate to sit for hours at a computer and watch trees on the off chance someone tripped one of their sensors.

Matthias looked down at the thin glasses in his hands. *Congratulations.* They were the kind of champagne flutes a person drank out of at their wedding.

Matthias glanced at the empty hallway. Had Bolton been married before? The man never talked about his past, but he also never used the internet connection in town and had told Matthias it was a security precaution. He had more concessions than anyone else—like his truck. He guarded the perimeter, and the military had granted him every piece of equipment he'd asked for. Bolton was the only person in town who was allowed weapons.

It wasn't the first time Matthias had wondered who this former DEA agent really was. Maybe he would never know; maybe Bolton wouldn't ever feel like it was time to share with Matthias about his past. It wouldn't be a commentary on their friendship, just a condition of what was likely Bolton's emotional recovery. That was something which happened a lot in Sanctuary. People either over-shared or they never shared at all.

Like Frannie.

The white frame of her bike was the first thing he spotted. Back-lit by the orange glow of streetlights from Sanctuary she rode down the ranch's mile-long driveway. Her skirt floated around her knees as she pedaled, and the shirt she wore had no sleeves. Thankfully she was wearing canvas shoes, since sandals or flip flops would have nixed the whole hiking idea.

She smiled wide as she stopped the bike in front of the porch and hopped off, a little out of breath. "Hi."

Matthias watched her walk to him, her red hair glinting in the porch light.

She giggled, taking the glasses from him and looking at them. "Special occasion?"

He slipped the backpack from his shoulder and put the champagne flutes in the folds of the blanket. She didn't know? He'd figured it was pretty well written on his face, and probably had been ever since he'd stood with her behind the counter of the bakery talking about his nephews.

Matthias settled the backpack back on his shoulder and flipped on the flashlight. "Ready for a little walk?"

Frannie's eyes were wide, and she cleared her throat. Maybe she had seen it. "Sure. That sounds good."

Matthias didn't wait for her to need his help, he held his hand out right then. They crossed the field to the path through the trees that led up the mountain. Rush was a twenty-minute walk along switch-backs and over fallen trees downed in last winter's storm. He noted a couple more they'd need to remove before winter so they could have firewood and the path would be secure.

They were almost there when he began to hear Frannie

breathing harder and harder. She wasn't out of shape, even working in a bakery. She clearly exercised, given the ease with which she'd ridden her bike to the ranch. When she coughed, he stopped.

"Are you okay?" He studied her face. "We can stop here, if you want."

The path was well grown with trees and bushes crowding them on both sides. There was nowhere to sit, so it wasn't ideal, but he wasn't going to push her if she couldn't make it.

Frannie pressed her hand to her front and sucked in a breath, coughing it out. "It's been happening all afternoon. I just can't catch my breath."

"We're almost there. We'll take it easy, okay?"

She nodded, and they continued walking at a slower pace. "I thought I'd be okay once I got some fresh air."

Matthias said, "Are you allergic to anything?"

"Only kiwi, and Dan doesn't grow it."

Matthias didn't like that she wasn't feeling well. If she'd told him, they could have stayed at the ranch. There wouldn't be much privacy between Bolton, Diego and Sean. But they could've still had a good time. Now he felt bad she was struggling up the mountain because of Bolton's stupid idea to—

Frannie gasped. When she pulled back on his arm, Matthias stopped. They'd entered the clearing that was Rush. At the far end of what was essentially a giant shelf on the side of the mountain, a twelve-foot-high fall of spring water tumbled down into a small pool.

"A hot spring?"

Matthias nodded. "It's why they decided to put Sanctuary here. The hot springs mean geo-thermal energy which means we don't need power lines. In terms of electricity, the town is completely self-sustaining with the added bonus of being off the power grid. Secure and energy efficient."

Frannie laughed, which turned into a small cough. "Win, win." She let go of his hand, wandering to the edge of the pool where she sat and looked around. "It's beautiful here, Tias. I'm glad you brought me."

He smiled at the sight of her sitting there. "I'm sorry you aren't feeling well."

She waved off his concern. "Don't worry about me. It'll go away. I don't have time to be sick."

Matthias wasn't going to argue with that. Frannie was a formidable woman—that much was clear. She'd have to be, considering she ran a business at her age that was successful both in terms of product and financially. Frannie had to bake well, and understand accounting. It made Matthias even more proud to get to be the one who gave her the space to relax and be herself even just for a little while.

FRANNIE PULLED the poker from the fire and blew out the flames on her marshmallow. "I meant to do that."

Matthias's grin was infectious. "Sure you did."

"It tastes better crispy."

"Whatever you have to tell yourself."

Frannie nudged his shoulder with hers. The trees were still, and the stars were bright. The fire and the moonlight made it so she could see almost as if it were day. Matthias had done nothing but smile at her all evening, like they shared a delicious secret and he loved that it was theirs alone.

She mushed the marshmallow between the crackers and bit down, loving the taste of chocolate in the middle. "Way better than cupcakes."

"Maybe you should sell these in Sweet Times."

She grinned. "S'mores are pretty good in the oven. I

haven't made them for a long time, though. I guess I just associate s'mores with the outdoors and a fire."

"You did that when you were a kid? Camping, and stuff like that?"

She laughed. "Uh, no."

"You didn't?"

"Only one time. It was a wilderness camp. I was thirteen I think, and I had to beg my dad for weeks to let me go with my friend Julia."

"I know your mom isn't, but your dad wasn't the camping type either?"

Frannie swallowed, feeling the scratch in her throat that hadn't gone away all day. Her nose burned, and there was this weird taste in her mouth she couldn't get rid of. She was trying to ignore it right now, or Matthias would think she wasn't having fun.

She looked at the flames, trying to figure out why watching them was so mesmerizing. "My dad was a mobster."

"As in...the mafia?"

She nodded. "La Cosa Nostra. It means, 'This thing of ours.' Which pretty much sums it up. The family." A spark popped from the fire, and Frannie brushed the ash from her skirt. "I hardly saw him, and when he was home he was always on the phone. It would ring, and he'd rush out no matter what time it was. Family comes first, just not the one at home."

"What happened?" Matthias's voice was quiet.

"He killed my uncle in our living room and then tried to kill me. The FBI raided the house, and I just...decided I wasn't going to live their way anymore. That I had to make my own choices, control my own destiny and all that."

Matthias had gone very still. Frannie looked at him, and for the first time she saw something dangerous in Matthias.

Everyone was capable of violence if they were pushed hard enough, but even with it there in his eyes she knew she would always be safe.

Only his lips moved. "He shot you?"

Frannie took his hand and lifted it to her shoulder, usually covered by her sleeve. She traced his fingers over the thin scar where the bullet had sliced through skin.

"Thank God he missed anything important."

She squeezed her eyes shut. "I'm not sure God had anything to do with it."

He was quiet for a second. "If God hadn't been with you, then your dad might not have missed."

"Maybe." Frannie mulled it over. "I used to think God was part of everything, but only because it was my father justifying the monster he was when he left our house to do who knew what. Now I don't know. If I believe God is there, then will I just be using Him to justify myself?"

"He is there." Matthias lowered his hand, keeping her fingers with his. He intertwined them, and held her hand down by his leg. "Lately I've been wondering if He shouldn't be part of everything, you know? Like if He really is who I believe Him to be, then I should live like that's true. I should talk to Him all the time, about everything." He stopped, and Frannie looked at him. "Maybe you don't want to know about all that."

Frannie shook her head. "I like that you want to share personal things. It's real to you, Tias. That makes it something I want to know."

His lips pressed into a small smile. "Thanks."

"You're welcome." She nudged his shoulder and then looked up at the sky. "I think being up here has helped. I haven't coughed once, even with the smoke."

He'd moved the log they were sitting on so the smoke

didn't end up in their faces. Which didn't work perfectly when the wind kept changing direction, but he'd considered her. At least they could have an actual fire up here, where the smoke wouldn't get trapped in the basin the town occupied. In the lower elevations they were restricted to grills, not open flames.

Matthias squeezed her hand. "I'm glad."

"So how do you feel about the play?"

Frannie wasn't sure she wanted to know what her mom had said and done at rehearsal. Matthias hadn't mentioned it, but she couldn't forget the way he'd looked at her and told her she was *everything* more than her mom. Did he really think that was true?

He said, "I think it'll be good to get the play over with, so I don't have to do it again for at least two years. And then maybe it'll be some tiny part with no lines."

Frannie laughed. Her throat caught, and she had to cough. "Shoot. I was doing so well."

He motioned to the trail with a nod. "We can head back, if you want."

She shook her head. "Not yet. Please."

Matthias touched the back of her head and leaned close, pressing his lips to her forehead. "Whatever you want."

Frannie looked aside, smiling to herself. It was almost too good to be true. Or was that her nature, assuming the worst was always going to happen to her? She shut those thoughts off before they could birth a whirlpool she'd have trouble climbing out of. Instead, she looked up at the trees.

"Someone should build a cabin up here," she said. "Rent it out as a vacation spot so people can get away for the weekend. Everyone needs to feel like they can escape life, even here where no one leaves except for a court appearance."

"If I was going to build a cabin up here, I'd live in it. I don't think I'd build one and then let other people use it."

"But you could make some serious money with a get-away spot."

Matthias grinned. "There's the entrepreneur in you."

"Hey, it's not being shallow. It's just good business." She laughed, and coughed.

Sighing, Frannie got up and walked to the hot spring pool. She sat on the edge of the rocks and skimmed her fingers in the warm water. It didn't smell good, but it wouldn't matter if she was up to her chin in the soothing water.

Matthias took the picnic blanket, dunked the entire thing in the pool and took it—dripping—to the fire, where he wrung it out over the flames. The fire sizzled and extinguished. He did this twice more, until it was all the way out.

Frannie watched him gather the left-over food packages and put them in the backpack, along with the glasses. When he zipped it up and swung it over his shoulder, she said, "I sort of don't want to go."

Matthias walked over. He opened his mouth, but someone made a noise in the trees. It sounded like two people, a man and a woman. Frannie moved closer to Matthias's side while the voices got louder.

Diego and Izzy stumbled into the clearing. Their eyes widened in genuine surprise, and Izzy laughed. "Cinderella!"

Diego laughed too, his eyes glassy. Come to think of it, Izzy didn't look entirely with it either. They didn't walk straight; they kind of weaved around as they made their way to Matthias and Frannie.

"Fancy running into you guys here." Diego's smile was aimed at Matthias, and there was nothing nice about it. "Taking the little woman out for the evening, are you?"

Izzy laughed. "Too bad Cinderella has no idea how to have fun."

Diego looked at Frannie. His gaze swept down and back up her. She felt Matthias stiffen, apparently as offended as she was.

"We're leaving." Matthias tugged on her hand.

"So soon?" Izzy pouted.

Diego said, "Stick around. We can all party."

"Matthias and I both have to be up early for our jobs." Frannie realized she was only confirming Izzy's opinion of her. But why did her little sister's impression mean so much— and hurt so much—anyway? "Maybe next time."

Diego leered. "Sounds like a plan, darlin'."

Matthias took a step. Frannie planted her hand on his chest. "Don't, Tias. Let's just go."

"Tias?" Diego erupted into laughter. Izzy giggled, but it sounded like she wasn't even sure what was funny.

"Pet names. Dude, that's so sweet."

Matthias shifted. "You'll want to remember who gave you that black eye."

Izzy gasped.

"Whatever, Dad. Push us all around like you always do. Thinking you're the boss of all of us when you're *not*."

"Diego—"

Frannie turned, standing in front of Matthias so he focused on her and nothing else. "Let's go."

This wasn't going to end well. Not when Diego—and probably Izzy also—were hopped up on something. Frannie knew next to nothing about drugs, since she'd come here as a late teen. It wasn't like this was a place where it was easy to experiment with meds. It was a "dry" town, but there were ways to get ahold of stuff. Still, her exposure to it had been minimal since she'd been working at the bakery and trying to finish high school.

"Tias." Her voice was a whisper. Hopefully Diego wouldn't hear her call Matthias that a second time. "Let's go."

He nodded. "You're right. This is a waste of our time."

Frannie heard them snickering. She glanced back and saw Diego swoop Izzy up in a kiss that made Frannie blush. That was why they were up here? Frannie swallowed past the grating sensation in her throat. Matthias was nothing like his brother, and she was nothing like Izzy. But it might be nice to be swept up in something that overtook her completely. Maybe just once.

CHAPTER 10

Matthias glanced back. Frannie had fallen behind, still picking her way along the path slower than him. He stopped and waited for her to catch up. "Sorry."

She shook her head. "Don't be."

"I'm mad. Did they ruin our night?"

"Not if you don't let them." Frannie put her hand in his, and they kept walking.

Matthias blew out a breath. "I had a good time, even though Diego and Izzy kind of wrecked it." Matthias didn't want her to placate him, but if he didn't know something was wrong then he couldn't fix it. "Are you sure they didn't mess things up?"

"Why does your brother get under your skin like that? Is it because he said you were like your dad?" She worked her jaw back and forth. "Unless...it's a family thing and you don't want to talk about it."

Had he conditioned her to think that? What else was he supposed to do? There were some things he just wasn't going to be able to talk with her about. Not ever. He didn't want to lie or keep secrets from her, but it wasn't like there was an alternative. Betray his family's confidence? Ruin the unsteady detente they had established?

"Partly." Matthias was going to have to tell her at least some of it, the stuff he was allowed to talk about. "There's been a rash of that lately—people saying I'm like my dad—and not just from Diego. My dad was a drug dealer. That's about the extent of the glamor of it. He'd have said he was an entrepreneur." He chuckled. "Though not like you."

"I can see why you'd get mad."

He squeezed her hand. "My dad got in deep with the wrong people, owed them a lot of money. They forced him to go bigger and bigger until he stepped wrong and the DEA caught up. So, let's just say I know exactly what it's like to have federal agents swarm your house. Mama beamed one of them with her rolling pin because he grabbed Antonia too roughly. They were both arrested, and the DEA got him to roll over on all the guys he worked with from Miami to Mexico. The whole operation. And we all got shipped to Sanctuary with him."

"Miami?"

He nodded. "Where are you from?"

"Baltimore." She shook her head, dissipating whatever had been occupying her thoughts. "You didn't want to come here?"

"I was eight, and it's cold here. Still, it wasn't like I had a choice. Mama would never have broken up the family, because God hates divorce."

Matthias didn't believe in it either. Though, he figured that was easy to say when he was unmarried. Marriage seemed like it would be pretty good—especially with a woman like Frannie.

"That seems like a bad reason to make everyone miserable."

"It is." Matthias sat astride a fallen log. He lifted Frannie over and climbed down on the other side. "And then Dad kept making us all miserable even after we were here. He'd run around on my mom with any woman who looked his way. She's changed so much since he died. I don't want to think he did us a favor, but sometimes it crosses my mind."

Matthias stopped and turned to her then. "Does that make me a horrible person? I don't want to hate my dad, but what else am I supposed to feel? He killed whatever love and respect I had when he started hitting Maria, Antonia and Sofia just because they were girls, and then yelling at me and Diego to make sure we became stronger men."

Frannie touched his face. "It's okay to feel what you feel. You have to feel it, because it's honest and denying it would be worse." Her hand dropped back to her side. "You can't stay there, though, you have to live here where life is happening right now or you're going to miss it."

He looked at the trees. Maybe that was Maria's problem, she hadn't ever moved on from the day their father died. She was stuck living there while half-living in the present, missing out on her sons' lives and the opportunity to make her marriage good.

Matthias swallowed against the lump of emotion in his throat. "Every time I think I can breathe free of him, something happens, and it's like he's this specter in the corner of the room that won't ever die."

"So look away. He'll always be there because he's your father, but you don't have to acknowledge him."

"You sound like you know what you're talking about."

Frannie gave him a small smile. "I know a little something about overbearing fathers who dictate everything and demand everything to be a certain way. Their way."

"I'm sure you do." He held her elbows then, remembering

what she'd told him. The mafia? He could believe that of her mother. Mimi seemed like the kind of woman who would jump at the chance to marry someone wealthy and powerful. The mafia had probably seemed glamorous to her. But this Frannie, the one with him now, didn't seem like the type at all. He could barely imagine her in that life.

"How did you do it?" he asked her. "How did you leave that behind and become...this?"

She laughed and swept her hand down. "All this? Not much to write home about, let me tell you."

"Why do you do that?" She winced, and Matthias realized he was gripping her arms too tight. He dropped his hands to the sides. "Why do you put yourself down? It ticks me off."

"Well, excuse me." She slammed her hands down on her hips. "It's not like eligible bachelors are lining up at my door to take the plain sister on a whirlwind weekend romance trip to—oh wait, we can't even leave town!"

"You're the one who wants to start a vacation business at the hot springs."

She glared. "You're the one who wants to keep the good things to himself. Let me guess, you were bad at sharing as a kid?"

"You're right. I don't want to." Matthias gritted his teeth. "Why would I share? If something is good then I'm not going to lend it out so anyone can use it."

She blinked, and something washed over her face. "Good."

"Now it's good?" He huffed. "I don't understand you at all. You just said it was bad. And why are we fighting about something this stupid anyway?"

Frannie stuck out her lower lip. "You started it."

"I'm pretty sure you did, actually." Matthias scrubbed his hands down his face, rubbing away the moment of humor.

Frannie was good medicine and a beautiful distraction, but the reality was his life basically sucked. "Why does Diego ruin everything?"

Frannie frowned. "Is there something I don't know about the two of you?"

Matthias shrugged. "Maybe it's just me, but it's like any time I set my sights on something. Or someone. He has to interfere."

"He stole your girlfriend."

Matthias nodded. "In high school."

"Who was she?" Frannie folded her arms, her gaze dark now.

"It doesn't matter. Cyan left town with her mom and never came back. I have no idea what Diego said to her, but one minute we're in love and talking about getting married after graduation and the next I find her kissing Diego. Two minutes after that, her mom moves her out of town."

"Wow."

"I know."

Frannie said, "You were really going to get married right after graduation?"

Matthias blinked. "And Diego stole her from me."

"She let him steal her."

"Excuse me?"

Frannie lifted one shoulder. "She couldn't have been all that in love with you if she didn't even stick with you. The first test and she bails on you?" Her voice was getting louder and louder. "I mean seriously, the girl can't have known what she had if she gave you up for *Diego*." She said his name like Matthias's brother was little better than a nasty virus. "And then leaving town, without even admitting she'd done wrong? I mean—"

Matthias touched the sides of her face and stepped close so their bodies were touching.

Then he kissed her.

In the dark, halfway up a forest trail, it was like dawn broke. The one who'd walked away seemed like a distant memory. Frannie filled every corner of him, like light touching every inch of land as far as he could see. Nothing inside him was left unaffected by the feel of her. All the clichés he'd ever heard about love, about feeling like at last he'd come home.

They were all true.

———

FRANNIE CLEARED HER THROAT, concentrating on putting one foot in front of the other. Matthias glanced aside and gave her a smile. She understood Izzy a little more now. There was a lot she would do to feel all that again, probably most of it stupid stuff with a doe-eyed look on her face. Who cared? Her lips still tingled from Matthias's kiss—she hoped it lasted a while longer just so she wouldn't forget it.

The trees ended, and they stepped off the path onto the field where cows grazed. The ranch land was a wide, dark expanse broken only by the porch light at the house, the barn light and another building. Matthias wound them across the grass, moving left and right every few steps. She presumed that was because he saw what she could smell, and he was keeping her from stepping in it. A fact she greatly appreciated.

As they grew closer, Frannie saw a helicopter on the landing pad across from the ranch house. The lights were off, and the rotors were still. Who knew how long it had been here? It didn't look like one of the usual ones that dropped off and picked up residents—those were nondescript. This was Navy.

"It's the president, I'll bet."

Matthias said, "You think so?"

Frannie picked up speed, hoping she'd get the chance to say bye to Susan and wish the first lady well on her visit. There were several people standing around the helicopter, talking. "Susan must be going to spend time with her husband. She told me they'd planned to have a visit, but she didn't know when it would be."

"You'd think he'd have more security than a pilot and co-pilot."

And those hadn't even exited the helicopter. Frannie could barely see them, but the light was on inside. They looked like they were drinking coffee.

A tall man stood beside the helicopter, talking with one of two women—Susan and Beth. John Mason and his son were there, too. As they drew closer, Frannie recognized the man. "Grant!"

She laughed and jogged to him.

Grant smiled wide. "Frannie." He hugged her while the first lady smiled. "How are you, girl?"

"I'm good." She tugged Matthias closer, hooked her arm in his and laid her head on his shoulder. "Just out for the evening."

Grant lifted his eyebrows. "Is that right?"

John chuckled, swinging his son Pat up onto his shoulders. Matthias nodded, shaking the director of the Marshals' hand. "Mason."

"Good to see you, Matthias. How's the family?"

Matthias nodded. "Good. Yours?"

Grant nodded, glancing at his brother—Sheriff John Mason—and nephew. "We're all good."

"How's Sarah?" Frannie hadn't had a letter from the deputy marshal originally assigned to her case recently. They'd only spent a few days together, but they'd agreed to keep in touch. Frannie's letters got routed through the marshals' service's mail system that kept the location of witnesses safe, but contact was contact—and friendship was precious.

"She had the baby. It was a boy. Riley."

Frannie clapped. "That's great."

Grant turned to the first lady and said, "We should get going now, ma'am."

"Are you leaving for your trip?" Frannie touched the first lady's arm.

Susan smiled. "Yes."

Grant said, "Hopefully soon things will be back to normal."

Susan gasped. "Really?"

The marshal nodded. "The investigation into the organization who tried to kill both you and Beth uncovered a widespread plot within more than one federal agency. But I think we're finally getting to the bottom of it. Shouldn't be long before you're back at home in the White House."

Susan clapped. "I could kiss you!"

Grant laughed. "I'm not sure the president would approve."

"Pshaw." Susan waved away his concern. "What he doesn't know won't hurt him."

Frannie giggled, glancing at Beth who was also laughing. Beth said, "There's my mom for you. Scandalous."

"Uh, sure." Frannie knew what scandalous looked like, and it dressed in way shorter skirts than the ones Susan wore.

Beth giggled. Susan looked at her. "I'll see you soon?"

Frannie glanced between them, her gaze settling on Beth. "Aren't you going?"

Beth shook her head, rolling her eyes. "The doctor advised me not to travel, and Mom and Dad need some *alone* time, if you know what I mean."

Frannie kind of wished she did, but that was a dream. It wasn't something she was going to admit out loud, though. Susan gave out hugs all around. Frannie was the one before last.

"Take care."

"I will," Susan said. "Olympia has already mentioned to a few people around town how you'll need assistance while I'm gone. So look for help. It's there for you."

"Thank you." Why did this feel like goodbye for good? Frannie shrugged off the ridiculous thought and moved back beside Matthias. He wrapped his arm around her shoulder and gave her a side hug, leaving his arm in place.

Beth and Susan said a teary goodbye, and the first lady got in the helicopter. Grant had a quiet conversation with his brother and then hugged Pat before climbing in too. They waited with Beth until the helicopter disappeared over the mountains.

John clapped. "Frannie, you need a ride back into town?"

"I have my bike." Plus she didn't want to say goodbye to Matthias in front of John, Pat and Beth.

"We'll throw it on top of the Jeep."

Beth grinned as she walked behind John. The sheriff was making a bee-line for his vehicle, swerving and making Pat— still perched on his shoulders—laugh like he was on a roller-coaster.

Matthias touched her shoulder. "You should get a ride back, then you can get some sleep."

"I look that bad?"

He made a nervous noise in his throat. "I'm not even going to touch that. I know you've had a long day, and tomorrow won't be any better."

She nodded. "We have rehearsal again. I'm gonna need a nap at this rate."

Matthias kissed her forehead. "I'll see you then, if I don't see you earlier."

John had already loaded her bike on the roof of his Jeep. He and Pat stretched cords across her bike and hooked them in the open windows.

"Can you drop me off at the medical center?" Frannie waited until John's gaze met hers. "I want to stop in and see Stella before I go home."

John nodded, and Frannie got in the back.

Beside her, Beth smiled. "How was your date?"

Frannie thought about the fire, sitting beside Matthias at the hot springs and his kiss. She felt her lips curl up into a smile.

"That's what I thought." Beth was smiling too, but her eyes didn't sparkle the way they had in the bakery kitchen. In fact...she looked sad.

"I'm sure your dad will be able to get a message to your husband."

John reacted—shifted in his seat—but she kept her attention on Beth. She guessed the woman hadn't told John about the baby, so she didn't mention it.

Beth looked away, out the window. Frannie wanted to draw her out, to let the woman know she could rely on her. If she even wanted to talk about it at all.

John pulled up outside the medical center. "I'll get your bike."

Frannie propped it against the outside of the building and

knocked. Xander hit the access button, and she went inside. "Good evening."

"Good evening, Ms. Frannie." Yet another person tonight who looked at her with sadness in their eyes.

"She's having a rough night?" Frannie squeezed his tree-trunk arm, and he nodded. "I'll see what I can do to cheer her up."

It wasn't until she stepped into Stella's room that Frannie released the breath she'd been holding. Father Wilson sat in the chair pulled up to Stella's bedside. His eyes were closed, and he prayed with lips moving silently. Stella's face was almost gray. She opened her eyes...and winked.

Frannie clapped a hand over her mouth to keep from laughing and managed to cough instead. Father Wilson lifted his bent head. Stella shut her eyes again, so that Father Wilson looked sternly at Frannie. "Amen."

Frannie nodded, trying to look respectful. "Father."

"Ms. Peters." He stood then, and Stella opened her eyes.

"Thank you, Father."

He nodded, but with his shoulders too so it looked like a bow. "I'll be by tomorrow." Father Wilson looked at Frannie out of the corner of his eye on the way past her, and then he was gone.

Frannie rushed to Stella, who held her arms out.

"So...a date with Matthias?"

Frannie leaned back. "How did you even know that?"

"Word gets around."

Of course it did. "I knew he must've been wrong. I knew you would never have agreed to let a crazy man kill you, like putting you out of your misery was something honorable."

Something shifted in Stella's eyes. "Plenty of people have probably wanted to put me out of my misery a time or two in my life."

"Not just you." Frannie settled on the edge of the bed. "When I read it in the letter, I didn't believe it."

"I heard about that, too. Are you okay? It can't have been a pleasant thing to read."

"It was weird, and creepy." Frannie shook off the cloud the letter had brought with it. She didn't want that in her life. "I'm glad John is working to figure out who it was in your room. That's probably weird for you, thinking about someone in your room when you were sleeping."

Stella's nose wrinkled. "Wasn't the first time. Not when I need meds at all hours."

"You don't know who it was...do you?"

"The sheriff asked me that."

Frannie watched her friend. "You don't want to have met him. Maybe he's even a bit crazy, what with wanting to end lives. Like that will make people happy."

"I'm not worried about dying."

Frannie swallowed. "It doesn't bother you at all?"

Stella took her hand. "It shouldn't bother you, either. It's not weird, or bad. Not really. Not when I'm sure of what my faith tells me. I have peace."

Frannie straightened. "I don't want any part of that if it means you're not going to fight."

"I'm too tired to fight." Stella rubbed the back of Frannie's hand with her thumb. "I'm asking you to let me go."

"You're going to let some delusional maniac kill you?"

"I told him I wouldn't do it until I talked it over with my husband, and with you."

Frannie shot off the bed. "You know who it is." She couldn't believe this. It was insane. Stella had talked to him. "You said you didn't see who it was."

"He was here before, and I never saw his face."

"Then he won't wait for you." Frannie sucked in a breath.

"He had a needle, he was going to do it before I interrupted him."

"Then you'd better get on board, darlin'. Because there isn't much time."

Black spots flickered in the edges of Frannie's vision. "This is... Don't do this. Don't let that monster do this to you."

"Ms. Frannie?" Xander stood in the doorway, glancing between her and Stella.

Stella shook her head. "Everything is fine, Xander. Thank you."

Frannie nearly choked. Nothing was fine. Stella was *inviting* death because... Frannie took her friend's hand. "I know you're scared, I'll be here with you."

Stella smiled, like Frannie was a confused child who didn't understand the scope of what she was saying. "You don't get it. I'm not scared at all."

CHAPTER 11

THE BELL over the bakery door rang, and Mimi sauntered in. "Hello, darling."

Frannie sighed. "What's up?"

"I'm here to work, of course."

This can't have been the help the first lady had been talking about. Although Frannie wouldn't have put it past the woman to go by Frannie's house and have a "talk" with her mom, she just didn't think it had anything to do with getting Frannie the help she needed.

"I'm glad you're happy, darling." Mimi squeezed her hand. "Matthias is a wonderful catch. A real man's man. You hook that one good and don't ever let go."

Frannie stared while her mom slipped on a pink apron. "I'm not sure that's exactly how it works."

Mimi gave her a look. "That's because you know next to nothing about men."

Frannie turned away. She didn't need that lesson from Mimi. Not when the tips and tricks she'd have to offer were the ones that had wreaked havoc on their lives for years.

Mimi came back from a bathroom break—not that she

called it that—later that morning, a white envelope in her hand. "This was on the floor inside the back door."

Francine snatched it from her, not wanting her mom to have to deal with it if it was another letter from the killer.

Then she froze.

After everything, her instinct was concern for Mimi?

Frannie would put up with a hundred of these letters if it meant she had proof she wasn't like her parents—that she understood how to think of someone other than herself all the time.

Frannie used the phone by the cashier's log. Dotty answered on the first ring. "Yes, ma'am?"

She probably thought it was Susan calling. "It's just me."

"I know, dear." Dotty chuckled. "You need the sheriff again? You didn't get another one of those letters, did you?"

Frannie sighed. "Can you just have him come by?"

"He's out at the reclamation center, but I'll radio him right now."

Frannie tossed the letter on the counter. "It's not going anywhere."

She hung up and looked around. The tables were clear, and there were only two customers in the corner huddled together in quiet conversation.

Mimi picked up the letter. "What's the deal with a letter, you have to call the sheriff?"

"It's from the person who tried to kill Stella. He's some kind of assisted suicide nut, but he's dangerous. He's killed before."

"What are you talking about?" Mimi looked baffled. "There's another killer in Sanctuary?" By the time she was done her voice was a screech.

"Mimi—"

"Open it!" She shoved the envelope in Frannie's face.

"You don't want to know what it says. He's delusional."

Not that Stella agreed with her assessment, but Frannie hadn't figured out how she was going to convince her friend when she was so obviously suffering. It was selfish to want to keep her around, but Frannie didn't have any problem being selfish in this instance.

Losing Stella was going to be incredibly difficult whether it happened today—because she chose it—or in a few weeks. What was stalling Frannie was the anger. Fury that this had to happen at all roared through her, and she wanted to push back against it. She'd been trying to stay out of it, but that was before she'd talked with Stella.

"Open it."

Frannie took the envelope from her mom and glanced at the window. The sheriff wasn't here yet, and he hadn't said she couldn't read it. Maybe there was something in there to help her convince Stella this guy wasn't the answer to her problem.

She ripped into it, pulling out the folded paper and shaking it out.

Her mom wafted a hand in front of her face and stepped back. "What is that?"

"It's just what it smells like." Frannie set the paper on the counter and coughed into her elbow. The scratch in her throat was back, not that it had been gone for long. Whatever it was that made the letter smell like this must be exacerbating the virus she'd caught over the last couple of days.

My dearest Francine,

She flinched. "Seriously?" Having a crazy man grow more attached to her was not a good outcome.

"What does it say?" Mimi was keeping her distance, probably because of the tangy chemical odor.

Was that what was making her sick?

Frannie held the paper farther away and read aloud. "I regret whatever harm I've caused you in the past. My work is important. However, your injury was the result of my impulsive actions. It is not in my nature to cause pain. I seek only to bestow peace to the suffering. Please grant me the gift of your forgiveness." She paused for a shallow breath, shaking her head.

The smell hit the back of her throat, and Frannie coughed. So much for trying not to breathe it in.

"Do not fear me. It is needless. I reside not with the living, but only with those close to departing. I—"

"Frannie."

She looked up. John stood in the middle of the bakery, his arms folded.

"You didn't say I couldn't read it."

"You're adding your fingerprints, which makes it harder for Grant to process considering your prints will get flagged as unknown and possibly being the killer's."

"He's testing the letters?"

John nodded. "Of course. The first one was sent off on Monday's transport. This one will have to wait until next Monday."

"Is he testing for—" Breath caught in her throat. She tried to suck more in, but couldn't get enough air. She bent forward and hung her head down, coughing and trying to clear her throat. Grant needed to test for poisons.

"Get her some water."

Mimi's heels clapped out into the kitchen and John came over to stand by her. "Give yourself a minute. If you stress out or freak because you're panicking, it'll take longer to get your breath back."

She nodded, working on taking in more air every time her

lungs hitched. It was like they were reaching for oxygen, trying to draw it in. Her head pounded with every cough.

When she'd calmed somewhat, Frannie straightened and took the water from her mom. John walked her to a chair, and she slumped into it.

"I'll take the letter." He looked at the paper on the table like he was trying to figure something out. "You should probably go home and rest. Let your mom look after the bakery."

Mimi blanched, but thankfully covered it up. She flicked back one side of her hair and said, "Of course. Darling, you should put your feet up."

If she'd finished fixing up the apartment upstairs, Frannie would only have had to walk up there. As it was, she pushed her bike back home. Riding seemed like it would take entirely too much energy and brainpower. It took some time, but she made it back to the house. She propped the bike against the wall beside the front door and just stood for a minute. One hand braced against the house, Frannie tried to figure out what she was going to do next. It felt like a jackhammer had taken up residence in her head.

"What are you standing out here for?"

Frannie turned her whole body so her neck stayed straight.

"Gees, you look worse than you did last night."

"You remember that?" Frannie quipped. "I'm surprised you even knew what was going on, given how stoned you were."

Izzy smirked. "So you're not as innocent as everyone thinks." She jerked, and turned aside.

Diego sauntered past her, planting a messy kiss on Izzy's lips. "Later, darlin'." He saw Frannie, and leered. "Sick and hot is still hot."

Frannie waited until he was out of earshot and then turned back to her sister. "Why do you hang out with him?"

Izzy bristled. "It's none of your business."

Frannie stepped inside. "How was that doctor's appointment Mom mentioned?" She looked at the stairs, but couldn't bring herself to put one foot in front of the other and climb them.

"What doctor's appointment?" Frannie glanced over just as Izzy shot her a weirdo look. "Mom probably had plans with her man. He won't let her tell anyone they're together. He wants it to be all secretive."

Frannie shook her head. The resulting pain was enough to make her clutch her forehead and almost fall. She braced her other hand on the wall and moved toward the living room. "I'm going to lie down."

"Whatever, I have plans anyway."

"Maybe you should go to work. Mom might need help."

"Nah. Mimi will be fine." Izzy's voice got quieter as she moved away. "The girls and I have plans."

Frannie tumbled onto the couch and the room spun.

The front door slammed and another wave of pain crashed over her. Nausea roiled in her stomach. Frannie clutched her abdomen and prayed she wasn't going to throw up. The scar on her shoulder tingled like phantom pain, remembering her father's eyes and the booming sound of the gunshot.

It was like something had crawled down her throat. Was this her punishment for wanting to have her own space, her own life...her own relationship? She would take it all back if it meant this would go away.

She wanted to sleep, but it felt like her head was going to explode.

When she opened her eyes again, the pain in her head

was down to a dull thump-thump. Frannie braced herself and opened her eyes. The living room was halfway dark, except for the lamp light. At least someone in her house was capable of being considerate so she didn't end up waking to complete darkness. Still, even the small amount of light exacerbated the pain in her head.

Frannie stretched. Her foot touched something solid, and she shifted to see what it was.

"Whoa, easy." Matthias grabbed her ankle, then let go to rub where she'd kicked his leg.

"Uh...hi."

He smiled at her.

Frannie saw the book in his hand. How long had he been there? "Tias."

He didn't move, his head still bowed and his eyes on the pages in front of him. "Hang on, I'm at the good part."

She looked at the book. Half an inch of pages were in his right hand, the greater portion of the book on the other side. Apparently the "good part" came near the end. When was the last time she'd read a book?

Frannie set her chin in her hand and snuggled into the couch cushions to watch him—which should probably have felt strange, but it didn't. Like she had nothing better to do than study the line of his jaw, and the way his hair kind of just fell wherever it wanted, even touching his ear.

His forearm flexed, and he set the book in his lap. "Feeling better?"

"I think so." She shuffled up and sat back against the arm of the chair.

"Your front door was unlocked. Is it okay that I came in?"

Frannie shrugged. It would've been weird if she was upstairs sleeping but didn't figure he'd have gone up looking. "How long have you been here?"

"Maybe half an hour."

"What are you reading?"

He cocked his head to one side. "You got another letter, and this is what you want to talk about?"

"I'm not in denial. I'm just not giving him head space I can't afford to lose." She tapped the side of her temple with her index finger. "Prime real estate, right here."

He smiled but said, "I'm sorry. I know how busy you are."

"You don't have to apologize. You rank higher on the list than a crazy madman." Even if the letter-writer considered himself to be of sound mind, she was still going to think of him that way. He might be trying to make her sick. Who else than a psycho would do that?

"Glad to hear I rank higher than the demented criminals of the world." He turned the book, pulling a bookmark from the front and settling it between two pages. When he tossed it on the table, she read the author's name. *Carl Gabriel.* Frannie had seen some of his historical adventure movies.

"Can I borrow that when you're finished with it?"

"Depends." He eyed her. "Do you fold the corners of the pages down to mark your place?"

Frannie said, "What if I don't have a piece of paper or something else handy to use as a bookmark?"

"You should write the page number on your hand."

"What if I take a shower and it washes off?"

He smiled. "You are feeling better. Are you hungry? I brought some tomato soup since I wasn't sure what you'd have." He stood, stretching his arms above his head.

"Sat for too long?"

"It was a good excuse to read, so thanks." He grabbed the book and stuck it in a black backpack by the door. Was he planning on staying a while?

"Soup?" She stood, pitched too far, and braced as he caught her.

"Easy, Frannie. Don't move too fast."

"Why am I lightheaded?"

His frown wasn't curiosity, it was genuine concern. "I don't know."

"I feel like I've caught some weird bug, but it isn't like anything I've ever felt before." She paused. "Although, I haven't had more than a cold since I moved here. Maybe it's an Idaho thing."

His lips twitched. "Maybe."

He kept his arm around her waist while they walked to the kitchen, and she settled at the table. "I feel bad making you take care of me."

"I don't mind." He stirred the soup on the stove and left the spoon in the pan, moving to the fridge where he drew out the butter. "Bread?"

Frannie pointed at a white container on the far end of the counter. "In there."

He pulled out the loaf and stared at her with no small amount of surprise. "Generic, store brand bread?"

"It's not betrayal. If there are leftovers that won't keep, I bring them home from work and freeze them. But I don't want to eat my bread all the time. Sometimes I even make a quesadilla from that sliced cheese where they're all individually wrapped."

"Fair enough." He chuckled and set to buttering four slices. "Do you have any cupcakes here?"

Frannie shook her head. "Sorry. Mimi and Izzy don't eat them." And her butt didn't need any more calories. She had so little will power when she was at work without bringing it home too.

"They don't eat your sweets?"

"Uh, no." Frannie rolled her eyes. "Mom wants the gluten free, sugar free, calorie free, dairy free, everything free, but still somehow tasty."

"She's allergic? I saw her eat a cupcake at the twin's birthdays."

"I think she'd like to be because then she'd have a reason to feel special. Who knows what's going on in that woman's head? I can't figure her out half the time."

Matthias poured the soup into two bowls and set everything on the table, the plate of buttered bread in the middle. "I didn't have this in mind for the first time we shared a meal together."

"S'mores don't count?"

"As a meal?" He looked offended she'd even suggest that. "No way."

"Do you cook?"

"A few things, enough so I don't starve and I get to eat more than just noodles or macaroni and cheese." He swiped up some bread, folded it in half and dunked it in his soup. "You?"

"A few things. I'm just usually too tired by dinner to do more than nuke some chicken and make a salad."

"It must be hard having rehearsals for the play in the evenings."

"Once we get further in, I'll know for sure. But it is only two weeks. After the play I'll take a couple of days off and crash, probably." Frannie took a bite, and had to cough before she could swallow.

Matthias frowned. "I figured you'd be okay since its smooth soup. No chunks."

"Don't talk about chunks right now." She groaned and shot him a smile. "There probably wasn't much else in the cupboard, either. I haven't been grocery shopping yet this week."

He looked like he wanted to say something about that, but he didn't—a fact for which Frannie was grateful. She said, "Is this a date?"

He swallowed and lifted his attention to her. "Do you want it to be?"

"Why are you here?"

Matthias sat back in his chair. "Maybe I'm just here because I want to be here."

"All of a sudden. Like, you just decided this week we should spend all this time together?"

"It doesn't feel sudden to me at all." His fingertips tapped the table. "It feels like it's been a long time coming."

She didn't disagree, but still. "There's a reason why I don't get involved. If we started...dating, or whatever, and then we broke up, it would be all awkward. We'd have to tiptoe around each other for the rest of our lives."

She would end up having to watch him marry someone else, knowing he slipped out of her grasp.

That would suck.

"Who says it's going to go bad?"

"You don't know that it won't."

"And you don't know for sure it will." He studied her for a minute. "Look Frannie, I like you. I wouldn't have kissed you if I didn't. But this isn't an ultimatum, and I can't promise a future I don't know for sure is going to happen. I'd like to spend time with you, get to know you better."

"And this doesn't have anything to do with the letters? Because all this seems like it happened at the same time."

Matthias's shoulders slumped. "You are the single most cynical woman I have ever met in my entire life. It's exasperating." He ran a hand through his hair.

"Why have I never seen you with another woman before? Why me? Why now?"

"I don't know." He turned his hands so, for a second, she saw both of his palms.

Was he going to give up? Was she driving him away? "I'm sorry. My head is all messed up from the headache, and I don't feel good at all." She pushed the bowl of soup away. "Ignore me."

He shook his head. "Don't think so. I think this is the most truth you've ever spoken to me."

"I don't lie."

"But you rarely ever admit you doubt so much about yourself either." Matthias waited a moment, and then said, "I can't give you self-esteem, Frannie. You have to find it in yourself, because you have to see yourself how God sees you."

"How does He see me?" God was—she didn't even know. Up there. Disconnected from what was happening on earth, or that was what it felt like at least.

"Trust Him with your problems."

Frannie shook her head. "Where is all this coming from? Why do you suddenly think I need fixing so badly? Is it that obvious something is wrong with me?"

"Nothing's wrong with you." He circled the table and crouched beside her, laying his hand on her shoulder. "Calm down, okay?"

That was when she realized her breath was coming in gasps. "What's happening to me?"

"I don't know. But be sure I'm going to figure it out. You can trust me, I'm not going anywhere."

"Are you sure?"

"I don't leave." His gaze held hers. "I'm not the one who leaves."

"Why did she do that to you?" Frannie felt warmth on her

cheek. He swiped it with his thumb, and she realized she was crying.

"I don't know." He gave her a soft smile. "I heard she's some famous Christian singer now. Maybe that's why. It's impossible to keep up with popular music when Hal only plays classic rock and old-man country on the radio station."

She smiled, but it didn't hold. "Is something wrong with me?"

He lifted her up so she was standing, and they walked to the hallway. "Let's get you settled back on the couch, and I'm going to make a call. Everything's going to be fine."

"Promise?"

Frannie laid back on the couch and felt his lips touch her forehead.

"I promise. Get some more rest, okay?"

"Wake me up for rehearsals."

———

Matthias gripped the phone until he picked up.

"Sheriff Mason."

"There's something seriously wrong with Frannie."

He heard John up and moving. "Tell me what."

"She took a nap. When she woke, her head was all messed up. She's dizzy, slurred speech. Talking in circles. She's fine one minute, then she's upset and crying."

Then I'd have to watch you marry someone else, knowing you slipped out of my grasp.

That would suck.

Matthias knew she hadn't planned on saying that—or the rest of it—out loud. The only thing he could think to do was pray. That's why he'd tried to get her, even in her confusion, to go to God. Because Matthias was scared out of his mind. He'd never seen her like this.

John said, "I'll call the doc. You want us there, or you want to bring her to the medical center?"

Matthias blew out a breath. "She's already freaked out. I don't know if it's a good idea to push her into a check-up in this state. We have an hour until rehearsal. Why don't you tell Doctor Fenton to swing by? At least he can observe her."

"I'll ask. But if he balks, you need to get her an appointment."

Matthias watched the slow rise and fall of her breathing, thanking God she wasn't coughing anymore. "Whatever gets her to the doctor, she needs to think it was her idea."

CHAPTER 12

"Precious."

Frannie spun in time for Olympia to swallow her in a warm hug. The woman held on long enough it could have been considered a snuggle. Eventually Frannie leaned back, and Olympia released her.

"Don't look so embarrassed, Precious."

Frannie sighed, glancing around the Meeting House where rehearsal was about to start. "Tias is acting like I'm glass that might break at any second."

Olympia's eyebrows rose, and Frannie realized she'd called Matthias by his nickname. "My boy, he treats the things he cares for very, very well."

Frannie didn't even know what to say to that. He really was taking care of her. It should feel suffocating, but it didn't. She wasn't used to attention. Or care. Maybe it was just the fact it was him that made the difference.

Olympia patted her cheek before moving back over to the kitchen, where she'd been preparing a late supper for everyone due at rehearsals. They'd even bought up everything left over at the bakery and had it brought over. Apparently

Mimi hadn't sold much that afternoon, but if the town was buying the remainder, Frannie didn't have anything to complain about.

"You all right?" Nadia Marie was frowning.

Frannie shrugged. "Are you?"

Nadia Marie glanced at the stage, where Bolton Farrera shifted boards and lined them up next to each other. He had a ball cap on instead of his trademark cowboy hat, and he'd shoved a pencil in front of his ear under the edge of the hat.

Nadia Marie sighed. "It's the tool belt. Gets me every time."

Frannie laughed. Matthias looked back from his spot beside Bolton and smiled. She smiled back, glad whatever weirdness that happened in her house had passed. She wasn't totally fine. The headache was still present, but she wasn't dizzy, and it felt like she could think straight now, at least.

"Good evening, ladies." Terrence sat in the row in front of them, a smudge of something on the front of his shirt. Apparently he'd eaten already.

"Terrence."

Nadia Marie nodded. "Terrence."

He looked around like he was searching for something to talk about, and his gaze settled on Nadia Marie's purse on the seat beside her. "Did you get mail this week?"

Frannie leaned over to look. The envelope was different than the two she'd received from the killer. Her stomach unknotted at least a little, as Nadia Marie smiled.

"That's cool." Terrence pulled it out of her purse and looked at the front. "I've never gotten any—"

Nadia Marie snatched it back. "Don't touch my mail."

"I was just looking."

"It's none of your business."

Terrence lifted his hands, palms out. "Relax. I don't care about your love letter from your *boyfriend* anyway."

Frannie glanced at Nadia Marie, shooting daggers at Terrence with her eyes. She looked like she wanted to jump up and scratch his face. "It's from my brother. Not that it's any of your business."

Frannie glanced at Matthias again, widening her eyes so he would know something was wrong. It seemed so natural to ask him for help, but why couldn't she deal with this on her own? What had happened to her that made her think she wasn't capable of managing her own life? It was like this virus made her forget who she was.

She turned to Nadia. "I'm sure Terrence didn't mean anything by it." Frannie gave him a very pointed look. "I'm sure he won't ever try to touch your mail again."

Terrence nodded frantically, looking scared of both of them. Was this the rush Andra got when she intimidated people? Whether she intended on following through with it or not, Frannie was discovering a little bit of strong confidence went a long way.

She said, "You had better not."

"Gees, you don't have to get all stressed out about it. It's just a letter, it's not like it contains state secrets. What's the big deal if I look at the envelope?"

Frannie nearly groaned. "You're not helping, Terrence."

"Why? Is it such a secret her brother's in the military?"

Frannie turned to Nadia Marie. "He is?"

Nadia Marie's lips curved into a small smile. "He's a staff sergeant in the Marine Corps."

Terrence had the decency to look a little impressed.

"Awesome." Frannie grinned, and Nadia Marie returned it.

"I know." Nadia Marie sobered. "He's deployed right

now, and my mom has his dog. He's freaking out because I can't go check on Dauntless, and mom is weird about dogs. But there's no one else. The marshals refuse to transfer the dog to Sanctuary every time Shad gets deployed, like a dog is going to tell my brother where WITSEC placed me."

Terrence snorted. "Your brother's name is Shad? And his dog is called what—Dauntless? What is that?"

"It's from a book, Terrence." Frannie sighed. She didn't read that much, but even she knew what a Dauntless was. "And what does it matter what Nadia Marie's brother's name is. Obviously it's going to be something cool. Your mom must be a character."

Nadia Marie snorted. "You could call her that, yes." She laughed. "Think hippie who doesn't like animals and is allergic to most herbs on the planet, with a Marine son who hates the name Shadrach, and an artistic daughter who sucks at painting."

Frannie smiled at her. "I have no idea how to picture that."

"That's the point. She defies understanding, and she loves it that way. But she doesn't really love Dauntless, more like tolerates him. And there's nothing I can do about it."

"It's just a dog." Terrence's face scrunched with what was probably supposed to be confusion. "What's the big deal?"

Frannie wasn't sure a dog was ever *just* a dog. Unless it was super annoying or something. "It's not tiny, is it?"

Nadia Marie shook her head. "German Shepherd, and he can sniff out IED's. He has medals for bravery, but he hurt his foot so he couldn't go this time. Plus he's getting older, so they're talking about retiring him."

"That's sad," Frannie said. "But maybe if he retires permanently the marshals might let Dauntless come here."

"True." Nadia Marie nodded, her eyes sad now.

Frannie squeezed her forearm, wondering why her friend had never mentioned her brother before now. Maybe it hurt too much to talk about him when he was in danger, and she couldn't even be somewhere she would receive word quickly. If her brother was hurt it would take time for the information to reach Nadia Marie through the marshals. There might even be days where she didn't know anything.

"It must be hard, to be here when he's in the line of fire."

Nadia Marie shrugged. "No harder than anyone else with a loved one who is deployed."

"Still," Frannie said. "It wouldn't ever be easy."

"It is what it is. Being in the Marines is what makes Shad happy, and until that changes, I'm going to support him." Nadia Marie sniffed. "It just sucks I haven't seen him since before I was admitted to WITSEC. I can't ever see him, even when he's home. Except for Skype and letters, but that's not a hug from my brother."

Bolton strode over, his attention so fully on Nadia Marie it was like no one else existed in the whole world.

Terrence got up, immediately backing away from the approaching man. Matthias sat beside Frannie while Bolton said, "Did Terrence say something to upset you?"

Nadia Marie shook her head. "It's okay. We were just talking about my brother."

"Yeah?" He looked interested, but didn't ask further. "You sure you're okay?"

"You need something?"

Bolton said, "Actually, since I have zero artistic ability I was thinking maybe you could help me with the set. The backdrop needs painting so it looks like a villa at a winery. You think you could help me with that?"

Frannie glanced aside to Matthias and grinned. Bolton wanted to work closely with Nadia Marie on the set? It might not be a date, but Bolton hadn't ever made a move to spend time with her before this. Was he changing his mind about them having a relationship, or had he just seen her upset and wanted to cheer her up?

Nadia Marie smiled, but it didn't reach her eyes. "Sure. I'm not Picasso."

Bolton flashed his straight, white teeth. "I can't draw better than a five year old, so you've got one up on me."

"I'm sure we can make it look good."

Andy clapped. "Okay, folks!" The room quieted down like a class of obedient first graders. "Terrence and Nadia Marie, let's do the first wedding scene."

Frannie glanced at Nadia Marie, who grinned back. "This will be interesting."

She walked with Nadia Marie to where they were going to stand together. It would be interesting to see if Terrence was even capable of the emotion it would take to scream at Nadia Marie during what was supposed to be their wedding. A scene that would turn into his grand revelation of her infidelity, which was going to then prove to be untrue. After Nadia Marie faked her own death, of course.

Bolton had stopped work, his eyes on where Terrence was making his way to Nadia Marie. The rest of the actors stood around, forming the congregation for the service. They all took their positions, and the scene started.

The door of the Meeting House opened. Doctor Fenton looked around, his eyes zeroing in on Frannie. Was he making a house call? She'd woken up feeling better. Had Matthias called him?

The doctor sat watching as they worked on the scene. Once they got through it Frannie could explain to both him and Matthias that she felt better. It might have been disorienting enough earlier, but she was fine now.

Nothing was wrong with her.

———

Thursday morning May and Elma, the elderly twins who lived with Elma's grown son, showed up at the door. Frannie unlocked the bakery and admitted them.

"We're ready to work!"

They breezed past her into the kitchen and came back tying aprons on over their velour pant suits—one pink and one purple. Their hair was matching white perms and their faces gave away how much they'd laughed through the years. Frannie had always admired their individuality.

"Olympia sent you to help out?"

"She sure did." May grinned. "She told us you just want to bake. We'll man the counter for you and serve the customers. Aaron and Pat will be in later to help bus tables and do dishes."

The door opened again. Matthias strolled in, a tan tool belt fastened low on his hips. Nadia Marie was right, it was very swoon-worthy. But maybe that was just Matthias in general.

Frannie sighed. "Hi."

May and Elma erupted into whispering giggles. Frannie spun around. "Don't you ladies have work to do?"

They both snapped to attention, saluting her. "Yes, ma'am!"

Matthias chuckled, his low voice reverberating in her chest like a bass guitar. "I'm going to head upstairs and get started on your plumbing." He glanced at the closed kitchen door and stepped closer, planting a light kiss on Frannie's lips. "Good morning."

"Good morning."

"How are you feeling?"

She said, "Just a tiny headache still, that's it."

"Good." He stepped back and turned to the hallway.

A pre-teen boy biked past the front window, tossing a thin newspaper in front of the door. Frannie retrieved it and went back behind the counter. She unfolded the half-dozen or so pages Nigel issued every week. Not that much happened in Sanctuary, but if the former editor wanted to re-live the past, she wasn't going to object. Although he could employ less fantasy and more reality. It was more like entertainment than news, even if he did sum up what was happening in the country and across the world. But that was like half a page. She lifted her cup and took a sip.

Sanctuary News Exclusive: The Angel of Death Walks Among Us

The scalding brew got stuck in her throat, and Frannie choked, wiping her mouth with her apron. It wasn't just a revelation of what was happening—it was an interview with the killer.

"Matthias!"

He came bounding in, closely followed by Elma and May. "What is it? Did you get another letter?"

She pointed to the front page article. "It's Nigel. He interviewed..." She looked aside at Elma and May.

Matthias snapped up the paper and read Nigel's interview with the killer. "I'll take this to John. We'll figure it out."

"Does he mention the letters?"

He scanned the article. "Not once. It could be fake, or the...guy Nigel spoke with might have simply not mentioned you."

Elma and May glanced between them, probably waiting for an explanation. Frannie didn't have the energy to go through all of what had been happening. They could read the article—fictitious or not—for themselves.

"I'm glad he kept me out of this. But how did Nigel get him to talk? Did he really figure out who it is, or did the man approach him?" Frannie groaned. "I feel like I'm in limbo, waiting around for whatever's going to happen next."

Death, maybe. If the killer decided she was next. At what point was he going to snap and abandon his principles? Who knew how many people would be in danger at that point.

"I'll be back soon, okay?" He squeezed her arm. "Don't worry about this."

Frannie nodded. May's presence crowded her, and Frannie blinked, her brain recalling the moment the killer ran at her, shoving her aside. She'd assumed it was a man, but what if it wasn't? May and Elma both had that short, stocky build. Their weight alone could give them the momentum to knock someone Frannie's size back.

"What is it, dear?"

"Yes, dear." Elma said. "What is it?"

Frannie stepped back. "It's nothing. This whole thing is just freaking me out is all. I'm going to go bake something." She moved toward the kitchen and looked at them both, so concerned for her. Was it false? "You ladies will be great out here, I'm sure."

Frannie waited until the kitchen door shut and blew out a breath. She was going crazy. They were just two concerned older women; they weren't killers. She'd been sure it was a man, now she thought it was twins? Only one person had been in the medical center.

This was crazy. They wouldn't hurt anyone.

Would they?

———

"So deputize me." Matthias slammed his hands down on his hips. "You've done it with Bolton, why can't you do it with me?"

Sheriff Mason leaned back in his chair. "Those were extenuating circumstances."

"Because it was your woman in danger, and now it isn't? It's just poor little expendable Frannie."

"I never said that." John stood. "*We* aren't going to go see Nigel. *I* am going to see him. Even if you were authorized, or qualified, you're still too close to this. I can give you reason after reason why I wouldn't let you get in the middle of it."

Matthias pressed his lips together. He was supposed to do nothing while Frannie was getting sick, and someone was killing people? She might be in danger even now.

It was the not knowing that bothered him so much. If she was at risk for sure, he would protect her. He'd stand between her and the gates of hell just to kiss her good morning every day for the rest of their lives. But the killer hadn't made a move. He'd only sent two letters—and what did that do? Maybe she wasn't in danger at all. Maybe he was worrying about nothing.

"I'm running through suspects, Matt. I'll find out everything I can from Nigel, and I'll talk to Stella again. I think she's the key, since she's the one we know for sure talked with him. Frannie told me Stella admitted to having a conversation with this guy."

"But she hasn't told you who it was?"

John shook his head. "She refuses to say, but made the point to tell me it didn't mean she condones his actions. I talked to her husband. He didn't want to upset her by being the one to try and get her to say who she talked to, either. It's like they're both okay with this guy helping their situation. Even if they won't say it was okay for him to kill any others."

"And Doctor Fenton isn't doing anything?"

"We're keeping watch on the situation. If the killer tries to meet with her again, then Xander or the day security guards will let us know. Doctor Fenton is trying to make things easier for her, but all that's left is to make her more comfortable."

"So it won't be long?"

Frannie had indicated as much, but Matthias was sorry to say he hadn't visited Stella or her husband to show his concern for her illness. He should ask Frannie if he could go with her next time.

"The doc said it may be days, not weeks."

Matthias blew out a breath. "Then Stella will pass away simply because of her sickness, and we'll never figure out who it is. The killer doesn't have to do anything."

"Not unless someone else in town is close to dying, or wants out of Sanctuary badly enough."

"Not really something we can fake."

John nodded. "I'll figure it out. Testing could come back with something from Frannie's letters to indicate who it is. Or he'll make a move and reveal himself somehow. Maybe this article is it, and Nigel will give up his source. But if no one dies, there's nothing immediate to investigate and little hope of new evidence. There are only cold cases, and it's not like I can start exhuming bodies on a hunch and some letters."

Matthias wasn't going to count on any of those things. "How do you do it? It's like you trust everything's going to turn out fine." It sounded a lot like naiveté to him, but he wasn't going to tell his friend that.

"I have faith. That's something new. I can only run down so many leads and ask so many questions in one day. That's how investigations are done. One person, one question at a time. It's not like I can wait around for crime to strike and jump in with my cuffs."

"Shame."

John laughed. "Don't I know it." He motioned to the now unoccupied deputy sheriff's desk. "You don't want a job, do you?"

Matthias eyed him. "Will you let me interview Nigel?"

"No."

"Then no."

John sighed. "It was worth a try."

"I'm going back to the bakery. You're going to figure this out, right? Because I need to know if she's in danger."

John's eyes narrowed with amusement. "I'll let you know when I know. For now just keep your eyes open. I know Bolton trained you in weapons and tactics, so I'm not worried about Frannie if you're there to help."

"Thank you." Matthias didn't mind all the hours of Bolton hammering home the methodology on fighting styles and handling everything from a steak knife to a high-powered rifle. Not if it meant Frannie would be safe.

"You should tell her that's why you're there."

Tell Frannie he was watching her? "I'm fixing up her apartment."

John shook his head. "Yeah, but you're also playing body-guard. So tell her that, because you suck at lying, and I don't think you've ever been able to hide anything important before."

"Since when?"

"Oh, so you are hiding something?" John studied him.

"Walked into that one, didn't I?"

"Why don't you start by telling me what happened when your dad died? Because I implied this "Dark Angel" is the one who did it, and you got this look on your face. Like there was no way, because you knew conclusively it wasn't true." John watched him for a minute. "Maybe it wasn't this suspect, but I'm thinking maybe it wasn't heart failure like the report says."

Not given how much blood Matthias had seen. "Maybe I killed him."

John laughed.

"Maybe I did."

John sighed. "You're not a killer, Matthias. But I think if it was someone you loved, then you would keep that confidence all the way to the grave." He paused. "Maybe it was self-defense. Maybe he was going to hurt someone—your sisters, maybe, and someone stopped him."

Matthias sank into a chair and ran his hands down his face. What was the big deal? John wasn't going to spread it around, not if it was truly self-defense like he said. John just wanted to know what had happened in town so he could be informed.

Matthias sighed. "I'll tell you what happened."

Matthias hung his head so low it was almost between his knees. For years he'd kept the secret of what happened the night his father died.

If John knew, would that mean he'd betrayed his family's confidence?

The sheriff's eyes sobered. "Whenever you're ready."

Matthias was glad his friend wasn't pushing him. He could get up and walk out if he wanted, but a heavy part of him wanted to stay—to speak the words and finally be free of the burden. The steel bands that tightened across his chest, cutting off his air.

John said, "I know it's easy for me to say you can trust me, even more so since we're brothers in Christ. But you have to decide for yourself. I won't be offended if you choose not to tell me."

"It's not even my secret to tell." Matthias gave himself a minute, time enough to contemplate the truth wrapped within the lie. "If it gets out it will affect all of us. Maria..." His voice trailed off, and he realized he couldn't do it.

"Did Maria kill him?"

Matthias froze, his hand on the doorknob.

"She must have been...what, eleven? Twelve? I can understand trying to stop him if he was hurting her. Or you. I can understand doing whatever it takes to protect the people you care about. That's a good thing, Matthias. It's an honorable thing, but it's not a burden kids need to carry. If you—"

Matthias stared, unseeing, at the closed door in front of him. "The screaming was so loud I ran downstairs. Maria was under the kitchen table, and Papa was..."

Matthias had grabbed the closest thing—a light-framed kitchen chair. He'd slammed it across his father's head and shoulders. How was he supposed to know the shock would send his old man into a heart attack? Or that his father would grab his hand and force him close...to watch him die.

He turned then. John had made his way over to stand in front of Matthias.

"It isn't like Maria changed. She was always different, even before." He didn't want to speculate on the why of it. "His death didn't help any, that's for sure. But it wasn't the cause."

When fall rolled around it was like she became more and more fragmented. Accusing Antonia of sleeping with Tom was only one symptom. Spring was when Maria seemed to heal. The weather got warmer, and she started to come out of her shell some. But first they had to survive the holidays.

John spoke then. "I know you were a kid, but do you know why it was covered up? If your dad was killed in self-defense there would be no reason to conceal it. There was no danger of anyone being convicted of his murder."

Matthias didn't know, and he hadn't asked. "The doctor came, then the sheriff. We never talked about it. There was never a reason to. Not when he was gone, and we were better.

Mama smiled. For a few months, Maria actually acted like an annoying big sister."

A thought Matthias had considered—not frequently, but enough over the years—came to the front of his mind again. Namely, how the way Maria was might not be isolated. It could be hereditary, considering his mom.

Though not to the same degree, Matthias's mom did have similar tendencies. This time of year was rough on all of them, but maybe the way Maria acted wasn't all her fault. She'd been through a traumatic experience as a kid, and the weaknesses in her personality made her the way she was. Mama was just able to hide it more.

"You realize it wasn't just them, right?" John studied him. "Your mom and Maria might have felt better after your dad's death, but you saw it too. You were just a kid, and you saw it. Your sister was traumatized by it."

"I'm not brushing it off. It just wasn't about me."

"You were there. I'm not saying you have full-blown PTSD, but that diagnosis even covers a wide range of...repercussions. It's conceivable you've been affected in some way after witnessing a shocking event at such a young age."

John didn't even know the extent of it, and he'd figured out what Matthias refused to acknowledge. Now he didn't know what to say. He shrugged one shoulder.

"Will you tell me if you need anything, or if you want to talk more?" When Matthias nodded, John said, "And I will be praying for each of you." He grinned. "I do that now."

Matthias laughed. "I bet you do a lot of things now."

"Thankfully pre-marriage counseling with Dan isn't too traumatizing, even if I have to talk about my *feelings*." John shuddered.

"Father Wilson isn't doing it?"

John shook his head. "I talked to him, but he never

followed up with me. I guess Dan is over that stuff, anyway. Small Bible studies, counseling of all kinds, anything people need beyond Sunday's service. He seems more like a pastor in a lot of ways, even though its Father Wilson's church. But I'm new at this. What do I know?"

Matthias hadn't really thought about it, but he supposed that was true. He must be one of those people who didn't need anything past Sundays and mass. "Is Dan good at that stuff?"

"Really good. It's been great getting to know him better, and seeing how he lives what he believes. It's not just all talk, you know? Everyone who works for him at the farm, they all get together every morning to pray before they take care of the crops."

"That's cool." What else was he supposed to say? They were talking about church, and all he could think about was his dad's dead eyes.

Bolton wasn't likely to have morning prayer meetings, ever. Matthias's boss must have had a bad church experience, because he was pretty adamantly against organized religion of any kind. Bolton didn't bad-mouth Matthias for his beliefs, but he made it plain he didn't understand why any of it was necessary.

"If you're going to be in town looking out for Frannie, maybe we could do that?"

"You want to pray?"

"Sure."

"Because of what I just told you?"

John shook his head. "No, just a start-the-day type of thing."

"Why?"

"Isn't that what church people do?"

"I suppose." But when had Matthias actually said a

prayer, aside from briefly a couple of days before? And yet, hadn't he thought about doing it more anyway? "Yeah, I suppose we could." Taking his faith more seriously probably wasn't a bad idea, and if praying helped keep Frannie safe, then why not? Matthias didn't figure he had much—if anything—to lose.

He lifted his chin. "When's the wedding?"

John immediately grinned. "Christmas eve. My brothers all did their duty the first time I was married, so it'll just be Pat standing up with me."

Matthias had been an usher when Maria married Tom, but that was years ago in the early days of her pregnancy with the twins. It hadn't been an altogether happy occasion when the bride threw up from morning sickness right before walking down the aisle. Plus Frannie hadn't been the bakery owner yet, so the cake had been so-so.

"Why do you look like you just swigged bad milk all of a sudden?"

Matthias shook off the detour down memory lane. "Just thinking about something."

The satellite phone on John's belt started ringing. "I'll catch you later."

Matthias left the sheriff's office thinking about Christmas lights and wedding cake. Only it wasn't John waiting at the altar for Andra in his mind. It was him, waiting while Frannie walked excruciatingly slowly toward him in a white dress that was demure and simple, but incredibly sexy at the same time.

Maybe it made him weird, but Matthias had always known a wife and kids and a happy home was what he wanted. He was a simple man who took pleasure in simple things, but not everyone understood. He didn't need to strive for more than what he had. The money he earned, he simply banked in investment accounts or used it to support people in town. He'd found he only needed to be good at what he did. Really good.

Matthias wanted to be with someone who loved him. His sisters knew and teased him mercilessly about it. Diego just plain thought he was crazy.

It had been a long, dry stretch of years since Cyan left Sanctuary. After her betrayal he'd almost thought his dream wasn't ever going to come to fruition. He'd tried to trust God would bring the right girl in time, like his mom said, but when things looked impossible it wasn't easy. Calling Frannie an answer to prayer wasn't something he was prepared to do, yet. Even if she seemed like it.

Matthias watched through the window, where Frannie was laughing with John's son Pat. The boy was animated and far more outgoing than Matthias had been at that age. Not that he'd been a particularly effusive person anyway, even before the night his father died.

Frannie looked up and saw him at the window. Her face broke into a wide smile, and she waved. Matthias smiled back as she walked over and opened the door for him.

"Everything okay?"

Matthias felt wrung out, physically and emotionally. Then he remembered the newspaper and the reason he'd gone to talk with the sheriff in the first place. "John's going to talk to Nigel about the article."

If he told Frannie what happened the night his father died, would she let him go? Maybe she would jump at the chance to avoid yet another crazy family. If he told her she might well turn out to be everything he'd ever wanted, would she freak out?

He didn't want to scare her away. He was going to have to tread carefully, at least for as long as he could.

———

JOHN LOCKED the front door of the sheriff's office. "I'm back. What's up?"

His brother's voice came over the line. "Are you sitting down?"

"Just tell me." Bad news was bad however you delivered it. Nothing was going to lessen the sting, and he needed to get over and talk to Nigel. "Is it mom?"

Grant sputtered. "It's not mom."

"Then what is it? What happened?"

There was half a minute of quiet and then Grant said, "It's still early, but I'm getting real-time updates. For now only a few people know, and they're going to wait as long as they can to announce it, but eventually it's going to come out."

John gritted his teeth and sat down. "What."

"As of an hour ago the undisclosed freaking secret location where the president was meeting with the first lady was sieged." Grant took a breath. "There was a period of time wherein every single secret service agent on the detail was out of contact. Local federal agents were tasked to visit the scene —a middle of nowhere chain hotel. They arrived six minutes after the last radio contact. No one was alive."

John could barely breathe. "What?"

"They were in and out within minutes, and they left no one alive. It gets worse. Indications are the president suffered some form of physical torture. I'm not clear on the details, but before he died he wasn't in a good way."

"The president is dead."

Grant's voice was quiet when he said, "And Susan."

Beth. John gripped the edge of the desk. "Find the SEAL."

"He's still out of contact."

"I don't care. Figure out where he is and go there yourself.

Get Beth's husband here. Now." John squeezed his eyes shut while his brain ran down the possibilities—and the implications. "So it's whoever wants Beth dead, too? They want to know where she is?"

"If they even had time to ask. It was minutes, John. What could they have gotten? But if I wanted the location of Sanctuary from the first lady, it's what I would do." Grant cursed.

"So they're looking for her still, and conceivably now know where she is."

Grant said, "We don't know for sure they got the information. Maybe there was no time so they killed them and got out. Maybe they were after something else, not just the location of Sanctuary."

"We don't know for sure either way. The whole scheme had to be way too elaborate for them to cut and run when time ran out, they had to have been sure they'd get what they wanted or the operation wasn't worth the risk." John got up and paced the room.

If the team who killed the president and first lady were now coming for Beth, the whole town was in danger. It would take hours to evacuate every resident and get them to a safe location.

"At this point, we don't even know if this is about Beth."

John frowned, glancing around his empty office trying to figure out what he was going to do first. "What do you mean?"

"It could conceivably be about any of the residents. At least three are high-profile enough targets it could induce whoever wants them dead to go after the president and first lady this way. And that's just the ones at the top. All of these people are with you because the people who want them dead are so determined we have to hide them in an inaccessible location, virtually cut-off from the rest of the country."

"Because where else do we hide important people?" John gritted his teeth. "Did we shoot ourselves in the foot?"

Grant cursed again. "That's why we took the precautions we did. I really want to know who leaked the first lady's location. I want their head on my desk."

"Where else could they go?" John sighed. "We couldn't have kept her here when they wanted a visit. It's been weeks, but maybe the secret service agent who betrayed them before wasn't alone?"

"I vetted this team personally." Grant groaned. "I have to go. The vice president is calling me."

"I'll break it to Beth."

"Give me an hour first."

John hung up.

———

"You really should put a scoop of mayonnaise in that, dear."

Frannie didn't look up. Elma and May were in her kitchen, and they'd been making comments through all three batches of cupcakes—red velvet, chocolate and now vanilla.

"It makes the cake moist."

Because her cake was normally dry? Frannie hit the button on the mixer and drowned out the old lady bleacher section. The whir of the mixer didn't help her headache, and she couldn't take more ibuprofen for another hour. Frannie grabbed the peppermint Olympia had mixed up and brought over earlier. Maybe it would ease the tension and help her stop coughing.

Frannie braced her hands on the counter and hung her head for a minute.

"Are you okay?"

She looked up. Matthias was at the bottom of the stairs. His T-shirt had smudges of something on it, where he'd wiped his hands. "Is the water running now?"

"I need a couple of parts from Lance, then it should work. Answer the question."

"I'm...okay."

Matthias came over. "Your head hurts?"

She nodded, and he touched her cheeks, running his hands back into her hair where he massaged her head. Frannie groaned. "I'm not sure that's supposed to feel so good."

Matthias chuckled. Frannie grabbed the sides of his T-shirt at his waist and held on. "Maybe you should go home."

"I have a few more things to get ready for tomorrow. Then I won't have to get here as early."

"Okay." His fingers slowed, changing to a softer motion. He was completely messing up her hair, but Frannie didn't care. She reached back and pulled out her pony tail.

"Any idea where you're going to get a pull-out couch from?"

"No." She sighed, unable to muster up the energy required to figure out what she was going to put in the apartment once it was cleaned out, functioning and freshly painted.

"Let me take care of it, okay?"

"Sure. Whatever you want."

He chuckled. "You might regret saying that."

The kitchen door swung in. Elma pulled up short, her eyes dancing with delight at Matthias standing close to Frannie, practically embracing her. Frannie dropped her hands from his waist. "What is it?"

"Three uh...*gentlemen* are here to see you." The older woman's displeasure was clear. "They're demanding you come out, and if you don't they intend to storm your kitchen like Rudy Giuliani in a Bronx Italian restaurant."

Frannie laughed. "I'll be right out." She turned back to Matthias. "Thank you."

"I'll come out with you."

She shrugged. "It's your funeral."

Frannie trailed out of the kitchen where Sonny, Louis and Michael waited. She raised her hands, palms out. "Guys—"

The bakery's front door swung open, and Sheriff Mason stuck his head in. "Is Beth here?"

Frannie shook her head while Pat ran to him. "Dad! School is done so we're helping."

"I know, bud."

"Ms. Beth might be at the school building still. She stayed there after we all left."

"Thanks, bud." John ruffled his son's hair and waved at Aaron, intently wiping a table like the germs were an invading army he was determined to eradicate. "I'll find her."

Matthias said, "Is everything okay?"

John looked at Sonny, Louis and Michael like he wanted to ask them that same question. "I just need to find her."

He left, and the three men turned to her. Frannie folded her arms. "Did I miss a meeting?"

Louis said, "You know it's not until Sunday." His T-shirt was a light shade of pink with three buttons at the collar. But it didn't make him any less lethal.

For half a second Frannie entertained the idea one of them could be the man who thought killing sick residents was a service. She dismissed it as quickly, since none of them would hurt her. Although, they would certainly kill—and had in the past—she knew the men wouldn't do so unless they were forced into it. And certainly not assisted suicide.

She was pretty sure.

Frannie cleared her throat. "Well then, what's up?"

"We heard about the letters." Michael's eyes were soft.

Matthias moved closer but didn't touch or embrace her. Still, it was clear what he meant by it.

Sonny's eyebrow rose. "Like that, is it?"

Frannie lifted her chin. "Whether it is, or not, is none of your business."

Michael stepped up to the counter and leaned toward her slightly, speaking low. "*Angela*, this man is not family."

Everyone heard him anyway. That was why Frannie said, "This is Sanctuary. We're all family."

"And who exactly do you think will be walking you down the aisle?" Sonny said. "You be very careful in your choice, Francesca."

Frannie was ready to explode. "He's right here. He can hear you, and who said anything about *marriage*?"

Matthias put his arm around her shoulders. "They care about you. If Sonny, Louis and Michael have something to say, they are entitled to their opinion. But it's your choice, and they're going to support you. Because *that's* what family does." He looked at the three men across the counter. "And she's right. We are all family."

Sonny stared at Matthias long enough Frannie shifted her stance, wondering what was about to happen. He looked at Frannie. "You know where I am if you need anything."

"I know."

Michael touched the back of her hand. "*Angela mia*."

"I'm okay." Frannie gave him a small smile, and the three of them left. She squeezed Matthias's arm and went to use the bathroom before she got back to work.

When she came out a white envelope lay on the tile just inside the back door.

Just like the other two, it was easy to try and convince

herself it was going to be a payment, or a bill. It wasn't mail day, and Aaron—who delivered all of Sanctuary's mail brought in by the Air Force—was out front cleaning up. She'd already had today's local mail delivery.

Frannie looked back at the kitchen. No one was around. And why did that make a difference? She snapped up the letter and slipped her finger between the flap and the envelope, ripping it open. She wanted to know what this guy had to say for himself this time. Even before she pulled out the paper, the smell hit her. The headache.

Frannie pulled out the paper and flicked it so it unfolded. The smell wafted toward her face. She inhaled, but the air got stuck. Her throat thickened.

Frannie turned and took a step toward the kitchen. Matthias...

Black spots sparked across the edges of her vision. She couldn't get any air.

And then everything went black.

CHAPTER 14

MATTHIAS HEARD the thud and raced into the kitchen. He'd figured Frannie dropped something heavy, but it was her on the floor. "Frannie!"

Elma and May came trotting in, too. Matthias crouched. She was breathing, but barely, and her heartbeat was weak. "Frannie." He patted her cheek. "Frannie, can you hear me?"

"What happened?"

"What should we do?"

Matthias kept his eyes on Frannie. Should he lift her? "Call the emergency number." They'd either get Dotty at the sheriff's office, or the sheriff himself. "Call the medical center, too. We need the doctor here."

May pushed back out the door. A letter lay on the floor beside Frannie. It was open enough he could see it was another one from the killer. Had she fainted from the shock? Maybe he just needed something strong smelling to wake her up. But for now he needed to get the thing put away so no one else touched it. John could take it as soon as he arrived, but right now it was Matthias's responsibility.

"Get me a plastic bag that seals."

Elma opened a low cupboard, searching around until she located one. Matthias grabbed the letter with two fingers. The thing smelled awful. No wonder Frannie was having headaches, and coughing. The disorientation in her kitchen had really freaked him out. He dropped the letter in and looked at his fingers.

White powder.

Anthrax?

Matthias looked at Elma. "Seal that up without touching it or breathing in the smell." He went to the sink and washed his hands before going back to Frannie.

May came back in, her eyes full of tears. "The doctor will be here in two minutes, but the sheriff will be longer."

He looked at Frannie. "The doctor will be able to help her." He hoped, at least. *God, where's John? Help us. Help Frannie. Get the doctor here.*

The previous letter hadn't had any powder on it, or any white residue. But the smell had been similar—although not as strong as this. How would they figure out what it was? Anything able to make Frannie this sick was either something she was naturally allergic to, or anyone exposed would react like this. Either way, it was methodical and intentional.

The killer had reached out, making contact with her—looking to confess his sins. But more than that, was he deliberately trying to harm Frannie?

"What happened?" Elma's knees popped as she knelt on the opposite side of Frannie, who still hadn't woken. "Was she hurt, or did she faint? What's going on?"

Matthias took Frannie's hand. "She saw someone at the medical center Saturday night. He was trying to harm Stella, and he hurt Frannie. Now he's sending her letters about how he helps those who are ill, or who want to die."

"Like euthanasia?" When Matthias nodded the older woman gasped. "That's terrible! Who would do that?"

"We don't know, but—"

The doctor rushed in with a bulky duffel bag. Matthias kept his hold on Frannie's hand, but moved aside so Fenton could kneel by her.

"You found her like this?" Fenton listened to her breathing with his stethoscope.

Matthias nodded. "I think she's being poisoned."

"Explain." He handed the doctor the bag. Fenton opened it and sniffed. "Einetine."

"What?"

"Sounds feminine, but it's deadly. Only thing in the world which smells like that." He handed it back. "Seal that up." The doctor unzipped his bag and pulled out a tablet. He tapped and swiped, and then said, "She's allergic to codeine, which makes the reaction even worse. Otherwise prolonged exposure would simply mean death from what would appear to be natural causes. She's reacting twice as fast, even with the significant amount on this letter."

The doctor shoved his tablet back into his bag. "Lift her carefully. We need to get her back to the medical center. She needs oxygen to start clearing the poison from her airways while I order the antidote. It'll have to be delivered on an emergency transport."

Matthias half-listened while he gathered Frannie up in his arms. She felt so frail the knot in his stomach tightened. Had the killer known she was allergic to codeine? If he did, he'd gone from trying to kill her gradually to a vicious amount intended to kill her immediately.

"Will she be okay until Monday?"

"I'll know for sure after I run a few tests." The doctor shot Matthias a look. "You realize if I'd known about this when you asked me to come and observe her, this wouldn't have happened."

He followed the doctor through the bakery and the sea of people watching. "I didn't know it was the letters. I only knew something was off when she freaked out, but she seemed fine later. You said yourself Frannie seemed like she was just under the weather."

Matthias climbed in the golf cart with her on his lap. "At least now we know, and she'll be able to get better. Right?"

What if the killer wanted her in the medical center so he could present his offer and kill her there? Then Frannie would be in even more danger when she was supposed to be healing.

"I can keep her comfortable enough until I get the remedy."

"Who in town would have the knowledge to do this?"

The doctor's eyebrow lifted. "Aside from me?"

"Do you know of anyone?"

"One or two, maybe. I'll speak with the sheriff after Frannie's stable."

A nurse, an older woman, came out of the medical center pushing a stretcher. Matthias settled Frannie onto it. "Take care of her, please. I have to make a call."

One foot in front of the other through the medical center proved harder than Matthias had thought it would be. There wasn't anything he could do for Frannie. Not medically. He'd only be in the way if he insisted on staying with her.

Another nurse sat behind the reception desk. He didn't know her name, but she did all the ultrasounds in town—she'd done his mom's when her gall bladder had to be taken out.

"Can I use your phone?"

She waved one hand, not taking her attention from the computer screen. "Sure."

Matthias dialed the extension for the ranch house, praying Bolton was there.

"Yeah."

"It's me. Frannie collapsed. Whoever's sending her the letters is trying to poison her. The doctor said it's Einetine."

"That would only work this fast if—"

"She's allergic to codeine."

"That'll do it," Bolton said.

How did he immediately know everything about this substance? Sure, he'd been a DEA agent, but what cop knew instantly about poisons? His boss was a curiosity Matthias didn't have time to solve.

"What do you need?"

Matthias pinched the bridge of his nose. "Around the clock protection, and a full investigation into whoever is doing this. I need to know who in town could have made or got their hands on this stuff."

"John's working on the case."

"More hands—and pairs of eyes—isn't going to hurt any."

"True. I'll see what I can dig up."

"Thanks." Matthias took a breath. "I'll take point on protection. I think he may have wanted her at the medical center. Maybe even so he can finish her off. Make her sick and then—"

"Make her an offer she can't refuse, one that ends her supposed suffering permanently."

"Is John there now?"

Matthias looked out the medical center's front windows but didn't see John's Jeep. "Not yet. I think he's on something else."

"I'll find him, and we'll meet you there in half an hour."

"Thanks."

"Don't thank me until the threat is over."

Matthias hung up. The front entrance door opened, and his mom rushed in. Matthias moved in for a hug. She gave him a squeeze, and said, "How is Frannie?"

"I don't know yet. She was unconscious when we brought her in."

"The girls are on their way. We'll wait with you until we know Frannie is all right."

There was next to no point in arguing with her. Not when she'd rallied the family to stand vigil. It was a solidarity born of where they'd come from—a time when they only had each other to rely on in order to survive the tight-handed reign of Matthias's father. Mama had relaxed some over the years, but she'd never lost the need to hold them all close as though they might slip away if she didn't.

It was part of the reason why Matthias had never left Sanctuary. He hadn't exactly told Frannie the truth about Cyan. She had apologized, and she'd begged him to come with her when her mom signed her out of Sanctuary as a minor. Matthias's threat meant he'd have been at risk then, the same as he'd be at risk now, if the men his father had double-crossed found out he was out in the open once again. But he'd thought about it.

He'd never told anyone Cyan asked him to leave with her. Love was worth a lot—even the risk his enemy might find him. But Cyan's betrayal had left its mark on him, even given her obvious remorse.

He'd never imagined Cyan might do something like that to him, but she had. Frannie seemed so different. It was safe to assume she wouldn't either, even if Diego had his eye on her. Then again, she very well might betray him exactly the same way Cyan had. Caring about her was easy, and protecting her was one thing. If he was going to get involved with Frannie, the risk of them killing the relationship was one he'd have to be willing to take.

His mom squeezed his arm. "She'll be okay."

"I hope so." He looked down at the bagged letter, halfway crumpled in his hand.

Could something so innocuous really be responsible for making Frannie sick? She'd been under a lot of stress lately, busy and exhausted. Perhaps what was happening to Stella was taking its toll on her. His experience with Maria as his older sister could easily be clouding his judgment. He had to remember not everyone was able to convince themselves the world was a certain way, despite reality.

The door opened again. "I need some help!" John strode in with Beth in his arms.

The ultrasound tech jumped up. "Come this way."

"What happened?" Matthias asked as he passed.

John shook his head. Mama followed John into an exam room while Matthias, dismissed, walked farther down the hall to the room where the doc had placed Frannie. The door was open, and he could hear the rhythmic beep of machines counting each breath.

Had the killer hurt Beth, too? He'd have to tell Bolton she'd been brought in. It wouldn't do the town any good if people started dropping like calves from some white chemical. His fists clenched by his sides.

The doctor could run out of medicine to treat it, and then where would they be? More would have to be flown in. The town would be in a full-on state of emergency.

The doctor stepped out. His gaze registered on Matthias's face. "You need to calm down. Frannie needs peace and quiet, so if you can't get a handle on this I will not hesitate to ask you to leave."

Matthias stared at him. The doctor had been through a great deal in the last few weeks, before and after his wife committed suicide—if that was even what had happened. The doctor could be facing the fact his wife's killer had struck again.

"Can I..." Did he want to ask this? "Could this have something to do with Harriet's death?"

The doctor's face morphed quickly, but Matthias caught the look of displeasure. Not grief. "It's possible, I suppose. I didn't do the final examination but I can get a copy of the doctor's notes and—"

Someone yelled, "Doctor!" It was the ultrasound nurse.

"Excuse me."

———

The first thing Frannie registered was the plastic touching her face. The mask surrounded her mouth and nose, and what she was breathing in smelled cold. She reached up and pushed aside the oxygen mask.

A gentle hand touched her wrist. "Leave it where it is." His voice was the warmth she needed to open her eyes. Otherwise, what was the point? There wasn't anything good to wake up to if Matthias wasn't here.

When she found his face, her heart pinched. He looked...concerned.

"I'm okay." Frannie's throat felt like trying to swallow sandpaper. He didn't agree with her. "I am okay, right?"

Matthias dipped his head to look at her hand. "You will be. The doctor wants you to keep the mask on until he says you're good."

That was when Frannie realized the beeping by her bed was a machine—her machine. Beyond it, Stella lay in bed.

The only spark of life was in her eyes, bright and fixed on Frannie.

"Stella." She tried to remove the mask again, and Matthias stayed her hand. She looked at him. "Am I going to die? Is that why I'm in here?"

He shook his head, and Stella started laughing, a wheezing sound that was a facsimile of what her joy used to sound like.

"Stella!" How could she think this was funny? "I'm dying! You're not supposed to be laughing."

Stella laughed harder. "You sound like your mother."

The doctor rushed in the door and pulled up short. A tiny smile curled his lips, and he stepped out again. Frannie grabbed Matthias's arm and sat up so she could glare at Stella. She swatted his hand away, and pulled the top of the mask down to speak over it. "Fine, so I'm not dying. But don't tell me I sound like Mimi."

Strength bled from her muscles, and she lay back.

Matthias glanced at Stella for a second, and then said, "She wanted you in here with her."

Frannie shut her eyes. "Tell her I said thank you."

Stella wheezed out a laugh. "You're welcome."

"Did you call my mom?"

Matthias squeezed her hand. "She wasn't home, and neither was Izzy. Do you have any ideas where they might have gone?"

Frannie shook her head and sighed. Were they even going to care she was sick in the medical center? Maybe her mom showing up and making a scene would actually be worse. Right then Frannie didn't have enough energy to deal with her mom's drama. She needed strength and a clear head to get back to work.

Frannie wasn't going to let a letter-writing murderer get

the better of her. Stella would never forgive her if she did give up. Not when her problems didn't even come close to cancer. The time for meandering instead of just moving forward with her decision was over. Frannie needed to make a clean break from her mom and sister and claim her own life.

Matthias touched his fingers to her forehead. Frannie took a breath and let it out slowly. It still hurt. Her head swam, and something was seriously wrong with her throat.

"Mama's going to be upset she wasn't here when you woke up, but she's next door. Beth was admitted. I'll find out what's going on and tell you more when you wake up again."

"Is it the baby?"

"Beth has a baby?"

Frannie nodded. "Pregnant."

"I'll go tell the doctor." She felt his lips press against her forehead. "You rest."

———

MATTHIAS RUBBED the tight spot on his chest. Heart problems didn't run in his family, thank the good Lord. But it didn't help that he felt like he'd aged ten years since morning. Maybe Diego did have the right idea, and he was missing out on life. Doing whatever he wanted had to be better than the heartburn of anxiety over Frannie, and Beth.

"I'd like to tell you the feeling will fade, but I'm not convinced it does."

He leaned against the door frame toward the frail woman with the wise eyes. "How do you live with it?"

"Knowing you've lost what might be everything you ever wanted is much worse. Especially when you know there's nothing you can do to ever get it back." Stella's eyes gleamed. "I don't have much time, so I'll lay it all out straight. If you mess with that girl, I will come back from the grave and haunt you for the remainder of eternity."

Matthias wanted to smile but this was hardly the time. "How can you be so calm about it?"

"I assume you are referring to my retiring from this mortal coil and thereby emerging in eternal glory to spend forever before His throne in worship."

He walked over and sat on the edge of Stella's bed. "I guess you could put it that way."

She cocked her head to the side. "You've never thought about it?"

"I figured I'd go there when I died, because I go to church. But not beyond that. I mean, heaven is heaven. Right?"

"I hope not. It would be disappointing if it was everything I'd hoped for when it could be so much more than I imagined." She grinned. "I've had plenty of time to think about it."

Whereas Matthias barely gave the next life any headspace at all. And why was that? He was a Christian, and he was trying to do better with it. John seemed like he'd found something worth being excited about—but when had Matthias felt that way about his beliefs?

He didn't know what to say other than, "I won't mess with Frannie. I'm not going to do anything to hurt her."

"As her mother is...not here, how about you tell me what your intentions are toward my girl. After all, that—" She motioned a bony finger toward the now sleeping Frannie. "—is the closest thing I have to a granddaughter this side of these mountains."

"I understand." Frannie had told him about Stella's son, who she and her husband were estranged from.

"Now spill."

Matthias felt his lips curl into a smile. "I intend to marry her, if she'll have me."

Her look turned stern. "It's a bit soon for that, isn't it?"

Matthias felt his cheeks warm. "She nearly died today."

"And marriage will lessen the risk of her expiring at any given moment?"

"No," Matthias said. "But it means there's no time like today to tell her how I feel, even if it scares the life out of her. She should know I'm serious."

"You love her?"

"I have for a long time."

All humor had dissipated from Stella's eyes. "Then get her away from those two shrews she calls family. If she stays there, if she continues to support them even though they never did one thing to deserve it, it's going to destroy her. Mimi and Izzy will tear her apart, and Frannie won't even see it coming."

Matthias held her gaze. What made him think he and Frannie could make a family of their own, let alone one that stayed together? He couldn't even count on them remaining happy forever. Their histories were too fractured for them to even know when their relationship was breaking down. Wishing and intentions didn't hold up against reality.

"You're having doubts. I can see it on your face. If you're not in this one hundred percent, then you might as well not bother. Don't give her false hope, that's worse than no hope at all. Maybe it's too late to hold off on giving her hope. I've seen the way you two look at each other. But that girl has had to withstand a whole lot in her life, and I'd hate to see her break now because of you."

"That won't happen."

"Says you."

Matthias lifted his chin. "I'm not allowed to be scared I'm going to mess it up?"

"Honey, you'll mess up every day. And every day she'll

forgive you for it. That's how marriages work. It's easy to say you'll never get divorced but harder to actually do it. There aren't any guarantees, even if you take your 'I do's' seriously. What you have to do is *show up*, every day. That's how you make it work."

"It sounds exhausting."

Stella's lips twitched. "Probably will be, with your family the way it is, and her family trying to get in the middle of everything. There will be things that have to give. But so long as you keep your priorities straight with God, then Frannie comes first in the marriage. And for Frannie, it's you who comes first. So are you going to stick it out, or will you fold?"

"Isn't true love supposed to be easy?"

Stella laughed. "People just say that because they're all high on endorphins. When the feeling wears off, that's when the real work begins. You take the sparks and the quiet moments, and you turn them into support and sacrifice. Until the day one of you has to stand back and let the other move on into the next life. You know you'll be parted for a time, but there's hope in the promise God has made."

"I don't even know where to get that much peace."

"Prayer. Helps when you can't even get up to tinkle without calling for someone to help. I've had plenty of time to come to terms with it, even if I wished Director Mason would be able to find my son. My husband, Harold, is determined Grant will get Steven here in time, but I know that's not going to happen. Not now."

"What can I do?"

Stella reached out her hand. Matthias came over and took it, careful to hold her fragile bones loosely. She glanced once at Frannie and then smiled up at him. "Honey, you're already doing it."

CHAPTER 15

FRANNIE LOOKED DOWN at the cards in her hand. The symbols and numbers all blurred together, and she couldn't even remember what game they were supposed to be playing. She tossed the handful on the wheeled table over her legs.

"I win." Michael grinned and tossed his cards on the pile.

"Yeah, right." Stella's husband did the same, giving him a look.

Louis sat observing, like always.

Sonny's attention was on Frannie. "Should we leave?"

"Leave?" Michael gasped. "We're not leaving. We barely got here." He was looking at Sonny, trying to communicate something.

"If Frannie wants us to leave, then we go." Sonny's word was always final.

Michael made a face that got Frannie laughing. "You guys don't have to leave. Maybe we should have our meeting. I doubt I'll be out of here by tomorrow night."

She rested her head back on the pillow. Their presence wasn't necessarily soothing, but it did serve to distract her from the fact her letter-writer was now out-right trying to kill her.

Sonny glanced once at Stella's husband, and then lifted one eyebrow to her.

"Okay, so we can't have the whole meeting. But still..." She saw on his face the moment he gave in to her request. It wasn't manipulation, per se. He loved her, but she didn't make a habit of banking on that fact to get what she wanted.

Sonny sat back in his chair, folding his arms over his tailored Italian silk shirt. As a condition of his WITSEC agreement he wasn't allowed to run a business in any area related to finance, so instead he acted as a consultant to all the businesses in town. For a small fee.

Sonny said, "Our requests for contract bids from residents to renovate the Main Street store fronts have gone largely ignored. I've spoken with the mayor several times, and he assures me it's in the works, whatever that means. He doesn't need permission from the marshals for us to use Sanctuary money, materials and workers to spruce up Main. And yet, for some reason he's stalling."

Louis's displeasure was plain. He looked like an old mobster contemplating how difficult it would be to take out the mayor and get away with it—which was likely exactly what he was thinking. He looked extremely out of place as the patron of the laundromat, but it made his wife happy to provide a service. Louis's devotion to his equally wrinkly wife was the only thing that made him seem remotely human.

"So where do we go from here?" Frannie glanced at each of them, her gaze settling last on Sonny.

"We pool our resources and set the whole thing in motion ourselves, which we've basically done already as the chamber of commerce. We approach the bank about forming our own corporation. That way we can hire contractors, and we all pay equally for the work."

"Or?"

Sonny's jaw flexed. "I'm willing to explore other options, like making renovations store-by-store instead of all at the same time. We shouldn't really need the mayor's approval. It was merely a courtesy."

"Doesn't he want the town to look better?" Frannie frowned. "Or does he want the work to be done on people's houses first?" The mayor's house had been commissioned; it wasn't one of the original buildings but a recent add-on.

"Your guess is as good as mine."

"Great." Frannie sighed and looked at the ceiling, remembering. She glanced at each of the men again. "Hey, you guys want to go to church tomorrow?"

Louis looked like she'd just asked them if they wanted to run down Main stark-naked with her. Sonny had paled, but Michael sat up and said, "You want to go to church?"

"Will the doctor let you out?" Sonny frowned. "Are we going to have to push you all the way there in a wheelchair?"

"I hope not, but maybe." Frannie squeezed her fingers into fists on the blanket. "I can't bake, so I figured we could go and just listen to the service."

Louis shook his head. "I'm sorry, but I won't go." He got up, gave her a quick peck on the forehead and then left.

Frannie looked at Sonny and then Michael. "Did I say something? Was it me, or the church thing?" She hadn't ever heard Louis mention a bad experience in church, but when would he have done that? The man was not the most verbose person at the best of times.

Sonny sighed. "It's Father Wilson he has the problem with, not church itself."

"Did they have a falling out?"

"I'm not certain. Whatever it was, it happened a long time ago."

Frannie mushed her lips together. "Well, I didn't know that."

Michael squeezed her arm. "Don't fret over it, *angela*. We'll come with you."

"We will?"

Michael shot Sonny a look, for once not seeming like the underling. "Yes, we will."

"Thanks."

She didn't mind going with Matthias, but he would probably be sitting with his family, and she wasn't about to get in the way of that. Church had been a "family" thing when she was a kid, but not in the same way. Michael and Sonny would provide a buffer so Frannie didn't have to sit by herself—or by someone who would check her reaction to everything Father Wilson was saying all the way through his speech. They didn't even ask her why she wanted to go to church all of a sudden.

Sonny stood. "We'll come by in the morning at nine forty-five, that way we'll have plenty of time if you're not feeling well."

"I'll be fine." She had no energy and her throat was still raw, but all she had to do at church was sit in a chair and listen.

Sonny chuckled and kissed her forehead. "I'm going to catch up with Louis. I'll talk to him."

Michael rose and said goodbye, too. "You'll be fine here tonight?"

Frannie hadn't even thought of that. She would be with Stella, and Xander would be here to keep them safe. They would be okay, but she probably wouldn't get any sleep regardless. Who would, wondering if a killer was going to show up?

Michael said, "I'll talk to Matthias. I'm sure he already arranged with the sheriff to make sure you're looked after."

It was like they all knew what was going on, and they'd drawn a host of conclusions. Had Michael, Sonny and Louis already met with Matthias? Frannie wouldn't put it past them to decide she was going to be protected and then act like it was a consideration after the fact.

She loved them, but they were definitely the kind of family that didn't take no for an answer. "Good night, Michael."

He chuckled all the way to the door, where Matthias stood with a backpack over his shoulder and two grocery bags. It was the same backpack they'd taken to the hot springs, reminding her of that night. Even with Diego and Izzy's interruption, and the first lady leaving on a helicopter, it had still been the best date she'd ever had.

Matthias's eyes narrowed with humor as he walked over, setting the bags down. "You look like you're thinking about something."

Frannie shrugged and kept her voice low as she said, "I was just thinking about our date at the hot springs."

He actually blushed. Stella and her husband were still in the room but talking low, giving them some privacy.

"It was a good date."

Frannie smiled. "What all did you bring?"

"Just dinner. I was actually trying to figure out what to bring when Mama called. She made chicken corn chowder and blended it so there are no chunks. She also made vanilla pudding from scratch, so there's dessert, too."

Frannie laughed. "You'll have to tell her I said thank you."

"I already did." He sat on the edge of the bed and started arranging food on the table.

Was no one going to actually mention the fact that, for all her visitors, Frannie's mom and sister hadn't even come? Even if they hadn't received the message she was in the medical center, shouldn't they be wondering where she was? Or did they really just not care about her at all...like seriously actually at all?

Frannie shook off the thoughts and took his hand. "Thanks for coming."

"Of course."

"You don't have to babysit me. I'm not going to get up to anything if you're not here."

"I know that." He glanced at Stella then back at their hands. "I'd be lying if I said I wasn't worried whoever wrote the letters might find you tonight, or another night. That's why I talked to Xander, and Bolton spread the word. People from all over town have volunteered to take a shift keeping an eye on the medical center and your bakery." He smiled. "But that doesn't have anything to do with why I brought dinner. If it did, I'd have brought a sleeping bag and I'd be camped out in the hall instead of hanging with you."

"I suppose."

"I did that last night." He slid the table toward her, not making her hold the mug of soup but giving her a spoon. Frannie sat for a moment and just breathed it in. It hurt her throat, but enough of the scent filled her that her stomach stretched and yawned in response.

Matthias dipped buttered bread in his mug and ate the soggy mass. "One day I'm going to grill you a steak."

"If we get there, it'll probably be the best thing I've ever tasted."

"If?"

Frannie shrugged. "I'm okay right now, but if I smell that stuff on the letter again before Monday I'm pretty much a goner."

He stilled. "Monday?"

"They won't bring the cure until the normal transport, because it's technically not a full-blown medical emergency. If I'm careful, I can wait two days."

"So you have to stay here?"

Frannie said, "I'm going to church tomorrow. That's non-negotiable." Why it was so important, she wasn't all the way sure. Did it matter?

"What if the killer's there? What if you smell it on his clothes?"

She sighed. She got that he cared; that wasn't the problem. "I'm too tired to argue with you about this."

"You're just going to risk it anyway, and who cares about the consequences?" Matthias paused.

"Does this whole thing freak me out? Sure. I'm scared. But maybe that's the perfect time to go to church. Everyone's been talking about it, so why not?"

"It can't wait a week?"

Frannie bit her lip to avoid glancing at Stella. "What if I don't have a week?"

"That's not a good reason to endanger yourself."

Frannie felt a rush of something run through her. An urgency like she'd never felt before. She wasn't one to put much stock in her instincts, but this feeling made her sit up and take notice.

"Go find Father Wilson. Tell him I want to speak to him right now."

———

Matthias was on his way down the hall when Dan—the town's farmer and his Bible study leader—came out of Beth's room.

"Hey." Matthias kept his voice low. "How is she doing?"

Dan shook his head.

What had happened to her? Everyone who knew was keeping it pretty close. If it was another attack, he'd have heard. Therefore, it must be something else, and it had him worried. "Does she...need anything?"

Dan swallowed. "The president and the first lady were killed."

Matthias just stared.

"Beth asked for space. The baby is fine, and your mom is planning on stopping by later. Beth asked for Olympia. I prayed with her, but I feel pretty helpless. Not sure what else I can do, and I know there's nothing I can say." Dan took a breath. "How's Frannie?"

His mind was reeling from the news, but he said, "She wants to go to church tomorrow."

"That's good."

"It's dangerous, is what it is." Matthias sighed. "I'm supposed to go get Father Wilson right now. Maybe then she won't feel like she has to be at service."

Dan motioned to Stella and Frannie's room. "Want me to talk with her?"

"Actually, that would be great." There was something about the farmer that was so much more approachable with spiritual things than the father. "I need to check the bakery and see if I can find Mimi and Izzy. I can't believe they still haven't been here to see Frannie. Half the town has been in and out since we brought her in yesterday."

"Does she know you spent last night in the hall with your sleeping bag?"

Matthias shot him a look. "I told her. Just go talk, okay? Do the thing you do that makes everyone feel better."

Dan grinned, but said, "You seem like you might need some of that yourself."

"Maybe later."

Dan nodded. "Very well."

Matthias kicked out his leg, forcing Dan to dodge out of the way even as he laughed.

Matthias walked through town to the bakery. The bare skin on his arms chilled from the evening air. On fall nights when the temperature would drop, warmth got trapped in the basin inside the mountains, so it wasn't too bad. They got some snow, but it usually melted pretty quickly—at least until winter hit in full force. It took people some getting used to, and Sheriff Mason was forever wearing a sweater with shorts because he couldn't figure out what temperature it was supposed to be.

He thought about Susan, and the impression she'd made on the people in town since her arrival. They'd all known Susan and Beth wouldn't remain in Sanctuary forever, but who didn't enjoy the company of the two women? Now Susan was dead, and Beth's family had been destroyed. What was going to happen to her? He couldn't even imagine what that kind of loss felt like.

Matthias approached the bakery. The residents of this town had banded together because of their shared experiences with WITSEC. There wasn't much else they could do, considering they had to live together. It was like a submarine or a remote military base...or a prison. There were always people who refused to join in, but for the most part, those who understood this was their life now made the best of it. Because what other option was there?

The front of the bakery was dark, but a light was on inside

toward the back. Matthias checked the front door and found it unlocked, eased it open and stepped inside.

"That's why we have to go in tonight." The high, tight voice belonged to Izzy. "We need more stuff."

"The medical center is crawling with people. There's no way we'll get in and out without being spotted." Diego sounded like he was trying to be the voice of reason.

Matthias stood in the dark and peered through the round window in the kitchen door.

Diego was leaning back against the broken oven Matthias had been meaning to look at, while Izzy paced and ran her hands through her hair. "But we're *out*."

"You wanna get caught, then you go in. See what you can get from the medical center before you're busted." Diego folded his arms. "There's no way I'm going down just because you're antsy."

The medical center had been broken into just a few weeks ago. After John had surmised the doctor's wife's death was the work of the letter-writer, they'd all assumed it was him who stole the drugs from the medical center. Were the ingredients for Einetine part of what was taken? Could it have been something as innocuous as Diego and Izzy looking for a fix? Either way, Matthias needed to know the truth about his brother and Frannie's sister. And where was their mom? Mimi had been practically AWOL for days.

"I thought you loved me. You would never leave me like this if you cared about me. It was all a lie!" Izzy stormed over and got in Diego's face. "Admit it!"

Diego practically shrugged, though he didn't move much. Matthias had seen that 'so what, who cares' attitude on his brother so often he could read exactly what Diego was feeling. Izzy was right; he barely cared about her at all. Possibly at one time but not now. Their relationship had evidently gone on long enough for Diego to grow bored with her, like the Christmas toy he'd stopped playing with by the first of January.

Why did Diego think this was going to fly in a town like Sanctuary? He couldn't love-and-leave here, where the string of jaded and wiser hearts he'd discard would always be at town meetings or at the grocery store. Matthias knew of two other girls his brother had tossed away like yesterday's pizza. And those were only the ones Matthias was aware of. Now there was going to be another?

Izzy wailed, tears running down her face. "What about the baby?"

For a second, Diego looked genuinely shocked. Then cynicism won out. "What baby?"

"Our baby! You said you would love me forever, I thought you'd be happy I'm having your child."

"If it really is mine." Diego didn't unfold his arms, no matter how much Izzy kept tugging on them, trying to get a reaction out of him.

She sputtered. "You think I cheated on you?"

Matthias shook his head. Now probably wasn't the time for Diego to make those kinds of accusations, followed closely by demanding a paternity test once the baby was born. Not a good plan.

"You think I would do that to you?" Izzy's voice was shrill. Matthias couldn't see any resemblance between her and Frannie, and not just because Frannie's hair was a gorgeous red color now.

"I know you'd do that to me, Iz." Diego's voice had dropped to cold. "I know it for a fact because Sean told me about the two of you. You think I'm that much of an idiot?"

Izzy wailed. "I love you so much, Diego. It was wrong, I know. But you weren't talking to me and—"

"I'm not interested in excuses. I've had enough lies to last a lifetime, Izzy." He shifted to the side, moving past her. "Goodbye."

"Diego!"

Matthias took two steps back so the door didn't hit him. "Diego!"

He pushed through the kitchen door and saw Matthias. "I'll kill myself! I'll do it! I will."

Not moving his eyes from Matthias, Diego yelled. "Get some help, Izzy. You sound like you need it." Without anything more, Diego walked to the front of the bakery and let himself out. Matthias ran to catch up.

"Hey!" Diego slowed, but didn't turn. "Will you wait a second?"

"What's the point? We both already know you saw that humiliating display back there."

"It wasn't too humiliating for you. Izzy seemed like the broken-hearted one. Do you think she's lying about a baby?"

Diego looked up at the sky.

Matthias said, "I did that the other day. Just looked up and realized—I don't know what, like I could just pray. By myself, because I wanted to."

"What does that have to do with anything?"

"You should try it. Might help."

Diego's chin lifted. "Doesn't seem like it's much helped the rest of you. Maria goes to church all the time. She meets with Father Wilson once a week."

"She does?"

Diego looked inordinately pleased. "Didn't know that, huh?"

Matthias wasn't going to respond to his brother baiting him—this time. "If Izzy's baby is yours, then it's up to you to do the right thing."

"Like marry her?" Diego snorted. "You want that woman at the table on Thanksgiving?"

Matthias would rather have Frannie there. If Izzy was across the table with Diego, what did he care? "She'll need your support."

"She needs someone's help, but it sure isn't going to be mine." Diego turned and took a step away.

"Did the two of you break into the medical center and steal drugs?"

He kept walking.

"You need to tell me. Someone's trying to kill Frannie, and if you stole medicine then that implicates you."

Diego lifted his hand...and his middle finger.

Matthias sighed.

"That's a nice guy, your brother."

He whirled around. John had one foot crossed over the other, arms folded and his hips resting against the front of the wall between the bakery and the store next door.

"I was going to come and tell you."

"That you suspect it was him?" John shrugged. "Hearsay from someone known to be an antagonist? You could just be trying to get him in trouble. Evidence would be better, which is why I've been looking."

"That's it? Looking?"

John shook his head. "Why does everyone think police work is rushing around town with the Jeep lights flashing, yelling at people to confess? I have to tread softly, ask questions and look for inconsistencies."

"If you're trying to sell me on the deputy position, you're not doing a great job."

John laughed. "Would that I was. I could use another pair of hands just to cover the emergency line so I'm not answering calls twenty-four/seven while working days on Frannie's case."

"You think it was Diego who stole the drugs from the medical center?"

"He's on my short list of suspects, but I need conclusive evidence. Without it my hands are tied, and I can't get an arrest warrant." John sighed. "It's still unrelated to Frannie's case."

"I really don't want your job." Matthias shook the sheriff's hand. "I'm going back to the ranch. Bolton is on shift at the medical center. Did he talk to you about who might have been able to manufacture or obtain Einetine?"

"He did." John nodded. "Two people. An off-the-charts genius, but she's unlikely to be the suspect. She's working on a contract for the Pentagon right now, something about breaking an unbreakable code."

"Remy."

"That's the one."

"She wouldn't have done it. Remy is way too oblivious of anyone or anything when she's working to get involved in individual's lives this way." The one time Matthias had met her, he'd barely understood what she was even talking about.

"She hasn't been here long enough to account for every murder we think the killer committed."

Matthias said, "What about the other?"

"An older man, former bio-chemist. I'm interviewing him tomorrow."

"And Nigel?"

John nodded. "I spoke with Nigel. The newspaper article on the angel of death wasn't based on an interview. It was only what was told to him by someone who claims they were there and read Frannie's letter."

"Only one?"

"Someone sold her story for cash, but Nigel won't tell me who."

———

FRANNIE STARED at the man sitting beside her bed, overwhelmed by the loss of Susan. She'd been a wonderful woman, and now she was gone? Frannie couldn't even imagine how Beth was feeling. Meanwhile, Dan waited for her to respond to what he'd told her about God. "He really did all that?"

The farmer smiled, like the news was exciting to him. "The Bible even says He didn't do it because we're worthy, or because one day we might be. It says He just loved us, even when we were sinners."

Frannie's head swam. She'd heard the story before, and she'd seen Jesus hanging on the cross all her life. He'd come down from that cross, been buried and risen to life because He loved her?

A tear slipped down her cheek, and she wiped it away.

"When we believe in Him as Savior, we share in His death. We die to sin, so we can share in His eternal life. That's the great hope we have. All we have to do is believe He's the Savior and hold that faith in the truth as part of who we are. Then He makes us righteous."

Frannie gripped the blanket. "Tell me how to do that."

CHAPTER 16

Bolton sat in the waiting area at the medical center early Sunday morning. Legs outstretched and ankles crossed, he had his arms folded and his eyes closed. A strip of morning light cut across the tile floor and half of Bolton's dark features.

Matthias approached. Was his boss asleep? What kind of a guard—

"Don't even think about it." Bolton opened his eyes.

"You realize anyone could walk in the back door while you're sitting there, right?"

"And anyone could walk in the front while I'm checking the back." Bolton uncrossed his legs and stood. "That's why Xander is at the other entrance, and you're going to quit questioning me."

Matthias took a breath, ready to fire back about sleeping on the job.

"Used to be no one questioned my methods and lived." Bolton sighed. "Now I have to deal with people who don't even know how good I am."

"Sorry you're stuck with us." Matthias held back his reaction. This was about the most personal thing Bolton had ever said about his past. "John seems to think when you're here no one is going to dare try and get by you."

Bolton said, "Any time you want the killer to show, I'll be happy to take the night off."

"No, thanks."

"I get you're just worried about your girl. She's fine. There was some laughing and singing around eleven, but after that all quiet." Bolton motioned to the right with his chin. "How's the ranch?"

"House, check. Cows, check. Barn, check."

"Which means you spent an hour before breakfast mucking out all the horses, or you wouldn't have an attitude."

Matthias smiled. "At least the cows just stand there, making steak."

"And sometimes baby cows."

He shuddered. "Don't remind me."

Bolton laughed. "For a rancher, you're pretty squeamish."

Matthias waved him off. "Looks like my near future involves being more of a baker than a cowman."

"Happy for you." Bolton nodded. "She's a good kid."

Matthias supposed, compared to Bolton who had to be forty or thereabouts, Frannie being mid-twenties did mean she was a "kid". He knew his boss didn't think of him that way so much.

"Unlike Diego, who is not so good." Matthias filled his boss in on his brother's latest activities and what Izzy had said.

Bolton tipped his head to the side. "Frannie may not be like them, but still. You're sure you want to get involved with that family?"

"I'm sure."

"I'll talk to Diego." He shook Matthias's hand and then gathered up four empty paper cups, tossing them in the nearest trash can.

"Thanks."

"Later."

Frannie was sitting up in bed fully dressed, on top of the covers, with a tray in front of her. The plate was empty and she was spooning tiny chunks of fruit into her mouth. She tossed the plastic cup and spoon on her tray and waved him over.

"How are you?"

One finger pressed to her mouth, she shushed him and motioned to a still sleeping Stella. Matthias nodded as he made his way to her bedside, where he whispered, "How are you?"

"You heard about Susan and the president?"

Matthias nodded. Tears sparked in her eyes, and he gathered her in his arms and held her for a minute.

Frannie shoved her hands between them and pushed him back, wiping her eyes. "You're never going to guess what happened last night." Her whisper was laced with a joy that didn't have anything to do with Beth's family. "Dan came by. You know that." Her eyes were sparkling for a different reason now. She looked...at peace.

"What did he say?" Dan had told her about Beth, but what else could he have said that made Frannie almost joyful even in her grief?

"He told me all about what Jesus did, and I couldn't really believe it. But it made so much sense. It was like, all of a sudden, it just...clicked." She grabbed his hand and pulled him down to sit on the edge of the bed. "I prayed with Dan, and I became a Christian."

Despite his worry, Matthias couldn't help smiling. "That's awesome."

"Now I need to go to church for a whole different reason. But I want to check on Beth, too." She sobered. "I can't believe

Susan is gone."

Matthias tried to keep things light. "I knew you had an ulterior motive than just realizing life was too short to keep putting it off."

"I can't wait to tell Nadia Marie. And Andra." Frannie took a sip of orange juice. "I just feel so...like I belong now, you know? I'm going to pray for Beth."

Matthias nodded, but he wasn't sure what she meant. He'd been a Christian so long he could barely remember praying that first prayer as a kid. His first communion had been lost in the confusion of his father's antics and WITSEC.

Since then church had become something he just did because that's what their family believed. Lately he'd been feeling the nudge to seek. It was entirely possible God would use Frannie's new relationship with Him to spur Matthias to find out if his own faith could be more than it was.

Their relationship had to be based on more than just attraction—which was there in spades. It had to have a solid foundation of shared interests. Not just favorite music, or movies, but shared beliefs, too.

Matthias leaned forward and kissed her softly on the lips. "Congratulations." He smiled, though his heart was still heavy with the news about Susan and the president. "Maybe that's not what you're supposed to say for something like this."

She shushed him again. "It works. Thank you."

"So you're ready for church, then?"

He'd never considered she might be opposed to coming with him to church. It was a gift, not only the fact she was willing to consider it, but she'd made the decision independently of his wanting her to share his faith.

"I guess." Frannie looked around, her gaze roaming all around the room. "The guys aren't coming?"

Matthias shook his head. "I gave them the morning off if that's okay with you."

Frannie swallowed. She looked around the room again.

"You don't have to be nervous. God doesn't throw you in the fire on the first day."

"I'm good." She pushed the tray aside, moving the rolling table out of the way, and then shifted to get off the bed.

Matthias found her shoes under a chair and brought them to her. He wrapped her arm in his and walked her to the ranch truck. The inside was free of food wrappers and the sweaters and jackets he discarded when it got too hot. But it was dusty. Not just dust, but the dust of walking around on dry dirt all day and then kicking it off his boots when he climbed in the truck. Why hadn't he cleaned the truck out?

"This is weird."

He glanced at her, sitting beside him on the bench seat. "It is?"

"Aside from the ride in the sheriff's Jeep the other day, I haven't been in a vehicle in nearly eight years."

"You should have asked. I would have taken you for a drive before now."

Frannie said, "There are probably a lot of people in town who miss it. Maybe you should start charging for rides. You'd probably make a decent chunk of change."

"With a side business as a taxi?"

"Or a scenic tour guide."

Matthias morphed his voice to sound like an announcer. "On your left, you'll notice the Laundromat. Louis isn't usually there, but if you're lucky his wife will scold you for whatever you've been up to that got your clothes those stains. And beware bringing in anything that has blood on it. She'll look appropriately disapproving, but she won't ask where you hid the body."

Frannie groaned. "Maybe not."

"There you go, being the entrepreneur again." He grinned at her. "I would never have thought of that."

"It's not like I sit around thinking up new ways to make money."

"I know." He glanced at her.

"But you aren't interested?" Frannie frowned at him like she wasn't sure if what she'd said was okay. "It's not like I'm only concerned with making money."

"I just don't really think about it. I get paid, and there's stuff I need. Mostly I break even after I stash part of it in two funds. One's for retirement and one is for someday. They aren't all that small since I don't have much to spend. I order supplies for the ranch, but that comes out of a separate account of both mine and Bolton's money which we cycle back into the ranch. When we sell beef to the diner or the grocery store, that's when we get paid. Trickles in, trickles out. That's about all there is to it other than the fact I sunk some money into the nursery so Sofia and Antonia could be comfortable." He grinned at her. "There you go. My financial status in two minutes."

She smiled back, but it was subdued. "So how does the cow get from your field to a steak on a plate at Sam's diner?"

"Your buddy Michael, actually."

Frannie gaped. "Seriously?"

He nodded. "The man might only have one arm, but he's the best butcher I've ever seen. It takes someone to help him, but it's worth it."

"Is it awful, watching them die?"

Matthias much preferred the end to the birthing process, though it was equally as messy. "It's never pleasant, but we make it as quick and painless for the cow as possible. That's all we can do."

Matthias pulled up outside the Meeting House. Frannie put one hand on the door handle and turned to him. "At least I don't have to murder anything to make a cupcake." She grinned, swung the door open and crumpled onto the ground.

Matthias jumped out and rounded the door to find her sitting on the pavement. "Need some help?"

"I can't believe I just collapsed." Frannie curled her lip, looking miffed. "If you carry me in there I'm going to be mad at you for eternity. I have one of those now."

"Eternity?" He reached down and hauled her to her feet. She nodded, so Matthias said, "All the more time for you to be ticked off with me."

"I figured it was going to happen every now and then, so I might as well get used to the feeling."

Still, he tucked her arm in his elbow, and they walked slowly. "Occasionally mad at me is okay." Just so long as those occasions spanned the next seventy years of their lives, Matthias was more than fine with it.

THE MINUTE THEY STEPPED INSIDE, Andy and Shelby rushed over. Frannie had her arm wrapped in Matthias's so it didn't look too much like he was holding her up.

Frannie locked her knees and held onto him. "Andy. Shelby. I'm so sorry I missed practice."

Andy looked like he might actually be mad about that, but Shelby gushed. "Oh, dear. Don't worry about the play. Your understudy is fully prepared to step in if it becomes necessary. All you need to worry about is getting better."

"My understudy?"

Shelby smiled. "Your mother graciously offered to take your place."

Matthias's body went as hard as granite against her arm. "My mother, huh." She tamped down the rage at a woman who didn't even come and see her in the hospital, but made sure to fill Frannie's spot in the play.

Frannie glanced at Matthias. "We should get a seat before they're all taken."

His smile was brittle. "Good to see you, Andy. Shelby."

Frannie's steps snagged against Shelby's ankle-length floral skirt as they passed, but she managed to get untangled even though the couple just stood watching them walk to their seats.

When they were out of earshot, Frannie said, "I really do need to sit." He took a step, and she stumbled. Nadia Marie jumped in on her other side, whispering, "Hey, girl," as she took Frannie's other arm and helped her to a chair.

Frannie slumped in the seat, drained. She blew out a breath as Nadia Marie sat by her. "I talked with Dan last night."

Nadia Marie grinned. "I'm glad he convinced you to come."

Matthias leaned forward and said to Nadia, "It was Frannie's idea. She became a believer last night."

Nadia Marie screamed. Every person in the room stopped what they were doing and turned to look. Across the room, Andra laughed. She walked over while Nadia asked a million questions and Frannie mostly just smiled so much her face hurt, and said, "Yes."

Nadia Marie wrapped her arm around Frannie's shoulder and squeezed, telling Andra what happened.

The former assassin frowned. "I thought she screamed because you told her you were kicking out your mom and sister."

Frannie cocked her head to the side. "Really?"

"This was better," Andra said. "But you should still do that as well."

Frannie wasn't sure. "Are Christians supposed to evict their family?"

Andra muttered, "If they're big leeches who deserve it."

Nadia shot her a look before turning to Frannie. "You can have boundaries, and you're allowed to be firm on them. This has been a long time coming."

Matthias told Nadia Marie and Andra about Mimi being Frannie's understudy for the play. He looked a little pale—at least as pale as someone with his coloring could look.

That was when Frannie remembered he'd have to kiss her mom in the play.

She gasped. "Uh..."

"Exactly." Matthias shook his head. "I'm not doing it if you aren't."

"Shelby and Aaron aren't going to like it if we're both out. They'll have to get two understudies."

Dan stepped toward the microphone up front and began to strum his guitar. He looked around, and Frannie saw the moment he spotted her because he winked.

Nadia Marie leaned closer. "Maybe Matthias could trade with Terrence. I'll play your part instead and your mom can kiss him."

Frannie nearly agreed...but that would mean Nadia Marie would kiss Matthias. Frannie glanced at her friend. Did she want to?

Dan started the song, an upbeat tune everyone seemed to know. Frannie looked at the words projected onto the screen at the front and decided she agreed with the senti-ment. She closed her eyes and allowed the singing to resonate in her.

Was she sure what Nadia meant? Did her friend intend to

kiss Matthias, assuming it was no big deal just because it wasn't Mimi doing it?

Gradually the tension bled from her, and Frannie simply enjoyed what Dan had called "worship." After he prayed, they all sat. Father Wilson came to the front. He read from the Bible, and Matthias tilted the copy in his hands so Frannie could see it. She leaned against his arm as she read, listening to the father talk about a king called Hezekiah.

Matthias touched the page with one finger, skimming down the text faster than Frannie could read. He stilled. His attention was on one verse and the words of Hezekiah's prayer. Matthias made a "huh" noise in his throat. Frannie straightened to see his face. His eyebrows were pinched together as his eyes scanned the passage.

He looked up at her. Frannie smiled and put her head back against the outside of his upper arm. Matthias shifted, and she felt the warmth of his lips against her forehead for just a second as she listened to Father Wilson talking about the purpose of prayer.

The father had them all stand, and Matthias held Frannie's hand as they bowed their heads with everyone else.

She needed to talk to Andra and Nadia Marie about what happened next. Dan had told her about reading her Bible every day, and praying as much as she could so her decision really sank in. Maybe the girls could show her how to do that.

As soon as they said, "Amen," Matthias squeezed her hand. "I'm going to go talk with Dan for a second. Will you be okay?"

Frannie nodded and watched him make a bee-line for the farmer while Nadia Marie spoke from behind her. "Well, well, well. You two looked pretty cozy."

Frannie turned, using all her strength to stay standing. She put her hands on her hips. "What's it to you?"

Nadia Marie's eyebrows rose. "Is something wrong?" She glanced at Matthias for a second. "It didn't look like there was."

"There isn't, thank you. That's why I don't appreciate you offering to kiss Matthias in the play instead of my mom."

Nadia Marie frowned for a split-second, and then burst out laughing. "You think..." She cackled. "You're mad... because you think I'm going to..."

Frannie glared at her. Then she had to sit down. Then she glared some more.

Nadia Marie pointed at her, even though it was rude. "You're jealous."

"I am not."

Nadia Marie wiped a tear from under her eye. "You so are. It's the cutest thing."

"And if Bolton agreed to kiss someone else, you wouldn't have something to say about that?"

Nadia Marie sobered. "I wasn't going to kiss Matthias. We could have worked it out and avoided that. Why would you assume I wanted to?"

Now she felt foolish. "I—"

Nadia Marie moved closer and whispered, "I don't want to kiss Matthias. Trust me. He's like my brother." She touched the sides of Frannie's face for a second before she let her hands drop back to her sides. "Understanding what God has done for you and being so thankful you can barely breathe because He saved you is an amazing thing. I'm so happy you made that decision."

"Me too."

"But you're still you. God isn't surprised when your fears surface. He wants to make you more like Him, but you start from here. From who you are now. We become Christians because we aren't content with this, with who we are. We want more, and God is the only one who can do that. But even more, He wants to give us even greater things than we can imagine. Not just victory over the sins we don't even think about committing because we're so used to them being part of our lives. But amazing gifts only He can give."

"How do I not mess that up?"

Nadia Marie smiled. "Pray. Read your Bible every day. Church. Andra and I are going to start a Bible study. Come with us."

"What about my mom? I don't know if I want to totally sever the tie, but what choice do I have? She doesn't care about me at all. She only cares about herself."

"It'll be messy, that's for sure." Nadia Marie worked her jaw from one side to the other. "Have you talked to Stan? If you sold the house and moved in with me, they'd have to either buy it or go find somewhere else to live."

Frannie had to sit. "I can move some of my furniture into the apartment above the bakery, but they would be homeless."

"Serves them right."

"Aren't Christians supposed to be compassionate?"

Nadia Marie said, "Not to the point we get walked all over. Jesus wasn't a doormat when He allowed them to crucify Him. And your family isn't allowed to treat you like one, either."

Frannie looked at Matthias, who stood across the room with Dan. The farmer had his hand on Tias's shoulder, talking low, and they both had their eyes shut.

She looked back at Nadia Marie. "I can't move any furniture right now."

"That's what your friends are for. You want to move into the bakery, give me your keys. I'll get your stuff over there, so when you're released from the medical center after tomorrow's medicine delivery you can go straight there."

"You would really do that for me?"

"Just don't ask me to make you any meals. You wouldn't need poison at that point."

Frannie laughed. "Good to know."

"I'll talk to Olympia about getting you set up for meals." Nadia Marie sat and squeezed Frannie's hand. "Don't worry about your mom. She's going to make it difficult, but at least it'll be done. Worse would be having her in your home for *decades*."

"Maybe I should just give her my part in the play." Frannie shrugged. "It's not like I can stand long enough to say all my lines. I can barely manage ten minutes right now."

"So you missed a couple of rehearsals." Nadia Marie waved away her concern. "We worked around that. After tomorrow, when you get the antidote, you'll be good as new."

"Francine." She turned and found Father Wilson beside her. He held out his hand. "So glad you decided to join us this morning."

"Thanks, Father." She squeezed his cold hand and let go. The question in the back of her mind slid up to the forefront. "I know this probably isn't a normal sort of question, and maybe there's some kind of privacy thing, but... The man I saw about to kill Stella has been sending me letters." He nodded, though he looked confused, so she continued, "I was just wondering if he's approached you at all?"

"Right," Nadia Marie said. "Like maybe to talk about what he's doing, or something he did in the past?"

Frannie said, "He indicated he has faith and that's why he's doing this. I just wondered if you had any clues as to who it was."

Father Wilson coughed, his hand to the front of his shirt. "Well, it is true that a great many people come to me to confess, or simply to talk. But I can't say this killer person has revealed himself to me. How very distasteful."

Frannie frowned. Didn't this man understand the worst things in people? They came to share their sins with him?

"I'd rather like to know if you have any questions about my sermon. Anything you'd like to know, or ask me about?"

"Uh...not that I can think of." He wanted to talk about that? "Beth might need to talk with you, though. She's still in the medical center."

Father Wilson continued like she hadn't even said anything. "It is crucially important that each person submit to the lordship of Jesus Christ in our lives before it's too late."

"I'm getting medicine tomorrow, I'll be fine after that. Beth needs more than I do right now, but she's not sick or anything."

"Not to mention Frannie became a Christian last night."

Father Wilson looked from Frannie to Nadia Marie, and back. "How wonderful." He smiled, but it was more like a grimace. Was his craggy face even capable of looking happy?

"Thank you." She didn't mean it to come out as a question, but the inflection was there. "I should find Tias and head back to the medical center now."

"Of course." Father Wilson laid his hand on her shoulder. "You feel better soon, Francine."

CHAPTER 17

Monday morning Frannie sat on the side of Stella's bed and wiped away a tear. Matthias squeezed her shoulder. "You can come back and see her later."

Frannie nodded, her gaze still fixed on Stella's closed eyelids. She'd worsened during the night, to the point she'd slipped into unconsciousness. The likelihood was Stella would only last long enough for Sanctuary residents to say goodbye. Her dream of hanging on long enough to see her son one last time was coming to an end.

"He must have done something." Frannie fisted her hand on her leg and looked at Matthias. "He must have come in here last night and done this to Stella."

"You were here. Did you see anyone?"

"I was asleep. He could have done something to me, too, but he didn't. Maybe he really does only kill those who are dying or who told him they want to die. But that doesn't give me a good reason why he's been trying to hurt me."

He drew her up then, and they walked to her bed. Matthias sat with her, holding her hand. "The delivery will be here in a couple of hours. You'll get your medicine, and then you won't have to worry about being dosed with that poison again."

"Stella—"

"She's ready, Frannie. You know that." He squeezed her hand. "The doctor recommended waiting until the medicine has had time to work before you leave. You're not supposed to be agitated right now."

Commotion outside the room brought both of their attention to the door. Matthias got up and strode into the hall. Frannie settled herself into the wheelchair at the end of her bed and followed, even though he was going to be upset about it. Maybe he needed a minute away from her and it wasn't just that he'd gone to see what was going on. She wasn't some fragile flower he had to protect. Frannie had been shot by her own father. Getting agitated was kind of relative after that.

The wheelchair was hard to maneuver, but she got into the hall and headed for the front of the building. Aaron paced in the waiting area, wringing his hands. He usually didn't get this agitated delivering mail. Matthias stood at the counter with Doctor Fenton who was using a knife to open a taped-up cardboard box.

Aaron saw her, and Frannie smiled at him. He didn't exactly acknowledge her—she never really knew what penetrated and what didn't—but he obviously cared or he wouldn't be upset. He did like her cupcakes.

The doctor lifted the flaps and rummaged. Stilled. And then rummaged again. He looked up at Matthias. "It's not here. They sent something similar, but it won't work." He swore. "I told them she was allergic to codeine."

Doctor Fenton shoved the box away. "They're going to have to special delivery the right medicine." He snapped up the phone. "I'll have the sheriff call director Mason." Before he dialed, Fenton said, "You absolutely cannot tell Frannie that Susan was killed until she gets that medication."

Frannie gasped. "Seriously?"

Matthias and Fenton both whipped around. "Frannie." Matthias started toward her.

She didn't even move. Her arms wouldn't function. "I already know. Dan told me."

That was right, wasn't it?

Why did it hurt so bad? Her head was pounding, the voice of her father loud in her ears.

She glanced at the doctor. "You weren't going to tell me?" Her voice was high and shrill, even to her own ears. "You weren't going to tell me Susan is dead?"

Matthias crouched in front of her, his hands covering where hers lay in her lap. "Take a breath and let it out slowly. Until you get that medication you can't get upset."

"Can't... I'm..." She tried to pull her hands out from under his. "Did you agree with him?"

"You knew Beth was brought in. You told me she was pregnant." Matthias shook his head. "I'm fine with the fact Dan told you. I wasn't going to keep it from you."

Frannie tried to remember telling him about Beth's baby, but she couldn't. "I can't even think, Tias." Finally she managed to get her hands free. She gripped the wheels and moved herself backwards. "You didn't want to tell me?"

Matthias took a step toward her. "It was Fenton's recommendation that—"

"No!"

"Fran—"

"Both of you would have kept this from me?"

He looked aside, his mouth moving, but she couldn't hear what he said. It was like the world was underwater.

The chair she was in spun, making her lightheaded.

Someone yelled. Frannie opened her eyes and saw her father again, his gun pointed at her.

"You killed Uncle Benny and now you're going to kill me."

Hot tears tracked down her face. Warmth surrounded her —strong arms and the smell of pine and molasses cookies, but Frannie didn't want to go. She struggled, but he didn't let her loose. She wanted to stay here with Tias where she'd finally found what she'd always been looking for.

God, help me. I don't want to leave him. Don't let me die.

She gripped the sides of her face. Her head felt like it was splitting open.

———

YOU KILLED *Uncle Benny and now you're going to kill me.* The wrenching words rang in Matthias's ears as he watched Doctor Fenton adjust the IV feeding medicine into Frannie's arm.

"What will that do?"

"Buy us time. That's all."

Matthias stared down at her, laid on the bed she wasn't supposed to be sleeping in any more. She should have gone home today.

Fenton said, "I've had to induce a type of coma, which will effectively shut down brain functions to help her body rest and heal at least some until we can get the antidote deliv- ered." He hesitated. "I really didn't want to have to do this, but it will slow the effects of the drug she previously inhaled while giving her the chance to heal and us the time to get the medicine here."

Matthias folded his arms. If the doctor hadn't wanted to induce a coma in Frannie, he shouldn't have said so bluntly that

Susan and the president were dead. She'd known, but hearing it aloud like that had clearly shaken her fresh with the news.

Matthias touched her hand, needing the sensation of contact with the warmth of her soft skin.

"I'll take care of her."

"You'd better." He said it before he could stop the thought from emerging.

"Excuse me?" Doctor Fenton's face registered extreme consternation that Matthias might question him. "I understand you care for this woman, but I am her doctor."

"You're everyone's doctor. None of us can go get a second opinion, even if we wanted to."

"Now you're questioning not just my methods, but my entire practice?"

"I don't think you're a bad doctor. I just don't want anything to happen to Frannie."

"A nurse will be monitoring her the whole time. She's safer right now than she was when you took her to church."

Matthias's stomach clenched. "We only have a problem because you so callously blurted out the fact Susan was killed."

Matthias was still having trouble believing it'd really happened. She'd been a genuinely nice woman, and the president seemed like a good man as much as you could tell those things.

"I refuse to argue with you in front of a patient." Fenton strode on his shiny black shoes out into the hall. He looked like a fancy high-roller doctor from TV, not a small town no one even knew existed.

"Frannie will be protected. That has been the case since we brought her in." The light in the hallway was different than in Frannie and Stella's room. Now Matthias saw the doctor's eyes were surrounded by dark circles. It probably wasn't easy being the sole doctor of an entire town. Especially considering he also did the job of a paramedic.

But that didn't mean Matthias was going to let his suspicions go.

He folded his arms. "It's awfully convenient, now I think about it. Your job is tough, so why not bump off a few people who you think might be better off dead."

"Ah, so not only are you accusing me of violating my oath, I am also now a murderer?"

If the expensive Italian leather shoe fits.

"I see," the doctor said. "Sooner or later someone was going to accuse me of harming people. After all, that's what we do in this town. Because my wife can't possibly have overdosed and taken her own life. No, she has to have been killed by someone who believes murder is mercy." His impassive face was red, and the only way Matthias could tell he felt anything about Harriet. "Even though she's dead, that woman is still ruining my life."

"I'm not like that mob who thought Andra was a killer."

"No?" Fenton's head jerked. "But you feel it's necessary to point out the fact I have both the knowledge and the opportunity to have committed these crimes."

"If you didn't do it, then you don't have anything to worry about."

"Matthias—" The booming voice came from behind him. Bolton was coming this way.

Fenton glanced over Matthias's shoulder and smirked. "Oops, Daddy's here."

Matthias's fist flew through the air, but didn't get that far. Bolton grabbed his wrist and yanked it back. Matthias spun, his other fist clenched. When he saw Bolton's face, reason stepped in. Nothing good would happen if he clocked his boss.

Matthias dropped his hand, panting hard when Fenton yelled, "I want him arrested for assault."

Bolton grasped both of Matthias's hands and pulled his wrists behind his back. "I'll take care of it."

"Tell the sheriff! I want to press charges!"

"I didn't even touch you." Matthias yelled back as he was walked away. Bolton gave him a shove.

Fenton yelled, "You would have if he hadn't stopped you."

Bolton marched Matthias through the waiting room, past gaping residents waiting for their appointments, all the way to his truck. He shoved Matthias in the passenger side and slammed the door.

When he got in the driver's seat, Matthias turned to him. "I—"

Bolton held up his hand, palm out. "Don't say anything at all."

Matthias clenched his fists. He'd almost punched someone. Again. His stomach roiled. First Diego, and now he'd been about to hit Fenton. What was his problem that the minute someone mentioned his father, Matthias lost his cool? Sure, his dad's verbal and occasionally physical abuse had left its mark on him. Of course it had. He wasn't naïve enough to think otherwise. Sheriff Chandler—John's predecessor—had looked the other way.

Was what had been wrong with his father wrong with him, too?

Bolton slammed the door again. Matthias let himself out of the truck outside the sheriff's office.

"You're not really arresting me are—"

Bolton grabbed his arm just above the elbow in a grip that managed to be painless and yet completely solid. He dragged

Matthias through the front door without saying anything. Dotty, the elderly dispatcher, gaped. John turned from the white board he was studying and watched as Bolton shoved Matthias through the door of the single cell and slammed it shut.

"You cannot be serious."

Bolton completely ignored him. He strode back to John and the two had a whispered conversation. John glanced once at Matthias, showing zero emotion on his face. And why did it bother Matthias the two of them might be disappointed in him anyway? So he got mad and nearly punched the doctor. This was a free country, wasn't it?

"This is a free country, son."

Papa's grip on his hair stung, but Matthias refused to cry. He wasn't going to be anything like him, not ever in his life. He'd seen Papa hit Mama last night, and now they were out in the truck on the freeway and Papa was acting like nothing was wrong.

Why did Papa bring him, anyway? Matthias had homework, but Papa didn't care about school. He didn't care about anything. He said he loved them, and then he yelled at Maria about her backpack. Like it was her fault Papa's hook fell off the wall when she hung it up.

All they ever did was tiptoe around him, dead scared they'd get yelled at next. Papa was like a time-bomb waiting to blow up all over them.

The truck edged off the freeway. Papa pulled in behind a closed carpet store and stopped alongside a shiny old Cadillac and a tall man got out of the back. The tall man's eyes made Matthias pull his feet up on the seat even though Papa would smack them back down when he saw.

He hugged his knees as Papa rolled down the window. Papa lifted the gun and shot the man through the window.

Matthias screamed. He felt the wetness on the seat of his jeans before he realized what he'd done. Papa swung the gun around and hit Matthias on the side of the head. His scream cut off, and he slumped in the seat.

The disposable cup was cold against his fingers.

"Take a drink."

Matthias looked down at the water and then lifted it to sip. Bolton had crouched beside him, the cell door open now. Matthias didn't look at his boss. He couldn't.

"It's okay to give yourself a minute."

Matthias took another sip of water. "And I don't need your sympathy."

"You need something."

Matthias looked at him then. There was no recrimination in Bolton's eyes, only the same sense of connection he'd seen in his boss from the first day he'd met him. "I suppose you know what that is?"

He looked beyond Bolton to where John stood at the cell door. Dotty had vacated her desk. She'd probably gone home when Matthias started to freak out, scared he was some kind of mental patient.

"What triggered it?" John's voice was calm.

Matthias shrugged, thinking it through. "Fenton blurted out about Susan's death, and Frannie started yelling. The drug was affecting her. She said I killed Uncle Benny, and I was going to kill her, too. I think she was talking about her father, like she thought I was him. Then it just hit me that Fenton could be the killer. Any of us could. That's why we're all here, right?"

What was the point of trying to hide it anymore? There was only one reason they sent people to Sanctuary, and it wasn't because they were innocent.

The door flew open, bouncing off the wall.

Matthias stood. "Mama—"

"Don't tell them." Her big eyes were tear-filled, and she clasped her hands in front of her belly, hugging her middle. "Please don't tell them. Things are fine. They can stay the way they are."

Bolton glanced between them, but he didn't look surprised.

Matthias turned his head to lock eyes with his boss. "You know, don't you?"

"Matty—"

"Mama, what's the point?" He spat. "They're not idiots. They probably figured it out already. Face it, it's never going to go away. I need to accept the consequences of what I did."

She pushed past the sheriff, filling the tiny cell with her girth. "You saved us. That's what you did. Don't you for one second think otherwise, Matthias Hernandez."

"I'm done hiding it. I can't do it anymore."

John's voice was completely even when he said, "You killed your father." It wasn't a revelation; it was a statement of fact. "I figured from the holes in your story there was more to it."

Matthias frowned. "You knew?" His mom gripped his hand, but Matthias was way too resigned to what was about to happen to accept her solidarity.

John shrugged. "It didn't add up, but it happened a long time ago."

"So instead of finding whoever is killing people and hurting Frannie, you've been trying to catch me in a lie? Is that why you were outside the bakery?"

"I am able to multitask." John motioned to the board and for the first time, Matthias saw the pictures and notes. "The list of suspects is dwindling, but I will find whoever's doing this."

"I want to help."

"I know you do."

Mama tutted. "Matthias, they're cops. You just keep looking after Frannie."

"No." He looked at John, and then Bolton. "I want in. I'm not just going to sit around and wait for her to die. I want to do something."

John said, "Fenton's too tall to be the person who ran at Frannie."

"And the old man, the bio-chemist?"

"Not mobile enough. He could barely walk, let alone run."

"So you're out of suspects."

John said, "Just because we don't know who it is doesn't mean we'll never figure it out."

Matthias let go of his mom's hand and folded his arms. "It wasn't me. I'm not the killer."

Bolton took a half-step toward him. "No one thinks that."

"And I'm not crazy, having psychotic episodes."

"That remains to be seen," John said.

Everyone looked at him.

John kept his gaze on Matthias when he said, "I want you to talk to someone."

"I thought that's what I was doing."

John smirked. "I mean a professional. Until you do, your judgment will be in question." His mom looked like she was about to say something, but John continued. "No arguments. You can be here, and you will be in the loop. But you don't call the shots."

"Done."

As long as he was helping keep Frannie safe, Matthias didn't care how tied his hands were going to be. They weren't questioning his judgment as such, but they would be—along with everything else he said or did. Because of what he'd done twenty years ago.

Matthias's cheeks warmed. "Am I losing it?"

Bolton shook his head. "It was going to come out, sooner or later. I'm honestly surprised it took so long before it reared its head. Matthias, you're not crazy but you do have a lot of junk to work through before you can get your temper under control. Until then, you have to check your reactions. You can't go lighting in to people just because you're mad."

He hung his head. "I'll apologize to Doctor Fenton."

Bolton squeezed his shoulder. "I'd be surprised if he lets you in to see Frannie after you accused him of multiple murders."

Matthias gritted his teeth. "I'll convince him."

"We'll all talk to him," his mom said. "We'll tell him you're only scared because you're in love with Frannie."

Matthias's head whipped up to look at his mom.

Her eyes were dancing. "A mother always knows."

Matthias nodded, but inside his stomach was wrenching. There might be a small chance Fenton would let him in to see Frannie. But when she woke up he was going to have to explain what he'd done.

Her father had killed her uncle and then tried to kill her. When she found out he was the one who killed his dad, Frannie was going to turn him away. She wouldn't want to be with someone just like her father. Not when Matthias couldn't handle his own anger. That was the worst part of it. Because there was no way he could ever let himself hurt Frannie. Until he got all this figured out, and got his feelings under control, there was no way Matthias deserved a strong, pure woman like Frannie.

It burned like fire through him, incinerating the hope he'd had that they could find a future together. Matthias had been kidding himself, refusing to see reality for what it was. Their dates had been amazing; there was no doubt about that. She might like him now, but once she knew the truth Frannie would walk away.

And he would let her.

His mom kissed his cheek. "Fenton will come around. Everything will be fine, you'll see."

Matthias didn't correct her. He knew what was coming.

The sheriff's radio buzzed. He grabbed it off the table and pressed the button. "Sheriff Mason."

"This is Sofia, um...sheriff."

Matthias and his mom both rushed to where the sheriff stood by his desk.

"Maria's at Antonia's house. She's going berserk. She's trying to kill them both."

CHAPTER 18

MATTHIAS JUMPED out of Bolton's truck before he'd come to a complete stop. Maria was on the front lawn, screeching at Tom and Antonia.

His brother-in-law looked like he always did. Beside him, looking disheveled and remorseless, was Antonia—barely covered by a silk robe.

Tom put both his hands up. "Maria, listen—"

"Oh, so now you want to talk? I haven't seen you in days, and you've barely acknowledged me in *weeks*."

Beyond them, Sofia stood on the sidewalk. Dressed in jeans and her nursery polo shirt, she still wore her gloves and looked like she'd run all the way from work. Probably the neighbors had called about the noise—but they hadn't been the ones to call the sheriff. They left that up to her.

Matthias's heart went out to his younger sister. Sure, he felt for Maria, but she seemed to be handling her anger justifiably. Sofia hadn't asked for any of this. She'd been a baby when their father died and didn't remember him or the impact he'd left on each of them, at all.

Maria strode over, hand raised to slap Antonia across the

face. Sheriff Mason got between them, forcing her to back up just out of respect for his size and position. "Tempers are high. I get that." Sheriff Mason kept his gaze on Maria. "Now isn't the time to have this conversation, and it shouldn't happen on the street." He glanced between all of them. "Let's not let this get any worse."

Maria said, "Well *excuse me* for disturbing your precious town. But I just found out my own sister is a traitorous, back-stabbing—" The word she used to describe Antonia made Matthias's cheeks burn.

Sofia whimpered.

"How dare you!" Antonia flew at Maria, but Tom held her back.

"Don't."

"You heard what she just called me!"

The intimacy between Tom and Antonia was obvious, and it made Matthias's heart break for Maria. At once the three of them were yelling, each trying to be heard over the other. Sheriff Mason did his best to interject, trying to de-escalate the situation, but they weren't paying him any mind.

Matthias stuck two fingers in his mouth and whistled as loud as he could. When he had everyone's attention, he turned to Antonia. "Go inside and get dressed."

He had nothing else to say to her. Not when her actions had torn their family apart, and not in any repairable way that Matthias could see. Antonia clearly hadn't been concerned with anything other than her own pleasure. The least of which was what would happen to her nephews.

He turned to Maria. "Where are the boys?"

"At the park with Aaron and Pat."

Matthias nodded. At least she'd had that figured out before she started this. His mom, who'd shown up sometime in the last couple of minutes said, "I'll go to them."

Mama hugged Sofia, kissing her on the forehead before she walked away down the sidewalk faster than he'd thought she could move.

Maria's tear-filled voice broke through his thoughts. "How could you do this?" It was barely a whisper, her attention fully on her husband.

Matthias turned so he could find out the answer. Tom's expression was brittle. "It's not what you think, Maria. But you can't understand that. Can you?"

Bolton huffed, like he had no patience for Matthias's brother-in-law. The truth was, his friend was more like family to Matthias than Tom.

Tom sneered at the rancher. "Why are you even here?"

Bolton didn't answer. He just looked at Tom.

Matthias turned back to his brother-in-law. "You're here with Antonia, who was half-dressed. What are we supposed to think?"

"I was trying to *stop her*." Tom rubbed his temple. "It's not me she's sleeping with. Maria—" He turned his earnest eyes to his wife. "You have to believe me, Maria. It's not me. He was here before you showed up. I was trying to convince Antonia it's a horrible idea to get involved with him, but she won't listen."

Maria folded her arms, not backing down. "Who is Antonia sleeping with?"

"I can't tell you."

Antonia came back out on her heeled boots wearing jeans that probably cost her a week's pay and a designer shirt that she'd told him was supposed to look like it was old. Everyone saw the look that passed between them. Tom said, "Tell them it's not me."

Antonia lifted her chin. "I won't say who it is. It's none of any of your business."

"You have to tell them!" Tom's face was red. "Maria thinks it's me!"

She slammed her hands on her slim hips and said to Maria, "So now you know."

That was it. No remorse. Matthias's heart sank. "Do you have any idea what you've done?"

She looked like he'd slapped her. "It's not like I planned it, okay?"

"You didn't stop it either." He glanced at Tom, the man's regret was almost palpable. "You're not even going to clear this up for Tom and Maria?"

Antonia didn't say anything.

"Seriously?" Bolton shook his head. "You've done a serious wrong to your family and your sister, and you don't even have the grace to apologize?"

Antonia glared at Bolton. "You don't get to judge me. My personal life is none of any of your business."

Matthias said, "It is if you're hurting Tom and Maria."

"I didn't ask for him to stick his nose and his opinion into my business!" She huffed. "Besides, we're in love."

"Are you serious?" Sofia shoved past John, making everyone gape. "Can you even hear yourself? You don't care about anyone. I don't even believe you know what love is, let alone being capable of feeling it for someone else. I've lived with you for years, Antonia. I know you. The real you."

Antonia butted in with, "Sofia."

Matthias shot her a look and she gave up what she'd been about to say.

Sofia shook her head. "Antonia comes in at lunch every Monday and Thursday. If it's just this one guy, it's been going on for months."

"So when I confronted her at the nursery, you knew?"

Sofia didn't say anything. "I don't want it to be any of my business. Not if it was Tom, or anyone else."

"You could have told me, you shouldn't have let me wonder." Maria moved toward Sofia, at once full of anger again. An aggressive anger.

"Maria." Matthias couldn't let this get out of hand.

Sofia glanced at him, wide eyed. "You always side with her. None of you care about me."

He tried again. "Sof—"

"No!" She turned to Antonia. "I'll be finding a new place to live. You need to find a new job."

"You can't fire me, you're not the boss!"

"I'm buying him out, and then you're fired."

Matthias shook his head. "You don't have the money to buy me out."

"I'll get the money. I'll talk to Stan and get a loan. I don't care. I won't work with her anymore." Sofia stormed away.

Antonia yelled after her. "You can't do that. You have no right."

"Antonia." Matthias was at the end of his tether.

In the balance of Maria's emotions and the family had Sofia been lost in the mix? Whether she had or not, she seemed to feel like she'd been forgotten or neglected. He would sell the nursery to Sofia for a dollar if it made her happy.

He stared at his sister. "I think you've done enough damage for one day."

Maria, who'd been staring at Tom this whole time trying to illicit some kind of reaction, finally said, "How could you not tell me? I thought she was having an affair with *you*."

Antonia didn't say anything. Tom looked at the ground for a second, and then back up at his wife. "Maria—"

"I can't live with this anymore. Your stuff will be on the front lawn." She turned and walked away.

Matthias followed, catching her around the shoulders with his arm. "I'm sorry."

"Don't be." Maria sighed as they walked. "I'm not a model wife. I know that."

"Your shortcomings don't have anything to do with not being able to trust Tom. He could have told you what Antonia was doing but he didn't. He may have been trying to help. But he should have thought about how it would've looked."

"I'm not blameless. But what's going to happen to Reuben and Simeon? I don't want them living in two houses." She stopped then, burying her face in her hands. "What am I going to do? It was hard enough to keep my life together when he was helping, and now it'll just be me. I don't want to be a single mom!"

The anguish in her eyes tore at his heart.

"Maria—"

"I don't want words, Matthias. You've always protected me, even when it was so hard it *kills me* to think about what you did."

It affected him, too, realizing he was no less of a monster than his father, so easily killing him. It wasn't solving the problem when he'd had to virtually destroy himself in the process. All that was left now was—what? He wanted to tell her they could work it out, that she and Tom could heal their relationship and fix what was wrong. But Maria wasn't going to listen.

Matthias walked her to her house. The door was locked and the lights off. His mom had probably taken the boys somewhere for dinner to give their parents time to sort things out. "Will you be okay?"

Maria looked up at him. The look in her eyes worried him.

More than just grief and guilt over what had happened, there was something else he couldn't identify.

"You've always been the strong one, Matthias. When I needed it most, you did what I couldn't. Now it's time for me to be strong."

Matthias hugged her. "You are. Even if you don't know it."

There was a lot in his sister that he also saw in Frannie. He could help them. He could defend them, but they both had so much courage. Courage he didn't even know how they possessed. It humbled him to realize how much they didn't need him.

———

Frannie looked the same, lying in the bed connected again to machines by wires and tubes. The light in the room was dim, just the lamp above the sink to cast shadows where there should be none. In the chair pulled up to the bedside was Beth.

Matthias didn't like how un-lifelike Frannie looked. It brought a lump up in his throat which threatened to choke the breath from him. Where was the medicine?

The nurse in the corner looked up from her magazine, but at the machine's readings. Not at him.

He perched on the edge of the bed, the day wearing heavy on his shoulders. Frannie's hand was warm, but he missed her fingers curling around his as she squeezed his hand. He missed that smile she always shot him—full of happiness, like she couldn't believe they were really together.

He held her hand and looked at Beth. Long blonde hair framed her face, making her eyes big and dark. The president and Susan's daughter looked gray and drawn out as though fifty years of life had passed since her mother left. Only days ago.

She smiled a sad smile.

"How are you doing?" Matthias wondered if she was even going to answer. Maybe he shouldn't have disturbed her.

Finally, she broke the silence. "The heartbeat is good. I'm concentrating on that right now. I spoke with Grant, and he's getting a lot of pressure to reveal my whereabouts so I can be 'made safe.'" One side of her mouth crept up. "I can't even go to the funeral. The vice president has been sworn in, but Grant is refusing to read him in on Sanctuary. He told me he doesn't care how much flack he gets, he's not breaching security. He's making excuses right now, delaying them."

"Do you need anything?"

She shook her head. "This town is incredible. People I don't even know keep showing up at all hours of the day to ask me that. The military is flying in a special delivery early tomorrow morning with Frannie's medicine and my mother-in-law." A smile curled the corner of her mouth for a second before she continued, "There was a delay of a few hours because Grant had to wait for something else. I don't know what it is."

She sighed. "Grant wanted to come himself, but he thinks he's being monitored. He has his whole family and the next of kin of everyone in Sanctuary under guard because he doesn't want what happened to my parents to happen to anyone else." Her voice broke then.

Matthias squeezed her shoulder. He had no family outside of Sanctuary, and was suddenly grateful for that fact even though it was selfish.

"The one thing I really need, no one can give me."

Matthias knew her husband was out of contact. Was that

who she was talking about? He didn't know what he was supposed to say, so he just let her talk.

"Sam and I... He didn't leave under the best circumstances. I tried to contact him as soon as I found out about the baby. It's the kind of mission where it could be weeks before he surfaces somewhere that actually has a secure phone. Grant promised me his brother will find Sam. Apparently he might be able to do that, even when no one else can."

She sniffed. "But it's too late. I needed him weeks ago. What if, by the time he gets here, I don't need him anymore? What if I find the strength to do this without him? What if I don't? What if Sam doesn't even want to come?"

Tears rolled down her cheeks. Matthias drew her to her feet and wrapped his arms around her. He would question how anyone who'd married Beth could ever choose not to be with her, but he didn't think it would help to say that. He just smoothed his hand across her shoulders and let her cry.

To his consternation, tears filled his eyes. Why did he feel such unity with a woman who had lost everything? Matthias had made a choice at ten years old to save his sister, to do everything in his power to rid their family of the cancer attacking them from within.

He didn't regret it, not even on the rare occasions he slept, when he dreamed of that night and woke with the memory of watching the life fade from his father's eyes. Maria had lived her life with her head in the past, where Matthias had done everything he could to pretend the story his mother told was the real truth. Frannie could never know. If she ever found out the truth of how much like his father—and hers—he was, Matthias would never forgive himself.

Beth stepped back, wiping her face. "It feels like the whole world has fallen apart, but I'm still just sitting here. Everything is different, and I'm just...the same."

Matthias looked again at Frannie.

"She'll wake up. The medicine will make sure she isn't harmed any more by the chemical."

"Your mother-in-law is a good woman?"

"She'll help take care of us."

Matthias looked at her. "He's a fool if he chooses to miss even a second of this."

She sobered then. "Thank you for that."

"It's the truth."

"Yes, I've noticed that about you, Matthias."

It was hard to lie about anything else when he'd had such a huge secret. Now it was out some of the tightness which always seemed to band around his chest had loosened. John and Bolton both knew the truth, no thanks to his freak out. It didn't seem to bother them what he'd been capable of doing as a child. Matthias wasn't naïve enough to believe they wouldn't be watching him now. He would keep an eye on him, too, if he was them. No one needed someone with homicidal tendencies running loose around town.

At least not any more than there already were.

Beth squeezed his arm and walked gingerly from the room, like she was purposely trying to be gentle with herself. Matthias watched from the door while she made her way down the hall. The security guard—Xander—strolled past, moving around the waiting area. Matthias's sleeping bag was rolled up on a chair in the hallway, his pillow on top, but he wasn't the least bit tired. He could still watch the room, though.

Stella and Frannie were resting, not that either could wake if they wanted to. Elma and May were keeping the bakery open during the day, but they weren't Frannie. Bolton, Diego and Sean were covering the ranch. Matthias wasn't sure what he was supposed to be doing; he was used to more action than being on guard duty.

The power went out.

Matthias spun back to Frannie's bed, but the monitors were still on, switched to battery backup during an outage. Frannie's heartbeat was steady. The rest of the building was dark, but the patients should remain undisturbed. He stepped into the hallway, ears peeled.

Matthias heard the nurse move behind him. The door swung shut, the motion pushing air toward him. The lock turned. Apparently she'd been briefed on the killer targeting the women she was caring for.

"Matthias?" Beth's voice betrayed an edge of nervousness, coming from down the hall to his left.

"Yeah, I'm still here. I think the power went out."

"Doesn't the whole town use geo-thermal—"

He pressed his lips together in the dark. "Yes. We've never had an outage that I can remember. It's not supposed to happen." And it meant the power had been cut.

"Matthias?" Farther to his left, down the hall, was Xander.

"Yeah?"

"My flashlight isn't on my belt. I don't know where it is. I had it—"

There was a dull thud, Xander's words cut off followed by a tumble as the big man hit the ground.

"Xander?" Beth called to him.

"Get back in your room, Beth. Shut the door."

"But—"

"Do it. Now."

There was a muffled thud.

"Matthias!" Beth screamed from behind her door. It sounded like she was struggling.

He ran in her direction, full speed to where her door was. Who knew what he was going to meet when the tackle came, but too much was at stake to worry about it. The person was shorter than him. Matthias hit a shoulder, taking the man down.

He grabbed for a hand, or arm, but his fingers glanced off the tile floor. He grasped a jacket and tried to get a grip to subdue the attacker. A boot slammed into the outside of his thigh. He gritted his teeth and finally found the man's head. Left hand on the side of his face, Matthias punched his attacker's cheek with his right.

A needle punctured the outside of his arm. He moved, but his attacker pushed the plunger on whatever was in there. Matthias grasped the man's hand and pushed the needle out. Dread swamped him and he was pushed aside. Matthias rolled. In the dark, he found a syringe on the floor.

His attacker got up, and took one step before Matthias kicked up his leg, tripping the man. He needed to see who it was. He couldn't let the guy leave.

Matthias tried to get up. He had to...needed to...

His head hit the floor. Pain reverberated through his skull and footsteps pounded the floor. The sound made Matthias grip the sides of his head. He groaned as the room spun under him even as he lay there on the tile floor.

"Matthias." His name was a whisper.

"Frannie."

She rushed over. "It's Beth." He felt her settle beside him, her hands moving over his shoulders and then his face. "I need help!"

"I'm not opening this door," the nurse yelled. "No one's getting in here."

"Xander and Matthias are hurt!"

"Until the doctor gets here, this door doesn't open."

"The phone won't work. I tried it, it's not working." Beth

turned back to him. "I have to go get help. It's so dark in here. Can you move?"

"Frannie."

Beth whimpered. "Please don't be bleeding out or something, okay? I'll be back soon." Her hands pressed on his chest on last time, like she was reassuring herself he'd stay there. "I'll be quick."

Her steps retreated. That was good. Matthias squeezed his eyes shut. Full dark wasn't good. It reminded him of all the things he didn't want to remember.

He sucked in a breath, trying not to panic. How was he going to react to the drug? Was it the same thing Frannie had been dosed with, or something worse? But he'd done his job. Frannie was okay. He'd kept her safe. He'd kept Beth safe. Surely Xander would be fine, just a lump on his head.

The burning in his arm was getting worse. So was the spinning. Matthias laid his palms flat on the floor. He was going to be fine. Right?

CHAPTER 19

Just after five in the morning Sheriff John Mason stood with his thumbs in his belt. Mostly just because that was what Idaho sheriffs did. Not that he'd ever actually met any, but he was one. For half an hour before the helicopter set down on the square stretch of concrete at the ranch house just after eight-thirty, John stood waiting...and praying.

Whoever had broken into the medical center the night before had cut the power, incapacitated Xander and first tried to enter Beth's room. Only after Matthias rushed him had the assailant gone after Matthias.

The substance injected into Matthias had been a powerful paralyzing agent. Thankfully his friend hadn't received too much of a dose. He'd been woozy and disoriented, but that was all.

John had kept to himself his suspicion the attacker intended to abduct Beth, for some reason, and not Frannie.

Wind whipped at the collar of John's jacket. He bent forward and moved to the helicopter's door so the stylish, late-sixties woman could exit. Her light blue pants and white blouse were covered in black and brown dog hair. One hand in his, she stepped out with her purse on her shoulder. Her eyes met his, even while her lip curled.

"Abigail Myerson?"

A German Shepherd hopped out behind her.

Abigail handed him a medical bag no bigger than an insulated lunch box. "Sheriff Mason, I presume."

"John is fine, ma'am."

One more person to protect.

The weight of each of their lives, and the lives of every family member they had outside Sanctuary, rested on his and Grant's shoulders. It wasn't something he took lightly.

If the president and Susan had given up the location of Sanctuary, it was only a matter of time before there was a physical breach of security. Until then, the military was watching the airspace and the NSA was tracking all movement on the ground. John wasn't going to rule out the possibility someone could get past their safeguards. It would be foolish to think that. But a full-scale attack was unlikely. This was targeted.

Any attack on Sanctuary had to be targeted.

But Grant—as always—had an ace up his sleeve. One that meant John was in a holding pattern until an indication they were under some kind of attack presented itself. Watching and waiting weren't something John truly appreciated, but covering it all in prayer was helping.

Abigail Myerson shook his hand, and then John crouched to meet the dog. It sniffed him in a hopeful way and then barked once and sat. John didn't know if that meant he was disappointed or not.

John rubbed the German Shepherd's flanks. "Dauntless."

The dog barked and jumped to set his paws on John's

thighs and make his greeting face-to-face. John chuckled. "Platz."

Dauntless pushed off and stood tall. He barked again.

Abigail laughed. "I suppose that means hello."

John looked at her as she flipped her blonde hair back over her shoulder and straightened. She reminded him a lot of his mother. "Shall we?" He motioned to his Jeep.

"Lead the way."

John walked beside her while the dog trotted after them, apparently content after the long trip and the relief he'd had on the side of the heli-pad. Bolton would probably object to the mess left behind, but John hadn't remembered to bring a plastic bag.

They drove straight to the medical center while Abigail asked about Beth's well-being, and John did his best to not betray the grieving woman's confidence. Whatever she chose to tell Abigail had to come from her, not John's concern.

"I just hope they find Samuel quickly." Abigail sighed. "My son is headstrong, and he hasn't always made the right choices in the past. But he'll want to be here for his wife and child. I'm sure of it."

Matthias was in the waiting area when they got there.

John waved at him. "Don't get up."

Matthias looked relieved, dressed in jeans and a T-shirt where John had half expected him in a gown. "Did you get it?" He didn't even spare Abigail a glance.

John nodded. He handed the medical bag to the doctor, who whisked it away, and then said to Matthias, "This is Beth's mother-in-law, Abigail Myerson. Abigail, this is Matthias Hernandez."

Matthias nodded. "Ma'am."

"Abigail?" Beth was back in that gray sweater John thought was ugly, the sleeves pulled down over her hands.

Abigail rushed to her and the two embraced, albeit awkwardly. Abigail leaned back. "It's nice to finally meet the woman my son spoke so highly of."

The timeline between the wedding certificate, Sam Myerson's mission and Beth's arrival in Sanctuary was less than two months. Until now John hadn't believed it could have been an elopement. Who did that anymore?

The dog barked once and then sat.

Everyone looked.

Matthias said, "Who is that?"

John motioned to the door. "I have to go talk to Nadia Marie. Are you waiting for Frannie to wake up?"

Matthias shook his head. "Not if you need me to come. The doctor said he'd have to take it slow letting her off the medication. I'd like to check in at the bakery."

He got up slowly. John wanted to rush over and help his friend, but what he'd learned about Matthias in the last few days told him the young man was eminently capable of taking care of business. If Matthias needed help, he only had to ask.

John was learning how to lean on other people. It was easier with his brothers, but being in Sanctuary he'd also learned to rely on the people here—especially to help raise his son. These people prayed with him, studied the Word with him, encouraged him, challenged him and stuck by his side. They were also planning the biggest event Sanctuary had ever seen, because Christmas Eve John was getting married.

Nadia Marie was due to meet him at the bakery in ten minutes. She had no idea why he wanted to see her. John had asked Andra to come, too. Nadia was going to need all the support they could give her when he told her the news.

He glanced at his friend in the passenger seat, trying not to look like he felt awful. "Who's on duty right now?"

"Frannie's friends are watching her. Sonny, Louis and Michael are old, but I figured there's strength in numbers."

John nodded. "Plus the fact that between them they've likely killed upwards of a dozen people means they're prepared to defend her if necessary."

"I'm glad they consider her one of them. It's safer than being on their bad side."

"For sure," John said. "Did you know all of them are ex-mafia?"

"Is there ever an "ex" when it's mafia?" Matthias's question made John wonder if the guy knew his girlfriend was mafia, too. Not by choice, but by birth—though no one would take one look at sweet little Frannie Peters and think, "La Cosa Nostra." She seemed to have successfully left that life behind, even if Sonny, Louis and Michael might not have.

"How's Diego?" There were a lot of people in town, but John liked to keep as apprised as he could on how they were doing.

Matthias shrugged. "Haven't seen him since that night you saw us in the street."

"And Izzy?"

"Same. The mom, too." Matthias shook his head. "I'm supposed to be at rehearsals tonight, but I'm going to tell Andy and Shelby they need to cancel the whole thing until Frannie's better or I'm out, too."

"They're not going to be happy."

"I'm not kissing Frannie's mom, even if she is the understudy."

John laughed, loud and hard enough Matthias glared at him.

"Andy and Shelby, and even Frannie's mom, are the least of my worries," Matthias said. "Someone keeps trying to get to

Frannie, and until we finally catch them—" He slammed his fists on his legs. "—I'm not losing focus."

"Good." John pulled up on Main Street, outside Sweet Times. Nadia Marie's salon was only a couple of doors down.

"Aren't you supposed to tell me to back off because you're taking care of it?"

John studied his friend. "Would you?"

"No."

And that was good. Because Frannie's well-being didn't matter too much if the entirety of Sanctuary's security was compromised. If they were going to solve all the problems they had right now, they'd need to pull together.

MATTHIAS OPENED THE JEEP DOOR, but stayed sitting in the passenger seat hoping no one noticed his lack of energy. He hadn't wanted to leave the medical center, but Frannie had adequate protection. The unexpected arrival of this particular dog wasn't good. Had something happened to Nadia Marie's brother, or had Grant done the impossible and gotten her request approved? Matthias figured it was the former, given the look on John's face.

It got worse when Bolton came out of the sheriff's office, talking on John's satellite phone. He ended the call and tossed the unit to the sheriff. All of them winced, but John caught it smoothly. The thing was a DOD prototype that was way more than a regular satellite phone—or a police radio—and who knew how expensive to replace.

Matthias felt the dog's fur brush his ear, and then a wet tongue swiped it. He waved the dog away and got out to pop open the back door.

Nadia Marie strode out of the salon in black fitted pants and boots with heels that brought her almost to Bolton's height. The question on her face evaporated when the dog jumped out and ran to her.

"Dauntless?" She sank to a crouch and greeted the dog, who nuzzled and licked her. "But Grant said—why is my brother's dog—?" Dread washed over her face.

Matthias walked toward her.

"Something happened to Shad."

Bolton got there before Matthias, putting his arm around Nadia Marie. John moved closer so they formed a huddle around her.

The sheriff's look wasn't encouraging. "Grant wanted to be here himself. He wanted to be the one to tell you, but—"

Nadia Marie gritted her teeth.

"Shad is missing in action."

She sucked in a breath. The dog moved closer to her, nudging her with the side of his head. Matthias grabbed her hand even though Bolton still had his arm around her. Andra poked Matthias in the side. He shifted, and she inserted herself in the huddle with a small smile for him, putting her arm around her fiancé.

"He's not dead."

John didn't disagree with her. "There's no body, but there are also no signs he was taken by someone, or injured either."

"I would know if he was. I would feel it." Matthias must have reacted in some way, because she turned to him. "Shad isn't just my brother, he's my twin. If he was hurt, I would know."

Matthias nodded. Bolton shot him a dirty look, despite the fact this was hardly the time to start getting territorial.

"And he would never walk away from his duty."

John said, "The Marines are doing everything they can to mount a search for Shad."

"What about Billy?"

John waited a second, like he was bracing himself before he told her. "I'm sorry to say Staff Sergeant William Martinez was killed in action."

"Eleanor." Nadia Marie closed her eyes for a second. "Shad wouldn't have left him. They're teammates."

"It's conceivable he had no choice, Nadia." John pressed his lips together. "Grant is going to forward me the report so you can read it. I know it's not much, but we have enough pull you can at least know the full story of what happened—as much as the military knows, or is willing to share."

She nodded, glancing at Andra for a second. "Thank you."

"The minute I hear anything, you'll be the first to know."

"And Dauntless?"

"Grant wanted you to have Shad's dog with you, since he'll need watching for an indeterminate period of time."

"You mean my mom found out Shad is gone, and she was going to get rid of him."

The side of John's mouth curled up in a small smile. "You don't get rid of a dog like this. Grant sent his wife to your mom's house. He says it took her all of five minutes to persuade her to give Dauntless up to you."

Nadia Marie laughed, though there were tears in her eyes. "I would've liked to have seen that."

They were all chuckling when a scream rang out. Then a crash.

A chair flew through the window of the bakery, taking all the glass with it. The spray of shards rained onto the sidewalk and the street in front of Frannie's store.

Multiple people screamed as John ran over to the bakery.

Matthias's boots crunched on the glass as he followed. He looked back to make sure the dog wasn't going to step in it. Bolton was already leading Nadia Marie away, clicking his fingers for the dog to follow.

When Matthias entered Frannie's store, John already had Mimi restrained. She was screeching, wrestling with him while multiple people looked on. May's arm was around Elma, who was holding her cheek with her hand as though she'd been struck.

He went to the twins. "What happened?"

"She went crazy," May said. Elma whimpered, her fear-filled eyes still on Mimi who was thrashing and screaming.

John set Mimi in a chair and got in her face. "Calm down." The authority in his voice was such that Mimi's howling cut off, and she choked on a breath. "I'm arresting you for criminal damage to—"

"She's cutting me off!" Mimi screeched. "I've taken care of Frannie her whole life, and this is how she repays me!" Frannie's mom motioned to a paper on the table.

Matthias grabbed it, scanning the printed words on the page issued by the Sanctuary bank. Stan evidently did not mess around, since Frannie had only approached him the day before about selling the house she, her mom and her sister lived in.

"She's selling the house out from under me." Mimi's voice was quiet now, full of tears no doubt honed through years of professional acting. "Izzy is pregnant, and now we'll both be homeless."

Matthias was pretty sure they'd been fired from the bakery, too, not that they showed up for work half the time. Frannie had been carrying them both for a long time, but now that time was over.

He was just glad Frannie wasn't here to see—

"Mom?"

Matthias spun back. Mimi started screeching again. Frannie stood in the doorway, Sonny at one elbow and Louis at the other with Michael behind them.

He took a step toward her, and the old-man posse reacted. Matthias stopped. "Should you be out of bed?"

Frannie didn't even acknowledge him. She let her friends walk her into the store where she sat on a chair. Her skin was gray against her red hair. The woman did not look like she should be up and walking around.

"Mom, did you break my window?" She sounded like she was choking back tears. Matthias took another step toward her, but the three old men all reacted. As though they needed to protect Frannie from *him*.

What was going on?

Mimi scowled. "I said you were going to destroy us if you testified, and I was right. You think you're so much better than me and Izzy." Her handcuffs clinked as she shifted in the chair. "And now you're going to ruin both of our lives."

"I'm sorry you think that." Frannie's voice was sad. "I'm sorry you think I've ruined your lives. But the only reason we're in Sanctuary is because you refused to live quietly. We could have been anywhere, but I had to make this decision when I was sixteen because you're too childish to appreciate the fact your life is in danger."

"Because of you."

"No, because of *you*. Because you married dad."

"If I hadn't, you wouldn't even exist."

Frannie didn't react. She looked like she only had enough energy to sit and talk, not to express any kind of emotion. Or there simply wasn't any left for her mother. Frannie waited a beat and then said, "We're done mom. I'm not going to support you anymore."

Mimi huffed, but there was a flash of fear in her eyes. "You can't kick us out!"

"I already have. I'm selling the house. If you can't afford the payments then you need to find somewhere else to live."

"You can't do this!"

John set a restraining hand on Mimi's shoulder.

She glared at him. "I want out of Sanctuary. Izzy and I can't live here anymore, not after what she's done."

"Izzy has to make that decision for herself," John told her. "If you're serious about leaving I can put in the request. It'll take some time right now, given we're still under heightened security."

"You can't keep me here. I won't be a prisoner."

Frannie looked at the ceiling. She still hadn't acknowledged the fact Matthias was even there. He felt like a specter in the room no one could see, only able to observe what was happening but not able to participate.

"Mom—"

Mimi winced. Izzy stepped inside the bakery, glancing around and seeing immediately something had happened. "Mom—Fran—what on earth?" Izzy looked like she barely had time for either of them.

Mimi said, "Izzy pack our stuff. As soon as I'm out of jail, we're leaving Sanctuary."

John turned to Frannie. "Do you want to press charges?"

"Not if she pays for the damage. I just want this done with." Frannie hesitated a second. "If they want to leave I won't stop them."

Frannie looked like her heart was about to break. The old men gathered around her, laying their hands on her shoulders in a move of solidarity. Izzy reached his side, sliding her hand through his elbow. When had she moved toward him?

Matthias shifted, hoping she would let go. She only smiled up at him and hung on.

"I'm not leaving, Mom."

Mimi's eyebrows rose at where Izzy was standing. "I see that."

Matthias shifted again, but Izzy didn't let go. It was like Mimi and Izzy were communicating without saying anything, like they were having a whole conversation just by looking at each other.

Mimi nodded.

Which couldn't mean anything good, now could it?

Izzy laid her head on Matthias's shoulder. "It's too early to tell, but soon everyone will know about Matthias and I. A baby is just proof of our love. That's why I can't leave." She beamed as dread settled on Matthias like a vice. "We're getting married."

Mimi's smile was like an evil victory.

They were seriously so vicious toward Frannie they would make an accusation like this? Matthias took Izzy's hand and pulled her grip from his arm.

"Are you kidding me?" He put all the disgust he felt over their actions into his question. How could they do this to Frannie? Only someone with no conscience would seek to harm another person—someone they should love—this way.

Izzy immediately produced tears. Matthias couldn't look at Frannie—not until Izzy admitted she was lying. While the tears rolled down Izzy's face, she covered her hand with her mouth and then said, "How can you say that? You told me you wanted our baby!" Her hands went to her flat stomach. "All that talk about marriage...it was just talk? How could you do that to me? You told me you loved me, Matthias. You told me you love our baby."

"Our baby?" He felt his eyebrows raise and shook his

head. "Seriously? You don't think you've hurt Frannie enough without dragging me into the drama between you and Diego?"

"He doesn't have anything to do with this. You told me you forgave me for that. I know it was history repeating itself for you, but I told you it won't happen again. I'm not like that other girl. I'm not the one who's going to leave you behind. Matthias, I love you. I love the baby we made together."

The door shut. Frannie was gone, along with the old men. Andra stood just inside the door, arms folded, looking like he was next on her hit list.

He moved to the door. Izzy grabbed for his arm, but Matthias shook her off. "She's gone?"

"You really think she was going to stay and listen to that?" Andra huffed. "She's nowhere near able to fight them off, and you should've had way more care with her feelings than *this*."

"But it's not true. She should know that."

"Matthias." John's voice was stern, making him back up a little. Getting mad at the sheriff's fiancé wasn't going to help.

He rubbed his head and tried to figure out what just happened. "She can't have thought that was for real."

Andra shrugged. "I don't think she knows which way is up right now."

"Why was she even out of the medical center?"

"I don't think that matters. Not when you've got more important things to worry about. Like making her believe you're the one telling the truth, and not—" She looked at Izzy. "—her."

Matthias ran his hands down his face. He must have swayed or something, because John grabbed his elbows.

"Andra, help him back to the medical center. He has business to take care of."

"No." Matthias shook his head, still deciding what he should do. "I'll have to wait until later. Frannie needs to rest."

"Are you sure?" Andra frowned. "You don't want her thinking this is true."

"There's no way she thinks that."

If she did, Frannie obviously wasn't the person he thought she was.

CHAPTER 20

Flashes of dreams from the time Frannie had been asleep wouldn't give up their grip on her mind. She didn't want to think about the word coma, a scary term for being anesthetized just to help her heal. Dan had been there when she'd woken up. He'd told her to simply close her eyes, take a breath and recite the Bible verse he'd shown her.

Stella hadn't worsened, but she wasn't better either. Frannie's lungs were clear for the first time in days. She finally felt like she was getting past the worst of the chemical's effect on her, even though her throat was still raw.

She glanced over at the guys, huddled together in the far corner of the room. Sonny, Louis and Michael were having an intense conversation with Hal—the Sanctuary radio DJ. The elderly biker was frowning, shaking his head.

Frannie sighed, raising her voice so they could hear her. "If you're planning on sticking close until kingdom come, you should probably note the fact I'm going home soon."

They all turned to her, but Frannie didn't back down. "Sheriff Mason will be here in a minute to pick me up. You'll need to re-format your plan to the apartment above the bakery."

She didn't want to be in the medical center one second longer. Not when all she could think of were crazy images of Stella sitting up—getting off the bed and walking around like the undead while Frannie couldn't get away.

The residue of nightmares had left her shaky and needing air.

Whatever things are true.

At least her nightmare images of the bakery were real, or as real as it could be when it was all Izzy's lies. Frannie knew that. She knew Matthias was not the father of her sister's baby, but it hadn't stopped the slice of pain that ran through her like a samurai sword seeing them standing together talking about a child. His face had told her the truth, but with all the other images—most of them unreal—swirling in her mind, Frannie hadn't been able to stick around and wait for him to explain what she already knew.

Whatever things are lovely.

Later, when they had some time, they could talk about it… after she'd slept for a year at least, first.

Frannie grabbed her bag, and the script she was supposed to be learning for the play. Half the stuff in her head was due to practicing her lines. Where else would all the stuff about dead people coming back to life have come from?

In the play, after Hero is accused of being unfaithful, the characters decide to tell everyone she has died until the truth can be revealed and her husband-to-be can prove himself honorable. And in the grief over his accusations, he unravels the truth.

It didn't make for happy dreams, even though Frannie and Matthias's characters were by-standers who fell in love during the emotional time where Hero—Nadia Marie's character—is being slandered. It made Frannie's messed up head wonder if she couldn't fake her death to draw out the killer and thereby prove Izzy's accusations to be untruth.

Whatever things are of good report.

But this was real life, not a story where the fairytale came to a "happy ever after" conclusion and everything was wrapped up nicely at the end. She had to live with the reality her sister and mother would do or say anything just to hurt her, simply because Frannie wanted to be free of them. And now they had sucked Matthias into their twisted plan.

Frannie kind of hoped they did leave town. Not that she wanted them to put themselves at risk. So long as they could be protected, she was good with them living far from here.

Hal wandered over. The aging biker's leather jacket had tassels on the sleeves and multiple patches signifying things Frannie had no idea about. His long hair was streaked with gray and tied at the back of his neck with a leather thong. "Darlin'."

"Don't try and change my mind, Hal." Frannie clutched her stuff to her front. "I'm going home."

His chest rumbled with laughter. "I was only goin' to offer to carry your bag."

"Oh." She shifted, and he took it from her. "Thanks, Hal."

"Not to worry, darlin'."

Sonny and Louis came over, helping her off the bed so she could walk with her arms through theirs.

She smiled. "I'm looking forward to being able to get around without a bunch of old men holding me upright."

Sonny patted her arm. "We'll always hold you up. You know that."

She did, but didn't have the chance to tell them so before they met John in the hallway. The sheriff rocked back on his boots and said, "Maybe you don't need my protection. Looks like you've got your own army of bodyguards."

She smiled. "Looks like it."

Think on these things.

"Still, I'll give y'all a ride anyway."

It didn't take long to get them all to the bakery, but it was squished in the car. Frannie left the lights off inside. She couldn't face whatever state the place was in, or the memories of Matthias standing so close to Izzy. She just walked straight to the stairs and flipped on the upstairs light.

John stopped her with a hand on her shoulder. "I'll go first. You stick here with the guys, and I'll be back down in a second."

She nodded, looking at the four men waiting with her. They really were an army of bodyguards. But more than that, these men were the closest thing to a real family she'd had since she arrived in Sanctuary.

The peace of God will be with you.

Michael sent her a look. "Don't cry now, Frannie. You look like you're gonna lose it."

"I am not." Even though tears welled up, she folded her arms and lifted her chin.

Louis snorted. "Whatever you tell yourself, Francesca. But you haven't lost it yet." He stepped closer, holding her attention in his silver gaze. "Don't break now, when it's almost done."

Hal reacted immediately. "Macho idiot." He elbowed Louis out of the way and received a scathing glare in return, but Hal didn't pay any attention to it.

Hal laid his worn hands on the shoulders of her T-shirt. "Darlin', you don't have to be strong. That's why we're all here. There's four of us standing with you, taking your back. Outside of here there's a whole town of people we had to fight away. You've got organized protection for the next month we had so many volunteers."

"Seriously?"

Hal nodded. "These people love you. They don't expect you to be hit with the weight of the world and stay standing. They're only worried about you getting hurt more than you already have been."

John appeared at the bottom of the stairs. "Hal's right, Frannie." He glanced at the men. "Apartment's all clear."

Frannie looked at her feet for a second and then back up. "I know what Hal said is right, and I'm grateful everyone cares. But this can't go on for a month. We need to catch this guy in the act. Maybe I can—"

All of them reacted. "No." The word was in stereo.

"I'm not sitting around doing nothing, waiting for him to come at me again."

"You're not going out looking for him either," John said. "Apart from the fact Matthias would tan my hide for not looking out for you, I won't let you do that. If this guy comes, we'll be ready. If not, this is your life. It's a precious thing, and we're not going to risk you for anything in the world. I think everyone here would agree with me."

They all nodded. Louis did not look happy.

Frannie sighed. It was nice they all cared so much, but it wasn't going to solve her problem. Frannie needed her life back. If she had to be in danger to make that happen, she was starting to wonder if it might not be worth it. Matthias would just have to understand.

Frannie tried to hide how strenuous it was to climb the stairs. She was ready to crash on the floor and sleep for a week. If only she could avoid the dreams. The guys were a good distraction, but they weren't going to keep the nightmares at bay.

Frannie stopped and looked around. A couch with comfy cushions sat facing a coffee table on a dark red rug, and a short unit topped by a widescreen TV that didn't overtake the whole room. Paintings hung on two walls, and a vase of flowers topped a small, two-person table.

"Holy cow."

John chuckled. The guys dispersed through Frannie's brand new furnished living room, Michael and Hal going straight for the fridge. He smiled at her. "I'll be keeping an eye on outside."

Frannie nodded, still unable to believe what Nadia Marie had been able to pull off.

A pounding knock on the door downstairs made Frannie jerk.

She moved to the office, which had been cleaned and organized. She looked out the window to the sidewalk below. "It's Matthias."

John's voice was soft. "Do you want me to let him in?"

She shook her head. "I don't want to see him right now." She could barely think straight, and he would want to talk.

John nodded. "I'll tell him on the way out."

Frannie didn't move from her spot by the window. She watched Matthias take a step back when John exited the front of the bakery. Matthias moved to enter, but John stopped him with a hand to his chest. John spoke close, like he was letting him down easy, but Matthias reacted.

Frannie's fingers tightened on the frame of the window until it bit into her skin. Matthias looked really upset. He glanced up for a second and saw her in the window. She saw his mouth move, yelling her name. Frannie didn't move. Seconds ticked by while she was frozen, watching the agony on his face that she wouldn't talk to him—that he didn't know if she believed her sister's story and couldn't convince her how he felt.

Frannie backed away from the window.

Matthias would stick with her, she knew it. He would hurt until they could straighten this out, just as she would. But Frannie couldn't give him what he wanted until she'd untangled the mess in her head.

All she could see was him in her face, yelling about her having been unfaithful. And the priest.

She really shouldn't have read the play before she fell asleep.

Publish it that she is dead.

THANKSGIVING PIE ORDERS had piled up while Frannie was in the medical center. A pile of them were stacked on the desk. She sorted through them, though they were the almost the same every year. The monotony of the task helped her thoughts to quiet. When she could breathe, Frannie looked out of the window again. Matthias wasn't standing by the door anymore. His truck was parked across the street and Frannie watched him drop the tailgate and climb in the back, where he rolled out a sleeping bag and settled down.

This was what he was going to do with his evening? Frannie sighed and shook her head.

In the living room she could hear the guys arguing.

"Hey, Frannie!" Michael called out. "You got any nacho cheese? Never mind, I found it!"

Frannie frowned. The cupboards and fridge were empty, weren't they? She didn't have anything edible in the kitchen unless someone put it there.

"You want some?" He yelled again.

"No thanks!" She slumped into the desk chair. The guys couldn't expect her to actually eat something spicy like nachos and then have a dream-free sleep, could they? They were supposed to be protecting her, not giving her heartburn.

The phone on her desk rang.

"Frannie?" Sonny stuck his head in the door.

She waved him off. "I got it."

Sonny waited.

"Francine Peters?"

"Yes." She felt her brow flicker, and Sonny noticed. "This is Francine. What can I help you with?"

"What makes you think I need any help?" The voice slipped, and a drawl emerged. Nigel was the only person in town with a Texas accent. So why was he trying to pretend it wasn't him?

Frannie looked at Sonny, and nodded. He needed to know this wasn't a normal phone call. His eyes hardened. She'd figured he would immediately go and tell all the guys, but he didn't move.

"Well then, what was your reason for calling, Mr..."

He didn't take the bait. "I don't think my name will make much difference at this point."

Except she was pretty sure it was Nigel. She could picture him in her head as he spoke.

"If you want, you may call me the angel of death."

Frannie froze. Nigel was the killer? The mental image of him running at her in Stella's room arrested her thoughts so all she could see and hear was that moment, and the rush of adrenaline forcing her heart to beat at hyper-speed. Had it really been the newspaper editor?

She tried to remember if the build was the same, but couldn't decide if it felt like it could have been Nigel in Stella's room that night, or not.

Sonny walked over. She heard his footsteps before he crouched, his knee joints popping. He set his hand on her shoulder, and Frannie sent him a look that was supposed to be reassuring. He didn't look convinced.

Clarity distilled her thoughts. "Are you saying you're the one who killed Harriet Fenton, you tried to kill Stella and would have if I hadn't intervened?"

"And why would I admit that, especially when your phone is likely bugged? This is hardly a confession."

Yet that was exactly what the letter had proclaimed to be.

She'd signed an agreement which meant the government could put her under whatever surveillance they wanted, even though it would be inadmissible in court. They didn't need a trial to kick someone out of witness protection. All that was part of living here; signing away the better part of her right to a private life meant they were safe.

Frannie didn't care if everyone was listening if it meant they found this guy. "If you don't intend to confess, what did you call for?"

"Now there's a good question." His voice was sardonic, as though this whole turn of events was beneath him. "There's a woman here I think you will be interested in, especially given the condition she's in. Whether or not she remains that way is up to you, Francine."

"Is she hurt?" She didn't want to ask if the woman was dead, that was unbearable.

Sonny's eyes scanned her face as she gripped the phone.

Nigel chuckled, a low and dark sound. "You could say that."

———

MATTHIAS SHIFTED LOWER in the sleeping bag with John's tablet out of sight and the brightness turned all the way down. He nodded even though the guys couldn't see him, and spoke into his headset. "If you're right and it is Nigel..."

John said, "I'll get him. I'm on my way to his house now." Matthias could hear him running.

Bolton chimed in. "Dude, your woman could've been a hostage negotiator. She's holding her own, don't you worry about that."

Matthias didn't really want his boss's opinion on the way Frannie dealt with a killer, but it was nice to know she was hanging in there. The woman was stronger than anyone he'd ever met if she could deal with a repeat killer and keep her cool without her voice even wavering.

John's voice crackled in the headset, his breath coming hard. "I'm on B Street."

Matthias tapped and swiped through the database John had stored on his tablet. "Six houses in on the left hand side, that's Nigel's."

There were a ton of places Matthias wanted to be, and none were in his truck on the street. Top of the list was inside with Frannie. He'd grab the phone from her so he could deal with this sicko himself. Second was in the basement of the library, hooked into the phone call instead of Bolton, listening to her voice for himself. But the guys knew he'd likely not be able to resist chiming in and telling Nigel exactly what he thought of the man terrorizing Frannie.

John's voice was steady. "I'm entering the house now."

Matthias wouldn't mind John's job right now either, feeling like he was actually doing something. Whoever this woman was Nigel had hurt, John was the one who was going to find and help her.

But Matthias's position put him closest to Frannie.

Bolton muttered into the radio, "She needs to get him to tell her who the woman is, and where they're at."

"Clear," John said. "Nigel's house is clear. They're not here."

"His office, then?" Matthias thought aloud.

"I'll head there next. Stand by."

Matthias looked back up at the office. If she'd let him in, he could tell her they needed more information.

"That's a girl," Bolton muttered.

If the tablet was physically connected to the town's internal network, Matthias could tap in and listen to the call. Sanctuary's internal phone system was constantly recorded, and periodically the recordings were sent to the NSA. Lately they'd had to be sent as physical copies—a box of CDs—since the president's family being in town meant security was even stricter and their satellite internet connection had been disconnected.

Who knew when it would be back up? But the town seemed to be doing okay going back to snail mail correspondence.

"There we go..."

Matthias gritted his teeth. "What? What did she get?"

"John—"

The sheriff interrupted. "Nigel's office is clear, too."

"Frannie asked for proof of life." Bolton said, "He's at Maria's."

Matthias's whole body went solid. "Maria?"

John's breath came fast. "I'm on my way." Matthias could hear the pounding of John's boots on the sidewalk as he tore across town, no longer concerned with stealth. If anyone could get there before his sister was seriously hurt it was the sheriff. John wouldn't waste time if it risked someone's life, but he had to balance against the threat.

All of which Matthias knew in theory, but these men had lived it. John had held down a high-profile, dangerous federal agent job, and Matthias didn't figure Bolton's was much different—not given everything the man knew. A ranch hand who'd lived his whole life in Sanctuary didn't quite measure up, even with the training Bolton had given him. They were content to involve him, to make him count, but Matthias was content to lean on them if it meant the difference between life and death for Maria.

Matthias said, "Bolton. Connect to the doctor's extension and tell him he might be needed."

"Good plan."

John said, "I'm at Maria's. House is dark. I'm headed inside."

Matthias held his breath and waited.

Seconds.

A minute.

"Drop your weapon, Nigel." John paused for a second. "Bolton, have the doctor meet me here."

"No! I'm the dark angel. She has to die, just like they all had to die."

"Nigel, drop your weapon."

Matthias's stomach clenched. He could hear Maria's cries in the background. He jumped off the bed of the truck and climbed into the cab. As soon as the engine turned over he hit the gas and drove as fast as he could through town. Frannie had protection. Maria needed him now.

The past played like a bad B-movie reel through his mind. His dad, fist pulled back ready to punch Maria again. His mom's scream.

Matthias gripped the steering wheel, feeling the wood frame of the chair in his hands. The thump as he hit his father.

"I won't go in. I won't." Nigel's protest was followed by a thud, and grunting.

Bolton said, "On my way."

"Me, too." Matthias turned the corner so fast the car almost tipped onto two wheels.

Maria was still screaming.

Nigel yelled, "I won't go down for this. She made me do it. She said it would be easy, that Maria's crazy." He was crying aloud now.

John's voice was level and clear. "Who?"

Nigel cried for a few seconds and then rallied himself to say, "She told me if I really loved her, then I'd do it."

"Who?"

"Mimi. She wanted me to scare them both."

CHAPTER 21

Frannie was back at the medical center, this time with it full of people. It seemed like everyone had turned out to see if Maria was okay. Her family was there, with the notable exception of Antonia. Tom looked chastised, mostly concentrating on corralling the twins who were playing tag in the waiting area. Father Wilson was trying to talk to him, but Tom wasn't really paying him any attention. Nadia Marie and Andra stood with Beth, talking low and keeping one eye on the boys every time they passed.

Frannie and her posse of old men bodyguards crossed the room so she could speak to Olympia.

Matthias's mom held her arms out. "Precious."

Frannie sank into the embrace, feeling the hot rush of tears hit her eyes as a lump filled her throat. Olympia made shushing sounds as she stroked Frannie's back. Why couldn't this woman be her mom? Instead Frannie had been birthed by a woman with no moral code and no sense of decency, who barely tolerated her existence. Had Mimi simply given Frannie's father what he wanted—a legacy?

Frannie leaned back before she dissolved completely. "How is Maria?"

Olympia didn't let her go all the way, for once giving Frannie the impression she needed the comforting physical contact as much as Frannie did. "Shaken, but not too badly hurt."

She looked over Frannie's shoulder, so Frannie turned and saw Matthias making his way to them. He kissed his mom's cheek and glanced at her with no small amount of longing. "The sheriff has Nigel in custody. Bolton is bringing in Mimi so they can find out the extent of what went down."

Frannie blinked. "You knew?"

"Bolton was listening in." Matthias's earpiece was still in one ear, the chord hanging down the front of his shirt to the radio on his hip. "He said you did a good job talking to Nigel. You got us the information we needed to get to Maria before it was too late."

He'd been involved, too? Frannie wasn't sure if she liked the fact Matthias had done that even after she'd told the sheriff she didn't want him there. The warmth of knowing he cared was overshadowed by fear of the killer hurting him because of their relationship.

If she was obviously attached to him, would the killer leave her alone because she had reason to want to live? Maybe his insidious attacks on her were about revenge, because she'd stopped him from "helping" Stella leave this earth peacefully. But despite Stella's condition, she was still alive.

If the killer wasn't Nigel, then it begged the question: what was the real killer planning? Frannie felt a shiver move through her just thinking about what he would do next.

Matthias touched her cheek. "Are you okay?"

"I'm not fine, but I am okay." Olympia put her arm around Frannie. "I can't believe Maria was terrorized. I knew my mom would retaliate after I told Stan I wanted to sell the house. But this is too much."

She didn't want to believe her mom thought Maria was the "weak link," but it looked like that was the truth.

He squeezed her shoulder. "You don't have to face her."

"Lover!" Izzy's shrill cry ceased all the conversations. Everyone turned to watch her totter across the tile floor in her stiletto heels. Her eyes were bright—too bright—and consumed with Matthias.

Frannie took an involuntary step back as Izzy launched herself at Matthias. He had the decency to catch her and managed to narrowly miss her lipstick being planted all over his mouth. Matthias set her away from him. "Give it up, Izzy."

She shook her head like she was oblivious. "What are you talking about? Why are you continuing to hurt me?"

"I'm not your lover. No matter how many times you say it, regardless of how many witnesses are there to hear you. It doesn't make it true, Izzy." Matthias's voice was softer than normal, but his tone still held an edge to it. He was trying to be nice, but he was completely serious. "I am not the father of your baby. Diego is. Your mom has already convinced Nigel to terrorize Maria because she wants to get back at your sister, and this is how you've chosen to fight your battle against Frannie."

He took a breath. "The reality is, I'm in love with your sister."

Frannie gaped. Izzy glanced at Frannie and back to Matthias, completely ignoring the fact his mom was standing right beside them. She sputtered. "Tias, darling. Don't do this."

Tias? How did Izzy know the nickname Matthias had given to Frannie—and only Frannie?

He glanced at Frannie, suddenly looking worried. "Seriously, Izzy. You need to have a long talk with Diego about what you're going to do. This is not a solution."

"You gave me a ring. You asked me to marry you. *That* was the solution." Izzy's voice was getting softer, her eyes now rimmed with tears. Evidently she was going for the opposite of hysterical in the hope her story was more convincing.

And it was a story, Frannie was convinced of that.

"Izzy." Olympia put herself in front of Frannie and Matthias, facing off against Izzy herself. "You need help, dear. This charade won't stand, not when all of us know the truth of Matthias's feelings for Frannie. I'm very sorry Diego has done this to you, it must be a very troubling thing, especially in your condition. But do not put this on Diego's brother now. You will not ensnare both of them with your lies."

Matthias's mom paused for a second. "This is not the eighteen-hundreds, where I force my son to do the honorable thing and marry you. Neither of them would consent when you are a strong woman, capable of raising this baby on your own. Diego should provide help, as needed, but as much as it pains me to say about my own son, it's likely to not be a help to you.

"If I were you I would avoid the hassle and wait until Diego offers you support. Until then my family is fully prepared to help you and the child you carry, if it truly does belong to this family. But what you cannot do is slander my other son and destroy your sister's happiness with your insidious lies."

Izzy lost it then, screaming like a banshee. "It's not a lie! Your son is the father of my baby!"

"Which son you are referring to remains to be seen." Olympia put her arm around Izzy and steered her away. "And now is not the time for this discussion. Maria is hurt and that's why we're all here. Not to cater to your emotional state. Have a care, darling."

They walked away, even though Izzy didn't seem much like she wanted to go.

Matthias looked at Frannie then, his eyes sad. "I'm sorry she keeps doing that. It's not true."

"I know."

If it was, Frannie would have every reason to want to exit Sanctuary...permanently. But it was exactly what Olympia had said, an insidious lie.

He moved closer but didn't touch her, as though he wasn't sure it was still something he was allowed to do. "Are we okay?"

"I don't know," Frannie said honestly. "I need all this to blow over so things can go back to normal. Until then, I have no idea what's going on even in my own head."

"Tell me."

"The coma was..." She took a breath. "I dreamed. More like nightmares, really."

"I'm sorry." He put his arms around her then, and Frannie wanted desperately to sink into his embrace.

"Don't." She pushed back. "It's like your mom said to Izzy. I need to be strong and capable."

"Only because Izzy's never been that way. You already are. It's okay to lean on people, Frannie."

"I can't." She shook her head. "Not when the killer might show up at any moment, or send me more of that drug and it kills me this time. We can't get attached to each other when I might not make it. Don't put that on me. I don't want you to be in love with me if I could die."

"All of us could die, Frannie. It's a fact of life. We could get hit by lightning or killed in an accident. This threat isn't unique. I know things are scary right now and your mom isn't helping. But I want to. I want to be there for you."

Frannie stepped back, aware there were people listening. She kept her voice low. "I can't let you do that, Tias."

It wasn't like she wanted to set herself up as a target for the killer, but she couldn't let her feelings for him cloud her actions. She might have to fight for her life, and she might have to let go if the situation warranted it. Her eternal future was secure now. What she couldn't die with was the knowledge Matthias would be left longing after her—wishing he could have done something to prevent her death.

"Frannie, don't do this."

"I want to thank you for caring about me." She tried to smile. Maybe it worked, but he didn't look comforted. "I've never felt so much care in my life than when I'm with you. It's a gift I appreciate, but can't keep. Not when I have so much hanging over my head."

Matthias blinked, and he saw a sheen of tears in her eyes. "If what Izzy said—"

"This doesn't have anything to do with Izzy. This is about us." Frannie wanted to cry at that word. Us. It tore her heart apart to even consider she could be part of something with Matthias. "There can't be a you and me. Not right now, and maybe not ever. I'm sorry, Tias." Her voice broke then. "I'm really sorry."

He touched the sides of her face then, his lips covering hers in a last desperate goodbye. "Frannie..."

She choked back a sob, pushed him away and ran for the door.

———

Matthias let himself in to the sheriff's office, his heart still reverberating with the aftershocks of what felt like an earthquake in his chest. John's face was an inch from Nigel's. "Understand?"

Nigel nodded.

John locked Nigel in the cell and walked straight to Matthias like he knew he'd come in. "How's Maria?"

Matthias blew out a breath. "Shaken up, but not seriously hurt. The bump on her head she says she got when she tried to run from Nigel. She slammed into a cabinet in her kitchen. That was what all the blood was from."

John nodded. "And Mimi?"

"Bolton's on his way now."

John grabbed his radio off the table. "Bolton, this is John."

It crackled. "Yeah, go ahead."

"Bring Mimi to the bakery. I don't want her presence here to affect Nigel. Not when I'm unconvinced I can make an arrest yet. Conspiracy to intimidate someone you don't like by using someone who thinks he's in love with a starlet to scare a third person you care about doesn't really hold much weight. Not when no real harm was done to Maria, its Nigel's word against Mimi's and Maria doesn't want to press charges."

Matthias shook his head. "And I don't want her anywhere near Frannie. Can't he take her to the Meeting House?"

"I don't want her harassing Frannie, either. But she's stronger than you think, and she's going to want to talk to her mom." John's brow flickered.

"At full capacity, maybe." Matthias folded his arms. "But Frannie's been through too much in the last week to want to deal with this."

John shot him a look. "Maybe we'll ask Frannie about that. And about you speaking for her. If there's one thing I've learned from Andra, it's that women rarely like being dictated to."

"A killer is targeting her, and her sister's telling everyone I'm the father of her baby. Now we find out her mom coerced Nigel into pretending to be the killer. There's not much more Frannie can take, and as much as I'd like to be the person there to help her pick up the pieces, I'd rather she didn't break in the first place. She's been through enough."

John's head tilted to the side. "What happened?"

"I'm going to go warn her Bolton is coming."

"He's probably already there." John caught up to him at the door. "Tell me what happened."

"She broke up with me."

"And you're still trying to protect her, even after she dumped you?"

"It isn't like that."

"Isn't it?"

Matthias headed out the door and jogged down the sidewalk to the bakery. John didn't follow, probably because he had to guard his detainee. Matthias's chest still felt like Frannie had stuck a knife in and turned it, but he hadn't lied. He was in love with her, and he had been for a long time. He'd been sure—as sure as he could be—that she felt the same way. Maybe she didn't. She was going through so much right now, but love shouldn't distract or get in the way of life. It was supposed to hold her up. The thought he might not be capable of giving her that kind of love crossed his mind.

He'd considered himself broken for a long time, perhaps it was the truth after all. Maybe, as much as he wanted it, Matthias couldn't love Frannie the way he was supposed to.

Bolton was standing over a handcuffed Mimi, who was lounged on a chair like she was in a swanky restaurant surrounded by adoring fans all trying to speak to her. She spotted Matthias, no reaction except her leg began to swing back and forth where it was crossed over the other one. "Tias, darling. How nice of you to join us."

Frannie, who stood at the opposite end of the room, flinched.

Matthias turned to leave.

"Don't go." Frannie's voice was hard, making him turn back. "Don't make her run you off when you haven't done anything wrong. She's the one who twisted Nigel and forced him to terrorize Maria. I saw the marks on her hands and arms. She had to defend herself against a knife."

"I didn't tell him to try and kill her."

"But you told him to scare her, and me. And pretend he was the killer."

Mimi rolled her eyes. "Says Nigel." She straightened and batted her eyes at Bolton. "I want a lawyer."

He didn't move out of his arms-folded, feet-spread stance. "Duly noted."

Frannie stepped toward her mom. "Who is it?"

Mimi's look turned sardonic. "Who is who, Francesca? No one knows what you're talking about."

Her voice was quiet when she said, "Who is the angel of death?"

Bolton glanced at Matthias, one eyebrow up. Matthias shrugged, he had no idea Mimi might actually know who it was.

Frannie's mom rolled her eyes. She opened her mouth, but Frannie cut her off. "You know just about everything that happens in this town. Considering the fact it was you who sold information about the letter and the killer to Nigel in the first place, I want to know who this angel of death really is."

Mimi shook her head sardonically, her eyes on the floor. Her face looked like she was having a whole argument against

Frannie in her head. She finally made a "pshaw" sound. "Who says I know anything? Maybe I just got everything from that letter of yours."

"Maybe you saw him, maybe you didn't." Frannie folded her arms. "But I think, either way, you know who it is."

Mimi lifted her chin, her attention square on Frannie. "You don't have a prayer of finding out who it is from me."

Frannie didn't even flinch. "You want him to kill me?"

Mimi shrugged one shoulder. "Won't be my fault." She glanced around, taking in Matthias and Bolton. Apparently the old men bodyguards were upstairs, because he couldn't see them. Mimi said, "Looks like you've got plenty of protection right here."

"But you don't care." Frannie shook her head. "Story of my life, Mama."

With that, Frannie walked out. Matthias looked at her mom, but he didn't see any remorse—or even a shadow of guilt over what her actions were doing to Frannie.

He turned to Bolton. "What happens now?"

Matthias's boss didn't take his eyes off Mimi. "When I'm satisfied I have everything I need, and John has everything he wants from Nigel, Ms. Peters will be released. The judiciary system within Sanctuary is such that she will likely be given community service for the harm she caused. Unless she really does sign herself out."

"And Nigel?"

"Something heavier. Justice Simmons and Sheriff Mason will decide whether it consists of being detained for a period, and community service following."

The elderly former superior court justice wasn't someone any of them were a huge fan of, not after Simmons tried to officiate a sentencing on John's fiancé with little to no evidence she'd actually committed the murder of the mayor's wife weeks ago. The man's motives—beyond using his former position to assert some authority in his retirement years—were suspect at best. John wouldn't like working with him.

"So Mimi will be released? A slap on the wrist after everything she's done to Frannie?"

Bolton looked at him then. "And what do you suppose I do, arrest every single jerk in the world?"

Matthias rolled his shoulders. "Fine."

"Go check with the guys, make sure Frannie is set for the night. Okay?"

Matthias nodded. He pushed his way into the kitchen where Frannie was at the counter, surrounded by ingredients and an open recipe book.

She looked up. Matthias's steps faltered he was so arrested by the look of longing in her eyes. Why did she have to look at him like that? It was her decision to walk away from him. She had to know they would see each other before this was over. He wasn't going to leave her safety to chance. There was no way he could do that, even if he was mad enough to spit nails right now.

Matthias kept walking. It hurt. Okay, it hurt more than he was mad. The anger came from the fact she'd essentially ripped out his heart.

He turned the corner and took the stairs two at a time. Michael and Hal were stretched out on the couch while Louis and Sonny sat in folding chairs. Someone had brought a TV in, because they were all watching a black and white show that was evidently funny.

Matthias put his hands on his hips. "And she's safe downstairs while y'all are catching up on your entertainment?"

"Now that's not fair." Louis got up, but Sonny stopped him with a hand.

Sonny got off the couch and came over to Matthias, trying

to look tough even though he was half a foot shorter. "We get you care for her, son. But the woman asked for space."

"I don't care what she asked for. She should have someone with her at all times."

He couldn't get out of his head the mental picture of Frannie on the floor in the kitchen, barely breathing. Or Frannie choking back a sob, walking away from him.

Matthias covered his face with his hands and rubbed. "Okay, look—"

A sharp scream pierced the air. Matthias hit the stairs before it even registered in him it was Frannie who'd screamed. His boot clipped a step and he tumbled, sliding down the last few steps until he hit the bottom, slamming his hand on the wall for balance.

The kitchen was empty. He raced around the counter in case she'd fallen. On the floor, a full bag of flour had hit the linoleum and spilled out. There was a scuff mark but no footprints in the dust.

Bolton flung open the door to the front, gun raised. His eyes were hard, as though the memory of a thousand bloody battles were there in his gaze.

"Frannie?"

Bolton shook his head. "Back door?"

Matthias moved to the back door. It was open wide, the dark night still when he emerged outside. He raced to the middle of the street, looked both ways, but saw nothing and turned back to the crowd at the door, heart in his boots.

"She's gone."

FRANNIE'S back was pressed against rough brick. The masked man who had grabbed her from the bakery kitchen leaned against her, pressing her hips back against the sharp surface of the building. His face was covered with a knitted mask, a hole for the mouth and two holes for the eyes.

Dead eyes.

His steady hand held a knife to her throat while his other hand covered her mouth, blocking air from escaping her nose. She struggled, barely able to breathe. He smelled like Einetine.

"Enough." The knife let up, and he dragged her farther down the street.

She'd heard Matthias come out, and the men shouting. They were moving now, fanning out to search while Frannie was dragged away by the man who'd nearly poisoned her to death. Einetine wouldn't work on her now. She'd taken the medicine. If he intended to kill her with it, the substance would have little effect on her—even given her allergy to codeine. Frannie didn't want to get dosed, but at least she would survive.

His grip on her was so tight she couldn't break his hold, no matter how hard she struggled.

"Do you know how much hassle you've caused me?"

He shoved her down an alley at the end of Main Street to where a lone golf cart sat at the end, parked out front of Sam Tura's gym. No one would be in there this late at night. Should she shout? Frannie figured she would likely get stabbed for yelling, but if she could draw enough attention to them, someone might hear her.

Frannie sucked in a breath to scream. A heavy fist thudded her in the stomach. Breath evaporated from her lungs in a rush, and she doubled over.

The killer leaned down and whispered in her ear. "You should know, I've done this before. Enough times you're not going to call for help. You're not going to challenge me. You're just going to walk where I tell you to and keep your mouth shut."

Frannie straightened to find the knife was in front of her face. She jerked her head in a nod.

"Now move."

He walked her to the golf cart and pushed her across the seat to the driver's side. With the knife pointed in her side, he said, "Drive."

"Where to?"

He slammed his boot down on her foot, slamming the tread of his sole into the skin on the top of her foot not covered by her ballet flats.

Frannie pressed her lips together to hold in the cry as they careened down Main. She gripped the wheel.

"Left."

The move would take her farther from Matthias and the men searching for her, but she did it. Where was he taking her? There weren't too many places to hide in town, and only a handful of buildings that weren't houses. She glanced at him, trying to figure out who he was. The build was of an older man, but still fit. Like an aging prison inmate whose only entertainment was using the workout equipment and jogging around the yard.

"Right."

Frannie swung the wheel, hoping he would lose his grip on the seat and fall out. As it was, he had one hand on her arm and the other held the knife in her side. Judging by the sting, it felt like he'd already sliced through her clothes to nick her skin.

The golf cart engine whirred as the killer's foot pressed hers. Frannie bit her lip to keep from crying out. Who knew the skin on the top of the foot was so sensitive?

Tears spilled out onto her cheeks as she followed his directions, past houses to the blacktop toward the water treatment plant at the base of the mountains on the north-east side. The siren from Sheriff Mason's car rang out. The rush of hope made her hands—slick from sweat—slip off the steering wheel. The golf cart swerved, the killer yelped and the knife stuck into her a little more. Frannie cried out. His boot moved off her foot and the blade was pulled back. He struck out, slamming the knife handle into Frannie's temple.

Then he gripped the steering wheel and took control. The two right side wheels hit the ground again, and Frannie clutched the side of her forehead with her hand. Warm, wet stickiness trailed down the side of her face.

She slammed his shoulder with her hand. "You hit me."

The pain in her head clarified her thoughts, sharpening her mind until she could only think of one thing—getting away. Frannie lashed out again.

The killer grabbed the back of her head and slammed it into the steering wheel.

When Frannie woke up she was lying on the floor. The pain in her head had magnified until she thought her skull was going to split open.

The concrete under her was hard and cold. Frannie braced her hand to lift herself up, but her arm gave out and she crumpled back onto the floor.

A low, dark chuckle penetrated the throbbing in her mind.

Frannie blinked and tried to focus. She could see him, shadowed in the corner.

Who was it?

"Ten for effort, but you will remain here. With me."

***

BOLTON STORMED out of the sheriff's office onto the street to where Matthias stood with Nadia Marie and Andra. "Mimi won't talk."

John followed him out, his attention on the earbud he put in his ear.

Bolton shot him a scathing look. "John won't let me cross his line, even though it would get us what we want."

Matthias watched Nadia Marie blink away shock, seeing something in Bolton she either hadn't known or hadn't realized was there. Andra was nodding. Evidently she felt she could get a result after a little time with Mimi, too.

"You're a scary guy," Matthias said. "But what's more scary is that I want you to do it."

John shook his head and looked up from the tablet he'd plugged the headphones into. "We have to keep our honor intact. Sanctuary has a lot of rules that are different from outside life, and everyone in this town signed away a significant chunk of their rights when they came here. But it's about protecting them. It's not for us to abuse that trust."

Matthias folded his arms. "Not even if it means the difference between Frannie's life and her death?"

"Not even."

"I know how to make the hard decision, John. I've done it." Matthias didn't know how much Bolton or John had told Nadia Marie and Andra about his past. "I'll do it now if I have to."

"I know you will. But if we give up our honor, what do we have left?"

Matthias could list a few things he would live with, even without his honor. Frannie being top of the list. But John was right, they didn't want to become the very thing they were hunting. Matthias had to prove—to himself and Frannie— that he was worth her love. She loved him, despite the fact she'd never told him, but there was so much in Matthias that was darkness, he couldn't let her light in even if he wanted to.

Matthias opened his mouth, but John lifted his hand, palm out.

"They're talking." John motioned to his ear-piece, and then at the sheriff's office. "I'll stay here and see what I can get from Nigel and Mimi. You guys go to Stella. See what you can find there."

Bolton nodded. "Got it."

Nadia Marie grabbed Andra's hand and took a step back. "We'll check in at the Meeting House, make sure everyone keeps searching."

John looked at each of them in turn. "Find them both before it's too late."

Matthias sprinted with his boss to the truck, jumped in and held on while Bolton sped through town to the medical center. The place wasn't so packed now; most people had probably gone home because it was late—although a couple handfuls of people were at the Meeting House being organized into search parties. That's where his mom was.

A blue light on the wall above the reception desk was flashing. Matthias started to run, heading down the hall. A nurse in pink scrubs ran out of one room, holding a small case, and ran to a room on the other side. Matthias could hear the continual buzz of an alarm—coming from Stella's room.

He stopped at the door in time to see the doctor shake his head. "No meds."

The nurse flinched. "But—"

"Stella's instructions include no life-saving measures."

The nurse stood still, while the doctor looked at his watch.

"Time of death, eleven-sixteen p.m."

Stella's husband slumped in a chair in the corner and started to cry quietly.

Matthias stepped back into the hallway, turning to Bolton. "Could the killer have done this?"

Bolton considered the question, but didn't answer before the doctor stepped out of the room.

"It was her time to pass on." The doctor didn't look happy.

Who would choose a career where people died while he looked on, helpless to do anything? Matthias understood John and Bolton a little more in that moment. Justice, fighting for what was right, for the life of someone innocent, was a far better use of time than this powerlessness.

Bolton set his hand on Matthias's shoulder. "Easy."

Matthias brushed him off. "Let's go. We'll have to find her ourselves."

He turned, almost bumping into Xander's chest. The bigger man rocked back and forth making his shoes squeak. "Ms. Stella is gone?"

Matthias nodded. "I'm sorry. We have to go find Frannie."

Bolton was studying the big man. "Was anyone in here before Stella coded? Did anyone visit her earlier?"

The security guard's brow crinkled as he thought. "Only Father Wilson. He prayed with Ms. Stella's husband."

Matthias shook his head and looked at Bolton. "Father Wilson isn't a murderer."

Bolton didn't give at all in his expression. "Let's go."

FRANNIE LOOKED around trying to figure out where she was. It looked like a warehouse, only smaller. Huge pipes laced the room, running up and down the walls and across the floor on the outside. The room couldn't have been more than twenty feet wide. It was part of the water treatment plant, she guessed. She'd only seen the outside once, on a tour of the facility they'd done when she was in high school—right after they arrived.

The killer stood across the room, watching her.

She felt seriously achy, like she'd been slammed against something. "Did you drop me?"

"You're heavier than you look."

Frannie touched her temple. It was still oozing blood, but she was done lying here, being helpless. Once she'd determined she was going to sit up, she didn't stop until it was done. No matter that it took five minutes, all the while the killer watched her struggle.

But she did it.

He clapped, slow and sharp. "Your tenacity is admirable, but it won't help you."

"Because you're going to kill me." Frannie studied him, trying to figure out who it was. His voice didn't give him away, even with that thick New York accent. There were variations around town, but no one spoke like this and it was too natural to be fabricated. If there was one thing Francesca Canetti knew, it was what a wise guy sounded like.

"Whether or not you die is up to you. We're all condemned. We've all fallen short and been sentenced to live out our days in this hole. Why not end the suffering?"

Frannie shook her head even though it shook her thoughts, too. "You can't just start killing people. It's not right."

"On the contrary. It was the job I have been given. A calling, you could say."

"I don't believe that." She needed to keep him talking, to stall long enough that Matthias and the sheriff would find her. "No one would ask you to kill people." He was just a deranged man whose mind was so twisted he'd convinced himself the despicable was honorable.

"Regardless of your opinion, I will do as I am called."

"And what is that? Killing more people who tell you they want out of Sanctuary instead of just letting them die naturally, with dignity. Or they could sign themselves out of the witness protection program to face the threat elsewhere, if they don't want to be here so badly. You don't let them make the choice. You take the choice from them."

"I have *never* killed someone who didn't ask me to!"

"What about me?" She gave him a look. It probably wouldn't help to give him attitude, but she was past sick of this guy. "You nearly killed me with Einetine."

"I had no idea you were allergic to codeine."

"You're going to apologize? You still caused harm. And I saw you nearly kill Stella."

"Yes, that was unfortunate, but Mrs. Noel and I have come to an agreement. She will be at peace soon."

"So you kill her, you kill me...and you keep killing, finding reasons to justify your disposing of person after person until… what? You're left alone in town. Is that what you want? To be the king of a ghost town?"

His chuckled echoed through the room. "An intriguing thought. But sadly, no. Our escapades have left me with little remaining of the Einetine I brought into Sanctuary. I can only do so much with the amount I have, so I decided to expand its reach one last time."

No wonder the sheriff hadn't been able to figure out who brought in the ingredients and manufactured the drug. It didn't have anything to do with the mail delivery, or the medical center break-ins.

"You brought it here."

"Disguised as aftershave, if you will believe." He dug into his jacket pocket—a brown suit coat that topped a yellowing shirt and brown slacks. His boots were in fact scuffed black shoes with thick tread. This outfit could belong to any one of the crabby old men she knew in town, or easily one of the ones she wasn't familiar with. None of her friends would betray her like this. She hoped.

He pulled out a flask that would barely hold a cup worth of liquid. "It took a considerable amount of research and several attempts to convert this Einetine to powder form. Your reaction was worth it. To watch you waste away, convinced you merely had a virus." His eyes gleamed like a cat's.

He moved to the pipes, looking at a horizontal one about hip height then crossed the room to pull a screwdriver out of the dusty toolbox.

"What are you doing?" She had to keep him talking, distracted. Come on, Matthias.

If there is any virtue and if there is anything praiseworthy —meditate on these things.

There was nothing good here. This man was only evil. *God, help me stop him.*

The killer went back to the pipe and the square panel on the rounded top. He started unscrewing the panel. He was going to put Einetine in the water?

She tried to get up. "No! What are you doing?"

He turned then, saw her struggling to stand. "Only what should be done. There isn't enough Einetine to last years, person-after-person. Decisive action must be taken. If I introduce it into the water supply those with health and vigor will survive. The innocent, who should never have been brought here in the first place along with those who are ready, will perish. This town should be for those who deserve it."

———

BOLTON WAS GOING to use the old-school method to open Father Wilson's front door. Matthias stood back, feeling two shades above a complete wreck, but he wanted Bolton to be proud of the way he was holding it together. Matthias felt like his younger brother most of the time. Not just friends, but family, too.

He didn't want Bolton to know just how much of a wreck he was—emotionally or physically.

Bolton kicked out with his boot, and the door splintered to pieces. He didn't spare Matthias a glance, just walked right in scanning the space with his gun held out in front of him. "Clear."

He turned back. Matthias stood in the doorway and raised his eyebrows.

"You want me to take chances with your girl's life?"

"Of course not." Matthias shook his head. "But Father Wilson is...a *father.* You can't just barge into his house."

Bolton turned away, taking the stairs two-at-a-time. He pushed open the first door: bathroom. He nudged the second door with his foot and it swung open to reveal what probably should have been a bedroom.

"Matthias! Get up here."

"I'm right here. What is..." He looked into the room. "Holy—"

"Yup." Bolton stepped in first.

The room had a bed but layered with grimy, mussed-up blankets. One wall was covered with a row of hung pictures. Photos. A row of photos of—

"Those are headstones."

"Yup." Bolton looked—disturbed. "I've never seen anything like this." He walked along the wall reading the names. Headstones in the Sanctuary graveyard. "Elliot Mercer, Harlan Tourneau..." He kept walking, reading name after name. There were eight in total. Bolton turned back. "There isn't one for Harriet Fenton."

"He killed all of the others." Matthias couldn't believe it was Father Wilson. "He killed them, and now he has Frannie."

"The question is where did he take her?" Bolton looked around

Matthias did the same, reading the room to try and figure out what Wilson's plan for Frannie was. If he was just planning to kill her, he'd have used the poison again. He wouldn't have abducted her, unless...

"His plan is bigger now. For some reason he needed Frannie...to finish what he started. Once and for all. Wilson is going big this time."

Bolton nodded. "I'm going to clear the rest of the house."

Matthias followed, trusting his friend's instincts more than his own need to save Frannie. Bolton had trained

Matthias himself, and he'd claimed Matthias was able to see everything Bolton saw. The difference here was simply the benefit of two sets of eyes instead of one.

Matthias scanned the kitchen and moved on to the dining room. A plastic sheet covered the doorway. Matthias pushed it aside and entered. Bolton went in after him. Was the man worried they would find something gruesome? Matthias didn't need to revisit his past—and they didn't have time for him to lose it in another flashback.

The table in the center of the room stood on a plastic sheet that covered the whole floor. Sheets covered the walls and ceiling, too. On the table was a bunch of equipment he hadn't seen since chemistry class. The whole room smelled like—

Matthias grabbed Bolton's arm and pulled him out. "Einetine."

He remembered the odor from the letters Frannie had received. The doctor had said nothing in the world smelled like that.

Bolton stumbled on his way out, grabbed the sheet to steady himself and ripped it from the tacks as he fell in a heap on the floor, wrapped in plastic. Matthias covered his mouth with his elbow and coughed. He could taste the smell in the back of his throat.

He fell to his knees and fumbled for the radio John had given him. He hit the button and opened his mouth, but nothing came out except a croak. Instead he paged John using the S-O-S from Morse code. That would give John some idea Matthias and Bolton needed help.

The unit slipped from his fingers. *Please God, let him get the message.*

Matthias tried to breathe, but it was like his throat was clogged. His head hit the floor, his body no longer able to sustain his weight. He tried to move so he could see Bolton on the floor beside him.

"Bolton, come in." John's voice was breathy like he was running. "Matthias, are you there?" He paused a second. "I can't get to you right now, I need you to tell me where you are. I'll send someone to retrace your steps and figure it out, but unless you can tell me right now, that's going to take some time."

A car door slammed, and John sucked in a breath. "Mimi gave me enough to go on that I think Frannie is at the water treatment plant. I have to go there and get her first, but I'll have Hal and the guys come to you."

Matthias could hear him driving, the sound going in and out like a bad speaker. He pressed the button on the radio and tried to speak, but all that came out was a croak. Black spots were beginning to prick along the edges of his sight.

"Stay safe." John's voice was unlike he'd ever heard it before. Torn, worried. "I'm sending someone to you now."

Matthias didn't know if he and Bolton would still be breathing when Hal and the guys arrived. But if John was going to get Frannie, nothing else mattered. She would be safe. Matthias could die knowing he'd tried to save her with everything he had. It wasn't enough to give them a future, but he'd done it.

To his last breath.

CHAPTER 23

FRANNIE SCRAMBLED ACROSS THE FLOOR. The killer had unscrewed a panel on the pipe that was as big as a tree trunk. The four screws lay discarded on the floor and he was looking inside.

He was going to pour that stuff in the water? She couldn't let him do this. "Don't. Please. They'll die."

She grabbed his leg, but he kicked out, catching her side. Pain bounced through her rib cage like a ping pong ball. His mouth curled into a snarl.

"Only the old and ready to depart. And some children, but there aren't too many of those in town. Innocents who should never have been brought here in the first place."

He would infect the whole town with Einetine so only the healthy who were able to fight off its diluted effects would survive? She thought, then, of Reuben and Simeon; exuberant boys who had enough to deal with without someone trying to kill them.

"That's not for you to decide," she said. "You're not their judge, jury and executioner." He was more like the grim reaper, dispensing some twisted form of what he thought was aid.

Frannie struggled to stand, even while he unscrewed the lid of the bottle. When he moved to pour it in, Frannie kicked the back of his knee with as much strength as she had. He started to fall and the liquid sloshed, missing the opening into the pipe.

The killer grabbed the pipe, lifted himself to standing and poured the rest in.

"No!" Frannie grasped him, using the grip to lift herself off the floor.

She slammed her fists into his back even though it was too late. He looked up at the ceiling and laughed, long and loud. The sound echoed in the cement room, permeating Frannie's heart with cold and darkness.

She turned and tried to run for the door. People had to be warned. There had to be a phone.

The killer grabbed her hair. The sharp pain halted her as he flung her backward. Frannie landed on the floor, and her back slammed against the concrete.

"You made me do it! You didn't have to interfere."

Frannie said, "I should have stood there and let you kill Stella?"

"She wanted to die!" His face was red now, the portion she could see around his mouth and those dead eyes.

Frannie looked at him then, really looked. "Father Wilson." She could hardly believe it.

He whipped the mask off. "She told me you would figure it out."

Frannie choked. Who was *she*?

"She claimed you might be clever enough, but that she was smarter. Too bad for her. If I'm going down then she's going with me."

Frannie's stomach sank. "Mimi."

"She was fun for a while, but all things must come to an end." He leaned forward, a shadow of the man who was supposed to love people and serve his church with honor. Now his face was twisted with rage, the same way his mind was twisted to believe what he was doing was the right thing.

He reached back into the waistband of his slacks and pulled out a knife. "I always carry my weapon with me. Even all these years later." He studied the end of the steel, nicked instead of smooth—and marred by something dark. "Seems it will finally come in handy once more."

Frannie curled up on the floor. He lifted the knife, and she wrapped her arms around her head. It wouldn't stop what was coming. Breath arrested in her lungs as she waited for the pain.

A gunshot split the air.

Frannie looked up from the shelter of her arms.

John stood in the door, a bullet proof vest covering his chest, and on his face, the hard look of a US Marshal facing down a suspect. "Drop the weapon, Wilson. It's over."

Frannie looked at Father Wilson. He wasn't hurt. John must not have hit him with that first shot. While the father's attention was on John, Frannie slid backward. When she was out of knife range, she said, "He poisoned the water supply. We have to tell everyone not to drink it."

John didn't take his attention from the father. "Drop the knife, Wilson."

It clattered on the concrete, ringing out a discordant sound.

John let go of the gun with one hand, pulled out his radio and tossed it to her. Frannie fumbled but kept it from falling. "Type two-zero-six-four and then hold the button down. It's like a walkie-talkie, but you'll intercom the whole town. Every phone."

Frannie's terror-filled brain managed to grasp what he was telling her. She typed the numbers and pressed the button on the side. "Everyone?"

A high pitched sound rang outside the door.

"This is Frannie. Don't drink the water." Her voice echoed in the hallway, proof she was getting through.

"Don't anyone drink the water." The words tumbled from her mouth as she gripped the satellite phone that doubled as his radio.

"Sheriff Mason is busy with his gun pointed at Father Wilson, who's been killing people for years, or he'd tell you this himself. Father Wilson poisoned the town water supply. Is everyone listening? Don't drink the water. Don't take a shower or wash your hands, or anything. Not until we know it's safe."

Frannie let go of the button. She didn't know what else to say, but prayed the message got through.

Immediately the phone in her hand began to ring. Number after number flashed on the screen of John's unit listing the residents' four digit extension numbers. Did they think she was going to answer?

John said, "Turn around. Hands on your head."

Wilson complied, and the sheriff took three steps toward him. He didn't lower his gun until the last minute before stowing his weapon and taking out handcuffs.

Frannie saw Wilson's face. "He—"

Wilson spun. His fist traveled with his momentum and caught John in the stomach. John punched back, completely unfazed. Wilson staggered. John hit him again and again until Wilson doubled over. "If Matthias and Bolton are dead, it's on you and that stuff you've been using to poison everyone."

Frannie whispered. "Matthias?"

"If anyone dies it's on you." John drew his gun again and Wilson grabbed for it. They wrestled, Wilson grunting and panting. "I'm not going to jail."

Frannie set her hand against the wall to steady herself. "You killed Matthias?" She stepped forward.

"Frannie," John warned. "Stay back."

She grabbed Wilson's arm. "Where is he? What did you do to him?"

He didn't even look at her, so Frannie shook him harder. "Where is he?"

The door flung open. Dan Walden, the town's farmer, filled the doorway.

"Frannie." John's voice made her back up. He started to restrain Wilson, getting one of the cuffs on the struggling man.

Dan rushed across the room, kicking the knife farther out of the way before going to a valve at the end of the wall. He gritted his teeth and turned it, putting what looked like every ounce of effort into what he was doing.

"I can help." She rushed toward him. "Tell me what—"

Wilson's arm wrapped around her neck. He spun them both, forcing her to face John.

"Let her go."

Wilson shook his head, his breath hot on her neck. "Drop your gun."

John stowed it in the holster on his belt.

Wilson said, "Back up or I snap her neck."

John raised both hands. "You've hurt enough people." His eyes flicked for a second over her shoulder, toward Dan.

Wilson jerked around, sideways so Dan was on Frannie's left and John was on her right. He inched them past John, toward the door.

His grip around her neck was solid. He smelled like the

chemical. The memory of what breathing in Einetine had done to her—coupled with his arm—was enough to close her throat. Matthias was dead? And Bolton? Her heart felt like it had been ripped to shreds. He'd been her only hope for a good future. Her only promise for a life more than the one she'd been living before, so empty and lonely. Matthias was what she loved most in this world. And now he was gone.

Frannie struggled, unwilling to let Matthias's killer get away. He shoved her and ran for the door. Frannie stumbled and fell down. John ran past her, narrowly missing slamming into her as he sprinted out the door after Father Wilson.

Dan left the pipes and rushed across the room to her. "Are you okay?"

The farmer's dark hair fell over his forehead. He looked like he'd had a long, hard day. He was several years older than her, and Frannie had liked him even before he told her about what God had done for her.

She smiled but didn't try to get up. Every bone in her body was sore. "Is Tias really...are he and Bolton dead?"

Dan squeezed her shoulder. "Let's get you some help, and then we'll find out. I had no idea what was going on until you made the announcement."

"Okay." She shut her eyes for a second.

Dan slid one arm under her shoulders and the other behind her knees and lifted her. "Let's get you to the medical center."

Frannie opened her eyes when they reached the door. Just in time to see John return.

"He's gone."

Dan stopped. "You lost him?"

"Rounded the corner and he just...disappeared." John shook his head like he couldn't believe it. "It was unreal, like the man's a ghost."

———

"WE NEED a way to draw him out." John leaned against the wall in the medical center room. Bolton was sitting on one bed, a breathing mask over his mouth and nose. Matthias was on the bed next to his, the same way but lying down.

Frannie sat in the chair beside him. She wanted desperately to hold his hand, just to reassure herself he was unhurt, but she couldn't. She'd pushed him away. And whether he needed her now or not, she wasn't able to take back the words she'd said to him.

No matter how much Frannie loved him she had to keep it to herself.

She looked around the room. Andra stood beside Nadia Marie, whose gaze was solely on Bolton. She looked like she was about to cry, and while Bolton hadn't made any move to reassure her he was okay, Frannie could see he was more than aware of Nadia Marie's distress over his condition.

Everyone else had been barred from the room, which was telling in and of itself. Still, as much as she wouldn't mind Sonny, Louis, Michael and Hal being here, she was grateful the four men weren't crowding her chair, studying her reaction to Matthias having breathed in the poison.

The doctor had given the two men each a dose of the drug that counteracted the Einetine, but they weren't the only ones affected.

As of minutes before, three people had been brought in because they'd ingested the poisoned water supply. Sheriff Mason had made additional announcements and sent a group of people out to go house-to-house and explain what was happening in case anyone hadn't heard. Director Grant Mason was having more medicine brought in.

No one had died yet, *thank you God*. But several people needed the same treatment Matthias and Bolton had received.

Nadia Marie broke Andra's hold on her arm. "I have to go let my dog out." She rushed to the door and ducked out. Right before it shut behind her, Nadia Marie let out a sob.

Bolton looked at Andra, a question in his eyes.

"You're not invincible, and neither is her brother."

"But I'm here." Bolton didn't look impressed by Andra's explanation. "I'm okay."

"Shad isn't, and there's nothing Nadia can do about it."

Bolton replaced his oxygen mask, then yanked it down. "Am I supposed to do something about it?"

"She knows you can't. That's why she feels helpless. You're fine now. The only connection she has to Shad is through Dauntless." Andra smiled. "And I happen to know she really does have to let the dog out."

Bolton's mouth worked behind the mask.

Frannie looked at Matthias and saw his eyes were on her. She mouthed, *What?* But he shook his head.

John folded his arms. "Bolton can figure out how to get Nadia Marie to sit still long enough for him to court her later—"

"Who said anything about courting?"

Bolton's words were met with immediate motion from John, and Matthias. Before either man could respond, Andra said, "You go after my girl with anything less than that level of respect and I'll bury you where your cows do their business."

Bolton's eyes flicked to her. He looked like he didn't know whether to laugh or be concerned because she was serious. The surprise dissipated, and he nodded. "Understood." He turned to John. "So how are we going to catch Father Wilson?"

"It's not like there are limitless places to hide, and he can't run." Andra shrugged. "It's only a matter of time before someone spots him and we bring him in."

John said, "Hal and the guys called a meeting with the general. They're going to organize teams to search the town and walk the paths. Those who are able will be part of teams hiking the less-accessible areas of the forest. But I'd rather he didn't face down someone with no training who is just going to get hurt."

"He doesn't have any Einetine left." They all turned their attention to her. Frannie felt her cheeks heat. She cleared her throat. "He's done the damage he wanted, even if it didn't work because we got the word out quick enough."

John nodded. "We have to ride that out, and Dan is heading up the team that's cleaning out the water supply, getting it all filtered so it's clear of the poison. I already called Grant with Dan's list of what he needs to do the job all the way, and fast. So we're on top of that, even while it's being worked on." John paused a beat. "But it only means Father Wilson has nothing to lose now, which makes him all the more dangerous. And off his plan."

Bolton lowered his mask. "So do we wait, or do we devise a plan to draw him out?"

"Draw him out."

"Draw him out."

John and Andra looked at each other, sharing a smile which made Frannie's cheeks heat again. Matthias reached out then and touched her fingers with his. She looked at him, and he reached up to pull the mask down.

"You have to leave that on." She wanted to stand, to move to him, but his grip on her hand held her still.

"He didn't intend to kill us. We walked in the room."

Bolton turned to look at Matthias. Out of the corner of her eye, Frannie saw him studying his friend.

"I don't want to talk about that." The fact he'd nearly died was too fresh in her mind. Matthias was trying to say something, but Frannie wanted him to rest. "I don't know what you want, but I don't want Father Wilson anywhere near you."

"He won't be."

Frannie shook her head, but it was John who walked over and said, "What's your plan, Matthias? What are you thinking?"

"Tell him I'm dead."

Frannie said, "It's not like we can text him, and there aren't any carrier pigeon's in town." They couldn't just tell Father Wilson that Matthias was dead.

"Frannie," Bolton said. "Hear him out."

"The play." His gaze bored into her, willing her to understand something she couldn't grasp. "Tell everyone I'm dead." He looked at John. "Have Nigel put it in the newspaper that I died."

Frannie got up from the bed and took two steps back. He was talking about the very same thing she'd been considering earlier. Only she hadn't been able to figure out how it would work.

Frannie pushed aside the fatigue, and the aches and pains, and rubbed her temples, trying to figure this out. "So Nigel puts it in the newspaper. Then what, we have a funeral? What are you going to tell your mom and your sisters?"

"Nothing."

"What do you think he'll do?"

Bolton was the one who said, "Wilson has a thing about headstones. He'll need to come by the graveyard and see Matthias's headstone for himself."

"I don't like it." It'd been her idea, originally. The fact he'd had the same idea said only good things about the affinity between them. But just because she'd wanted to pretend to be dead in order to draw out the killer didn't mean she had to be okay with Matthias doing the same thing. After all, he was lying there still suffering the effects of inhaling Einetine.

Frannie sank into the chair and rubbed her face. "I know why you want to do it, but I'm the one who has to go through the motions. And your family is going to think you're dead." She looked at Matthias. "You really want to do that to them?"

"What if I do it?" Bolton shifted on the bed. "Have Matthias take a turn for the worse, but tell everyone I reacted to the medication and died." He shrugged. "Who's gonna care?"

Andra shot him a look. "I'll talk to her."

"And we can all act really sad, like crying at your funeral." Frannie liked this idea much better than Matthias pretending he was dead. Then she realized what she'd said sounded liked. "Not that we wouldn't be sad if you died."

Bolton's lips twitched. "Don't sweat it, Frannie."

Matthias said, "I like this plan. Frannie and I can stick together, in case Father Wilson comes. Safety in numbers."

He was going to push for them to spend more time with each other? Frannie knew how he felt. It'd been obvious he didn't want her to walk away from him, but what other choice was there? Matthias wanted something she didn't have the time, or the energy, to give him. He wanted forever, and she didn't even know if that was available. But it didn't mean she stopped caring about him.

Frannie didn't want to be alone if Father Wilson was going to come after her again. But that didn't mean she wanted to spend every minute with Matthias—realizing how easily he could have been more seriously hurt today.

John looked between them. "I'll have to convince Nigel."

"And Mimi." Andra's face portrayed how well she

thought that was going to go down. "Nigel has to publish the paper, but Mimi has to not tell everyone..."

"That she's been sleeping with Father Wilson, too."

Everyone looked at Frannie.

"What?" John's voice didn't betray any surprise, just intense curiosity.

"Father Wilson told me...before you came in. He said Mimi thought I would figure it out, but that she was smarter than me—"

Andra stiffened. "She's not."

Frannie shot the woman a smile. "He...implied they were close."

"Which begs the question of how much your mother knew about Father Wilson's activities and never mentioned it to anyone."

Frannie's heart sank. "I knew she was selfish, but knowingly standing by while he murders people?" She blew out a breath. "I had no idea she was even capable of that."

Andra squeezed her shoulder. "John will get to the bottom of it."

"She thinks I can perform miracles." John chuckled, making Frannie smile. "But I'll talk to your mom."

"You mean interrogate her?"

He nodded. "As much as is in my power, I'll find out how far her involvement goes. But first we have to get Nigel to write tomorrow's paper announcing Bolton's death."

"What about Izzy?"

Matthias said, "Or Diego?"

Frannie said, "I can't believe neither of them knew what Mom was up to. They hang out so much. I'd think Izzy, and maybe Diego, too, might've had an idea. Izzy knew she was seeing someone."

"I can talk to them," Andra said. "If they know anything,

I'll find out." John shot her a look that made Andra lift her hands, palms out. "I'll be nice."

John slung his arm around her shoulders, drawing her close to his side.

"Okay, okay." Bolton's protest was coupled with a smile. "Enough of that romantic stuff. I'm busy expiring over here."

Frannie looked at Matthias. He motioned with his fingers, so she walked to his side and set her hand in his. "Are you okay with this?"

She nodded, despite her reservations of spending so much time with him. "I just want Wilson to not hurt anyone else." And if that meant someone pretending to be dead, she wasn't going to argue with the plan. But the fact was, Matthias was too well loved by the town and his family to be the one to be "dead."

Frannie couldn't say the same about herself. The only problem with her being the one to do it—apart from convincing Wilson it was true—was the drama it would cause when Mimi and Izzy were told. Even if they believed her to have been killed, and not that it was a ruse, Frannie's mom and sister would still milk the occasion for all the attention it was worth. It seemed like that was the only reason they did anything.

"Will you stay here with me, until I can go home?"

When he asked like that, his voice soft and him looking so vulnerable lying in a medical center bed, it was impossible to refuse him. Which didn't bode well for the future, however things turned out.

Frannie sucked in a breath and looked around—at her friends. "Can we pray first?"

John nodded, his arm still around Andra. "That sounds like a great idea."

CHAPTER 24

Stella's husband leaned sideways toward her and bumped Frannie's shoulder with his. "She loved you."

Frannie wiped a tear from under her eye. "I loved her, too. Very much."

"I know you did, kiddo. Stella knew that."

Frannie looked at Stella's still, pale form on the bed. "What will you do now?"

Harold swallowed, the weight of his grief evident in the slump of his shoulders. "I'll be escorting the body to Mountain Home Air Force base. After Stella has been cremated, I'm going to go find my son." Silence filled the space between them for a second. "Perhaps he'll be able to say goodbye to her after all."

Frannie slipped her hand into his wrinkled, rough palm and held on. "Is it safe for you to leave Sanctuary?"

He made a sound that was half-laugh, and half-sob. "It's difficult to grasp the risk when you no longer have anything to lose. Let's just pray I get to Steven before it's discovered I'm in the open."

Frannie gave him a small smile. She didn't like what he

was planning to do, or the risks it entailed. But there was no way she could stop him trying to find his son. "I will pray. I do that now."

He smiled back. "I heard."

"There you are." Mimi stood in the doorway, hands on the hips of her rhinestone encrusted denim mini skirt. "I've been looking for you all over."

Frannie squeezed Harold's arm. "Excuse me." She jumped up, bodily forcing her mom out of the doorway just from the speed at which she was walking.

Mimi sputtered. "What are you—"

"That man's wife just passed away." Frannie kept her voice low. "You should have a lot more respect for his grief than the display you just put on. But that would require you to be a decent human being, capable of considering someone other than yourself."

"Ha. Says Little Miss Selfish over here." She motioned to Frannie with her red-tipped fingernails. "You're the one who only thinks about herself."

All the frustration, all the years of working twice as hard so her mom and sister didn't have to feel the effects of her testifying hit Frannie like a tsunami.

"Why are you still here?"

Her mom blinked. Some of the bravado she toted around on those stiletto heels slipped.

"Do you get a rush out of stirring everyone up, playing people against each other and seeing just how far you can push every single one of us?" Frannie folded her arms. "I don't think you get much out of us, except pure amusement. That's what it is, isn't it? You're like that kid with the ant farm. You watch us all trying to make the best of our lives, and you just... poke, for the sake of seeing us scramble. You're in the middle of all of this. Spreading your wares around town like you're the Tuesday special. Nigel, Father Wilson. I'd wonder how many others there were, but I *really* don't want to know." Frannie shook her head. "You knew Father Wilson was a killer, and you never said anything. You made Nigel terrorize Maria—"

"Neither of those little...factoids can be *proven*."

"You need to leave." Frannie took a breath and prayed for strength. "I wonder that you've stayed so long, but it's time for you to get out of Sanctuary. Forever."

"And what about your father? He'll find me and kill me."

Frannie shook her head. "It's me he wants dead."

"I'm supposed to put myself at risk because you don't want me in *your* town?"

"You never wanted to be here in the first place, and you've made that clear every day since. So take the Marshals advice and get a new look. Maybe if you lay low, no one will even notice you."

Frannie knew that was never going to happen, but her mom had to take control of her own life for once.

Mimi's eyes narrowed. "If I'm going to put myself at risk then I'll need some walking around money."

"What?"

"Cash, darlin'. And lots of it."

Frannie gaped. "You want me to pay you to leave?"

"A hundred grand."

Frannie opened her mouth to tell her mom where to go. "Done."

She spun around and saw Matthias using the door jamb to hold himself up. "You can't pay her."

His gaze flicked toward Frannie. "I can."

"You don't have that kind of money."

"And you do?"

Frannie pressed her lips together. If she did, she'd be able to afford to replace her second oven. "Not even after I sell my house. I'll barely break even, and I'm going to spend the rest of my life living above the bakery."

Matthias's eyes flickered. She saw something there that looked a whole lot like a promise, and for once it didn't scare her. The idea of it matched something in her, deep in the place she'd buried trying to convince herself she neither wanted nor needed that kind of connection.

He smiled. "This isn't pity."

"I don't care who pays me. Soon as I get the money, I'm out of here."

"Fine." Matthias, again.

Frannie glanced between them. She knew what that determination on his face meant. She'd seen it on Bolton's, too, and wondered if the two men knew they shared it as a result of their friendship.

Mimi spun around and strode out, her heels clacking all the way down the hall.

Frannie moved to Matthias, wrapping his arm around her shoulder so she could take some of his weight. They walked to the bed and Matthias huffed. "I'm not worse than you are, but thanks."

Frannie waited while he settled back onto the bed. Her whole body did ache, but she wasn't going to hold back from helping him. "Are you trying to tell me you have a hundred grand to spare?"

He held her gaze with his. "Let me do this for you."

Frannie sighed. The newspaper Nigel had produced at the last minute the night before lay on the end of the bed, but Frannie didn't want to read the fictitious story of Bolton's death again. On the bedside table was a copy of a Carl Gabriel novel—the same one he'd been reading at her house.

She sat back on the chair, and closed her eyes.

"You okay?"

"I'm not super excited for Father Wilson to show up here."

"Bolton's hiding out downstairs in the morgue. He'll be ready if Wilson shows up down there to see his handy-work first hand. John and Andra are in position, and Hal and the guys are watching Beth and her mother-in-law, because John thought it might be important."

"Why does he think that?"

Matthias shook his head. "Don't know. But do you know what really has been bugging me?"

"What?"

"The break-in's here at the medical center."

"That was Izzy and Diego, right?"

"I guess, but it just doesn't seem to make sense. I heard Diego mention one, but there were more. Wilson didn't do it. If he brought the Einetine with him, he had no reason to."

"So who did?"

"That's what I'm trying to figure out."

She shifted on the chair and felt her brow crinkle. "Who does John think did it?"

"He was thinking Diego, but I haven't had the chance to ask him more about Harriet Fenton's murder."

"What does the doctor's wife have to do with anything?"

"It was murder."

"And Father Wilson did it, right?"

Matthias shook his head. "There was no picture for Harriet Fenton on Wilson's wall in his room. He didn't take credit for it, and I'm not convinced he did it and just didn't get the chance to put the picture up yet."

"So who did kill Harriet Fenton?"

Matthias's face was dead serious. "The only other person I can think would benefit from her death is Doctor Fenton."

"You think he killed her just because she was rude and a pain in everyone's butts?"

Matthias's mouth twitched.

"Yes, Matthias." The doctor's voice came from the doorway. "Do you think I killed my wife?"

He shifted on the bed, placing himself between Frannie and the doctor. "I'm not the Sheriff." Matthias's voice was steady. "What do you care what I think?"

Fenton held his tablet low in front of him with both hands. "Answering my question with a question. Interesting."

"This isn't a game," Matthias said. "Not when people have died, and other people's lives have been threatened."

"But you think I'm part of it, despite swearing an oath otherwise?"

Matthias kept his attention on the doctor. "That's between you and the sheriff."

"I will not have my good name and my reputation maligned by some too-tanned rancher."

Frannie shot up. "You did not just say that."

Matthias's arm came out, holding her back from stepping between him and the doctor.

"I think you'll find I did." Fenton looked at her. "Too bad, like all of this, you can't prove a thing."

Matthias got off the bed. "However beneath you that you consider me to be, it doesn't negate the fact your wife was murdered."

"So you say. I've heard nothing about a murder. Harriet committed suicide."

"The sheriff never said that was the case." Matthias's stare challenged the doctor to contradict him. "He's always maintained there was more to your wife's murder than a suicide."

Frannie studied the doctor, looking for any sign of grief over Harriet's death. But there was none. She could appreciate the fact he'd needed—or wanted—to continue working even after Harriet died, given he was the only doctor in town.

"Well, thank you for this enlightening discussion." Fenton sneered. "I'm going to return to treating my other patients. Hopefully none of them will accuse me of murder."

"Doc—"

He turned back at the door. "Oh, and it was Bolton's suggestion the two of you return to the ranch."

"You talked to him?"

"I checked on him a few minutes ago under the guise of securing the body."

Frannie didn't envy him that job. Matthias opened his mouth to say something, but she touched his arm. "Thank you, Doctor."

Fenton left.

Matthias turned to her. "You don't have to be nice to a murderer."

She shot him a look. "Maybe I do. You don't know for sure he did it."

"I don't think I'm ever going to understand you. Am I?"

"Do you think maybe we should go back to the ranch?" There was safety here, being alone with him in a semi-public place. The ranch would be more private. Not that she thought she wasn't safe from Matthias—at least not in the danger way.

He studied her, like he saw something on her face. "We could head to my mom's, if you want? Or Maria's. Maybe Mama's there with the boys."

Frannie nodded. "I'd like that."

———

MATTHIAS'S TRUCK was parked outside the medical center, his keys in the visor. But that wasn't why he was grinning.

Frannie wanted to go with him to spend time with his family. That had to mean something good, didn't it? For all the pushing him away she'd done, her actions told him a different story. Past the drama and the pain they'd both known in their lives, she wanted there to be something between them—and whatever it was going to be, it would mean a lot to both. He knew that. He'd probably always known that.

His mom answered Maria's door. Matthias grinned bigger, expecting her to be ecstatic at the sight of Matthias with Frannie's hand in his. But she wasn't. Her eyes were distant in a way he hadn't seen in a lot of years, back to the days he tried not to think about. Days that seemed to be coming up more and more recently.

Olympia put on a forced smile. "Come in, both of you." She latched onto Frannie's arm. "I'm so glad you're here, Precious." Frannie frowned, but let go of Matthias's hand to be pulled close to Olympia's side. "Come into the kitchen, won't you? Matthias, you go greet our guest." She shot him a look he understood instantly.

"Sure, Mama." He leaned close to her and whispered, "The twins?"

"Upstairs."

"And Maria?"

She motioned to the living room with her head.

"Okay." He looked at Frannie and said in a low voice, "Go with her." Frannie's eyes were wide, but he figured she was grasping what was happening. "And call the sheriff."

His mom nodded. "I was just about to when you got here."

"Go, do it now." Matthias strode toward the living room, trying not to betray how rough he felt after having nearly died from inhaling Einetine. His body was sluggish, but he figured he could off-set the effects with enough will power.

But that had been how he'd always done things. Matthias took a breath before he stepped into the living room. *God, I need Your help. I always have, I've just been too stubborn to ask. I'm sorry I waited until the people I love are in trouble. Help me now. Protect us all, especially the boys.*

Father Wilson sat perched on the edge of the couch like this was just another day in Sanctuary, just another pastoral visit. Maria was across from him in the armchair, wringing her hands together and betraying her nervousness.

He wanted to cross the distance between them and punch the man for his audacity, to scream at him to get out of his family's house. But he needed Wilson to stay put until John got there. What on earth was he doing here?

God, this can't be good.

Instead, Matthias planted his feet and said, "Can we help you?"

Maria's head came up, and almost at the same time she stood. Her body shifted like she wanted to move to him, but held herself back for some reason.

"Matthias." Her voice came out high-pitched. She cleared her throat. "Father Wilson came to talk about what happened with Tom and Antonia. He heard about it."

Matthias half expected the man to shrug off the ruse that had gained him entry. He could picture Wilson jolt into action, like a flash of prophetic knowledge, pulling a gun from his jacket and shooting them all. But there were no guns in Sanctuary that weren't accounted for, given it was impossible to sneak one in when all the mail was screened. Whatever this was, there was no way it was going to end peaceably. Even with John on his way. *God, let him be close.*

Matthias lifted his chin, trying to reassure Maria just by being confident even if he was shaking inside. "I'm sure his words will be very soothing, but Father Wilson isn't going to have the chance to perform his pastoral duties today."

Wilson unfolded himself from the couch, his gaze pinning Matthias to the spot. Before the man could say anything, Matthias said, "Why are you here?"

"I would have thought that was obvious, Mr. Hernandez."

"Enlighten me." Matthias only had to get him to talk long enough for John to get there. He wasn't in any condition to restrain the man, though Wilson didn't know that. "Considering you've recently murdered my boss and best friend, I'm all ears. What exactly do you have to say to justify yourself for trying to poison the whole town?"

"Yes." He almost grinned. "That was brilliant. It's a shame no one who deserved to die has actually done so yet."

"Except Bolton."

"Mr. Farrera deserved the judgment for the crimes he has committed."

"The crime of doing the honorable thing?" Regardless of how messed up their pasts were, everyone in town was here for testifying—doing the right thing. Some of the people here were former criminals, sure. But Bolton wasn't like that. "Be that as it may—"

"How dare you." Frannie stood just inside the living room. His mom was behind her, and when their eyes locked, Mama mouthed, *sorry*.

Matthias shook his head. It was better they had all the exits covered than Wilson had another chance to get away. "None of us are interested in hearing this. Why are you really here?"

Wilson grinned then, the sneer of an evil person convinced he'd succeeded in doing exactly what he'd planned. "My genius plan to poison the town didn't work, as well you know. I had to come up with a new plan."

Given his background, Matthias's mind raced through the options of what Wilson could have done.

"There was really only one way to dispose of all the terminal and unstable patients at once. Ms. Hernandez here —" He motioned to Maria. "—will have to accept my apologies for not including her. Your arrival tonight interrupted that plan."

"Get to the point."

Matthias agreed with Frannie. They needed to know what they were dealing with.

Wilson shot her a disgruntled look and flicked out his wrist to check his watch. "You have ten minutes."

John strode past Matthias to Wilson. He said nothing, but his face plainly stated he was not in the mood to be messed around with. He handcuffed the minister's hands behind his back while Wilson sneered at them. "Ten minutes?"

Matthias said, "Ten minutes until you do something to the medical center?"

Wilson nodded, starting to laugh.

John said, "So either you planned to be there to participate, or it's on a timer." Matthias shot John a questioning look to which he replied, "I was in the hall for the last five minutes."

Wilson didn't say anything, his low chuckle audible now.

Matthias strode over to stand eye-to-eye with a man he'd respected for a lot of years. A man who had only been lying to all of them when he pretended to be upright and righteous. "You planted a bomb at the medical center."

The women gasped. Frannie paled, but Matthias couldn't go to her. As much as he wanted to.

"Where is it?"

Wilson's body shook with amusement. "Tick. Tick. Tick. Boom."

Matthias hit the front door at a run.

———

Nadia Marie didn't much like being out of the loop. So here she was walking the streets of Sanctuary after eleven at night, on a Wednesday, trying to convince herself she was just exercising the dog.

Dauntless strained against his leash, eager to be moving around. The dog always wanted to be somewhere else, permanently on a mission to do something...or he was sleeping. That was it, just those two modes: work and unconscious.

Nadia Marie let Dauntless lead her to the medical center. She'd probably have to tie him up outside if she wanted to go in. Not that she should be looking for Bolton when he was supposed to be dead. Everyone in town likely expected her to be distraught, so if they were going to pull this off she should probably act her part.

Still, she wasn't about to leave Dauntless outside by himself.

It no longer bothered her the town knew. Not the depth of her feelings for the mysterious rancher—they couldn't know that. But it was expected for her to be grief-stricken at Bolton's death. Even though by some silent agreement they'd barely spoken. Something was holding Bolton back from pursuing her. That was all she could figure. She wasn't happy about it, but it wasn't like they didn't have forever ahead of them.

The closer she got to the medical center the more Dauntless strained against his leash. At the front door he ducked his nose to the ground and turned right, making his way around the building to a side door that was a fire exit. He sat. Barked once.

Nadia Marie looked at him. "Was that a question, or a statement?"

Dauntless cocked his head to the side.

"Fine." She tried the door, and it swung out. No alarm sounded. Had someone disabled the bar on the door that triggered the warning noise whenever someone used it?

Dauntless rushed in, nose to the floor.

"Whoa." Nadia Marie was dragged along behind him. "Dauntless, stop." She tried to remember what she was supposed to say. "Uh... Fuss. Dauntless, fuss." But the command to heel didn't mean much when he was determined to find what he was looking for.

He dragged her around the corner, and Bolton stepped into the hall at the far end.

"Nadia. The sheriff said Wilson is at Maria's house." His eyes flicked to the dog, who had sped up. "What are you..."

She and Dauntless got all the way to the door of the storage closet. Dauntless sat and barked once.

"Oh, no." Bolton ripped open the door to the closet.

Before she even got the chance to look inside, he was pushing her. "There's no time. Oh, God. All these people."

Nadia stumbled. Bolton grabbed her around the waist and lifted her, running and bearing her weight. She looked over his shoulder. "Dauntless! Hier!"

The dog raced after them.

They were almost to the end when all the air was sucked out of the hall, pulling Nadia's hair across her face. The fire started at the closet, rushing out toward them like an action-movie bomb exploding in slow motion.

They were going to die.

CHAPTER 25

Frannie gripped the dash as Matthias sped down Main Street, her eyes on the column of black smoke trailing up to the sky. She'd heard the boom and so had everyone else, judging by the amount of people running after the truck.

When the medical center came into view, all she could do was stare. The windows had been blown out. Glass littered the sidewalk out front while smoke and flames poured from the windows. Fire was bad under normal circumstances. Fire in Sanctuary was ten times worse. Their fire department—which consisted of volunteers—were among the crowd, and she saw Maria's husband Tom already yelling orders to his team as they sprinted up.

Xander ran out the front door, his white shirt blackened from smoke, carrying an older woman wearing a hospital gown in his arms. Both of them were coughing, and Xander had a cut on his forehead trailing blood down the right side of his face.

Matthias pulled up and jumped out. "I have a blanket. Put her in the back." He lowered the tailgate and spread the blanket so Xander could lay the woman down. She didn't look good.

Frannie looked at the building. "Where's the doctor?"

Xander shook his head, his eyes glassy. "I don't know."

Matthias grabbed the big man's arms. "Stay here."

Frannie ran after Matthias, not about to let him go in there alone. Tom and another guy yelled after them, but Frannie just ran. People were stuck in there, people who might not be able to get themselves out.

Flames licked the furniture in the waiting area. Smoke laced the air with black clouds that smelled like tar. Frannie lifted her shirt collar to cover her mouth and held it there. She followed Matthias, one hand on his shoulder, over to the single hallway that led to the rooms. They reached the reception desk, and she looked behind it.

Doctor Fenton lay on the floor, blood pooling from the back of his head. Frannie's knees hit the tile beside him, and she pressed two fingers to his throat.

Nothing.

She swallowed. "I think he's dead."

Matthias put his hand on her shoulder. "Go back out and get help. We'll need to take him outside anyway."

————

MATTHIAS WATCHED her disappear into the smoke and then turned back to search for Bolton. Visibility was so bad his eyes blurred and watered, stinging from the toxic air.

His foot hit a solid object that grabbed him. Matthias crouched, finding his boss on the floor. Bolton's eyes flew open. "Nadia..."

Matthias surveyed him, trying not to think about any number of injuries he'd sustained that couldn't be seen.

Bolton's face was blackened, there was a knot on the side of his forehead and his lip was split.

"Nadia."

"I'll have someone go find her for you, but first we have to get you out of here. Can you walk?"

Bolton grabbed his arm, squeezing Matthias with more strength than anyone should have when they'd just been blown up. "Nadia's...here."

Ice settled in Matthias's stomach. He crawled past Bolton, the direction his boss indicated, and found her clutching the German Shepherd. Why was she at the medical center? How many other people were here and no one even knew?

Bolton slid across the floor, dragging his lower body behind him. He leaned close, wincing, and studied both Nadia and Dauntless. Apparently satisfied, Bolton lay back with his eyes closed. "Get them out of here."

Matthias didn't like the sound of that. "I'll be back for you A-SAP."

He didn't know how he was going to get both the woman and the animal out, but his only regret was he couldn't take Bolton, too. Where was someone to help him? There'd been a crowd of people outside. Apparently, no one had followed them in.

Matthias coughed into his sleeve. The air was getting bad. "Can you walk?"

Bolton shook his head. "Tell whoever comes in they'll need a backboard, or a stretcher."

He rolled fractionally onto his side and lifted the back of his shirt. The skin there was red and warped, gnarled by scars that covered his entire lower back. Matthias sucked in a breath. Bolton rolled to his back and looked at Matthias, daring him to show pity.

"Ouch."

Bolton's lips twitched. "You have no idea."

Matthias had a million questions about what his boss had gone through in his old life, and why he'd chosen to share now, but it was totally not the time. "I'll get them out of here and be back myself."

Bolton nodded. "I'll be here. Praying the building doesn't fall down on me."

Matthias lifted Nadia and the dog. He gritted his teeth and blocked out the weight of them, the strain on his arms and shoulders. He kept walking until he tasted fresh air.

Andra gasped and ran over. "John went inside with Frannie to look for Bolton."

"Where's Wilson?"

People were everywhere. Their volunteer firefighters—who included his brother-in-law Tom—had hooked up hoses to the water supply and were starting to spray down the building.

"John left him in the jail cell." Andra shifted to avoid the spray from the hoses. "Don't get the water in your mouth."

"I have to get back to Bolton." Matthias looked at Nadia, being assessed by a man and a woman who were both former military. He glanced back at Andra and shook his head.

She leaned close, yelling over the crowd and the noise. "Don't get the water in your mouth."

"The Einetine?"

She nodded. "If your hands get wet, don't rub your face. The water's tainted but they have to put the fire out."

Matthias nodded, turned and ran back toward the building. He had no idea where Frannie was, but prayed she knew to be careful of the water. Rising smoke would get trapped in the air above the basin Sanctuary sat in. With the height of the ring of mountains, it took a significant weather system to clear out any cloud cover. Inversions were something they dealt with regularly, and smoke would be way worse.

———

FRANNIE KNELT BESIDE JOHN. "What can we do?"

Bolton gritted his teeth. "Whatever it is, do it fast. I can't go anywhere. You'll have to carry me, and my spine has to stay completely straight."

Frannie bit her lip. It probably took the big rancher a lot to admit he was basically helpless. She wracked her brain, trying to remember where stuff was kept in here and how to get to it.

How could Wilson have blown up the medical center? He had no consideration for the people who would get hurt while he was killing, or those who needed treatment and now had no medical center—or doctor.

John looked up from Bolton and shook his head. "We need a backboard."

Frannie jumped up and ran for the supply closet. Two people exited a room, slamming into her. They didn't slow down, just kept moving for the front door. She didn't blame them given the circumstances, but still. "Be careful! Bolton Farrera's on the floor!"

Frannie felt her way past the worst of the building's damage to the closet. Cans and bottles had tipped off the shelves and left a toxic smell. She grabbed a backboard that wasn't warped from heat damage and prayed it was strong enough to hold the big rancher's weight. Had he fallen? She didn't even know why he couldn't walk.

They rolled Bolton together, very carefully, and then Frannie lifted her end of the board. John led the way outside, where firefighters moved their spray angle to allow them to pass. Still, the mist of water hit them anyway. Frannie held one hand over Bolton's nose and mouth while the muscles on her other arm screamed in protest.

Matthias grabbed a hold of the backboard, taking the weight from her. "Are you okay?"

Frannie nodded. "Nadia?"

"Dazed, but she seems good. Dauntless, too. He won't back up long enough for Nadia to be examined."

"Who's the doctor?"

"Remy apparently has a medical degree."

The woman in question ran up, latex gloves on her hands. She was wearing cargo shorts and a drab T-shirt with bright red suspenders. On her feet were ugly sandals, and her eyes were wild behind her red-rimmed glasses matching her shoulder-length frizzy hair.

John and Matthias slid the backboard onto the back of Bolton's truck, parked farther up from Matthias's. Nadia Marie looked up from her spot to watch, while Dauntless didn't take his attention off her. Remy climbed up. All her usual awkwardness dissipated as she got close to Bolton's face and they had a low conversation.

After a quick minute, Remy removed Bolton's shoes and ran her knuckles up and down the soles of his bare feet. Matthias stepped in Frannie's line of vision, his face fierce as he stared down at her.

She frowned. Was he okay? "Are you—"

His wrapped her up in a hug that lifted her feet off the floor. Frannie sucked in a breath, and her throat clogged with tears.

"Matthias."

He leaned back. "We're okay. Wilson's in custody, and your mom is going to leave town."

"What about Bolton? People died tonight. Why are you happy?"

"I don't know what's wrong, but I know he's going to be okay. He has to be."

Frannie put her hand on his cheek then. "How can you be optimistic after everything that's happened?"

His arms tightened for a second. "This is why."

Before she could register what was happening his head descended and his warm lips touched hers. Things were far from over, but if this was an indication of what was to come, Frannie would hardly be in a position to complain.

He stilled the kiss, waiting beat after beat while their lips touched but neither of them moved. She could feel his breath on her cheeks—long, cleansing exhales that relaxed her. Frannie wasn't going to ask what he was doing. It would break a moment so sweet she wanted to cry.

Finally he eased back, his lips curled in a slight smile. Frannie studied his face and the steadfast love she saw there.

"You never doubted, did you?"

Matthias shook his head. "It was hard at times, but no. Not once."

"I think that's why I love you."

He bent his knees, lifted her and spun her around, his face buried in the hair at her neck. Someone whistled, but Frannie didn't look to see who'd done it. Matthias set her on her feet and released her to touch the sides of her face. "I love you, too."

Frannie grinned. "I've waited a long time for you to say that to me."

"It won't be the last time. Not by far."

Frannie looked around then. She saw Nadia Marie stroking Dauntless, her eyes on Matthias and Frannie, grinning wide before she turned to maintain her watch on Bolton. Andra had climbed up onto the truck bed beside her, with

John's son Pat and Aaron, the special young man who delivered the mail and had a room at John's house.

Frannie looked beyond them to the crowd of people watching to make sure everyone got out of the medical center alive. The firefighters, working despite the risk of being exposed to the chemical from the water they were using.

These people, this town. She hadn't known before she came here she'd been searching for something—a home, a God who loved her enough to die for her, a man who had stuck with her throughout all the craziness of the last few weeks. And a group of people who had their foibles, but who she was proud to call family.

She looked back at Matthias, pulling his head close so she could kiss him quickly. "Let's go see who else needs help."

———

JOHN WALKED through puddles of poisoned water, praying no one was harmed by exposure. So far a couple of people had been coughing, but Remy had organized a group to take them to the Meeting House. All the medical equipment in town was damaged, but a couple of older folks had volunteered their oxygen tanks. Remy had also explained an elaborate decontamination procedure for those who'd touched the water. John figured if it saved someone's life, it was worth it.

The fire was out. The building had been cleared. There wasn't much left but to figure out how he could have prevented this.

Andra's fingers laced between his, and she smiled up at him. "Need anything?"

John looked around at the chaos and shook his head. "I already put in a call to Grant and explained what happened. There's a chopper on its way for Mr. and Mrs. Carlyle."

"It's that bad?"

"Mrs. Carlyle's room was two doors away from the closet where Wilson planted the bomb. Both she and her husband were pinned under debris from the ceiling. Remy suspects they both have internal bleeding."

"Will they be okay?"

John drew her to him, more for his own comfort than for hers. All of these people had become important to him since he arrived, months ago. Now he was going to lose some of them. "They need surgery, but it'll be hours before they get it."

Andra ducked her head and pressed her forehead to his chest. John held on, squeezing his eyes shut.

"Sheriff?"

Tom stood in front of him, but John didn't let go of Andra. The firefighter cleared his throat. "Fire's out. Once Dan gets us decontaminated water we'll wash everything down. Remy gave me the name of a chemical that will kill all traces of Einetine. Dan has the compounds, and she says she can make it."

"Can it clear the water?"

Tom shook his head. "It can't be consumed, so we can rinse the buildings and the street with it so it doesn't seep back into the water table. But it can't be put into the water that's fed to residences."

"Okay." The genius-IQ woman had been a gift of God. They wouldn't have been able to get through the night without her.

"What about the building?"

"My advice would be, don't let anyone inside. We have no idea if it's structurally sound unless we can get an engineer in here to assess the damage."

John nodded. "I'll let Director Mason know, see what he

says. I'll also get some tape and rope it off so no one goes inside."

Tom shot a sideways glance at where Maria stood by her mother and sons, and then walked away in the opposite direction.

The mayor stood at the edge of the crowd, an almost pleased expression on his face. John hadn't seen the man much since his wife had been killed weeks ago, and he'd blamed Andra for it. Despite his attempts to draw the man out and get him to reconnect, the mayor hadn't responded. John had figured it was just grief keeping him apart from a town getting on with their lives, but it could be something more. He would have to keep his eye on that.

Beth and Abigail were here also, along with their old-man protection detail. John needed more information from his brother about the president and Susan's death. They would also have to prepare for the SEAL's arrival. That was a sticky situation if ever he'd been in one. The red tape alone was like a spider-web of complications. But if it kept them safe, so be it.

Andra walked with him to Nadia, still in the back of Matthias's truck. The lovebirds were there, too, hugging each other and not paying much attention to anything else. Dauntless sat beside Nadia, ears pricked knowing something was going on.

Remy strode over and hopped up beside Nadia. "Sorry it took so long to get to you. How are you?"

Nadia blinked. "I don't think I've ever heard you say that many words at once."

Remy laughed, a tinkly-bell sound. "It seems like a night for firsts all around. How are you feeling?"

"Bruised, but not worse than that. Thank God."

Remy nodded. "You have someone who can stay with you tonight?"

"That's me," Andra said. "I'm staying with her until the wedding."

"Right." Remy didn't especially look like she thought the idea of anyone getting married was a good idea. She shined a pencil flashlight in Nadia's eyes. "If you get any dizziness, nausea, disorientation, slurred speech, any of those things, let me know. I'll be by my phone."

Nadia nodded. Andra said, "Got it."

John gave his wife-to-be a squeeze, but asked Remy, "How's Bolton?"

She glanced at the rancher, a frown suddenly marring the skin above her hideous glasses. "He needs tests from equipment I have no access to, but he's refusing to leave Sanctuary for treatment. He wants to wait until the swelling goes down and accept the consequences of his injuries." She sighed. "He has some sensation in his feet and legs. There could be more when the bruises heal, or he could be immobile."

Nadia Marie gasped.

"It's an old injury, but that's all I can tell you."

Apparently sensing the gravity of what was happening, Dauntless shifted his head to sniff Remy's hair. She chuckled. "Don't get fresh with me, boyo." She pushed his muzzle away, froze, and then turned her full attention to the dog.

Seconds later, she shook off her reaction and said goodbye.

John looked around, but no one had seemed to notice. Matthias and Frannie were oblivious to anything but each other.

Andra caught his gaze and nodded slightly. John shrugged with his mouth.

A helicopter flew overhead. Even in the darkness it was obviously a military chopper.

"Gotta go."

Andra pulled him close for a kiss. "I'll be praying for the Carlyle's."

"As will I."

———

REMY STRODE BACK to the spot where the Carlyle's lay ready to be transported to hospital. She would pray they made it, but they might not want to. She didn't pay much attention to the people in Sanctuary, choosing instead to concentrate on her work. If that made her awkward and anti-social, so be it. She was at her limit of what she could handle from people.

But the dog? That was a whole other story.

He'd recognized her scent—that much had been obvious from his reaction to her. She didn't know why, but it pleased her the animal remembered.

She couldn't forget.

When every piece of information she'd ever taken on board was stored in her brain, the one thing that eclipsed it all was a pair of dark brown eyes. She should be above it, and the fact she wasn't grated on her. Romance wasn't part of any equation. Infatuation, regardless of the fact it refused to die, wasn't going to get her anywhere.

Not when the report said that he was missing in action.

———

JOHN SAW the helicopter off and then drove back to the sheriff's office. It was going to be a long night writing reports and talking to people who didn't plan on sleeping because a bomb had just gone off in their town.

Tomorrow he and Andra were supposed to have another pre-marriage counseling session with Dan. John twisted the door handle, wondering if the farmer was going to take over leadership of the church. It seemed like a simple enough idea to him, since Dan had been doing a lot of the heavy lifting already. Now Wilson had been exposed as a killer, it made a whole lot more sense. But maybe it was more complicated than Dan just taking over the position. What did John know about church leadership?

The office smelled. John's gut clenched, knowing immediately what had happened. Father Wilson hung from the bars in the cell, his feet hanging inches off the ground. John covered the distance between them with no rush, knowing it was too late.

He was dead. Wilson had killed himself. Hung from his cell with his own shoelaces.

John rubbed his face with his hands and reached for his phone.

It was going to be a really long night.

CHAPTER 26

Matthias perched on the dresser in Bolton's room where his friend was laid up on the bed. "Were you ever going to tell me?"

Bolton didn't look happy, but he also didn't shift like he was going to be evasive. Probably because he couldn't move. "Maybe. Probably." He scrubbed his hands over his face. "I doubt it."

"We've worked together for years. I could have taken some of your duties so you didn't have to face the threat of being paralyzed every single day."

"But I didn't get hurt ranching, I got hurt because the medical center exploded."

Matthias studied his friend, laid up for at least a week or two waiting for the swelling in his spine to go down. "I really don't think this is safe. What if something goes wrong?"

"It's not ideal, I'll give you that. But it's the best I've got, Matt." Bolton shrugged one shoulder. "I can't leave Sanctuary. Ever. Not even for a major medical emergency. The threat is sufficient no one can even *see* me outside this town."

"Seriously?"

He nodded.

"Wow." Matthias scratched the back of his head. "So you just lay here, and I pray?"

Bolton's face morphed into a half-smile that said he was definitely up to something. "I'll need some T-L-C, of course."

"Let me guess, Nadia's coming over?"

"I can't be alone, you know."

"Right." Matthias huffed out a laugh. The man was incorrigible. "All this time and you're using an injury to get her here?"

Bolton pretended to be offended. "I'm hurt over here."

"And I'm perfectly able to help you."

"Sure, I'll need you for the...uh, delicate stuff." It probably galled the big man he couldn't use the bathroom or shower by himself. "But I'll need someone to bring me meals. And keep me company."

"In your bedroom." Matthias shot his boss a look.

"She's made the boundaries clear. That's why Dan's coming, too. There's actually a whole schedule your mom worked up, as well as Remy checking in every day."

"Good." The rancher was usually so removed from town, rarely driving the short distance unless there was a meeting or other community event he couldn't get out of. Unless, like rehearsals, Nadia was part of it.

Matthias was glad he was relying on people, because if personal experience had taught him one thing it was that he could be around people his whole life and never really connect. Not until he made the decision to let them in.

"I should go and check on Frannie."

Bolton waved him off. "Fine."

A dog barked from the front of the house.

"Sounds like your company is here."

Bolton huffed. "That dog doesn't like me at all. He's pushed me away twice."

———

THE BAKERY KITCHEN was packed Friday morning. Frannie stood elbow-to-elbow with women from town, all pitching in to help her fill the Thanksgiving orders. The room was saturated with the smell of apple pie, pumpkin pies and all kinds of bread for rolls.

Frannie looked up from her cheesecake filling at Olympia, making some kind of complicated Greek dessert she'd never heard of.

Matthias was at the door, arms folded and leaning against the frame. He shot her a wink and several women in the room sighed.

Frannie's shoulders shook, and she smiled. "Come in."

All of her assistants were doing a wonderful job. She almost didn't need to be back in the kitchen, a fact which would have bothered her only a week ago. Frannie removed her apron and smoothed back strands that had come loose from her pony tail. She washed her hands at the sink and then said, "I'm going to go out front. Give me a shout if you need anything."

Her helpers waved her off, and Frannie went out to the packed customer area. Despite the small crowd, the noise level was surprisingly low. She spotted Beth and Abigail in the center, ensconced at a table surrounded by people giving condolences.

Frannie ducked back into the kitchen and pulled a chilled bottle from the fridge and grabbed a stack of small clear-plastic cups. She set them on the table between Beth and Abigail.

"Everyone grab a cup. Let's make a toast."

Beth looked up, tears in her eyes. Abigail smiled, but it was plain she didn't know what to make of the people in Sanctuary. Frannie poured a cup for everyone in the room and then lifted her glass. The kitchen doors swished open, and all of her helpers poured out to watch.

Frannie lifted her cup. "Susan Sheraton was a wonderful woman I was proud to call my friend."

The room was silent.

"And I never met the president, but he seemed like a pretty cool guy."

A ripple of chuckles moved through the room, and Beth smiled.

Frannie lifted her cup higher. "Here's to parents who love fiercely and without condition. To people who stand up for what they believe in and have the courage to make our world a better place."

Beth and Abigail both stood.

"To Susan and Thomas." Everyone in the room echoed the words. Beth moved to Frannie, circling her with slender arms.

"Thank you."

Frannie smiled, trying not to get choked up. "You're very welcome."

Matthias came over and pulled her into his side and whispered, "Good job."

"You really think the world is like that?"

Everyone turned. Mimi stood in the doorway in her trademark outfit. But Frannie was not in the mood for another showdown, least of all one that took place in public.

Mimi set one hand on her hip. "The world you live in isn't a real place, it's nothing more than a childish fantasy. No one "makes the world a better place" like that. They're all just in it for themselves. Nothing more."

Frannie shook her head. "It's Sanctuary."

Mimi really wanted to do this where everyone could see them?

Frannie said, "It is a real place, where good people live." And finally she felt like she was one of them. "Maybe it's not the world you're used to, but I want to live here." She slipped her arm around Matthias's waist and hugged him back. "I want to build a family here."

"Father Wilson was a murdering psycho. He tried to kill you!" For the first time it almost seemed like her mom actually cared she'd been hurt.

"If he hadn't tried, I would never have had the opportunity to hear Dan tell me about what Jesus did." Her mom started to roll her eyes, but Frannie wasn't going to stop. "He told me what a great sacrifice it was, all because God loves me." Frannie took a breath. "I know you don't want to admit you need help, but I've found peace. I feel secure now, and I know my strength isn't enough. God's strength is what brought me through this, not my faith in myself."

"You're right. I don't want to hear it." Mimi's hard stare flicked through the room and came back to rest on Matthias. "I've already started the paperwork. As soon as I get my money I'm out of here."

The door clicked shut behind her.

"She's never going to yield, is she?"

Matthias's soft gaze was all for her. "Maybe not, but it doesn't mean you stop believing it's possible."

Louis strode over. Frannie saw him beside them and jerked around. "You need something?"

He motioned with his head to where her mom had gone.

"You want me to whack her before she leaves? Or after. I still have connections."

"Uh, no. But thank you for your kind offer."

He nodded. "No problem."

Sonny came to stand by him, looking down at Louis like a king does an unruly subject. Louis slinked away, and Sonny turned to her. "Money?"

Frannie leaned in to Matthias's body. He said, "We're fine."

"However much it is, the chamber of commerce will pay half."

"No, you won't." Matthias shook his head. "I've got it covered, but if you want to help, Frannie needs a new oven."

"Tias!"

He lifted one eyebrow.

Frannie sighed. "He's right. I didn't want to ask for help, but I guess its past time to admit I need it."

Sonny touched her face then, something he'd never done before. "Don't do that again." He walked away, leaving Frannie to listen to the rumble of laughter in Matthias's chest.

"He's right, you know. If we're going to build that family you'll need more staff." Matthias's face dared her to challenge him.

"I wanted to do this on my own. The guys approached me initially. They helped out, investing so I could buy the bakery. I paid the loan off as fast as I could, and I promised myself I wouldn't ask them for more money."

"Maybe in the real world. But this is Sanctuary." His eyes gleamed. "We help each other out here."

"I know that."

"Which is why I think you should hire me as your office manager. I'll do all the books, invoices, accounting. All of it. And I can split my time between here and the ranch."

Frannie eyed him. "And how am I supposed to pay you? You'll need it, after you've given all your money to my mother." She still wasn't happy about Matthias funding her mom's departure, but Mimi wouldn't be able to ask for more, and he'd said he was comfortable giving it to her.

"You can just give me a kiss every day. At least for now."

Frannie laughed. "You realize that's extortion."

His head descended. "Only if you report me to the sheriff."

The rotors of a helicopter spinning rose in volume until Frannie could hear it over the hum of conversation in the room.

"Looks like Grant is here." Matthias looked at his watch.

"You have something you need to do? You don't have to stay here all day if you don't want to."

Matthias kissed her cheek. "I would love to stay here all day, but I need to go see a man about a thing."

"Uh...okay." Frannie laughed. "I'll see you later?"

"You certainly will."

***

Grant strode through the sheriff's office and sat in John's chair. John raised his eyebrows, but his brother just shot him a look like: *what are you going to do about it?*

John sat in the chair that would be his deputy's—if he had one. "We'll bury the doctor here next week...and Wilson. There's no need for the bodies to be taken out of town. How are Mr. and Mrs. Carlyle doing?"

"Mrs. Carlyle didn't make it through surgery."

John groaned.

"Mr. Carlyle is hanging on, but it doesn't look good."

John wanted to swear, but that was his old way of reacting. Good thing God didn't mind him being disappointed in the outcome. God wasn't surprised by it. *Help us heal from this.* All totaled there were a dozen minor injuries, two major ones—Bolton and Mr. Carlyle—and three dead. It wasn't the outcome John would have preferred, but he could only roll with what he'd been dealt.

Grant shifted in his chair. "I'll scout around WITSEC for another doctor I can transfer in, but right now you're going to have to put up with as much as the nurses can do. Remy's expertise should be saved for trauma. I'll talk to Mountain Home Air Force base and see if they can send a doctor with the mail transport. That way you'll at least get a few hours a week of clinic."

John nodded. "I'll tell the nurses to set up appointments. They can use the Meeting House until the medical center is rebuilt."

Pat's footsteps bounded down the stairs from the apartment they'd renovated, followed more sedately by Aaron. They were a strange friendship, a nine year old boy and a twenty-two year old man, but in this instance it worked.

"Uncle Grant!" Pat dived on John's older brother, causing a pang of guilt in John over the fact his son hadn't seen much of his extended family outside of secure phone calls in weeks now. Hopefully they'd be able to get together over the holidays. Security permitting. John and Pat couldn't leave, and getting multiple members of their family there under the radar would be interesting. At least most of them would be there for the wedding.

Grant gave him a long squeeze and ruffled his hair, then shook hands with Aaron. "How are you, Aaron?"

The young man with unkempt hair and a jumble of teeth in his mouth held out his hand, his gaze darting around the room. "All Aaron."

John chuckled. Grant looked at him and nodded. Aaron had been doing well lately and still loved his job as the mailman.

"Dad!" Pat jumped over, his energy level making John feel tired and old in comparison. "We're going to play at Reuben and Simeon's because Olympia said they need to have fun since their mom and dad aren't talking to each other. We're going to help them write letters to Santa!"

"Awesome." John hugged his son. "Have fun."

The door shut behind them and Grant said, "He seems to be enjoying himself."

John nodded. "Beth is a good teacher."

"She'd have to be, after the last teacher abducted Pat and held him at knife-point." John didn't share his brother's smile. Grant cleared his throat. "What time are you expecting Beth and Mrs. Myerson here?"

John checked his watch. "Any minute. How's Mom?"

"Fine."

"And Nate?"

"He says he's fine, but I think his knee is bothering him. Mom said he was talking about having to have surgery."

Nate was the quarterback for the Miami Dolphins. Having surgery not halfway through the season could be detrimental to his contract and the team's chances. "That's rough."

"Ben's last contact was six hours ago. The mission was in Syria, so he's making his way to intercept Lieutenant Myerson and his team. For now, he's dark until he finds Samuel. Then I'll meet them for a sit down."

"Very good."

John still didn't know precisely what Ben did to earn a livable wage. Or maybe he had enough money already, and he didn't need to work for pay. That was possible. There were some mercenary gigs that paid a lot, but John had always kind of figured his brother was one of the good guys. Like CIA, or whatnot. Maybe that was just wishful thinking.

Whatever he did, Ben had a whole lot of skills that surpassed even what a Navy SEAL was capable of.

Beth tapped on the door. She smiled, but her eyes were sad. She'd been quiet even before her parents were killed, but if possible she was even more subdued now.

"Come in."

Abigail followed her, clutching her purse to her side. She gave him a polite nod.

"How are you?"

Beth settled in the waiting area, which was a solid six feet from his desk where Grant sat. She sent John's brother a smile while Abigail walked over and presented her hand to be shook by the director of the US Marshals.

Grant was a perfect gentleman. "Mrs. Myerson."

"Has my son been located?"

Grant waved her to a chair. "I'll know as soon as he has, and I'll pass the information along to Sheriff Mason. After that it will only be hours until he arrives."

"If he wants to come."

Everyone glanced at Beth. John wondered if maybe she hadn't always been so subdued. Perhaps this Beth was only reacting to what had happened in her life...and her marriage.

Beth sat a little straighter in the chair, assuming the stance of someone born to privilege—something she didn't need much of in Sanctuary. "It's up to Sam if he wants to be here. I don't want him pressured into coming. He has to be given the choice."

Grant's gaze was steady on her. "His life is in danger even if he knows nothing about the threat that exists against you. He needs to be protected, just as you do."

"He's a SEAL, director. I'm sure he can take care of himself."

"Be that as it may, witness protection is the safest option. Whoever killed your parents will turn to other sources to discover your location."

He was downplaying it, given they didn't even know if the president and his wife had given up the location of Sanctuary before they were killed.

"They didn't tell anyone about Sanctuary. They wouldn't have." Beth's façade looked so brittle it was in danger of snapping at any moment. "My father was military. My mother was the strongest woman I ever knew. There is no way they'd have given me up, even under threat of torture."

John's eyes widened. They hadn't told Beth about that, but apparently she'd figured it out.

"It's not rocket science, gentlemen. They were murdered, along with their entire protective detail. Why else, but for my location?" Beth paused. "When you find Sam, I don't want him to be pressured. I don't need a husband who's only here out of guilt, and neither does this baby need a father who feels that way."

Grant said, "I'll give him the choice."

"I don't want him here if he doesn't want to be part of this." Beth laid a hand low on her stomach where her pregnancy wasn't yet obvious.

Abigail glanced between them, but she didn't say anything. She and Beth had either had this conversation, or they were going to have it later in private.

Grant popped open his briefcase and pulled out a CD in a paper sleeve. He set it on the desk. "I had the funeral recorded."

Beth stilled. "Were you able to attend?"

He nodded. "It was beautiful."

"Thank you."

Grant nodded again, and there was a long moment of silence before he said, "I'm resuming Sanctuary's internet access, effective immediately. The threat against you is still very real, but the people here need the limited contact they get with the outside world beyond snail mail."

Beth said, "I understand. It will make school easier if we can check in with the online public school program we're using."

"We're still operating at heightened security, though. And I'm not reading the president in."

John had never met the new president, formerly the vice president. And had only spoken to Beth's father a handful of times. This new commander-in-chief was an unknown quotient who could either reinforce everything they were doing in Sanctuary and help keep these people safe, or he could undermine it all and put them in danger.

"President Gunderson is a good man, but he's old school. He doesn't like conspiracies, or anything he can't stick his finger into." Beth gave Grant a slight smile. "I could speak with him, if you want. Explain the particulars of Sanctuary."

Grant shook his head. "Thank you for offering. I don't want either of you to worry. We'll keep you safe. All you need to do is live your lives, love this baby. And if Sam comes, promise me you'll honor his choice."

Beth looked like she wanted to object, but Grant continued. "I know you didn't ask for this life, or for any of this to happen. But Sanctuary is a good town full of good people."

John smirked, remembering how he'd teased his brother months ago about writing the brochure. Grant was good at his job. The threats against Sanctuary were many, and they were real. But conversely he had also built something here people valued, a community of friends and families who cared for each other.

Beth smiled, shaking her head. "I know that. You're right, I didn't choose this. But if I'd have known, then I would have. I would have chosen Sanctuary as the place I wanted to raise my family."

"So long as we get a doctor to deliver it," Abigail said.

John chuckled. "Yes, ma'am."

John had the feeling Beth's mother-in-law was going to prove to be a firecracker. Even if she had agreed to live here for an indeterminate period of time, which could very well end up stretching into the rest of her life, Abigail wasn't going to let anything get past her.

The two women left, and John and Grant stood on the sidewalk watching them walk away. A crowd of people hung around the bakery and other spots on Main Street. Life was continuing, even after the events of recent days. Construction had started on rebuilding the medical center, putting many of the residents to work where they'd previously been between jobs.

"I should go. The helicopter will be ready to leave in a few minutes."

John hugged his brother. "Christmas?"

"You think I'd miss your wedding?" Grant scoffed. "Where is your fiancé, anyway? I haven't seen her."

John scowled. "Go home to your wife, where she can keep you out of trouble."

Grant scratched his clean-shaven chin. "Maybe I'll stop by Nate's on the way."

"Because Miami is between Idaho and D.C.?"

"I just want to make sure he's okay, and I have some business in the neighborhood."

"Whatever, just take care. And don't stay away too long, Genevieve will be wondering where you are."

"She wants me to retire."

John lifted his eyebrows.

"I'm thinking about it."

"Who will replace you?"

"That's what I'm thinking about."

John didn't even want to know how hard it would be to break in someone new. "But I've barely settled in."

"I know." Grant's chest puffed out. "You need me."

"Don't fool yourself. Any old dude could replace you."

Grant took a playful swing, and John ducked.

EPILOGUE

Two Weeks Later

THE MEETING HOUSE WAS PACKED. Nearly everyone from town had turned out for Thanksgiving dinner, dressed in their "special occasion" clothes. After they all ate, the tables would be cleared away and the projection screen would be lowered from the ceiling so those who wanted could spend the rest of the afternoon napping in front of a football game.

Matthias put his arm on the back of Frannie's chair. Without breaking her conversation with Nadia Marie and Andra, who sat across the table, she leaned into his side. He looked around at people finishing up their meal.

Izzy sat beside Sofia, more subdued than anyone was used to. Diego was at the other end of the table, making a point not to look at Izzy once. It wasn't obvious she was pregnant, but she did look pale, and he'd noticed her go a bit green at the sight of all the food.

Mimi was gone, having transferred out of Sanctuary days before. Matthias didn't know if she'd gotten her wish to go to Miami, but prayed John and Grant had put safeguards in place to prevent her from putting anyone's lives in danger by revealing the whereabouts of Sanctuary. He wasn't convinced making her sign an amended confidentiality agreement would do it.

John stood, tapping a butter knife on the side of his glass. No one paid him any attention, so he set them down and stuck his fingers in his mouth. The whistle was ear-piercing, but after the reactions died down, there was quiet.

"Since the mayor isn't here today, it falls to me to tell you all thank you for coming." John glanced around the room, his gaze taking in every person. He set his hand on his son's shoulder. "Since Pat and I arrived, we've felt like this was the place we're supposed to be." He smiled. "Okay, so I'm not good at eloquent speeches. But we consider each of you to be our family, and we're blessed to spend this day with all of you. Since today is a day for giving thanks, I would like to say thank you to each of you. We've had our ups and downs."

Andra snorted. John smiled, and she reached and grabbed his hand, holding it in hers.

"But I'm praying the worst of it is over. And we're looking forward to many years of peace and safety in this town. Thank you for making Sanctuary a wonderful place to live."

Frannie leaned her head against Matthias's shoulder while everyone clapped. He squeezed her shoulders and turned to whisper in her ear. "Come with me?"

Frannie shifted so he could see the question in her eyes. He held out his hand, and she put hers in it. Matthias walked her outside to his truck.

"Where are we going?"

He smiled at her. "I want to show you something."

At the ranch, he saddled his horse and pulled her up behind him. Frannie's arms settled around his waist, the warmth of her pressed against his back. He touched her hands, linked on his stomach and felt how cold they were.

"Where are your gloves?"

He felt her laughter. "Where are yours?"

"My hands are warm." The horse took the trail easily, winding through the trees until they reached the hot springs where he'd brought Frannie on their first date. It seemed like weeks ago now, given so much had happened since.

Frannie walked immediately to the area of grass at the far side of the clearing. Stakes dotted the ground, tied together with pink string that marked where walls of the structure would be built.

She glanced back, frowning. "What is it?"

Matthias just stood for a moment, watching her there in the place he was carving out for her. "Tomorrow we're going to break ground on a vacation house. Not a tiny cabin, but not a big house either. Room enough for two, with a sitting room and a decent size kitchen. Maybe some bunk beds, if someone has kids. You can make it whatever you want. Rent it out, so couples or even small families have somewhere to get away from town."

Frannie rushed at him, jumped into his arms and kissed all the thoughts from his head. She leaned back, both hands on his face so that he was holding her up. "Can we live here sometimes?"

"Depends."

She cocked her head to one side. "On what?"

Matthias set her down then, drawing the tiny box from his pocket. Frannie gasped even before he got down on one knee in the cold grass.

"Will you marry me?"

Frannie hiccuped a sob but smiled at him. Matthias

returned the smile, unable to believe it was possible he could be this happy.

Frannie said, "Absolutely yes."

I hope you enjoyed this story, please leave a review at your favorite retailer, it really helps!

Please visit my Website and Subscribe to my Newsletter to get FREE books, be included in events, and stay in the know of NEW RELEASES and PROMOTIONS!
https://authorlisaphillips.com/subscribe

Continue reading the WITSEC Series in book 3: *Sanctuary Breached*

Read the complete WITSEC series by Lisa Phillips:

1 - Sanctuary Lost

2 - Sanctuary Buried

3 - Sanctuary Breached

4 - Sanctuary Deceived

5 - Sanctuary Forever

And Complimentary Books:

Sanctuary Christmas

———

Learn more about Lisa's small town series, Last Chance County. Home of several book series, including: Last Chance County, Last Chance Fire & Rescue and Chevalier Protection Specialists.

The Last Chance County saga begins with Expired Refuge, which you can find here: books2read.com/ExpiredRefuge .

For Lovers of Romantic Suspense check out Lisa's new series

-Benson First Responders-

The series starts with Allegiance, which you can find here:
books2read.com/BFRAllegiance.

For Lovers of clean Christian thrillers check out Lisa's series of thrillers

-Brand of Justice-

The series starts with Cold Dead Night, which you can find here:
books2read.com/ColdDeadNight.

ABOUT THE AUTHOR

Find out more about Lisa Phillips, and other books she has written, by visiting her website:

https://authorlisaphillips.com

Follow Lisa on Facebook and Instagram to stay up to date and find out about sales and giveaways when they happen!

facebook.com/authorlisaphillips

instagram.com/lisaphillipsbks

bookbub.com/authors/lisa-phillips

goodreads.com/lisaphillipsbks